IT WAS ONLY A KISS

RUINED RAKES BOOK ONE

SHANNON GILMORE

Copyright © 2021 by Shannon Gilmore

All rights reserved.

No part of this book may be reproduced in any form or by any electronic or mechanical means, including information storage and retrieval systems, without written permission from the author, except for the use of brief quotations in a book review.

For the sake of fantasy some liberties have been taken with respect to place and time. This is a work of fiction. Any resemblance to characters, places, and events is coincidental and a product of the author's imagination.

Developmental Edits by: Sue Brown-Moore

Line / Copy Edits by: Anne Victory

Proof Edits by: Linda at Victory Editing

Cover created by: SRGallagher

Illustrations provided by: Deposit Photos / Period Images

KEEP IN TOUCH

Subscribe to my Book Boudoir **Newsletter** for announcements, giveaways, and a **free reading journal** from me to you. And don't forget to stop by Shannon Gilmore's Book Boudoir Facebook group and connect with other historical romance readers like yourself.

Happy Reading!

~Shannon

*For Mom and Dad
I love you both to the moon and back!
Thank you for always believing in me
and for exemplifying true love in all its wonder.*

***Read past chapter 14 at your own risk.
Don't say I didn't warn you.***

INTRODUCTION

He was good at hiding his true self
She had a lifetime to find him

CHAPTER 1

*L*ondon, February 1821

Before Grant could change his mind, he released the brass knocker on the front door. If *headache* had a sound, he'd describe it as the clang of brass meeting brass. Or duchess meeting duke. Or grandson meeting grandmother.

He was no longer the heir. He was now the duke in *need* of an heir. Which required the socially acceptable wife, which in turn sent Grant's already-cynical nature into a well-practiced, guarded equanimity.

He'd arrived at his grandmother's London town house in an indigo carriage sporting the crest of the Duke of Havenly and drawn by two sleek, shining bays with white stars. He'd answered the summons a fortnight late, avoiding the duchess's tiresome lecture on the duty and diligence of his newly inherited title. Namely, an heir.

The great door opened.

"Your Grace," the butler intoned.

The fresh scent of lemon polish greeted him even before the butler closed the door. Grant tugged off his gloves, tossed them in his hat, then passed them off along with his coat to

Branson. He arched his left eyebrow and, with a quick jerk of his head in the same direction, indicated the open parlor door.

"Her Grace is waiting," Branson said.

"Patiently?" Grant asked with the hint of jest.

"As you would expect." After missing two seasons, Grant welcomed the butler's noncommittal monotone; it made life seem almost normal.

The clip of his dress boots heralded his arrival as well as if Branson had boomed his name in the echoing foyer.

"Havenly, I knew you'd show today even if you arrived unannounced," his grandmother said without a glance. The woman's hearing was not in question. She sat rigidly, a steel rod for a spine that would be impressive at any age, but at seventy-two she made it an art.

"I've no doubt you know my every move, Grandmother." Grant initiated a calm greeting before the inevitable storm.

"Would that were so, my dear boy."

Ignoring her brusque attitude, he leaned over the back of the burgundy and cream-trimmed sofa, pressing a light kiss to the duchess's cheek. With her lips pursed, she watched him through squinted eyes while he made his way to the sideboard and poured a cup of steaming black coffee.

"A year ago I would not have been surprised to find your name on a list of the dead from the wreckage of a sunken smuggler's vessel."

"Or a merchant ship perhaps?" His fingers twitched, gripping the handle of the coffee urn. He was annoyed at the involuntary subtle reaction to his grandmother's innuendo regarding his decision to practically disappear for the past two years. He cleared his throat, setting the urn down. "Last I checked, the spice trade was legal, and I'm thinking of expanding to cocoa." Grant took the chair draped in gold chintz, set next to a polished oak side table, and placed his coffee on a tea napkin with tatting lace trim.

His grandfather had left this earth ten months past. The ton might attribute the duchess's stone-like reaction to her usual cold, austere countenance, but Grant knew better. She saved emotional outbursts for angry retorts—one thing they had in common—and tears were never in vogue.

He adjusted his mouth into a benign smile, propping a booted foot across the opposite knee, the scent of perfectly brewed coffee beans wafting under his nose. "My apologies to have kept you waiting, although I'd guess that your spies are better than mine if you knew I'd be here today."

She stirred her tea without a sound, then rattled her spoon against the rim of the rose-printed teacup like she no doubt wished to rattle him. "I have my sources; you'd be good to remember."

With a determined casual gesture, he clasped his hands against his middle, his elbows supported by the arms of the chair, his position one of relaxed cordiality. "Ah, women with nothing better to do than keep eligibles like me in line."

"I understand duty. Sometimes I wonder whether you have any notion what that means."

He lifted a brow. "To which duty do you allude, madam? The one that keeps your income steady, your house in good repair, or your future secure?"

"All of the above and then some. The future of Havenly is up to you. Why should that come as any surprise?"

"I'm not surprised, Grandmama, I simply don't care enough to engage in a conversation directed at begetting heirs. I guarantee your future; why must you hound me about mine?"

"Because, dear boy, your future *is* mine." She set the cup down smartly, sending a small amount of tea over the rim, which she effectively ignored.

He shook his head, biting back the pulsing nerve in his cheek. With an effort, he unclamped his jaw. "It's my business."

"It's family business. Our family. Yours as well as mine."

"It's not happening. Ever. Or do I need to remind you why?"

She served him an icy glare, which he parried with his own bone-chilling determination not to be browbeaten.

"Gadding about the wharves like a stray dog is unbecoming and does not suit your station. Months have passed without my seeing you, and you can no longer ignore the season. Or me."

He could no more ignore her on an entire continent, much less in the same city. Refusing to rise to her bait, he squelched the defensive tone fighting to get out and massaged the stiffness in the back of his neck. "Gadding?" He allowed an aggravated, humorless laugh to escape. "Gadding? I have more than doubled this estate, the one you are so intent on finding an heir for. This society craves money, but no one wants to work for it. You think investments care for themselves? Or would you prefer I trust your assets to solicitors who don't give a damn what happens to them or you?"

"Stop. You think I'm angry because you work?"

"I know you're angry because I work."

"Nonsense. I'm angry because you'd prefer this all go to some distant sniveling relative. Honor is of great consequence in our circle, as well you're aware."

"And you are suggesting… What? That I am not honorable? Look to my teacher." He couldn't help the smile that crept up, because the woman could throw daggers almost as well as he. Besides, Grant couldn't stay angry with her for long. They were too much alike.

"You're a scoundrel if anything. Sparring with you exhausts me."

"Sparring keeps you young. Your cheeks are glowing with youthful exuberance, like peaches and cream."

"I am immune to your flattery." The duchess blushed to the roots of her finely coiled snow-white hair, then dug in her heels, folding her arms while adjusting her unbending posture with a scowl.

"Grandmother, that look bothered me when I was ten. At eight-and-twenty, it amuses me. Save it for those who live in fear of you." He seized his coffee and took a sip, watching her over the rim.

"You should have never grown up, boy."

He threw her a sideways glance as he set his cup back on the saucer. "I didn't have a choice, now did I?" Smoothing a hand down the front of his waistcoat, he settled back into a leisurely position that belied the irate beating of his heart.

"And your father should have never died."

"What about my mother?" His grandmother had never accepted that his father had married a woman of Spanish descent. His parents had fallen in love, but without a blessing from the duchess, they had eloped. The scandal that ensued was something she had never let them forget.

"Of course I mean them both." Her harsh reaction did not bode well this morning. "I know you think I'm happy your mother's gone, but really, how could I be?"

"How? Because you hated my mother." His tone was matter-of-fact, but he was anything but. By the age of twelve, his life had turned into one long day. Even now he didn't dare look too far ahead lest he be disappointed. Oh, the irony. By his grandmother's actions twenty-plus years ago, she'd sealed her fate and his. He would not raise a family at Havenly. He'd never allow such unhappiness to shape the future of another generation.

The duchess arranged her starched taupe skirts. "You should worry about yourself and how I feel about you."

"I know how you feel about me."

Her gaze snapped to him, but his never wavered. Grant knew his grandmother loved him. At times like this, however, it was best to get in a good round or two before she made her demands.

He rubbed his jaw. "What now?"

"You could apologize for being disagreeable," she said with indifference. One thing his grandmother had never been was a simpering female. At least not in his recollection.

On a quick sigh, he stood. He couldn't help chuckling at her look of triumph while he crossed the short distance from chair to sofa to place another kiss on her upturned cheek as a peace offering.

"I accept your truce, Grant."

He smirked and sat again, his hands folded and resting against his midsection.

"Where were you last night? I expected you at the Rowleys'. Lady Rebecca Sherrington was there."

"How nice."

"She's perfect, Grant. Everything we're looking for."

"You mean everything *you're* looking for."

"You know what I'm saying."

Grant bit down, impeding the inappropriate nature of his retort behind his teeth. "I didn't attend the Rowley ball because I knew you were there, and it is a foregone conclusion that wherever you land, whether party, tea, or piano recital, there is some insipid debutante waiting for a proposal. Besides, I don't know Lady Rebecca and I'm not interested."

"With your dark hair and her mahogany tresses, you'd make a lovely pair." She spoke as if he hadn't just discouraged her meddling.

Mahogany? No. Hair the color of dark honey perhaps.

But what he really wished, if he were being truthful, was an encounter with one Miss Nicolette Thomas, although he'd be the first to admit his interest in the lady was particularly complicated. He'd been following her for several weeks, knowing she might hold the answer to a haunting mystery he'd been chasing for two years. But the woman was young. A girl. A first-year debutante, making it that much more difficult to secure a private word with her.

"Grandmother, I concede. Perhaps your approach has some merit," he announced, a little too loud for his own ears. If anyone could put him close to Miss Thomas, it was his grandmother. He'd already arranged a dinner a week from now with Miss Thomas's uncle, Lord Walborne, but answers to his questions required a confidential conversation with the woman. An alcove, an unchaperoned stroll through a garden, anywhere but a small dinner gathering would do. He sat forward, elbows to knees.

The duchess's eyes went wide. Her tone softened. "You'll meet Lady Rebecca?"

"No, but I am willing to consider your list of balls, soirees, teas, and anywhere else you think appropriate for me to meet an eligible young woman."

She tilted her head, a wary gleam in her eye.

"Let me be clear. I'm not interested in Almack's."

"As if they'd have you. I doubt even my good name could produce an invitation."

He knew better. The biddies at Almack's might turn up their noses at an heir apparent, but they would never snub an eligible young duke. All the same, he wouldn't set foot at one of their gatherings. Not even for Miss Thomas. But he wasn't above waiting outside. He smiled to himself.

"Do you play with me, or do you truly want a list?" she asked, her hand reaching for the bell on the tea table.

"I truly want a list."

She plucked up the bell, giving it a dainty shake. "I'll have Branson gather the invites." Her gaze stayed locked on his as if she had a difficult time discerning the truth. In the end, her will for victory won.

"I'm also not interested in pursuing women of your choosing. I know what I like."

She gave a regal nod but unnecessarily added, "Titled, good family, acceptable dowry, and young enough to give me a half dozen great-grandchildren."

"Would you like me to divide my children into three boys and three girls?"

Branson materialized, the only clue that he'd heard that last comment was two quick blinks and a ghost of a glance toward Grant.

"You may divide them however you please, just make sure at least two of them are male." The duchess went on as if they were still alone.

"I'll do my best." He put his coffee aside and stood. With a click of his heels and an exaggerated bow, he left the room.

He waited in the foyer, mulling over where he might casually run into Miss Thomas in the following week, expecting Branson to appear with the promised cards at any moment. Instead, his grandmother entered the echoing space, holding a handful of invites offering at least a dozen prospects.

With his grandmother's list of debutante-approved entertainment, he was sure to run into Miss Thomas before the scheduled dinner party, quite by chance of course. He felt his mouth pull into a slow, arched grin over that bit of strategy.

When he bent once more to kiss his grandmother's cheek before leaving, she reached a hand toward his face. He eyed her like a horse avoiding the whip.

"Grant, my dear grandson." She cupped his cheek affectionately. "Plan with care. I've known that mischievous smile since you were two, and it doesn't work on me anymore. Save it for your admirers." She raised a brow that dared him to speak truth.

"I'm sure I learned it from you."

"No, son, you inherited that one from your father." Then, with a smart pat on the cheek, she bid him good day.

CHAPTER 2

Finding Miss Thomas had not proven easy. At least not in a place where he could speak with her in private. Grant had questions. She had answers. Perhaps.

He'd been watching her from his private theater box for an hour.

Clattering applause combined with the whoosh of sparkling taffeta, and a thousand voices breaking into a wave of whirring chatter signaled intermission. He observed Miss Thomas and her friends disappear from the first-tier stall along with Lady Walborne, who was acting as chaperone. If he hoped to explore the mystery behind the little pewter jewelry box that had unexpectedly come into his possession, he needed a word alone with Miss Thomas.

What intrigued him most were the words hidden under the blue velvet lining. They appeared to be Gaelic. Scottish or Irish, he couldn't tell, and he wasn't about to ask a stranger for fear that he'd lose it to its rightful owner, Miss Thomas herself. He couldn't be sure it hadn't been stolen because he'd won the damn thing in a game of cards playing against a man he suspected was not entirely honest. Revealing himself as the owner too soon might keep him from finding the truth of it. The mystery. The key behind it.

For some reason, the whole affair piqued his interest. It had become something of an obsession to find its origin. Which brought him to seek out Miss Thomas.

As he made his way through the congested theater saloon, he paused periodically to accept congratulations on his title from people he'd known his entire life. They greeted him as if they'd never met. The ton considered the climb up the social ladder a public event. His grandmother considered the public pawing a rite of passage.

He grabbed a flute of champagne and took a detour to the back staircase, the one attendants and theatrical personnel might use. He had a better chance of making it to the lobby unhindered through the bowels of the theater than to chance being stopped by every broody hen who wished to foist an unmarried daughter upon his title.

The dimly lit stairwell swallowed his shadow while he crossed round to the next set of stairs and then the next. Muted conversations from the foyer grew louder as he closed in on the ground floor. Rounding the last flight, he stopped short because near the bottom of the steps sat a woman. In a slouching, bored posture, she pressed her chin into the palm of one hand, elbow against one knee. Not a ladylike, debutante, practiced position. All the more reason he approved.

Before he could take another step, she whipped a wary look behind her and practically jumped to attention, scrambling to her feet.

With his right hand pinching the wineglass between his thumb and forefinger, he raised his hands for her to stop. "Sincere apologies for startling you. I hadn't expected to find anyone."

"Nor I," she said, a slight quiver in her voice.

She was unmistakably Miss Thomas. He knew it. She knew it. But she didn't know that he knew it.

Lord, what a tangle.

Any young woman born and bred among the ton would have fled even before he uttered a word. To be found alone would ruin her and elevate him.

He wanted neither.

For some reason, she stayed. Perhaps the same flaw of curiosity plagued her in the same way it plagued him. In this, it was easier to be a man. That, he would admit.

She pulled at her cream taffeta skirt in an obvious effort to smooth the wrinkles. After swatting at an errant fold, she stopped trying, her doe eyes meeting his.

Taking great precaution not to spill his drink, he set the glass on the floor, resting it against the wood-paneled wall, as if he relinquished a loaded gun in lieu of surrender. He held up his hands again when she looked as if she might bolt.

The last thing he wanted was to frighten her. The light was too dim to distinguish the color of her eyes, but just bright enough to cast her in a romantic glow. Her hair shimmered like a halo.

"It appears we've both discovered the same hiding place." Once again, he initiated conversation without an introduction, hoping she wasn't aware of his identity. He didn't feel as if he had time for the usual appropriate beginnings.

"I beg your pardon, sir?"

"The noise can be unbearable. I took the back stairs, eager for a moment of peace. I assume you're here for a similar reason?" He padded down the steps, stopping one step up, afraid if he passed her, she'd feel threatened.

"If I were looking for peace, it would appear I have chosen poorly." Her lovely, upturned face, devoid of emotion, heightened the air of mystery surrounding her. "Besides, I imagine one would expect a theater to be filled with noise."

He thumbed a nonexistent speck of dust from his trousers, then eyed her from under his lashes. "And would that *one* include yourself?"

That pulled an unexpected smile from her, softening her features and transforming her from unapproachable hauteur to relaxed cordiality. "Touché."

He liked her instantly, something he had not anticipated. The woman was young. A girl. A first-year debutante. But she was refreshingly candid. He followed her unhindered, albeit inappropriate, approach and leaned against the wall, folding his arms. "I assume there is a chaperone somewhere in this building worried about your person."

"Not likely. Not yet. I am taking refuge where all women find refuge—theoretically speaking." Her statement was followed up with an innocently demure fold of her hands. This he supposed she had practiced since it seemed more forced than natural.

"Ah, in the arms of a wealthy, titled gentleman, you mean?"

She rolled her eyes on a heavy sigh that challenged him to keep his eyes trained on hers and not her lovely décolletage, to which his position unfairly provided visual access.

"You must be the lord of somewhere or something if you suggest that wealth and title are every woman's dream." It was not a caustic statement, just an observation.

"And you cannot be from this social sphere with such radical ideas." His brows were raised high on his forehead, a gauntlet of sorts. In truth, he'd almost forgotten why he was there. He couldn't decide whether he thought her adorable, cheeky, or rude.

Or all three.

"If it's all the same to you, I choose to consider that a compliment."

"You do me a service… Miss?" He leaned slightly forward,

encouraging her to answer. Oh, he knew her name well enough, but she didn't seem to know him at all. Etiquette called for a proper introduction, but if he waited for that, he might lose her to a chaperone or a sudden return of womanly wisdom.

"Thomas." She almost stuttered, as if she had to think about it.

"Would that be your Christian name or your family name?" He grinned, intending to restore the ease of conversation, but the stern slant of her mouth told him it was not appreciated. Hell, he might be losing his charm.

"My apologies, Miss Thomas. I can see I've confused you with banter better left to friends, and we don't know each other, do we?" Tapping a knuckle against his mouth, he made a reckless decision. "I have the perfect place if you're interested in avoiding the crowd."

She bit her lip and examined him warily. "You, good sir, may be a smiling crocodile leading a duck astray."

Palms up, he showed empty hands. He tugged at the opening of each jacket sleeve. "No magician's trick. Nothing up my sleeves."

She shook her head as if he were all nonsense and gunpowder. Unpredictable. But although she pressed the back of her gloved fingers against her lips, she failed to stifle a grin while her ocean-blue eyes studied him. He could see the wheels of contemplation play across her face. Her eyes darting between his in silent debate.

"The Duke of Havenly, at your service." He gave an abbreviated bow. The last thing he wanted was to draw attention, but he couldn't hold back his identity if he expected her to trust him at least a little.

Completely unaffected by his title, she appraised him, even going as far as ignoring the obligatory curtsy. "What do you have in mind? Something nefarious?"

He had not expected to be captivated by her charm. And Miss Thomas was charming and something of an enigma. She'd grown up on a merchant vessel but spoke cultured English. She was the daughter of John Bradenton, the previous captain of the *New Horizon*, a ship he now owned, but her family name was Thomas. What little information he'd gathered on her was not enough. He needed this introduction but now found the idea of coaxing her for answers unappealing.

His shoulders rose on a deep breath. Was this banter? "Have you seen the stage from the actor's perspective?" When she looked skeptical, he added, "You have my word—"

"As a gentleman?" She viewed him askance. Her eyes simply exuded curiosity. She inhaled deeply—a telltale sign of someone gathering courage—and he knew he'd won this battle.

He fanned his fingers for her to follow. "Come with me, Miss Thomas. But not too close, lest we risk the gossip sheets ruining our reputations."

"I've little doubt yours hasn't far to go."

He chuckled, then walked away, leaving her to follow or lose her nerve and stay. He counted on the determination he'd seen in her eyes.

Lord, her eyes. They mirrored the sea she'd grown up on, and her lashes were thick and unforgiving in their beauty. At the moment these were not good thoughts.

Without checking behind him, he shortened his stride for her sake. He double-checked the corridor, then peeked at Miss Thomas. She shooed him with a flick of her wrist to keep moving. It was a short distance to the paneled door that led backstage, and she followed him, unafraid, like a curious kitten. This girl was delightfully unimpressed. Not once had she deigned to curtsy to him. He was only slightly conscious of their lack of chaperone, and Miss Thomas didn't seem to be mindful of it at all. Then again, he was harmless, at least when it pleased him to be.

He had no intention of seducing her. But she didn't know that. And yet she must trust him on some level, because she did follow, unchecked, unfaltering, even moving him along with a flick of her hand. His pulse picked up, a nervous rhythm thumping in his chest, either for the adventure or because a decidedly attractive young lady had joined him for it.

NICOLETTE THOMAS HAD NOT BEEN LOOKING for trouble in the empty stairwell when she'd managed to steal away from her friends during intermission. They'd been husband hunting for an hour instead of watching the play, a less-than-interesting rendition of Shakespeare's *Taming of the Shrew*. Perhaps it had been the constant noise of the crowd or the tittering excitement from Frances and Pleasance regarding some duke she'd never heard of. Then again, her knowledge of dukes and ladies was rather limited, and gladly so. Her friends were consummate husband hunters, an apparent disease that had infected debutantes for ages and one that Nicolette was blessedly immune to.

But here, now, directly in front of her, was the very duke her friends had feverishly sought... no, dreamed of... being introduced to. And she, simple Nicolette Thomas, the one debutante this season who had no fanciful dreams of dukes, earls, titles, or uninteresting gentlemen, had come upon him in an empty stairwell where he apparently had been seeking a bit of peace, the one thing that had eluded her for weeks.

But he was nothing like she'd imagined. Better yet, she'd not imagined him at all. He was not boring or stuffy or the rake she'd heard far too much about. Nor was he a proper gentleman exactly. No gentleman would have invited her to follow him unchaperoned through the bowels of the theater, seeking adventure. She would admit that he was a scoundrel for asking, but she was not ready to admit that she was something of a fool to have followed.

Just now, her pulse quickened with every step.

For the adventure? Or for him?

He was devilishly handsome. His voice rich and hypnotic. His eyes a warm amber. And his smile… lethal. The singular dimple in his right cheek made her heart skitter, a pang that thrilled her into motion.

When she lagged behind, he glanced over his shoulder and shortened his stride. Her legs were no match for his height, which must be over six feet, a far cry from her five feet four inches.

With few sconces to light the way, the dark wood-paneled door seemed to appear from nowhere. The duke turned, tilting his head toward the threshold while opening the door, a clear invitation to precede him.

He was a silhouette, an outline, a shadowed phantom against the light from the other side. When she reached the doorway, she dodged past him. They ascended a short flight of stairs. In front of her emerged a great room with a handful of heavy curtains hanging from the ceiling, dividing the sides of the intimidating stage. The floor was polished wood, scuffed near the center front and worn in places where sets might have been dragged across. The smell of dust and working bodies filled the place and carried the scent of well-worn fabric. It wasn't unpleasant, just different, like an attic. But nothing held her in greater awe than the pulleys and rigging, the gangways suspended from the ceiling, and the people who traversed them like acrobats.

She'd almost forgotten the duke until he offered his arm while she stared into the rafters. Without a glance in his direction, she took it, following his steps like a dance. He led her to the front of the stage.

"Did you see the ropes, the intricately mastered rigging? It was like that of a ship." She glanced up at him and then was caught by the intensity with which he returned it. His gaze followed her hairline to her eyes, her nose, and rested on her mouth like a kiss. Holy Moses, this man was dangerously charming.

She sucked in a gasp.

"What would a debutante know of halyards, masts, and shrouds?"

She blinked twice in lieu of shaking her head clear. "What would a duke know?"

"Touché." He smiled and pointed to the giant curtain enclosing the front of the stage. "A peek, Miss Thomas?"

She could feel her mouth parting, questions hanging on the edge. She nodded without a word. Gently gripping her shoulders, he spun her about, directing her toward the side of the famous red velvet curtain. With the touch of his hands on her shoulders, her breath hitched, her heart slammed recklessly. Standing in front of him, close enough to feel the heat of his chest at her back, and daringly close enough to be intoxicated by the scent of the man, she gathered her courage.

"You first," she said, tilting her head back, looking at him upside down. The duke was a full head taller than she, and for a moment he looked as if he would kiss her forehead. Instead, he pulled the curtain a smidgeon, for his eyes only. "Be sure to check for old quibblers napping behind their lorgnettes. They feign sleep so they needn't take part in inane activities."

"And how do you know this?"

She gawped at him as if he were a nodcock. "Everyone knows that."

"Oh, of course. My mistake." He looked down at her with

exaggerated wide eyes. "It's safe. No nefarious activities at play, my lady," he said, using his best stage whisper.

She scowled at him and then ruined it by winking. She drew back the fabric, careful to hide everything but her eyes.

"And?" he asked when she failed to ooh and aah.

She drew the curtain wide. "What on God's green earth?"

He followed her gaze, gripping the red velvet next to her hand. She could feel the tickle of his chin on the top of her head. There was, in fact, one dozing matron wearing a chain about her neck with a lorgnette attached. It did not hang; it rested on her bosom like a jewel upon a pillow, rising with each breath. Perhaps the most interesting oddity was her hat. Pinned to the top of her head among a spray of ribbon was a huge peacock feather.

"What manner of bird do you think is nesting on her head? That cannot be a hat."

"I'm afraid it is. And quite fashionable, I'm sure. Thank the saints that the milliner did not include the entire wing."

"It could double for a family of tiny birds, or perhaps it's a very long, elaborate quill. Do you think her a theater critic? Perhaps she hides a pot of ink in her ample bosom," he said with believable gravity.

Laughter bubbled up her throat with the ludicrous suggestion. When she saw a couple enter the gallery, she slammed the curtain shut, but she could not squelch the mirth over the poor woman's hat. "A... a nest," she sputtered between guffaws. "Eggs, perhaps"—she gasped for air—"or"—she hiccuped—"or an actual peacock." Her voice went up a notch as she laughed enthusiastically, bending over with her arms wrapped about her waist.

He slipped a hand around her wrist while she gasped for air and ushered her toward the stairs that led down to the ground floor.

She was still chuckling when they stopped at the place

where he'd originally come upon her. She turned to see his amber eyes lit with something else besides humor. It was deeper than that, almost carnal. She swallowed a giggle and cleared her throat.

"Does that happen often?" he asked, not unkindly but a little off-kilter.

She bit her lip. "Possibly. Often when I'm nervous."

"Are you nervous now?"

Her heart felt like a trapped bird, fluttering madly for a way out. Oh yes, she was nervous, a different kind of nervous. She watched his mouth and found herself wondering what a kiss felt like.

Without checking herself, she laid a hand against his chest. "Thank you, Your Grace. I know I've not behaved honorably, but I haven't enjoyed a night like this since arriving in London. You were quite a gentleman."

He swallowed hard and, as if he'd done it a hundred times, he took her hand from his chest, pressing her fingers to his lips. "My pleasure."

THE SOUND of her conscience outweighed the projecting voices of the actors, and Nicolette reminded herself to appear calm, breathe evenly, and *not* look in the direction of the Duke of Havenly's theater box.

Had it been her imagination when Aunt Lydia eyed her speculatively after inquiring where she'd been? Frances had searched for her in the women's retiring room, and Nicolette had put her off with a lie, telling her friend that they must have crossed paths. Frances didn't seem skeptical. Nicolette didn't care for lying, especially to her friends, but the prospect of fielding questions regarding her scandalous behavior with one notorious duke turned her stomach into a nervous roil.

Nicolette gave a thoughtful sigh. Frances reached over and squeezed her hand, and Nicolette patted her friend's hand in return. She wobbled a smile, hoping her deception didn't show. It had not been her intent to lie. Frances was her dearest friend, but such adventures were unacceptable in this world, and her behavior, if discovered, could hurt her friend's reputation as well as Nicolette's. Scandal had a way of clinging like static to everyone within a mile of the storm.

Nicolette swallowed down her guilt. After a glance at her Aunt Lydia to be certain she was otherwise occupied, Nicolette peeked at the duke's box.

There was no mistaking that dark head of hair, so dark it was almost black, like sinfully rich coffee. To his left sat a woman with pale blond hair. That surprised her. Without knowing why, she'd pictured him there alone. By the casual way he draped his arm over the back of the empty chair to his right, leaning away from the woman, he appeared bored. That did *not* surprise her. From their abbreviated meeting, she suspected he had the heart of an explorer. In this they were very much alike.

CHAPTER 3

Restless sleep had not changed the events of last night. They did not magically disappear like Nicolette wished she could. Her stomach churned with anxiety, an unsettling queasiness that lasted through the morning while she concocted believable excuses for avoiding the small dinner party that evening. There was little hope of crying off, knowing full well that Uncle James would insist upon her attendance.

He was proud of her. He'd said it often enough, and Nicolette was certain of her uncle's hope to use the evening as a softer launch into society. Little did her uncle know that she'd already been hard launched into a social dilemma where one handsome duke with eyes like molten amber had enticed her into a private tour of a theater stage. Due to the fact that she and the Duke of Havenly had not been properly introduced—curses to Debrett's for that bit of etiquette—she couldn't admit to her friends who'd searched for the man all evening, nor to her aunt and uncle, that they'd already met.

After all, she had allowed the duke's inappropriate invitation to see the gallery from the actor's perspective. Without much persuasion, she'd willingly gone backstage with him. And in all truth, he'd been a saint. Well, not exactly, but he'd definitely been a gentleman.

She'd been fighting the same type of dilemma for three years. Too many rules. Too much to learn. And a natural curiosity that did not lend itself to this properly stale society. She'd been educated well enough, but most of her life experiences were tied to the rigging of the *New Horizon*, the merchant ship her father had captained and the one she'd lived on between the ages of ten and sixteen, at which time she'd come to live with her aunt and uncle.

For three years Aunt Lydia, her cousin Arlienne, and Miss Blanchfield, governess extraordinaire, had done their level best to turn a sow's ear into a silk purse. But despite the hours upon hours of instruction, Nicolette could not identify every use of any number of forks. She could not dance as smoothly as Miss Blanchfield demanded. And fluency in French had escaped her. In her unappreciated opinion, it had all been a waste of time because although the rules were part of a bigger plan to lure a husband, she had no intention of making a match that blazed a trail through the season as her friend Frances would say.

But blazing such a trail through dinner tonight with the infamous duke was liable to burn her hide.

If her inability, or unwillingness, to adhere to the rules specific to the ton were any indication of tonight's questionable success, she was bound to make a notorious ninny of herself.

Did the duke know her uncle? Did he know she was his niece? Had he known it last night? These questions and more could only be answered in private. Most of all she feared that the Duke of Havenly would reveal her faux pas. Pinned in by chairs, a table, and manners, she'd be hard-pressed to escape the embarrassment of such a confession tonight. The mere fact that she'd been escorted by him, unchaperoned, was cause for these good people to judge her ruined. Perhaps not her aunt and uncle, but the ton, to be sure.

Oh, how she wished she'd said no. Everything she'd been taught had slid away with the duke's dimpled smile. A mere month into her first season and she felt exhausted and out of place. And now, tonight, she'd be forced to share a family table with the man and try to converse without tripping over words or spilling a drink.

Sitting on a lace-and-lavender counterpane with a hand pressed to her forehead, she checked for a nonexistent fever, then shivered.

"Are you chilled, child?" Miss Blanchfield asked, strolling unannounced into Nicolette's bedchamber, wearing her governess-approved, moose-brown, bombazine skirts as stiff as her chignon.

"I'm not. Just considering dinner attire." The dress that her maid Claudia had laid out earlier destroyed the feeble lie.

The governess turned a dubious eye toward the dress lying conspicuously over the vanity chair, then slowly met Nicolette's eyes. No words were needed.

Nicolette squeezed her hands together in a wringing grip and cleared the lie from her throat.

"I assume you're privy to this evening's dinner guests." The governess opened the top drawer of her bureau and brought out Nicolette's most prized possession, a shapeless crystal necklace. "And do not ask to wear this. I cannot fathom what your aunt was thinking to allow you to pack this garish bauble for the season." She dangled it between two fingers, staring at it as if she could not quite discern its secret power or why Nicolette should care so much for the admittedly unsightly jewelry.

She hurried forward, taking the half-inch, misshapen gem from Miss Blanchfield's grasp. However ugly the bauble might be, it was priceless to Nicolette, for the beauty lay in the giver, not the gift. It was one of the few things she had left after her father died.

Miss Blanchfield then pulled from the dresser a pair of soft white silk stockings and proceeded to lay them out with the dress.

Nicolette gently wrapped the pendant in a handkerchief embroidered with her initials, framed by tiny pink flowers, and placed the treasure back in the corner of her top bureau drawer. For the next while, Miss Blanchfield and Claudia fussed over her gown, her hair, and a last-minute lesson on silverware. This fork for that, that fork for this, and on and on.

An hour later she was seated in the sunshine-yellow parlor, wearing a dusky pink gown with her hair neatly twisted into a single coil that lay over her left shoulder. She sat with her cousin at the settee while her aunt sat primly in the adjacent yellow paisley chair. She listened half-heartedly to a debate over whether women should be allowed trousers under riding habits. Although she had arrived on the Thomases' doorstep three years past, carrying a valise stuffed with boy's breeches, those days seemed a lifetime ago. That girl was now buried deep inside this shell of frippery. Still, she had little use for this debate over riding habits since she could not sit a horse.

The foyer echoed with voices. The front door let in the unmistakable sound of gushing wind. Laughter, the scuffing noise of shoes on the marble floor, and the distinct tap of an umbrella spine echoed off paneled walls. There were several voices, but only one struck a chord. The baritone lilt of one particular duke.

Aunt Lydia gave her a reassuring look like a pat on the knee, as if she expected the evening to go well.

From behind, she heard the guffaw of male voices mingling in some kind of shared ritual that only men could comprehend. Arlienne, Aunt Lydia, and Nicolette stood when the men were announced at the parlor door.

"His Grace, the Duke of Havenly," the butler said.

Nicolette's pulse thrummed wildly in her throat while she kept her eyes downcast in what she hoped would be viewed as demure and not disrespectful. Her stomach did that rolling thing again, and she lived in mortified terror that it would churn out a sound like a croaking frog.

"Captain Robert Donovan," the butler announced.

At that, Nicolette's knees nearly buckled. Her head snapped up and her eyes burned with a shock of tears. It was Robert. Her father's faithful friend. The man who'd been like an uncle. The last she'd seen of him had been the day he'd dropped her at Uncle James's doorstep. His thick red hair now streaked with gray, his bushy eyebrows like a wave of fat caterpillars, his eyes dark as the sky, Captain Donovan gave no hint of pleasure at seeing her.

Somewhere inside, she wondered whether he recognized her at all. And if so, did he see the strides she'd made, the woman she'd tried so hard to become? Or did he still see the child she'd once been who wore boy's breeches and helped with some of the less taxing deck chores? Her father had allowed her at least that.

She followed Arlienne's lead. She looked toward the duke, who stood proud, tall, every inch his title from his dark coffee-brown hair to his amber eyes with tiny dancing flames to his larger-than-life presence rounded off by shoulders wide enough to put other men's padded coats to shame. She could still feel the hard muscle of his forearm under her hand when he'd escorted her last night.

Focused on the floor, she stepped in front of him and gave her best imitation of a ladylike curtsy, which one might describe as a bobbling mess. The heel of her left shoe lost its grip on the floor while she lost her grip on reality. The duke firmly caught her elbow to hide a near catastrophe. She glimpsed him from under her lashes and saw the corner of his mouth twitch. Last night she'd failed to curtsy to him, as was his due, and she had the distinct impression that he preferred it that way. Heaven knew she certainly did.

She swallowed hard. "Your Grace." She left off the *nice to make your acquaintance* part to save herself from the outright lie.

"Miss Thomas." He bowed over her hand.

Next, she turned her attention to Uncle James's familiar warm hazel eyes and salted brown hair. He stepped forward, a protective smile on his fatherly face, then folded her hand over his arm and led her to Captain Donovan.

Like the booming creak of a falling mast, her stomach lurched. No doubt too quiet for anyone closer than her and Uncle James, it nonetheless sounded like cannon fire and did no favors for her runaway heartbeat.

Captain Donovan, his hands clasped behind him, wore a scowl etched in his weathered forehead. He reminded her of her papa, who'd been of a similar age.

At his look of supposed disapproval, her heart plummeted, the pain bit into her sides threatening to splinter her apart until the odious man broke into a broad smile and opened his arms.

"Come, love, ye've grown up." Robert laughed.

Nicolette could have cried with relief. Forgetting every rule, she boxed his chest with a fist instead. "I wasn't sure you'd recognize me."

"I couldn't be sure meself. I half expected to see a little hoyden, not a grown-up moppet."

It was an inappropriate jest by proper standards, but the endearment made her want to weep.

"And yer quite a pretty lass at that."

Robert embraced her. The act was unheard of, but they were more than this social air of inequality. They were family, and she'd missed him dreadfully.

Her finger shaking, she swiped a single tear from her cheek.

She turned to her uncle. "I apologize, Uncle James. It's just that…" The words grew thick in her throat as she fought for control.

A warm smile pressed little crinkles at the corner of his eyes. "No apologies necessary, my dear."

"I should say not," Aunt Lydia said. "Captain Donovan, it's been too long."

Nicolette's aunt saved her any further embarrassment by filling in the short interim before dinner with all the appropriate pomp. The clasp of a hand, the smile of welcome, the invitation to toast with wine. She made it look easy, flawless.

When they were seated for dinner, Nicolette bit her lip, waiting for the duke to announce their familiarity. But he did not.

Every time the duke turned his head in her direction, she felt her face flush while her pulse thumped quite primitively in her throat. She felt conspicuous and out of place, staring at her plate with two knives, three forks, and a spoon that she'd rather describe as a ladle. Why did the gentry require so many utensils?

Out of self-preservation, she avoided eye contact with the duke, who sat directly across from her. Robert sat to her left, smelling of sweet pipe tobacco and causing a wave of nostalgia to break into her private thoughts. She'd lost track of the conversation almost instantly and remained in a relative fog through two courses.

"The *New Horizon*." The deep vibrating voice of the duke prevailed over her preoccupation with which fork to use with the roast duck.

Why on earth would the Duke of Havenly be mentioning her ship? She'd been so happy to see Robert that she'd failed to question why the duke and Robert would be invited to the same dinner. A duke and a sea captain had little in common.

She'd missed the beginning of the conversation; her ears pricked to hear the rest.

"Captain Donovan and I," continued the duke, "are considering chocolate. Cocoa, to be precise. America is a hotbed of trade, and with peaceful waters between us it's a good time for expansion."

"Chocolate?" Uncle James leaned back, allowing a servant to clear his plate.

"Chocolate." The duke repeated with confidence. "It's said that chocolate may surpass tea as the favored drink in America."

"What are your thoughts, Captain Donovan? Is it a good risk? Can we turn a profit within a year?" Uncle James asked in all seriousness. This was not small talk; it was business.

Nicolette's gaze swept the table, settling on the duke. Unlike the theater, tonight he had an air of regal formality about him. There he'd been more relaxed. Now he looked every bit a man of title. Without his hat, his hair curled at the ends, a testament to his nonconformity that softened the whole regal effect, and a part of her wondered which man was real and which was facade.

"And what is your opinion, Miss Thomas? Do you think chocolate especially pleasing?"

Her face warmed at the duke's question. "I'm not sure anyone would turn away chocolate, Your Grace. I certainly have no objection to it."

A smile lit his eyes, and his gaze stayed with her for a hair's breadth too long. "You see, Walborne"—he gestured with his hand toward Nicolette—"even your niece finds it favorable."

"So she does." Uncle James looked pleased with her answer.

Now that she'd joined the conversation, she changed the subject, unwilling to wait another moment. "Robert, how does my father's ship fare?"

"The *New Horizon*?" the duke interjected.

Her eyes snapped back to his, confusion settling in her stomach like a cherry pit, small but uncomfortable. "Yes, Your Grace. The *New Horizon*. What would you know of it?" The question was simple and innocent, but her tone was anything but. He'd mentioned it before, but she'd had no reference point. Perhaps now she'd find out where his interests lay.

He leisurely leaned his elbows on the table and clasped his hands. "I own it."

The muscles in her face strained and stretched until her ears felt as if they'd moved an inch. She turned to Robert. "What say you, Captain Donovan? Does he speak truth?"

He. She'd said *he*, not His Grace, not the duke, not even Havenly. Just *he*. The sick churn in her belly returned and brought a foreboding pall over her good sense. Had he followed her to the theater? And if so, had he or had he not known her identity?

She'd been wrong to follow him. She'd known it then and she knew it now, but until this moment, she'd had no regrets.

"Aye," Robert answered without looking up.

She forced back nausea. "I beg your pardon?" She blinked.

"I own it," the duke said again, this time punctuating each word, all the while locking gazes with her.

"What a coincidence." No matter how hard she tried, she couldn't keep the snark from her voice.

"Coincidence?" Uncle James asked her with pointed confusion, then turned a glare on Havenly. "I don't understand."

Havenly gave her uncle his attention, then turned back to Nicolette, his eyes bright with anticipation. Did he not realize the consequences if he revealed how they'd met? Perhaps because he was a duke, he'd be forgiven. But not Nicolette. And if society caught hold, her reputation might be affected. Worse than all that, however, was the disappointment it would bring from Robert. Never in the past three years had she wanted to shine like a polished penny. Normally she didn't care, but tonight she wanted Robert to be proud of her because she needed her father's approval, and this was as close as she'd ever come.

"It's a trifle odd that His Grace should turn up here, at this very table, as the owner of the ship *where I grew up*." She enunciated the last four words with enough force as to leave no question regarding her feelings. Irritation sprang from the grief she'd never surrender. Separating her father's memory from his ship could not be done. Or better, *would* not be done.

"So you own the ship that Robert captains? How fascinating." Aunt Lydia pierced her husband with a knowing gaze while addressing the duke in a perfect monotone.

It would seem that Nicolette was the last to know.

Arlienne cleared her throat, reminding Nicolette of her presence. If Arlienne had known, she would have said something, wouldn't she?

Yes. Nicolette must believe that or she'd lose confidence in her cousin, and she trusted Arlienne more than anyone.

Her aunt's gaze perused the table, then she notably relaxed, adjusting her napkin on her lap. "Your Grace, my niece's father was captain of the *New Horizon* prior to our Mr. Donovan. Nicolette has been under our care for many years."

That answer could not have been more vague, which brought Nicolette more questions about everyone's seemingly odd behavior. Or perhaps her aunt was uncomfortable with her ill-mannered boldness.

"Thank you, Aunt. I've overstepped—please continue with your discussion about chocolate." Nicolette took a deep breath and counted the minutes until she could return to her room. A footman cleared the last remnants from the table. Six courses, and Nicolette couldn't name one. It took everything in her to stay seated.

Under the table, Robert squeezed her hand. "Your father's ship is flourishing."

"And I would expect no less with you in charge." She directed the compliment to Robert but pointedly glared across the table at the duke because in her book of checks and balances, the Duke of Havenly had lied to her. He'd done it by omission, she'd allow that much, but he'd purposely done it, of that she was sure. But why?

"Miss Thomas, what an interesting childhood you must have had. Should I presume you know a little about ships?"

"You may presume that I know much about ships."

"And the rigging? Can you tie all those knots?"

She'd mentioned how the pulleys in the rafters of the theater looked like ship rigging, and he'd asked her if she'd ever sailed. The devil with him. He'd already known.

"I can tie a knot that no man can undo." The discussion was more than improper. She was suspicious why Uncle James allowed it to continue, but she was also too caught up in twisting information from Havenly to care what her uncle thought.

"I'd ask you to prove it, but I'm afraid it would be quite scandalous."

"Scandal is the perfect disguise for fear. I bow to your discretion, Your Grace."

"Touché, Miss Thomas. I have no doubt that fear rarely plagues you." He sucked in a cleansing breath through his nose, the kind that prefaced a change in topic. "If you're interested, I'd be happy to share how I came upon the *New Horizon* and Captain Donovan."

"If one could tie you to the truth, I'd be curious to know."

He held her gaze, and while war brewed behind her facade, he beamed with approval. He lifted a brow and almost imperceptibly bowed his head and eyes as if this were a game she had won but would encounter again.

"Suffice to say, Miss Thomas, Captain Donovan and I have considered broadening our spice trade to include cocoa and at least one trip a year to the Americas."

"How fascinating," she intoned in the same bland voice her aunt had used earlier.

It was clear to Nicolette, no matter where this evening ended, she'd be seeking him out to finish what he'd started. He'd answer her questions, or she'd... she'd... Oh, hell's bells, she would tie him up in knots as he'd just done to her.

Her heart then thrummed with foolishness and pride, and any concern she'd had for her reputation was obliterated by overwhelming curiosity and not a little anger.

She took a deep breath. "Exactly how did you come upon my family home?"

"Nicolette," her uncle warned in a fatherly tone.

"I grew up on that ship, Uncle James. I considered it my home. If His Grace cannot answer the question, I bow to your judgment and I'll remain silent, but I fear he came about *it* unscrupulously." The emphasized *it* had nothing to do with the ship and everything to do with their meeting. She pointed the challenge at the duke.

He accepted with one dark brow arched and a triumphant half-cocked grin on his piratical face.

When Uncle James made a sound of protest, Havenly waved it away, watching her all the while. "Your niece is not ill-mannered, just young."

She clamped her jaw. How dare he call her a child? The impulse to throw her napkin on the table like a gauntlet was squelched by her aunt's timely interruption.

"Cook prepared a lovely dessert. I think I'll check on that," Aunt Lydia practically blurted. Robert rearranged his remaining forks. Uncle James placed his napkin on the table and then went about straightening his silverware. And Arlienne continued to watch with a disturbing sort of concentration.

Havenly sat back with a slight tilt of his head, regarding her without shame. If he had crossed his arms smugly, she would not have been surprised. The pulse in her neck ran amok.

The silence proved louder than the conversation.

Dessert was served by fastidious servants invisibly shuffling in and out. A delicious, flourless chocolate confection—oh, the irony—with raspberry compote. It was rich and decadent. It seemed apropos. While everyone enjoyed the cake, small talk resumed, pressed and trailing at times.

When she finished, Nicolette purposely scraped her fork with a tooth-jarring screech across her plate.

"Miss Thomas, let me satisfy your curiosity. I came upon the *New Horizon* in a game of cards."

"Who would foolishly bet an entire ship?"

"A small fleet actually."

"The entire fleet? You own the entire fleet?" It was beyond thinking.

He nodded. "It's but three ships; we're hoping to add another. And let me clarify, I didn't win the entire fleet, only the *New Horizon*. The others were purchased later. However, regardless of how I came about them, they are mine, make no mistake."

"His Grace secured the *New Horizon* first because it was the best." Robert apparently assumed that bit of nonsense would placate her. "He only purchased the other two last year."

"Small pockets, Your Grace? I assumed with your grand title and leverage, you might have taken them all for a *steal*."

"I assure you I stole nothing."

Except my trust, she thought with anger.

"Nothing, Miss Thomas."

She felt more than saw the understanding they shared.

Aunt Lydia dropped her fork. The clatter of silver against china was enough to turn everyone's attention. "Wouldn't it be nice to exchange pleasantries in the drawing room?" She pointed the remark at Nicolette.

Nicolette felt only a touch of guilt, but the minuscule reprimands this evening were not enough to smother the burning need to finish the conversation.

"Tea and coffee, or perhaps a glass of sherry?" Aunt Lydia rambled, excusing herself, breaking any number of rules of etiquette. The drawing room was connected by a pocket wood-paneled door, opened to welcome after-dinner amusements. The small ensemble followed her aunt, everyone but Havenly.

As the guests retired to the drawing room, Grant gave a nod to Lord Walborne, a silent wish to have a word with his niece. Walborne affirmed the request with an equally discreet nod.

Before Nicolette escaped into the drawing room, Grant stayed her with a hand, surprised and relieved when she didn't object... until she trained her stormy blue eyes on him. He tugged her elbow, taking a few steps back into the dining room. Far enough for a word.

She jerked her arm from his grasp. "Any reason why you didn't tell me?" She hissed, a heated air of unresolved panic behind her tone.

"Would you believe I didn't know?" He reached for a lighthearted exchange equal to their conversation at the theater.

She clamped her teeth together. Eyes wide, she verily screamed at him.

"I understand you want explanations, and I'd love to give them."

"And I wish to know if you followed me into that stairwell? If you knew who I was? If you were playing a game for the sport of it?"

"Of course not." He had never considered this a game.

The inscription on the pewter jewelry box, the item that had pulled him into this chase, included what looked like a name along with the Gaelic script. At first sight it looked as if the letters had been worn away, but on closer inspection, Grant had noticed small etchings in the metal that pointed to them being removed, scratched out, perhaps on purpose. It was the name he sought to find next.

An errant golden wisp of her hair pulled his attention from her piercing gaze. He would have reached out and gently placed it behind her ear if she were any other woman.

"I am not convinced, Your Grace."

"Because you're bright. I like that about you, Miss Thomas, and I'll admit that I hadn't expected it. I didn't follow you into that stairwell. But I did know who you were. I won the *New Horizon* two years ago from Emmett Craddock's nephew and then purchased the rest of the fleet from the same man last year."

"Mr. Craddock owned the fleet. He died shortly after my father. And you appropriated the ship a year after I left, so how is it you know me?"

"Captain Donovan, I'll admit, was very reluctant to speak of you, but eventually the tale unraveled how your father had been killed on the waterfront by thieves and his only daughter had been taken to live with relatives." He chanced taking one of her hands between his. "Miss Thomas, I would love to share the rest with you, but not here. There's too much to tell."

Her nostrils flared, and for a moment he thought she would rail at him. After a short pause, she breathed out a long sigh, relaxing her shoulders along with the hard line of her mouth. "I imagine that would be the proper thing to do. Although I'm loath to understand why propriety has overcome you at this late date." Her tone settled back into something more agreeable.

He narrowed his eyes, unsure if she was angry or jesting.

"I think we're being missed," she said with a shadow of a smile.

Without a by-your-leave, she walked ahead, leaving him staring after her, speechless. Grant wasn't used to being dismissed.

Indeed, he liked her. He liked Miss Thomas very much.

When he entered the drawing room, a servant handed him a glass of sherry. The women sat side by side on the settee, Lady Walborne and her daughter, Lady Lawrence, flanking Miss Thomas like protectors of the realm.

Walborne watched him outright and then motioned him toward an overstuffed armchair in wistful colors of pale blue paisley that matched the settee. Grant nodded toward the ladies, then took his seat. The sherry he set on the table beside him. Opposite the length of the large blue Aubusson carpet sat Captain Donovan in a chair that mirrored his own.

Unsure whether this was a safe place for gathering information, he chose to brave ahead nonetheless.

"Now that we all know each other, I wondered if you might clear up a question for me, Walborne?"

"If I can." Walborne took his place by the hearth like an orchestra leader.

While Nicolette Thomas's hair was the color of spun dark honey, her uncle's was medium brown. It wouldn't be unheard of for Walborne's niece to have a lighter version of his medium brown, but they looked nothing alike, which explained the confusion of her name, the one thing that had hindered him from finding her.

"I would apologize to the ladies now for my forwardness." He regarded them, then focused his question on Walborne. "I'm curious about Miss Thomas's name?"

If he had not been looking directly at Walborne, he might have missed the twitch of his cheek and the stiff set of his jaw.

"I don't mean to disparage its legitimacy, but I do know that the previous captain was named Bradenton."

Walborne and Captain Donovan exchanged looks.

"Thomas is my surname," Walborne said, stating the obvious. "When Nicolette came to live with us, we thought to give her the freshest start. I discussed it with her father long before his death. Nicolette didn't come to us because he died. She came because John, her father, wished her to have a good life, something better than he could offer. The name was born from that. We all felt—Robert, Lady Walborne, and John—that changing her name might curb curiosity and harmful questions." He gazed fondly at Miss Thomas. "The move wasn't easy for her."

"Uncle James and Aunt Lydia were gracious enough to lend me their name because society would make me a pariah if they knew where I'd come from. Not that I'm ashamed of it, mind you, but—"

"But the ton would have made you the gossip fodder of the season," Grant finished. Damn the haute elite and damn society. He could see that although giving her the name Thomas was a kindness, it was also a hardship. The story would make perfect sense if he had not witnessed the exchange between Captain Donovan and Walborne. A speaking look of concern marred Walborne's forehead and the grim set of Captain Donovan's mouth. There was more to the tale, and more time, now that he'd found her, to uncover the answers. Pushing any further tonight would do him no service.

"I kin vouch for her education." Captain Donovan's sudden contribution made Grant feel boxed in. "Her mother and father were good people and they spoke proper. They made sure that Nicolette's education was complete. She didna come here unpolished. She's always been a pretty penny." Donovan's protective gaze softened on Nicolette.

Grant felt like a heel. "My question was not in good form, Captain Donovan."

"I would enjoy another topic." Miss Thomas looked at him with disapproval. Her cheeks flushed a rosy pink, and Grant couldn't know whether it was from embarrassment or resentment.

"I agree." Lady Walborne held out her empty sherry glass for a refill.

The hour following, Grant played his part as he'd been taught, speaking benignly and letting all talk of business ventures, and Miss Thomas, fall away. In proper time, he stood to bid them good night but first asked Walborne if his niece might walk him to the door. Lady Walborne didn't seem to approve, but Lord Walborne nodded. And Miss Thomas, as if duty called for it, preceded him, demure and quiet and completely out of character as he'd seen thus far.

Grant had come to trust James Walborne and was pleased to see that Lord Walborne returned it. Now if he could just convince Walborne's niece.

When they reached the door and Grant had taken his coat and hat in hand, Miss Thomas raised her chin and he saw the spark return. The flame that led her to venture behind the curtain, the one that gave her the courage to spar with him at a full table, burned bright in her eyes.

"I wish for you to know something, Your Grace."

He raised a brow and nodded for her to continue.

"I consider my home stolen. I consider you the thief. But more than that, my uncle may not have any reservation in sharing my personal information with you, but I do not feel the same. You have no right to my name. No right to ask."

Guilt doused him, and once again he felt like a cad. No mystery was worth the pain he heard in her overconfident voice. The jut of her chin, the glower, the harshness of her words were a barrier against something bigger than his stupidity. "I never meant you harm."

"No? Then why pry? You, who live a pampered, titled life, cannot possibly understand what it is to lose everything dear to you. You cannot know the heartache of having your life torn out from under your feet, quite literally. For the whole world to change in an instant. Do you know what sea legs are?"

He nodded, swallowing hard, realizing too late his curiosity had made a mockery of the life she'd left. The life she'd lost.

"When I came to live with my aunt and uncle, I was land sick if you can imagine. My world was literally tilted, my legs felt like jelly. That's how much time I'd spent aboard the *New Horizon*. It was"—closing her eyes tight, she shook her head—"*is* my home. Do you understand?"

"Better than you know." He knew far too well, but now was not the time to share his story. This title that she so easily dismissed had been in his family from time out of mind. It was a title that his father had deserved but never carried. It was a title that his grandmother would have stripped from her only son, if indeed she could have, just because he married a nobody. Unfortunately, his father died before he could inherit. Grant felt it a privilege to take his father's rightful place. But he would never grace his grandmother with the marriage and grandchildren she wanted. There was no way he'd be foolish enough to bring unhappiness into the world. He knew what it was to lose one's parents young. And he knew what it was to live someone else's definition of life.

She examined him, her eyes taking in every nuance of his face. Searching for sincerity.

"Let me apologize, Miss Thomas."

"You may try." She folded her arms, which unfortunately for him, accentuated the delectable swell above her bodice, something he shouldn't be noticing when he was desperately fumbling his way toward absolution.

With his kid gloves in one hand, he placed his hat on his head with the other. "I want you to know that my behavior at the theater was abominable. And I'm quite sorry." He sighed. "No, sorry would suggest that I feel regret, and I admit that I enjoyed myself very much. More than I have in quite some time. But if I could do it again, I'd..." His mouth quirked up into a reluctant smile. "No, that isn't right either. I'd have done the same, because Miss Thomas, I wanted to."

"Do you get everything you want?"

"Usually. But not this time."

She unfolded her arms, letting her hands slide until her fingers were laced together at the center of her waist. "I suppose I must accept your apology, because in truth I enjoyed myself too. I'll share a secret with you, Your Grace."

"Ah, be careful, kitten, lest I know too much of you." He coaxed both a smile and a blush.

She leaned close and whispered, "I loathe the theater. Not the drama from the stage, you see, but the drama from the gallery. It's exhausting. And boring. Do you think it's social sacrilege?"

"Absolutely."

She gave him the look of a conspirator. "Should I apologize?"

"For the love of God, no. It's refreshing."

"Truce, Your Grace?" She looked up from under her lashes with a mischievous hope.

Her straightforward temperament made him smile. "Havenly," he suggested in lieu of his title. "And yes to the truce."

"Are we to be friends then?" She cocked her head playfully; her tone matched the spark in her eyes.

"I can't recall a woman daring enough to ask such a question."

"Do you have no women friends?" A blush rushed up her cheeks.

"I think I do now." He brushed a kiss to the back of her hand.

The room felt warm despite the drizzling rain he could hear outside. He forewent his kid gloves and ran a finger along her jawline, relishing the soft perfection of her skin, stopping when he reached her full bottom lip. His gaze rested there like a kiss and then met her eyes. He smiled with some regret. "Friends… Miss Thomas."

CHAPTER 4

When the Duke of Havenly traced a finger along Nicolette's jaw, her skin came alive. It tingled, sending her heart into a fluttering sensation that brought on a plague of gooseflesh. And the way he had stroked her bottom lip made her wish they were more than friends. The biting hurt and anger she'd felt all evening was forgotten, at least for now.

After he bid her good night, she stared, teetering on a precipice of emotion, at the back of the heavy oak door. She let out a pent-up sigh, planning on a hasty retreat to her room only to be waylaid by Arlienne's knowing gaze from the gallery above. Her right eyebrow arched while a knowing smile played about her mouth. It was embarrassingly apparent that her cousin had witnessed at least part of her too-familiar conversation with the duke. Had she seen the whole of it? The way he'd touched her, the way his eyes had watched her mouth, the way he had kissed her hand?

There was nothing for it now; she took each step toward her room in silence. Behind her, the sound of Arlienne's satin shoes shuffled in pursuit.

With an elbow draped over her eyes Nicolette fell onto the bed in a heap. "Come in, Arlienne, I know you're there."

Skirts rustled and the door fell into place with a smart click. "Are we speaking of it yet? Or will you make me wait in suspense?"

"Wait in suspense," Nicolette said without removing her arm from her eyes.

"I knew it."

At that remark, Nicolette pulled her elbows down onto the bed, bracing them beside her chest, and scooted herself up until she could see Arlienne.

"The man watched you all through dinner. And my goodness, what was that exchange?"

Before she could answer, Aunt Lydia tapped on the door and let herself in. Nicolette wasn't sure it was the reprieve she needed. Leaning over, she grabbed a throw pillow, then flopped back onto the coverlet with a little bounce.

Aunt Lydia sat beside her and patted her leg.

"Aunt Lydia," she said, muffled by the pillow over her face. "I do apologize for my behavior tonight. I know it bordered on rude."

"It was an unusual discussion; I will give you that." Her aunt's voice was ever soothing.

Nicolette sat up. "I know it sounds silly, but I feel as if Papa died all over again. Hearing his name. Hearing *my* name. Seeing Robert." The painful words filled the room with nostalgia.

"It isn't silly, darling. You've endured more than most people ever will. How could you not feel that way?"

Nicolette peeked at her aunt. Behind Aunt Lydia stood Arlienne with her hand resting over her mouth.

"Get some sleep." Her aunt rose.

"Do you think Uncle is terribly angry with me?"

Aunt Lydia turned around, her lips pressed and thoughtful,

her unwrinkled skirt gently swaying. "I am at a loss as to what your uncle was about tonight, but I assure you he is not angry. He adores you like a daughter. All he ever wanted was that you be happy. If anything, Uncle's worried that perhaps you're not."

"Oh, but I am, Aunt. You must tell him so. It's only that I hadn't expected to be quite so overwhelmed by the season."

"I'm not so old that I don't remember my first season." Her aunt still held the beauty of her youth with only a whisper of gray in her mahogany hair. She leaned in and gave Nicolette a kiss on the forehead. "You're doing fine. Get some rest. We have a ball here in two days."

Arlienne waited to speak until Aunt Lydia left the room. "Is there anything you're not telling me?"

"I can't think of a thing." Nicolette watched her feet dangle over the side of the bed. She knew Arlienne waited for a confession.

"Have you no attraction for him at all? He's devilishly handsome."

"You have the devil part correct, I'm afraid." She hopped off the bed and sat at her vanity, where she started pulling each long hairpin out one at a time. "It's difficult for me to be unbiased. He stole—or procured, I suppose—my childhood memories."

"He purchased a ship. He made an investment."

Nicolette closed her eyes. "I know what you say is true. And I know I'm not seeing things reasonably, but I can't help but feel betrayed."

"How could he betray someone he didn't know?"

Nicolette turned half around, her hands perched on the back of the vanity chair. "That's just it, Arlienne. I'm not convinced he didn't know who I was."

Arlienne's mouth fell open. She blinked hard, then slowly took the seat beside the vanity. "You cannot leave me on pins with that statement. I'm staying right here until you tell me everything." She wriggled her bottom on the soft padded chair. "Why would you think he knew you?"

Nicolette swallowed, her throat knotted with secrets. "Because I inadvertently met him at the theater yesterday. And do not look at me as if you know the whole of it. I can see you're fairly bursting." She glared at Arlienne from under her brow.

Arlienne crushed her lips together and nodded, a silent promise to remain neutral, as if she could. When Nicolette turned back to unpinning her hair, Arlienne placed her elbow on the side of the vanity, leaning in until her face partially obstructed Nicolette's view. "And? You cannot expect me to be silent. Mother mentioned nothing."

Nicolette flopped back in her seat, her hair loose about her shoulders except for one piece still pinned to her head. She looked like Medusa, in which case she'd have frozen Arlienne's next question on the spot.

"Who introduced you to him?"

Nicolette rolled her eyes shut. She heard her cousin gasp. The back of Arlienne's chair bumped the wall when she sat back too quickly. Nicolette trained her eyes on the tiled ceiling. "Exactly, Arlienne. Can I trust you to say nothing?"

Arlienne nodded. "Only if you tell me how it happened."

"It was completely innocent, really. But you know the rules."

"Yes, and how you like to break them." Arlienne said this without blame.

"I prefer to think of it as having not mastered them… yet." Nicolette giggled, drawing a smile from her cousin.

"The Duke of Havenly is not just any duke, my dear. He's known for—"

"Being a rake? A rogue? A scoundrel of the worst kind?" Nicolette asked without condemnation in her voice. "I know.

I've heard quite enough from Frances and Pleasance, but he has been nothing but kind and"—she tipped one corner of her mouth—"gentlemanly." Even she thought that sounded unconvincing.

"What do you mean by gentlemanly? Has he done something questionable?"

"No," Nicolette said too quickly, her voice a pitch higher than normal. "What I mean is, he's witty and he banters as if he's studied the art for years."

"As I said, he's a rake, darling. That's what they do."

Nicolette cocked a dubious brow toward her cousin. "And how many do you know, Arlienne, that you should recognize such a man?"

"One." Arlienne looked sheepishly at her. "I married him."

Now Nicolette giggled. A burst of laughter climbed up her throat, and she pressed four fingers against her mouth to squelch it from recklessly pouring out of her. "Arlienne, your husband is completely harmless."

The man doted on Arlienne, and Nicolette had never witnessed anything remotely scandalous in his behavior. Then again, she hadn't grown up among the ton. She hadn't known Richard Lawrence until her aunt and uncle had taken her in at sixteen. At that time Arlienne and Richard had only just married. Now they'd been married three years and had a two-year-old little boy. Perhaps that had mellowed Richard.

"He's harmless now," Arlienne said. "Because I trained him." Her cousin's eyes went dramatically wide and a smile just as large appled her cheeks. "It wasn't easy, but it can be done."

"Well, I'm not interested in taming a beast. Besides, the duke is not interested in me, nor I in him." Nicolette dismissed the subject.

"Will you at least tell me how you met?"

"I'm trying to get to that."

"Well, try harder," Arlienne said.

Nicolette bit her lip, grasping for a proper way to tell a most improper story. "I met His Grace at the theater purely by chance. I had excused myself to the ladies' waiting room but decided on a detour since what I really wished for was a moment alone. After finding a private stairwell, I positioned myself near the bottom, not expecting to see anyone, much less a nobleman." She sighed, wrapping her arms around her middle. "Apparently, the Duke of Havenly was looking for the same thing."

"Are you certain of that? Or do you think he followed you?"

"I don't know. I wouldn't have thought so until tonight. He knew my name, Arlienne, but at the theater he acted as if he didn't know me at all." Nicolette pulled her loose tresses over one shoulder, rubbing the fray at the ends while she perused her memory. "I thought it unlikely that he'd seek me out. I'm an unknown. Besides, later I saw him in his box, seated next to a woman with blond hair."

Arlienne froze. "Miss Featherbe."

"Who?"

Arlienne blinked twice. "Miss Joanna Featherbe. The woman seated next to the duke. It had to be her. But she's nothing to worry over. He lost interest in her years ago if one can believe the scandal sheets."

"Arlienne!"

"I don't read them as a rule, but one does need to keep up with current events."

"Why do you think she was there?" Nicolette could not resist the question.

"Aha!"

"Stop. I'm simply curious."

"If the gossip of three years ago is true, then Miss Featherbe and the duke were very, very close."

"Mistress?"

Arlienne nodded. "But no more. If it was an affair, it ended a long time ago."

She couldn't be jealous. She hardly knew him. Then Nicolette remembered how bored he'd looked and how he leaned against the opposite chair, away from this Miss Featherbe.

Poo. If she were not jealous, why did she now feel relieved? What a ninny. He was kind and handsome and had all the prerequisites the ton demanded, but he was surely as pompous as the rest. She wanted what her parents had: love, contentment, a partnership. And then she thought how judgmental that sounded to assume that aristocrats could not fall in love. She kept that to herself.

"What happened next?" Arlienne said, breaking into her thoughts.

"He seemed surprised to find me sitting alone. He introduced himself." She sent up a silent prayer. "And then he asked if I cared for a tour."

Arlienne failed to look scandalized; in fact, the edge of her mouth quirked with mischief. "Did he? And what did you say? Yes, I hope."

"Arlienne," Nicolette chided, then admitted in a small voice, "I did."

"Aha!" Arlienne yelped again.

"You misunderstand. He wished to be alone."

"Then why did he ask to show you about? Please tell me he did not introduce you to anyone without approval."

"No. Although he was scoundrel enough to ask if I wanted to see the stage from behind the curtain."

"And?" Arlienne nearly leaped from her seat, an unmistakable gleam in her eye.

Nicolette gave up sitting. She pulled the last pin from her hair as she stood, then began to pace while wringing her hands. She stopped briefly. "And I said yes." She stole another peek at

Arlienne. "He was a perfect gentleman, and I might add there were any number of actors about."

"Not many, I hope. They have their own gossip mill, and the duke would be recognizable even if you were not." Arlienne tapped her lip. "On second thought, the stagehands wouldn't know you, so any gossip would go unfounded. No name to deposit into bending ears, no return on the investment. I'd say you're safe. How did it end?"

"Before the end of intermission, he escorted me back to the stairwell where he bid me goodbye. It was all very innocent."

"No flirtation?"

"None. At all." She felt her face flush and her palms sweat. In truth she couldn't say because she had never been versed in flirting and certainly had no experience being on the receiving end. Feeling somewhat relieved after such an embarrassing confession, she let her body wilt into a very unladylike slump. "Arlienne?"

Arlienne simply looked at her with rapt attention and an expectant raise of her eyebrows.

"Tonight he called me his friend."

"Oh." Arlienne almost looked dejected. Almost.

"Do men have women friends?"

"Not that I'm keen to. If I had to guess between the byplay at dinner and the clandestine introduction, I'd say his interest is more than friendly. He did say he knew your family name, so there's that."

"Which leads me to wonder if he did in fact follow me to that stairwell, if not the theater altogether." Her lungs filled with relief, her confession complete. "No, we're just friends, else I'd have to believe he saw me from afar and fell deeply in love." She said that last part with a dramatic swooning voice to emphasize the ridiculousness of the entire conversation.

"I'd venture to say that your position, if known, would be quite envied."

"By whom?"

"By every eligible miss this season."

Nicolette remained silent on the matter. She folded her arms tight and squeezed her elbows while delivering Arlienne a hard look.

"I dare you to prove me wrong."

CHAPTER 5

Two short days later, Nicolette examined herself in the full-length mirror, feeling a nervous detachment from the reflection of the woman who looked back. She wore a midnight-blue ball gown. It was beautiful and expensive and the most daring thing she'd ever worn, with silver braided trim at the hem and a provokingly tight, fitted bodice. She'd considered wearing a fichu, but even the fussy Miss Blanchfield had suggested going without. Claudia went to great pains to pin her hair up in a sophisticated chignon, leaving wisps of hair at her nape and ringlets at her ears.

When the time came to join her aunt and uncle in the receiving line, she did so with trepidation. Knowing the Duke of Havenly had been invited, she'd as soon lose herself in the crowd before he arrived than face yet another unsettling introduction. Thank goodness she had only to spend an hour greeting guests. As soon as the bell tolled ten o'clock, she was permitted to leave the line and join her friends on the third story, where the ballroom was located. Before she sought out Frances and Pleasance, she visited the retiring room and checked her hair and the fit of her gown. Even though she was duly cinched into the darn thing, she felt as if she might pop out of the bodice at the slightest movement. How on earth did her friends manage such gowns with ease?

Nicolette pinched her pale cheeks and made a turn for the ballroom. She bit her lip, stood on the tips of her toes, and searched for her friends over the sea of bobbing, coifed heads. Across the crowded ballroom, she spied Pleasance's burnished coil of curls. Frances was certain to be close by. Focusing her full attention on them, she sidled through the crowd.

She grabbed a glass of champagne from a passing footman at the same time she caught sight of the Honorable Gerald Clifton—who frankly was not so honorable. He rushed between people, making his way toward her with his lanky arms pinned to his sides, his face a mask of determination, his blond hair so light it appeared to be thinning. Perhaps he would be handsome if not for his abominable personality. Her friends had warned her about Mr. Clifton. It was rumored that he sold fodder to the gossip columns. Nicolette was not only new to the season, she was also new to this austere society and vulnerable to attack.

Good Lord, he'd be upon her in two yards.

She mentally rummaged through countless lessons on deportment—anything to halt his advancement and probable dance request. Without taking into consideration the crush, she pivoted on her heel, missed a step, and with a full glass of champagne slammed into the hard chest of a towering man with sandy-colored hair. The sparkling gold wine spilled down the front of his beautifully tailored waistcoat, thoroughly saturating the dark garnet embroidery that adorned the expensive fabric. The taupe satin shimmered with little popping bubbles while the gentleman did his best to hold back his tailcoat to avoid ruining the black superfine as well.

"Oh my heavens." Nicolette's cheeks flushed warm with sick embarrassment. She might have successfully avoided running into Mr. Clifton, but now she'd done the unthinkable and quite literally run into a stranger.

Clothed with caution, she tilted her head back and looked up at the unusually tall man.

While her mouth gaped like a gasping fish, the tall gentleman brandished a handkerchief. "May I offer my assistance?"

Nicolette looked at her dress, not a drop shone, furthering her embarrassed guilt. "I seem to have avoided my own misjudgment, much to my chagrin. I do apologize."

The gentleman wiped down his waistcoat. "It's nothing. Let me replace this." He took the empty wineglass from her hand, then waved over a footman and traded it for a full one.

She accepted it with some reluctance. "I'll do my best to pay better attention. Thank you."

"Nonsense." With a generous smile, he stuffed the soggy linen back into his inside breast pocket. "It was my fault. Besides," he offered lightheartedly, "I don't even like this waistcoat."

With that they parted ways, Nicolette once again moving toward her friends. As soon as she approached them, it was obvious they'd borne witness to the whole debacle.

Careful to steady the champagne, she held up her empty hand. "Don't say it. My humiliation is most complete."

"What happened?" Frances asked with a soft, sincere tone.

"I managed to outfox Clifton by way of mortifying disaster."

"Well," Pleasance said, "at least you lost Mr. Clifton. I'd say it was worth it." As befit her name, she smiled pleasantly.

"Yes, entirely worth it," Frances echoed with excitement. "Nicolette, do you know who that was?"

She shook her head on a heavy sigh. "No one of consequence, I hope." She knew better. The man's expensive clothing bespoke wealth and probably title too. The lord of somewhere or something, as she was wont to say.

"The Earl of Richfield," Frances finished on a dreamy note. "And you know what that means?"

Nicolette had no time to answer because as Frances's eyes went wide as saucers and Pleasance's hand went to her chest in awe, a familiar, resonating timbre vibrated through her.

"I'll take that," Havenly said, reaching from behind and plucking the glass of champagne from her hold. "Miss Thomas, it would seem I've been given permission to dance with you. If you'll have me." He bowed to her.

She closed her eyes, blocking out the questions on her friends' lovely faces. Since the dinner party, a notable theme had emerged, one that involved her uncle agreeing to every close encounter with the Duke of Havenly. Uncle James would not matchmake. He had promised that she could pick her own husband when the time came.

That time was not now.

Not during her first season.

Not to a man with shallow ties to the aristocracy and knotted to the mast of the House of Lords.

"Ladies, if you don't mind."

Pleasance and Frances, as if connected by some mystical perception, shook their heads in unison.

The duke handed her glass of sparkling wine to Pleasance, then placed Nicolette's hand on his arm.

"I heard you were having a difficult time holding your drink this evening. Is this true?"

The witticism was not lost on her. No doubt Mr. Clifton was fast spreading rumors.

She eyed him, but his focus was the dance floor where a waltz had just begun.

"This is a waltz," she said with some alarm.

"Is it?" He smiled down at her, the dimple in his cheek

making her heart skip, at the same moment he pulled her with fluid grace into a turn.

"And did my uncle give you permission for a waltz?"

"Is a waltz not a dance, kitten?"

She wrinkled her nose. The pet name was too much, and by the wolfish grin he wore, he knew it too. She ignored it. "I assume you refer to my embarrassment over a spilled glass of wine. But I tell you that I was dodging an unseemly beast, and by pure accident—"

"You stumbled into Richfield?"

"You know him?"

"Very well. Should I be jealous?" His tone teased her as much as his half-cocked smile.

"You are friends? Perfect." She bit her lip. "Please apologize to him. I only meant to dissuade Clifton's unwelcome presence."

"Yes, and that was my goal as well." He turned her effortlessly. "The toad was on your heels."

She made a cursory glance about the edge of the dance floor and saw the grim line of Clifton's mouth, his squinted eyes boring a hole through Havenly. She made a misstep, but the duke's superb skill righted the bobble with one expert twirl.

She returned her focus to her dance partner. "I fear you've made an enemy of Mr. Clifton."

"Mr. Clifton does not deal in anything so inconsequential as friend or foe. He's an opportunist, a walking theatrical tragedy. And I'm afraid I'd have to break his wrist if he dared lay a hand on you in that dress."

The reference to her gown heated not only her cheeks but every inch of her skin.

"I pray you've not attempted a curtsy in that gown because the position would cause a physical assault to the senses." He said the statement with such dire gravity that she couldn't be sure whether he teased or was truly appalled.

"Yours or mine?"

"Mine," he said with theatrical overtones, very Shakespearean, as if she'd wounded him.

"What's wrong with my dress?" She couldn't keep the defensive, hurt tone from her voice. A woman's plague, no doubt.

"Absolutely nothing. On the contrary, the color is a complement to your blue eyes and caramel hair."

"My caramel hair?" She sputtered, unable to hold back a smile. "Was that a compliment, Your Grace?"

"I am trying, sweet. The next time we meet, I'll be sure to bring caramels so you might see what I see. Besides, that dress is a sin. While I applaud the seamstress, you should be aware that it plants the seed of wickedness."

She gasped from shock but couldn't deny that she feared the same thing. "Are you calling me wicked?" She tried for coy but couldn't tell if she missed.

"No. If for one second I thought you were aware of the womanly attributes you'd reveal wilting like a lily to the floor, I would revoke our friendship and replace it with something else indeed." His eyes flashed with mischief, sending warning bells in her head.

"I see. Then I am at a loss as to where that leaves our truce, Your Grace."

"You may call me Grant. It is my name."

"I couldn't. First names are reserved for friends and lovers." Before she could stop, Nicolette realized the impact of her words and that their light banter had taken a dangerous, flirtatious turn.

The duke hardly blinked. "And your pick would be?"

"Friends." Nicolette laughed, bending her head, avoiding the duke's perceptive gaze. She felt it nonetheless, as constant as the warmth of his hand at her waist, a sensation that penetrated layers of fabric and petticoats.

It took a long thirty seconds of silence to find her tongue. "What could you be thinking to ask me to dance a waltz, of all things, in front of my friends?"

"I was thinking I wanted to dance with you." He watched her, and for a moment she thought she saw truth in his eyes. "Do you think your friends disapprove?"

"I believe a proper introduction was in order *before* you approached me for a dance. One would think a duke would know these things." She feigned a scolding tone meant to disarm him and set him off-balance, hoping to even the playing field because just now hers felt a little tilted.

"I rather enjoyed our first introduction. You know, the very scandalous secret one that only you and I are privy to?" He bent his head close and whispered the last part.

No one was privy to that secret but Arlienne. And she had yet to tell her friends about the dinner party. No one, save her family, knew they'd ever met. Nicolette grasped for a lifeline, seeking some kind of witty banter that would take the devilish grin from his face and cool her heated cheeks. "It really isn't proper that I should be dancing a waltz with you at all. But if you don't mind your reputation being tarnished by a first-year debutante, I don't mind."

"And what do you know of my reputation?" he asked. "Has someone filled your head with lies?"

She skipped another step, and without so much as a stumble, he caught her up to tempo.

"Let me see." She contemplated her next words, stalling to gather momentum and steady the rush of blood in her ears. And then with enough cheek to rival the best gossip rags, she answered, "I am not much for gossip, you understand, but I have heard of your charm, your legendary dashing good looks, your recklessness—"

At the mention of good looks, both his brows shot up.

"Not to mention you're an accomplished flirt, Your Grace.

Seduction is your favorite game. But make no mistake, it is always a game."

"Are you listing my crimes or describing my charm?" The way he watched her, the way he appreciated her with a glance, caused her heart to trip, something her feet had become quite accomplished at. He'd twice successfully rescued her from a physical fall, but this internal tripping was something else altogether. If anything, she needed rescuing from herself.

She continued, "Your reputation has been married to the scandalous term *rake*. And now to be dancing with me, I believe you may have ruined it all." She tried a coy look to match what she hoped sounded like innocent banter. "Can rakes be ruined, Your Grace?" She'd held his gaze the entire time, but now she looked away. The sound of her voice saying such things caused a stir in her belly, or perhaps it was the way his eyes smoldered with glinting amber flecks.

When the silence between them drowned out Mozart, she stole another glance at him. He was watching her, studying her almost, as if she confused him. He was distractingly, deliciously handsome. What had Frances called it? Rakishly handsome? No truer words spoken.

The Duke of Havenly was the most rakishly attractive man she'd ever laid eyes on.

The hand at her waist tightened, causing her throat to squeeze shut and her breath to catch. He held her too close. She could feel the power in his arms. Whether she was able to put a voice to it or not, a feeling of security surrounded her. Which made no sense at all because this man was not considered safe company even if her uncle approved.

"Do you believe everything you hear, Miss Thomas? Or did you spread such lies about me?" His eyes devoured her. His smile coaxed her to play.

"I, sir, do not lie."

"Ah, tread carefully, kitten, or I may hold you to your word. Remind me again how old you are?"

"Your manners are in grave question if you think it at all proper to keep calling me kitten." She couldn't help but be stirred by his voice. It vibrated through her, piercing her heart, sending blood rushing to all the places he touched.

His chuckle was rich and approving. "You play this game well. Too well, love."

"I don't play games, Your Grace. And I don't accept invitations to use proper names from improper gentleman. Especially rakishly handsome ones."

"How provoking you are, Nicolette."

If she were honest, and right now she preferred not to contemplate the idea too hard, she would admit that provoking him had become a goal. Perhaps she *was* playing a game. His game.

She slanted a smile and gave him a playful glare. "I have given no invitations this evening."

"I certainly hope not, Miss Bradenton."

"And since no one else is privy, the use of that name is far more intimate than my proper name, Your Grace."

"Then my question still stands. Friends or—"

"Do not say it again."

"The least you could do is call me Havenly."

The word was a little too close to heaven for her senses. She chose silence instead.

"I'd say this conversation requires more privacy, *kitten*."

Against her will, a pleasing thrill tickled her insides when he called her kitten. Before she could respond, he stepped from the dance floor and guided her through the open veranda doors. The balcony was in full view of the ballroom, and several couples were enjoying the torchlit terrace.

"The pet name fits even though I know you are a year late for your come out and not quite a kitten."

"Rudeness is not at all attractive, Your Grace." She tried for solid conviction, but her voice sounded thin, airy, like someone out of breath. Dash it, they'd been dancing. Why wouldn't she be out of breath? "Besides, not as if it's your affair, but my governess deemed me"—she looked toward the stars and took a deep breath—"not ready."

She left his side and walked toward the terrace balcony. Once there, she pulled the glove from her right hand and ran her bared fingers along the cold, solid balustrade, enjoying the feel of something anchored down. The only gloves she'd worn aboard a merchant ship were for work. These thin, stark white silk dress gloves were meant to keep worldly sensations from corrupting young minds—according to Miss Blanchfield. Nicolette's response to her governess had been, "And I thought they were merely to keep one's hands clean. Who knew?" Her wide-eyed cheekiness had not been appreciated.

The duke quietly walked up behind her. "You look very ready to me."

She pulled her hand from the rail and faced him, bending a playful brow. "Truthfully, in the words of my governess, Miss Blanchfield, I am hopeless at dancing—which I believe you've witnessed—and an embarrassment to the French language."

He pressed a hand to his chest in mock surprise. "You still have this evil governess?"

She couldn't help but giggle. Miss Blanchfield was steadfast, unmovable, and focused without a fault, but evil she was not. "Miss Blanchfield is also my companion when my aunt is not available. And she's quite harmless, I promise."

"And where was she several days ago when I met you in a deserted stairwell? She sounds remiss in her duties. Why, her charge might have been ravished by an unprincipled libertine." He gave a mocking bow, then looked at her from under his lashes, the devil of a look about him. "Like me." His face positively exuded wicked delight.

Even with the chill of late winter, she felt warm. She touched cold fingers to her cheeks and knew they were red as roses. Perhaps she appeared cold and not flushed with desire to continue this energizing wordplay.

"I think I'm pleased that this Miss Blanchfield is not a fit chaperone." His eyebrows rose with simplicity, an innocent tone covering the daring statement.

She swallowed hard. "I'll be sure and let her know."

"Promise me you will not be too honest with this dragon of a governess, else we'll never enjoy another private moment." His voice softened conspiratorially. "If she breathes fire, send me a note and I'll meet you right there." He pointed to an overgrown shrub in the far corner of the garden two stories below.

"You would hide in a shrub? How undignified. I hope you're not allergic."

"Not to my knowledge."

For a moment she wondered how many potted shrubs he'd hidden behind. How many ladies whose hearts he'd ravaged because she could not, would not, believe that he was capable of such a thing. Hearts crushed? Yes. But he didn't strike her as the kind who would press his suit upon an unwilling lady. He could have done so with her many times by now. Inwardly she grimaced. Perhaps he didn't think her worthy of pursuit.

Then it dawned on her what she'd been thinking and hoping and wondering. It shouldn't matter if His Grace found her interesting or attractive, but with some strange instinctual feeling, it did matter. It mattered too much.

"The invitation to stroll the gardens is not extended to your Miss Blanchfield. But I'll leave the invitation open to you. Whenever it pleases you."

She clucked her tongue. "Your Grace, you are dangerously close to being slapped."

"How brash to consider such violence on my person." His

voice rumbled with merriment. His devilish chuckle soared straight to her core. "Slap me here and the scandal will dog you well past the season. Gerald Clifton would assign an entire page in the gossip sheets to it. But then I'd say it might elevate his toady position, and he'd thank me for it." His eyes flashed with mischief. Humor created the perfect foundation for that fascinating dimpled cheek.

"That sounds very much like a dare. I don't think you want to do that. Not really. You don't know me that well." A swell of confidence worked through her veins, and she tilted her head shyly.

"I know you very well, Miss Bradenton." His voice was a persuading whisper, as clandestine as their first meeting.

Her brows hit the ceiling, metaphorically speaking.

His voice was like silk. "I know you are beautiful. Your hair is the color of dark honey…"

She looked at him skeptically and smirked.

"Your eyes, a deep blue ocean. And your mouth captivates me every time you speak."

The playfulness of a moment ago turned to heat, and she felt as if they were the only two on the balcony. Her lips parted when his shameless gaze fell to them.

A whisper was all she could manage after such a lethal attack on her senses. "Those are things you can see. But you cannot know me."

"Then I'll have to work on that." He rested a hip against the balustrade and folded his arms. "Tell me something about Nicolette Bradenton."

Grant stood there on the balcony, wondering over his preoccupation with Miss Thomas. After all, his first encounter with her had been for the sole purpose of discovering what she might know regarding the jewelry box and its interesting inscription. Thus far, he'd failed his mission. This guileless woman in front of him had charmed him into forgetting why he cared. He'd met his share of beautiful women, but none could hold a candle to this one, and not because she was a diamond of the first water. Nicolette Bradenton Thomas was definitely enjoyable to look at, but it was her damned innocent, reckless, candid responses that drew him. Her banter was not practiced. Her skill as a debutante was practically nonexistent. And for all that, the effect was utterly refreshing.

"Who is Nicolette Bradenton?" he asked her again.

"You ask me about a girl I hardly remember."

His heart twitched uncomfortably at her response. He knew something about forgetting oneself. He knew too well what it was like to lose a family. He'd lost his parents as a child and had worked hard at keeping the few memories he still held buried where they couldn't hurt him anymore.

Before he could respond appropriately, Lord Walborne darted through the terrace doors, heading straight for them. Grant's first thought was that Miss Thomas's uncle might not approve, but as the older gentleman drew closer, he recognized the fear in his quick stride and the determined set to his mouth.

Something was wrong.

"Havenly, I need a word." Lord Walborne addressed Grant first. "And Nicolette, your aunt needs you. She's in the rose parlor. Can I trust you to go straight there?"

"Of course, Uncle. Is she unwell?" Nicolette picked up her skirts and moved toward the ballroom before her uncle answered.

"It's nothing, darling. She just needs your help."

Grant guessed those words were meant to calm Miss Thomas, but he knew that Walborne would not have taken the chance of making a spectacle of himself, or of appearing overprotective, which was exactly how it looked to Grant. He followed James Walborne to his private study on the second floor.

When Grant stepped into the dark paneled room, he heard the lock settle in the door. The hairs on his neck stood up, and he took a calming breath before he turned around. He wasn't quite sure what to expect. There were many reasons why people locked doors, and all of them involved some level of protection, from without or within.

With eyes round, unsettled, and unfocused, Walborne paced the length of the room while Grant settled himself into a leather wing-back chair, willing to give Walborne a moment to put his thoughts into sentences. Grant noticed the contract of investment lying on Walborne's desk that would align Walborne with his own merchant shipping company. It was stacked neatly, just as it had been when James Walborne had signed it two days ago. Had he trusted the right man? He decided to give Walborne another minute before starting his own interrogation.

Ten years ago, dealing in covert affairs surrounding the numerous little battles that had broken out during the Napoleonic wars had taught Grant how to recognize fear. And something was scaring the devil out of Walborne.

Grant settled his elbows on the firmly stuffed arms of the leather chair, his hands clasped at his middle.

"Grant," Walborne said, his breath heightened.

That Walborne addressed him in the familiar gave him even more pause. "Why don't you sit, James," he said, his tone level and stable. They were business partners; making use of first names was not out of the question, but until now that had not been their practice.

"Perhaps I should," James said in a rush, then sat in a matching chair opposite a large rectangular Persian rug. "I didn't know who else to ask, and I apologize in prelude to what

I must say." Restless, James sat forward. "Someone has started a rumor. A dangerous one."

Grant gave the older man his full attention. He motioned for him to continue.

"If you didn't start it, who could have? I don't mean to suggest that you did it on purpose." James raked a hand through his hair and stood again. The pacing took the same route as before.

Grant asked, "Do you plan to tell me so I can defend myself, or do you blame without cause?" Now he was getting a little annoyed.

James rounded on him, then sighed, his shoulders drooping under the strain. He had always seemed a virile man, but now he looked older than his fifty-two years. The gray at Walborne's temples seemed more prominent with worry.

"I apologize. It's just that you're the only one who knows Nicolette's family name, and it appears that Clifton has become privy to it. I've stopped him momentarily from spreading it far and wide, but the little toad is more likely to keep it quiet now so he can profit from the scandal later. I'm afraid the damage may already be done."

"I've told no one your niece's family name."

"Of course you haven't." James scratched his forehead and searched the ceiling for the right words. "It's Clifton that worries me."

"Clifton's a weasel. He's rarely believed. How would he know her name, and more importantly, why should he care?" Then it dawned on him. He sat forward. "Dammit. I called her Miss Bradenton in conversation. A private conversation, mind you. I can't believe he heard. I do understand your anger with me, but I don't understand what difference it makes. There's nothing untoward about her having a different family name. Or am I missing something?"

Instinct told him there was much more to Lord Walborne's

overreaction. Grant waited for the explanation, and when the man was through, Grant planned to wring Gerald Clifton's scrawny neck.

"There's more to her surname than I told you. Perhaps I should have told you the whole story after you'd discovered her real name. But I feared for Nicolette."

"So tell me now." Grant's tone came close to demanding an answer to this nervous premonition of bad news. He leaned his elbows on his knees, resting his mouth against his gathered hands.

"Bradenton." James almost whispered it, then drew a handkerchief and dabbed his sweating brow. He sucked in a shaky breath. "What I am about to say I haven't repeated to a soul in twenty years. I trust you, Grant; otherwise, I'd be removing my niece from the city. I shouldn't have chanced it, doing business with you and Captain Donovan. I'm too close. I never dreamed that joining forces with your shipping company would put her in danger."

Grant's stomach turned. An almost physical weight settled on his shoulders. "Your trust isn't misplaced. I only wish you'd done this days ago. Please"—Grant gestured toward the adjacent chair—"have a seat and explain."

James ignored the request but did stop his pacing when he reached the hearth and gripped the mantel with both hands. "Nicolette's life depends on your silence."

"James," Grant said calmly, hoping to coax the nervous man into speaking clearly and evenly. At the mention of danger to Nicolette, however, fear seized him. "You have my full confidence." Grant quelled the rising surge of nerves, forcing his fingers from balling up. His concern was genuine, but calm was in order.

"What I'm about to tell you, Nicolette knows naught." James cleared his throat. He leaned an arm across the mantel and fumbled with a porcelain figurine, a bloodhound frozen in a state of howling. A call for action. "Elisabeth, Nicolette's mother, was much like a sister to me. We were cousins, raised in the same household. Nicolette's mother's last name was Moulin—that much Nicolette knows—Elisabeth was orphaned as a babe. My mother and hers were sisters, which is why our surnames are different. Moulin and Thomas. This is why Nicolette is safer here than anywhere, because her mother's name could not be easily traced to ours."

James took a moment to glance at Grant and then continued, "Before Elisabeth married John—Nicolette's father—he warned her of the life they'd lead. Sheltered from family and old friends, there would always be a marked distance kept. John also confided in all of us—me, Lydia, and my parents. We have never betrayed that trust. Nicolette had never met us until three years ago when her father died. John had already arranged for her to come live with us, you see, and then it was suddenly and achingly necessary after he'd been killed."

Grant breathed deep and tried to keep his curiosity in check. James wasn't making much sense. Not yet.

James went on. "John Bradenton's death was not a random act of robbery. It was not a mistake. It was, in fact, not a robbery at all. It was murder. That's why the coachman's purse was not stolen. That's why John's funeral was so private and at an undisclosed location. His crew didn't even attend, save for Robert Donovan. Not even Nicolette was allowed."

"How much does Captain Donovan know of this?"

"Robert knows everything. He and John were close friends. They were friends before I ever met either one of them."

"Why was Nicolette's father killed? What does his death have to do with her now?"

"It's the name," James said. "It's tied to superstition, a mystic secret, or myth, or perhaps even truth. God only knows. I cannot say much more, but I can tell you this—whoever is behind this means to eliminate the Bradentons completely.

John and his family are gone. His parents, his aunts and uncles, his wife. Nicolette may be the last." James looked expectantly at Grant. "If there are murderers still lurking and looking for some mythic treasure, I'm afraid Nicolette's name will draw them out again. And if Clifton is itchy for gossip fodder to sell to the bleeding scandal sheets…" James shuddered a breath. "I can't take the chance."

Grant contemplated the jewelry box in his possession and realized that perhaps it was more than a simple mystery. Could it have something to do with this? God help the bastard if Clifton decided to use what he'd overheard. He'd enlist the Earl of Richfield to take care of Clifton. Grant and Mitchell were closer than brothers. With one word, one request, Mitchell would silence Clifton without question. He wouldn't even require a reason. Their bond was that solid.

"I have an idea how to stop Clifton for now. Do you have a plan to keep Nicolette safe?"

"If you can stop Clifton, perhaps everything will return to normal, but we won't know right away." Walborne sat again, then placed his head in his hands. After a deep breath, he scrubbed his palms down the length of his face.

"And what of the authorities?"

Walborne's head snapped toward Grant. "No! John feared corruption from the local magistrate. No judge would dare open the case against John's attackers even if they could be found. The only lead Robert had was Craddock himself, the owner of the fleet prior to your purchase, but Craddock died of apoplexy shortly after John's death."

Grant had his misgivings concerning that tale. Perhaps Craddock knew too much. But that was the least of his problems. Minimalizing Clifton's damage came first. Clifton would either lose the story or lose his barbed tongue, Grant cared not which.

CHAPTER 6

Grant left Walborne to find his niece and have her sent to her rooms, to lock her in if he must. As for Grant, he sent a note to the Earl of Richfield. Richfield would stop the gossip from spreading. He was a man of great persuasion. His height alone scared most men into compliance, and Grant trusted him with his life. The two had been friends since boyhood. They'd joined the Royal Navy together. They'd saved each other's lives more times than he cared to remember. Richfield's trust required no explanation; the request alone would be honored without question.

If Nicolette's father had been murdered for his name, and if Craddock had been killed for any supposed knowledge, which according to Walborne there was reason to believe, then the danger to Nicolette was real. Too real for Grant to stand by and do nothing. Determined, albeit a little reckless, Grant penned another note, this one to Walborne. He then went in search of Nicolette.

With midnight nearly upon them, Grant wanted her safe before another surge of guests arrived. There would be little time for explanations, and he'd given little thought to what he'd do if she refused or if her uncle balked at his idea. To ensure Nicolette's safety, he first needed control over the situation and that meant reducing her contact with the outside world.

He planned to steal her away.

He tried every door on the second floor until he heard her voice, but not from behind a door—it came from the gallery below. With long strides, he reached the polished mahogany balustrade. Midnight-blue silk disappeared down a corridor, and then he heard a sharp yelp. It could have been her tripping or stumbling. It could have been a squeal of laughter. It could have been something completely benign, but to Grant it sounded like a scream. He took the steps two at a time, bounding down the staircase, not another soul in sight.

Chasing after a phantom, he spied a service door at the end of the hallway. He broke into a run, dashing past an empty parlor. The sconces on the wall flickered as he rushed to catch up with the person who'd screamed and the one who'd caused it. He grabbed the door handle, flinging it open so hard that it banged against the inside wall.

Two paces out the door, down the short steps, was Nicolette, hanging over the shoulder of a man he could not distinguish in the dark. A gag was tied around her mouth, and her hair fell from the pins.

"You should fetch a tidy sum, Miss Bradenton." The man barked out the name, and Grant's stomach lurched.

His stride ate up the ground. Coming up from behind, Grant jerked the kidnapper's forearm, twisting it into the small of his back. "You'll not get a farthing, you bloody bastard."

He labored to keep his grip on the man while he stretched to catch Nicolette with his other arm. His hands were full. The kidnapper pulled away, tearing out of Grant's iron grip. When he did, Grant fell backward with the weight of Nicolette on top of him. He hit the gravel walkway with a sharp grunt.

With his arms around her, the weight of her falling body

had thrown him off-balance. Her full skirts impeded his view. He took the brunt of the fall, and his right elbow stung from the impact with earth and stone. He was thankful that they were far enough from the steps to miss them altogether. Above him he saw her eyes wide with shock and her mouth still silenced by the gag.

The sound of horses' hooves on stone, the jerking roll of hacks passing up and down the streets were white noise during the season, but there was no mistaking the halting jingle of rigging or the puff of snorting nostrils from a horse reined in. Grant didn't need to look up to know that the man had escaped. He caught sight of the unmarked hack but nothing else. It had been too dark to see the man's face or the driver of the hack.

Nicolette pressed her hands against his chest in an attempt to stand and barely missed jamming a knee in his groin. Grant struggled to right himself, gained the ground on his haunches, then with a grunt stood, holding Nicolette pinned to his side.

He reached behind her head and untied the gag.

"Are you hurt?" He swallowed the explosive anger at losing the man, softening his tone when he saw the stunned, vacant look in Nicolette's beautiful blue eyes. Running his hands gently over her cheeks, he forced her to look at him. "Nicolette, did he hurt you?"

With the barest blink, she shook her head. "I... I don't think so," she stammered, her voice quivering.

Grant pulled her close with gentle support while she found her legs, then helped her inside. He didn't exactly expect the lunatic to return, but he couldn't be sure he wouldn't. Time was of the essence.

"Where are your rooms?" he asked while his mind began putting together a plan of action.

She answered without bothering to ask why, which was a definite sign of her mental state. "Second floor. West wing."

Walking alongside him, she led Grant to her bedchamber. "Miss Blanchfield should be about somewhere. I want to see Aunt Lydia." Eyes pleading and innocent and frightened gazed up at him.

"Not now, love." He opened the door to her room and led her through it. "Trust me." His words were soft and calm, but his voice was firm and resolved. He took a moment to cup her cheek and rub a thumb over her silky skin, smiling into her eyes, hoping to instill confidence and strength.

Nicolette didn't argue.

Through a connecting door, a woman wearing brown bombazine, her hair in a tight bun and a stern and unforgiving look upon her face, strode into the room. This must be the infamous Miss Blanchfield.

"You, sir, do not belong in here!" The older woman's eyes blazed, raking Grant from head to toe. But when she looked at Nicolette, the governess's face dropped and her mouth fell open. With a hand to her chest, she glanced back at Grant. "What happened?" She rushed to Nicolette's side.

"More than I have time to explain. Pack your lady a small traveling bag. And for your charge's sake, be quick about it," Grant commanded the governess. If he expected immediate capitulation, he was wrong.

"I will not. Not without an explanation," she said fearlessly. He was sure if the protective governess had a blade at that moment, she'd have run him through on the spot.

"We don't have time for this." His patience was coming to an end. He crossed to the wardrobe and dropped a peach dress on the bed, then turned back for more. While he whipped the room into action, Nicolette stood woodenly by, in shock, her gaze frozen and unwavering.

Miss Blanchfield stared worriedly at Nicolette and then took one look at Grant trying to pack. "No, not that one. Let me do it." She appeared to comply, absently packing the bag without much focus. "I could scream and bring the entire house running." Her thoughts were surely wrapped around saving her charge from certain ruin.

"You could do that, Miss Blanchfield, but it would only endanger Miss Thomas's life."

The governess turned suddenly, a stunned look freezing her otherwise severe features into a sheet of concern. She closed the satchel while keeping an eye trained on Nicolette. Her angry retorts stopped. How much of Nicolette's story Miss Blanchfield was privy to, Grant couldn't know. It was safer to keep the details of tonight between him and Lord Walborne. He'd already sent Nicolette's uncle a note. If Walborne wished to stop the plan from moving forward, he'd do so. But Grant couldn't allow Miss Blanchfield to delay him any longer.

He didn't waver. Nicolette glanced up at him while he silently wrapped a sable-lined cloak around her quaking shoulders.

"I'm not cold," she whispered.

"You're shivering, and we're leaving." So saying, he grabbed the bag containing the few items that Miss Blanchfield had packed and headed for the door. He held Nicolette's elbow and rushed her out of her bedchamber.

"Oh no, you don't, I'm coming with you. You'll not leave my presence with my charge." The governess was obviously panicked, but Grant had to hand it to her—she was determined.

"You are not coming." Grant's tone brooked no argument, not even from a steely, tenacious governess.

"I most certainly am, young man!" Miss Blanchfield shouted.

Grant stopped mercifully, for the sake of the affectionate woman who only had Nicolette's best interest in mind. "Miss Blanchfield, I know you mean well, but you will only slow us down. Find your employer. He'll know what to do. And tell no one else." He held her with a steady unwavering glare, refusing to accept nothing less than complete obedience. "Do you understand?" he said forcefully but not unkindly.

Acceptance shone in her resolve, and she turned a hopeful look toward Nicolette for an answer.

Shocked and silent, Nicolette nodded.

"As you wish, Your Grace." Miss Blanchfield's shoulders deflated with her hushed reply. Worry lined her forehead, but she did as Grant requested.

Leaving through the main foyer was out of the question. From Nicolette's bedchamber, Grant poked his head out the door and checked the hallway, then proceeded left toward the servants' stairwell.

The young woman whose feet stumbled alongside him made no attempt to speak, but she trembled beneath his hands. After requesting a word with the butler to have a rented hack brought round to the mews, he ushered Nicolette through the kitchens and waited. He pulled the hood of her cloak up around her face and secured the frog at her throat. When the hack arrived five minutes later, he assisted Nicolette up onto the worn leather seat, then took his place beside her, watching her lovely, bewildered face slowly show signs of recognition.

A puzzled crease formed between her ocean-blue eyes. "Why would someone wish to kidnap me? Why would they do that, Grant?"

Although he loved that she used his name, he also understood that it was brought on by trauma. She'd been through a terrifying ordeal. That she could speak at all surprised him. Traveling alone with a man was grounds enough for ruination, but Nicolette didn't seem overwhelmed by that fact.

Shocked? Yes.

Confused? Yes.

But trust was not born from fear or shock or confusion. It was born from something else. Something that had been missing from his life since he'd lost his parents. Something she apparently understood better than he.

"I'm not sure, love," he answered. "Right now my concern is your safety."

Her eyes frantically scanned the scenery out the window, her breath coming in frightened gasps. "I want to see my aunt and uncle. Take me back." Her eyes were wide and managed to pierce him with an equal measure of fear and demand.

"Nicolette." He kept calm.

"Take me back." She searched his face, panic shining in her eyes. "Take me back, Grant."

"I don't think that's a sound idea. And I think your uncle will agree this is the most effective solution for now." He did his best to soothe her without sounding condescending. He knew she needed answers, but now wasn't the time.

She placed a hand against the cold window, making an imprint on the frosted glass. "Where are you taking me?"

"Somewhere safe and secure." He knew the words were empty, but he had no others to give. Not yet.

She hissed with exasperation. "Do you think me an imbecile? There is no one else in this cabin. Surely you can tell me where we're headed. Is it to your home?"

"No. And before your imagination runs away, I promise that your reputation is safe. Only your family is aware of this trip, and of course your governess and the butler. I seriously doubt they'd risk their jobs for gossip."

She glanced his way, clear annoyance written across her brow, and then rolled her eyes with a sigh. "Obviously I trust them."

"Ah, it's just me you don't trust." He was baiting her, hoping to turn fear into strength.

"I suppose I have little choice." Irritation tinged her voice, but the fear was gone.

A quarter hour passed in virtual silence, and Grant

watched her furtively, avoiding an obvious stare, and waited for her to fully relax. He watched her throat bob after a stuttering breath, watched her tuck an errant hair behind her ear, watched her smooth her skirts absently like it was second nature, an extension of habit. She put a gloved fist against the cold, misty window and rubbed a wide circle to see better. Light and shadow passed over her face while they traveled between streetlamps. The clip of horses' hooves was a rhythmic reminder of where they were.

With her head turned away from him, he caught the scent of honey and lemon in her hair, a marked difference to the musty, dank smell of the rented hack. He stretched his fingers, then clinched them back into his palm, squelching the itch to twine the fallen curls at her nape around his fingers or to assist her in fixing them back atop her head. Instead, he grabbed the leather thong beside his head meant to steady the occupant from flopping about when the wheels of the carriage hit a pothole. The street was smooth enough, but Grant's rash decision to intervene had him feeling like he needed something to hang on to. He took note of the increase in traffic, curricles, carriages, and even a few young dandies on foot. Midnight was hardly late for those seeking amusement during the season.

As they made progress toward the outskirts of town, he directed his focus back to her.

"You're taking me from the city." Her body jerked round in her seat. Her eyes glazed with accusation. "Don't deny it."

"I'm not."

"You don't deny it, or you're not taking me from the city? I have the right to know."

"You're wrinkling your skirts." He pointed a look at her gripping fingers.

She looked down at her hands, at the fabric bunched into a tight ball. With a flick of blue silk, she smoothed the fabric over her knees, then drew the ends of her cloak together.

"We'll speak of the destination when we're closer." He said each word clearly, calmly, evenly. "Why don't you rest? You've been shaken, Nicolette." In truth, his own nerves were anything but steel at the moment.

"I don't need a rest. I need to go home." When he didn't comment, she continued, "I could scream." Her eyes searched his.

"And like Miss Blanchfield, you'd only draw attention. Attention we don't need or want."

"*You* don't need or want."

"When you're safe, we'll talk of it. Right now I won't take the chance that the driver, however unlikely, should overhear any details."

Defeated, she looked away.

"Nicolette, be reasonable."

She shrugged, her eyes unblinking, her face a numb mask.

"I sent word to your uncle. I'm not kidnapping you."

"If I thought you were kidnapping me, I'd have jumped from the cab by now."

He couldn't help the chuckle after that announcement. He half turned in the seat and folded his arms. "Are you strong enough for a question or two?"

"What do you think?" she nearly snapped.

"I think you're scared."

She looked away, biting her lip. "Ask."

"Have you ever seen the man who attacked you? Did he look familiar?"

She shook her head. "He asked if I'd help him find his spectacles, said he'd left them on the first floor, perhaps in the cloakroom. I thought him a little strange but didn't wish to embarrass him. So I took him to the first floor, and when we were out of sight, he grabbed my wrists. He dragged me down the hallway, out the door, and gagged me. It happened so quickly I hadn't a chance to think."

"Thank you for screaming, by the way."

She looked nonplussed. "You're welcome."

"I only meant that you did the right thing."

She stared at him like he'd grown another head. "You make it sound as if I used great intellect to do what came naturally."

"No. I'm sure anyone would have screamed." Feeling vulnerable and helpless, he watched her with narrowed eyes. "Honestly, Nicolette, it scared the devil out of me." He swallowed a lump.

She raised her brows. "What do you think he hoped to gain? I cannot be worth so much as to risk life and limb to steal."

"You must be worth something since I am apparently risking my life and limb."

She harrumphed. "Then you lie if you say my uncle agreed to this."

The challenge of trust did not go unnoted.

"Perhaps it was random?" Now she sounded hopeful. Pleadingly hopeful.

It wasn't random, of that he was sure, and equally sure that the man wanted her dead. Maybe it would be best to discuss it with her.

"It's clear you were the target. My guess, it had something to do with your name."

"Thomas? Or Bradenton?"

"Bradenton."

"Bradenton? How can that be?" She pressed her back against the hard cushions. Confusion took her voice up a notch. "No one but my family is privy to the name except for you. How did this stranger know?"

"I presume you know the lengths Gerald Clifton will go for a good story?"

"One need not be among the ton long before one knows

Mr. Clifton. He is none too kind. He takes great pleasure in using his words and influence over the gossip sheets to bring women to heel. And does his best to emasculate any man who lacks the strength to beat him senseless."

"He has the propensity for unusual gossip, and I'm afraid you were his victim tonight."

"Me?" Nicolette pressed a hand to her chest, her eyes round with surprise. "Why me?"

"Because his insatiable curiosity led him to eavesdrop on our conversation. He must have overheard me address you as Miss Bradenton." He curled his lip in disgust.

"When we were on the balcony."

His eyes closed in momentary self-loathing for his part. He turned away, uncrossing his arms, letting his hand rest on the seat between them. "He's not entirely to blame. It was my indulgence in our wordplay that started it. If I hadn't done that, then Clifton would know nothing. The weasel would sell his soul for information."

He felt dainty gloved fingers squeeze his hand. A jolt of shocked pleasure seized his heart as he switched his gaze from the scenery to her hand clutching his. The simple gesture of genuine compassion sent a ripple up his spine. He sucked in a breath and, damn it all, felt gooseflesh under his collar.

For God's sake, gooseflesh.

How in the hell had this girl coaxed such a response with an innocent touch? Gloved at that.

"You mustn't think this your fault."

Was she trying to soothe him? It took all he had to keep his wits and remember who was protecting whom.

"Besides, what could possibly be so sinister about my surname?" she reasoned. "What does the name Bradenton have to do with any of this?"

"It apparently has everything to do with it. And when I'm done with this little mystery, the man or men who purposed to harm you will be gravely put to rest." He forced the threat through clenched teeth, then patted her hand and released himself from the torture of her touch.

"You'd harm someone for me?" She visibly shuddered, but something in her eyes spoke appreciation.

"I would see you protected, yes. I believe the kidnapper meant you more than harm. I think his aim was murder." He watched her for signs of panic.

"You sound sure." She swallowed, turning her attention out the window again, although she didn't appear to be looking at anything. It seemed more habit than interest.

"He did give his name."

Without commenting, he tilted his head for a better view. Her face a ghostly reflection in the glass, he watched for any change in her expression and waited patiently for her to continue.

"He said his name was Douglas Manning. I suppose that could be his real name. If he meant to do me permanent harm, I can't imagine there would be much reason to lie." She glanced back at Grant and held his gaze like she was drawing strength from it. "If he meant to kill me, then who could I possibly tell, right?" Her voice shook on the word *kill*. Her body trembled.

There was still time for details. The man would be a fool to give his real name, but he didn't argue with her. He couldn't do anything until they reached their destination, and he realized her growing fear was perhaps more than he could calm. He worked on brightening the pall that descended over the tiny compartment. "Why don't we talk of something else for a while?"

She nodded. With her hands braced on the seat, she shifted her derriere and relaxed against the worn leather.

"You lived on the merchant ship your father captained. That's unheard of. How old were you when you first sailed?"

He must have hit upon the correct subject because her face was transformed as if she'd already left the night behind. She positively glowed.

"I was ten." She pressed a knuckle to her smiling mouth. "Papa refused to allow anyone else to raise me after my mother passed. She'd been sick, and my father nursed her to no avail. It crushed him and it devastated me when she died. He went to Mr. Craddock, the owner of the fleet at the time, and begged him for permission so I might stay with my papa. Mr. Craddock agreed to allow it for a year. But after the year was up, I'd become like one of the crew. We were a family. Papa handpicked the crew, and they all welcomed me. They were kind, and Mr. Craddock couldn't bear to take me from my father." She swallowed. "I know it sounds terribly odd." She stole a rueful glance at him.

He raised both brows, shrugging his mouth into a smile. "That sounds very normal to me," he said playfully. "Continue please."

She almost laughed, and he took joy in that.

"I know you tease me," she said with a little shake of her head, but a gentle curve still played about her sweet mouth. "I realize how it must sound to a man of your import. Girls do not live on ships."

"Apparently they do." The sheer delight in her eyes at the mention of her parents steadied him, anchoring the moment. Conversing with her felt natural. The sound of jostling coach wheels on cobblestone and the jingle of horse tack faded until it was as if they were sitting in a cozy parlor.

"I loved it. I loved being with Papa, and I loved the crew. Whenever possible he would take me back to the home where I'd grown up. I know he was trying to provide stability, but truly I preferred the dip and pull of the ocean."

She was like no woman he'd ever met, and he had to

remind himself again who she was. Young. Innocent. And above all else, scared.

The coach lamp swung as the road changed from well-placed cobblestone to rough and unkempt. Grant steadied the lantern. Nicolette didn't seem to notice at all, except she unconsciously braced herself for one particularly rough dip.

"Who educated you before you came to live with your aunt and uncle?"

"Papa was an educated man, and my mother was educated as well. They did what they could for me. But I'm afraid their lessons did not include waltzing or determining the proper use of every eating utensil ever imagined, nor did they include lessons in fluent French. Although my mother was French, she rarely spoke it. She grew up in England with Uncle James's family. They were as siblings. I loved my life on the ship, though I never dreamed I'd spend six years there."

"And what of this life? Did you never dream of being a debutante?" He put a hand to his chest as if it were of vital import. "Speaking proper English?" He mimicked the heavy accent used by the patronesses of Almack's. "And behaving without so much as a personality to spare?"

His gestures mocked the ton. He hoped to encourage her to keep speaking.

"I never wanted this." With a hand, she gestured from her hair to her clothes. "I was sixteen when my father died. I felt as if I'd lived my dream. I guess I wasn't old enough to know what I wanted then."

"What do you want now?"

Her gaze fell away, her smile unsure. "I guess I'm still not old enough to know."

He sat forward, his elbows to his knees, the action commanding her attention. "Perhaps it would be easier to list the things you don't want and then look for what's missing."

Tapping her pouting lips, she looked into his eyes. She bit

the tip of her finger. It was an action of thought, but his pulse quickened watching her do it.

She finally pulled her mouth to the side and answered. "I don't want to disappoint my parents."

That answer surprised him. "How could you possibly do that?"

Nicolette sniffled, not from emotion but from the difference in the chill outside and the increasing warmth of the cabin. He brandished a handkerchief and handed it to her.

"Thank you," she said while swiping it under her nose. She then held the handkerchief around her nostrils and blew.

Proper women claimed daintiness over comfort, but not this one, and Grant found himself liking her even more for it.

"As you can see, my mother was not successful with me," she muttered from under the handkerchief.

"Most of the women I know are obsessed with their own beauty, or lack thereof, and they live with their own misconception of what that means. But not you." He was mesmerized by her, or perhaps it was his reaction to her. He grinned unrepentantly as she tried to hide a blush and shy away.

"That was a compliment in case you wondered." He straightened.

Nicolette tried without much success to keep her smile at bay by using the handkerchief as a barrier. "Your compliments are like a maze, Your Grace. How many women have made the wrong turn and ended up on the wrong side of your personality, I wonder? Do you think that's why you're not married?" Her eyes sparkled.

"Nicolette." He used her name, hoping she'd go back to using his. "Your wit has yet to disappoint." He paused to tamp down the uncomfortable, bitter taste left from the discussion he'd had with his grandmother regarding marriage, then continued, "At nineteen, this should be your second year—has your uncle given any hint or chosen a suitor for you?"

"Uncle James will not choose for me without my consent." With her head held high, she made the proclamation with confidence. But Grant knew differently.

"No? Has Miss Blanchfield failed to teach you how marriages are typically arranged among the upper echelon? They are decided *for*, not *by*, those most affected. I've no doubt your uncle will have the last say." It wasn't that he wished to dash all her fanciful dreams if she had any, but it was the simple truth.

"I don't care how it's done here. I'll marry for love or not at all." She said that with such conviction he almost believed her.

"Love? You actually expect to love the man you marry?" Shaking his head, he held down his mirth. She was serious.

With narrowed eyes, she scrutinized him like she was plotting something. "What might your age be, Your Grace?"

Laughter chased him whenever she was present. He had no idea where this line of questioning was headed, but he was just fool enough to find out.

"How old do you think I am?"

She closed one eye and used the other as if she wore a monocle that made him automatically transparent. "You're certainly old enough to have fallen in love." A long, slender finger tapped at her bottom lip.

"Eight-and-twenty," he said with a chuckle. Did she think him as old as he thought her young? For some reason that gave him pause.

"Twenty-eight?" Her astonishment was unmistakable. "Well, you have nine years on me, sir, and I quite expect to fall in love long before I'm twenty-eight."

"I hate to disappoint you, but the ton do not marry for love, as I've said. I can't even think of one couple who is *in* love. Title. Wealth. Beauty even. But not love."

"That's very sad if you think that's true." Her gaze

searched his, and he feared this conversation would not end well.

"Name one couple you know to be in love. Affection does not count, nor a fondness for, and forget a tendre. I mean truly in love." He expected the answer to take longer than their coach ride.

"I will admit that in your world, this might prove a challenge." She seemed to ponder it carefully. "Aha! My Uncle James and Aunt Lydia. They remind me of my parents, and I assure you that my parents were very much in love."

Not ready to surrender this argument, Grant parried. "Yes, but your parents were not a part of the ton."

"But my aunt and uncle are." Triumph bloomed in her eyes, and she smiled with victory. "Besides, what do you know of love if you've never felt it yourself? Perhaps you don't recognize it. Although I'm certain you're rarely without the company of a beautiful woman." She paused, biting her lip while she searched the far corner of the cabin. She breathed in deep at the same time her eyes darted to his.

This did not bode well for him.

"May I ask you another question?" Her posture exuded energy. Her folded hands were more than the calm facade of a proper lady. They lured the audience into thinking her incapable of mischief.

Conversations ending in questions had a way of traveling south quickly, but the scent of fresh sweet lemon that he'd come to recognize as hers muddied his brain. He smiled wickedly and against all wisdom allowed his curiosity complete control.

"What do you wish to know?"

She filled her lungs with a steady breath like the prelude to a serious, perhaps difficult, discussion. "The other night, after we met at the theater and I returned to my seat and you returned to who knows where."

"I believe I returned to my seat as well."

"Yes, of course you did. I saw you."

"You were watching me?" The irony was not lost on him. He'd gone there to watch her.

She cocked her head. "You are difficult to miss."

He folded his arms, regarding her. "Hm."

"And so was the woman seated next to you."

His back straightened, his hearing muffled by the roar of blood rushing in his ears, and he crossed his legs, which made the cabin feel more cramped. For some bloody reason, his conscience crowded him.

"Do you recall? She was blond and from a distance looked very pretty."

Joanna Featherbe was not pretty. She was strikingly beautiful. And a pain in the arse, even more so now. Why did he feel as if he'd just been snared in a trap? Good Lord, who had Nicolette been speaking with? True, Joanna had joined him for the theater, but only because she'd begged him for a favor. She'd hoped that being escorted by a duke might bring Mr. Knightly to heel. Jealousy was Joanna's weapon of choice, although it had never worked on Grant. Regardless of his escort, no one believed he had any interest in her. Not now. Perhaps three years ago when they'd ended their relationship, but he'd been gone for nearly two years, and they'd not been seen in each other's company for some time, not until last week.

Damn it. Nicolette was staring at him, waiting for a response. He nodded.

"Was she perhaps your mistress?"

"Nicolette," he warned in a low, commanding voice, one that usually intimidated. This discussion was wholly inappropriate.

She shrugged; even the toes of her shoes rocked up with

her shoulders. "I know it's not at all in good taste to ask, but rumors have it so. And I do have a point to make."

"What is it?" His voice came out clipped.

"My point is, I don't know whether she is or she is not. Miss Featherbe I believe is her name. I would be hard-pressed to recognize a courtesan if I saw one. But I'm sure you would." She paused and took a breath. Pulling in her chin, she watched from beneath her perfectly winged brows.

Her daring unsettled him even more so because she did not hail from the fast-paced world he'd been raised in where true innocence was rare. He bit down on his next words, noticing, not for the first time, the soft swell above her neckline where her cloak fell away. It stoked a fire in his blood and reminded him she was a woman.

An unwise woman playing with fire.

"I've changed my mind. I should have included your stifling governess on this trip."

Nicolette grinned and brashly said, "I'm glad you did not. She'd have put a halt to this conversation, and I'm rather enjoying myself."

This young woman didn't know how flirtatiously dangerous she was. He would need to work extra hard at keeping her at arm's length because his reaction to her innocent banter was purely automatic.

"Are you going to answer the question?"

"You've failed to make your point." He hoped that would put an end to it.

"If she is your mistress, I wouldn't know. I know men keep them—I'm not completely ignorant. But if I had not heard the rumor, I wouldn't have guessed because I've never been exposed to it."

Grant all but choked on her reasoning. He squeezed his eyes shut and hung on to a calm he didn't feel.

"Don't you see?"

"No. I do not," he said emphatically.

"I don't recognize what I have not been exposed to."

"Yes, Nicolette, I get that. What does that have to do with anything?" Exacerbated impatience clouded his thinking, and if he admitted the truth, he'd have to say he was completely embarrassed.

"In the same way, you have not been exposed to a couple in love, so how on God's green earth would you ever recognize it? Unless, of course, you are in love with Miss Featherbe." She fell silent, but her eyes spoke volumes.

Unsure what to address first and not sure whether he should address anything at all, Grant waited a full minute before responding, his pulse galloping.

He took a deep breath. "I am not in love with Miss Featherbe. She is not my mistress. I can't believe you would ask that." He shook his head and sighed. "And I'm fairly certain I would recognize a couple in the throes of love because there are some things I do know about it." Hopefully that would put an end to the discussion. Even as jaded as Grant was, he would never have introduced such a topic.

"I don't think you do." She appeared quite pleased with herself, shifting in her seat and arranging her skirts. He noticed her crossed ankles and her heels tapping the floor.

Grant closed his eyes for a moment and contemplated his next sentence. These were personal matters, and he wasn't accustomed to sharing his private life with anyone, least of all a woman. Against his better judgment, he was about to break his own rules.

"My parents were also very much in love." He raised a hand against her next comment. "My mother was not a part of the landscape here. She was Spanish, and as you know, we have at times been at odds with Spain. My grandmother was quite biased and didn't care for my mother. My grandmother would never approve of my father's marriage, and in complete disregard for my grandmother's wishes, my parents eloped."

"How very romantic." Nicolette nearly gushed.

"Love cannot hold the storm of prejudice, and it couldn't squelch the scandal that an elopement caused. My grandmother never forgave my father for it. My mother and father came home to England to live as rightful heir to our family title and estate, but my mother was never made welcome, and because of an unfortunate circumstance, my father never attained the title due him." The words came out bitter. He'd tried for unconcerned, but every time he spoke of his parents' marriage he was reminded of how angry and how impossible his grandmother made it for him to wed. He'd never risk bringing a wife into his home, not with his grandmother's strict principles and harsh judgment.

"Is that why you're the duke now?"

"No, love. Titles are inherited not by will but by right. My father simply didn't live long enough to attain it. But I guarantee had he lived that long, my grandmother would have loved nothing more than to keep the title from him for the sake of spite. Now that the title has come to me, she's desperate for it to stay in her immediate family. I am the last of that line."

"I'm so sorry." Her eyes shone with tears, making them appear a deeper blue, like the sea on a moonless night.

Pity is not what he wished from her. He didn't wish it from anyone. He waved the subject aside. "It happened a long time ago." The darkness outside distracted him, and he imagined it enveloping his grief and guarding him against it.

"At least you had the opportunity to witness your parents' love. That should give you hope."

"No, it reminds me what a waste of time it is." He tried to smile. The conversation weighed heavy. With his arms crossed, he blew out a long sigh.

"How can you say it's a waste of time? Don't you want to

have a family and bring the kind of love your parents shared back into your home?" Her enthusiasm regarding his imaginary yearning for hearth and home eclipsed anything he ever felt for it.

"I have no intention of marrying and raising a family under that roof." It came out harsh, but he couldn't help it. "My grandmother still only approves of title and money. And I don't believe in love, at least not the kind you speak of."

"What about your parents?" She wouldn't let it lie.

He stared directly at her, trying to make her understand without getting angry. "It cost them peace and a good life, and I can't see how it was worth it."

"Can't you? You are a direct result of it. I think you're destined for it because you're a product of it."

That bit of nonsense made him laugh, which he needed badly right now. The deep chuckle broke the heavy spell and the serious tone of the unconventional discussion.

"You, sweet, are a dreamer." He smiled and softened his gaze.

"Yes, I suppose I am. My father always said it was one of my finest qualities." Her tone dared him to reply.

"It would almost have to be." The comment seemed to surprise her. "How else would a young girl manage to survive what you have? You have no idea how brave you are, do you?" He hadn't meant to say so much, to reveal so much, but neither would he take it back. He caught her gaze and refused to let go.

CHAPTER 7

The Duke of Havenly caught Nicolette completely off guard. He was nothing like the roguish stories she'd heard. Yes, his high-handedness was overbearing at times, but he had a gentle kindness behind his eyes. That molten amber of passion was perhaps a defense to cover the vulnerability that lurked beneath.

He'd called her a dreamer, then suggested she was brave.

To date, the bravest thing she'd done was to engage him in wordplay. The thought made her smile, which she was sure he would misinterpret since he was watching her intently.

Sitting beside him in the tight-fitting cab, she *bravely* held his gaze until he rubbed the place between his eyes. His whole being sighed, from his closed eyes to the lift and fall of his wide shoulders, and she couldn't blame him. This could not be what he'd expected from the evening any more than she.

Ironically, she endeavored to put *him* at ease.

She cleared her throat. "Would you care to play a game with me?"

The question was innocently asked, but from the bend of

his brow, she realized how it must have sounded. He folded his arms, an air of confident arrogance about him.

"I'm not sure I should agree. The last time you spoke of games, it didn't bode well for me. What did you have in mind?" His tone held playful relief. Teasing and humor were also his defense.

"It's just something I played with my father when I was young. One person would make a prediction, and the other would forfeit something whenever it came true."

"What was the forfeit?" His carefree smile increased the attraction of that boyish dimple.

It dawned on her that the forfeit had always been a familial kiss on the cheek. In her rush to escape his discerning scrutiny, she'd plumb forgotten about the kiss.

"A trade of a chore?" She cringed, wanting to squeeze her eyes shut when one side of his mouth slanted devilishly while his gaze told her that he didn't believe her.

He was kind enough not to ask. He did however suggest, "Why, Miss Thomas, that sounds like a wager. Currency is sometimes literal."

"Money?" She brightened. Now why hadn't she thought of that? "I do have an allowance, but you are a man of wealth. Is one pound enough to hurt your pocket, good sir?"

"Perfect. A crushing amount. Now what is your prediction?" He warmed to the game. Stimulating energy egged her on.

"I predict you will marry a woman you're madly in love with because you were born of love and you are destined for it." She gave a sidelong glance and batted her eyes with comic emphasis.

"That's hardly fair since I told you I don't believe in love. You are bound to lose, sweet."

"It's not necessary for you to believe it because I do. And it's my prediction." She took a haughty stance. Besides, the game was meant to pass the time. She had no intention of ever collecting on it. Or paying the price for it.

"I believe that sounds more like a death knell." His tone was amusingly dire. "How long do I have to live?"

A rogue giggle escaped, and she brought the handkerchief that he'd given her up to her mouth, smothering her response without much success. "Really, Your Grace, what would Miss Featherbe say?"

He shook his head and rocked a finger back and forth. "Oh, Miss Thomas, you do not play fair."

"I have no incentive to play fair. I'm trying to win." She bit into the smile that stretched her cheeks.

"In that case, am I allowed to make a prediction of my own?"

She gripped the edge of her seat and leaned in close, curious what outrageous prediction he'd make. "By all means." She flared her eyes innocently wide and strove for guilelessness.

"I predict your uncle will choose your suitor before the end of next season."

The playful, carefree mood fell away. Her stomach lurched, the wheel of the coach hit a rut in the road, and Nicolette automatically put a hand on her head to hold down a nonexistent hat.

He nervously rubbed his palms together. "Let me amend that," he said, instant regret in his tone.

"It's too late." She threw him a defiant look and swallowed down the terrifying prediction. She supposed she deserved it. She'd brought on the subject and even mentioned Miss Featherbe, knowing full well he'd not take it kindly. Her back went rigid while she fought her mood into a forced smile. "I'm only happy that you'd allow me another season of unattachment."

Next she did something completely out of character for a proper lady but something completely familiar to her. With a lofty shake of her head, she sent several wayward curls, mussed from her near abduction, back over her shoulder, then shot out a hand in the small space between them and waited.

Without faltering, he grasped her hand and shook it up and down in a gentleman's agreement.

She did smile then.

And he returned it.

"Where shall this transaction take place when you lose?" he asked good-naturedly, encouraging the light mood they'd shared moments before.

"How dare you suggest I'd lose, Your Grace," she said in a tone of bristling outrage and then ruined it by laughing. "I want somewhere public and humiliating." It was shameful for her to even suggest it, but she couldn't resist the taunt.

"Grosvenor Gate?" he proposed impishly.

She replied in kind. "Take the path until you come upon the first green bench. It's public and decent. Of course, when you hand over your forfeit, it will be quite scandalous, but you'll be in love and you won't mind."

"You, Miss Thomas, are impressionably young. I shall keep that in mind." He bowed his head.

"You may try. When you lose, you may send me a note at my uncle's. I shall endure the scandal of such a thing for the sake of your forfeit."

"Very gallant."

"Indeed. Are you afraid?" The question was innocent and playful.

"Of you?" He laughed. "No. I believe we've made a gentleman's agreement. I'm good for the money, Miss Thomas. I hope you are."

"I shan't need it."

While distracted by the game of forfeits, they'd apparently crossed a bridge. A whirl of panic interrupted every carefree thought. Answers were overdue.

"Do you plan to tell me where we're headed?" Anxiety

IT WAS ONLY A KISS

picked up pace with the smell of rot and decay from the river. Years had passed since she'd sailed, but the imprint of stench on her sinuses triggered memories that brought a flood of interwoven emotions. A full moon, reflected by the Thames, lit up the harbor. When the wharf came into view, it was all she could do not to desperately seek her father's beloved face.

"I cannot tell you exactly where we're headed—"

"You're stalling."

Before he could respond, the coach halted.

"Woolwich."

She shook her head and pulled back into the seats. The sounds of drunken men boisterously singing was deafening, and the smell of rotting fish was so strong she could almost taste it.

The duke didn't wait for the driver; he opened the door himself and forewent the steps. He jumped from the carriage, stuck out his hand, and expected her to join him. Nicolette slapped away his offer of help. It was one thing to travel by hack alone with a man but quite another to be seen traveling by ship with him. If the ton were to hear of this, her reputation would be in tatters.

Heavens, not just tatters—to travel alone with this particular man, one of England's most notorious rakes, would ruin her for good.

"Nicolette, come. We don't have time for games," he said sternly.

"Good, because I'm not playing one. And I'm not getting out of this cab." Protesting held no power over this man. He reached for her hand and pulled her forward. Not waiting to see if she would obey, he simply tossed her over his shoulder and carried her up the gangway of a large ship, her screams now cut off by the strong arm working to compress her midsection. The unperturbed crewman who carried Nicolette's only piece of luggage followed on their heels as if this were an everyday event.

She beat him with her fists, kicked her legs, and fought the air with her feet, to no avail. From her vantage point, all she could see were the feet of half a dozen crewmen parting from the duke's long stride. They were obviously aboard one of his ships. But which one remained to be seen.

Down a corridor of stairs and a sharp right, he kicked open a door and tossed her on a clean bed. Her mussed hair impeded her view.

Without thinking, she pulled off a shoe and threw it at him. "How could you?" she stormed.

Her unbound hair cost precious seconds. Her fingers caught in the tangle of curls as she swiped them from her face. Before she could pin her abductor with a scathing look, he'd already reached the door.

"Where do you think you're going, sir?"

Putting a finger to his lips, the duke motioned for quiet. "Keep this up and the whole ship will think I've stolen away with an unwilling companion."

"And have you not?" She refused to be daunted by his crass comment, but the man only encroached upon her loud retort. He even managed a smile.

"If you don't mind waiting until I leave?" He opened the door and quickly shut it just before her other shoe struck the thick oak.

Next, she heard a key turn in the lock from the outside.

Desperately she searched the wall for a peg where another key might hang. Outside, she heard the familiar sounds of running feet, the creak of pulleys and rigging, the faint sound of hollering voices. And then the all-too-familiar lurch that signaled a break from the dock.

Somewhere inside, a dam of pulsing nausea broke, and she settled herself on a chair set around an empty table. She slumped over, her head between her legs, while the sway of the boat forced her stomach into a roll. It had been some time since she'd sailed and an even longer time since she had succumbed to seasickness. It was a good thirty minutes of resting her head in one direction and then in the opposite to equalize the pitching. When Nicolette finally stood, she felt better.

Not great, but better.

Turning full circle, albeit slowly, she surveyed her surroundings. A large bed in one corner, butted against one wall, a host of windows where streams of moonlight illuminated everything made up another, and an unusual half wall built up in the adjacent corner with shutters to the ceiling was on the far side. There was an opening to this peculiar little alcove, and she stole a look inside.

It was amazing, astonishing, and completely out of the ordinary. It housed a tub and a basin with a full pitcher of water set into a washstand. Brass fittings held the door to the chamber pot. It was almost as modern as an English home.

She found a tinderbox and went about lighting the lamp oil.

Another take around the main room and the subtleties in wood began to remind her of her childhood.

And then she knew. This was the *New Horizon*.

Nostalgia buckled her knees and sucked a gasp from her. She staggered toward the bed and leaned against it. To crawl atop would take more strength than her lungs could gather at the moment. Her stays felt tighter with her chest heaving while thought collided with emotional baggage. Why would he do this? And where were they going?

Somewhere topside, a duke impeccably dressed in black formal attire was shouting instructions and setting sail to only God knew where.

For two hours she stared out the stretch of mullioned windows and watched as they made progress toward the open sea. How they maneuvered through the crowded Thames at night she couldn't know, and she wondered again when Havenly might return. He owed her an explanation. Did he expect her to fall asleep like a child and accept her plight without question? After three years observing ladies and gentlemen perform their daily duty with ton-approved proper etiquette, she still had no idea how women could sit passively by and watch every decision made for them, either by their elders or more often by men.

Even when she'd been taken from this ship at the age of sixteen, she'd not gone quietly. And she had no intention of going quietly now.

A key upset the lock in the door, reminding her with a jolt that she'd waited for two frustrating hours to confront her captor.

The heavy door inched open, pushing one blue silk slipper along the floor where she'd thrown it earlier. The hint of a navy wool seaman's peacoat appeared. Another cautious inch and a whole man slipped inside the cabin.

"Robert!" she blurted, clobbering the man with a hug before he shut the door.

Robert took the full force and wrapped her in a hug. The comforting scent of sweet pipe tobacco clung to him.

"Do you know what happened? What *he* did? It doesn't matter what he told you, we must go back." Her disjointed plea seemed to have no effect on her old friend.

"Nicole." He called her by her nickname, steering her away from the door. "Let's sit."

Had it only been two days since she'd seen him at dinner?

"I don't wish to sit. Are you worried for your position as

captain? Is that it? I can understand that, but surely the kidnapping of me carries some weight, does it not?" Frantic pangs of foreboding had her pulling at her hands, squeezing her fingers to keep them from fluttering about like a game of charades.

A knock sounded, and she whirled around to see the immoral beast of a duke peek his head in.

"Is it safe?"

"Not quite," Robert answered. To his credit, his forehead was wrinkled with worry even if he did seem to be in tandem with the duke.

Two quick steps and she was at the door. She smacked both hands against Havenly's broad chest. Hard muscle took the full impact with ease. He didn't put his hands on her or try to carry her again, but he did walk forward like a moving bookend, pressing her back toward the table while Robert shut the door.

With gentle care, Robert took her hand, guiding her toward a comfortable club-sized chair covered in red damask fabric that matched the curtains.

"I take it you haven't spoken with her yet?" Havenly asked.

Robert shook his head. "I only jest arrived."

"If what he has to say came from *you*, then I'm not interested." She tightened her arms across her chest and twisted her mouth.

The duke stood a yard from the table, his hands braced on his hips. He shed the formal jacket he still wore and threw it over the back of one of the chairs. "Are you hungry? Thirsty?"

She glared at Havenly, willing him singed on the spot.

Havenly sighed, a decided weariness about his eyes. "I'll go find something appropriate." After a step toward the door, he pivoted back and pointed a finger at her. "You stay put and listen to the man. He's your ally, not your enemy." He had the gall to give her a quick authoritative nod with a piratical quirk of a brow.

She didn't need or appreciate the lecture.

When the door shut, she slumped with defeat, her mouth pulled into a frown.

"It's time, Nicole," Robert said.

"For what?" When she looked at him, her temper fell away as it had always done. She let Robert's presence quiet her. The familiar, short version of her name reminded her of home.

"It's time ye understood that we have yer best interest at heart. You've had a scare, love. The anger's understandable, but we need ye to be calm and listen."

"We? Are you speaking for *him*, Robert? Do you know what he did? He stole me from my uncle's home. He carried me in here over his shoulder like a doxy. He's a complete scoundrel," she finished, her ire on the rise.

Robert watched her speak, heard her out, as he had always done. She'd exhausted herself from the inside out, gulping for air like a fish on deck. Folding her hands in her lap, she swallowed hard, surrendering the conversation, hoping that Robert could piece the puzzle together.

"Is it not enough I'm worried about ye? If I thought the man who'd tried to kidnap ye from yer uncle's was some random scoundrel, I wouldna have agreed to this. Ye must understand, my sweet, I do agree with His Grace, Commodore Havenly. Ye need protectin'."

"Commodore? How can you call him that?"

"Because he owns this fleet, and when he's on board, he's captain or commodore or His Grace, whichever you prefer. But make no mistake, the men here trust him. I trust him. Yer lucky he was there to help ye."

Pressing her fingers to her temple, she shook her throbbing head. This was not happening. Robert supported the brute. "Can't you see how worried Uncle James and Aunt Lydia will be when they find me gone? Are you not concerned?"

"Everyone is *concerned* about ye. And before ye spout off

again, your aunt and uncle know exactly where ye are and agree this is the safest place fer now."

Robert stretched his arm across the table and put his hand out. Nicolette hung on to his callused fingers and let the comforting strength he offered breathe life into her.

"His Grace has put his name behind findin' this bad man, but it'll take time, love. We all feel it best that ye be anywhere but home."

After everything he'd said, it was the word *home* that brought her around. "This is my home. You are my home, Robert." Burning tears threatened to spill.

A soft knock on the door and a wary peek announced the duke's return. Robert waved him in. Havenly placed a plate with toast and jam on the table to her left and set a hot teapot on a side table.

"How's the patient?" Havenly tried to smile amiably. He swiped his hands together and smoothed his dress trousers, which were no doubt damp from the spray of the ocean.

"We're makin' progress," Robert put in.

Nicolette disagreed. "I'm not hungry." It was a lie, but her pride would not accept any comfort from this impostor.

Robert stood, then came to stand behind her. He kissed the top of her head before leaving her with the stubborn man, shutting the door with an ominous click. Havenly was still dressed like he'd come from a ball except now his clothes were windblown and out of place, yet somehow he managed to look as fiercely handsome as ever.

Too handsome by half.

Nicolette glared at him, clamping her teeth together, all the more irritated for noticing such things.

"What do you plan to do with me now? Ravage me? No doubt the crew thinks you've done so already, being the scoundrel that you are." She hoped to infuse enough indignation into her speech to toss him mentally from the room.

He sat adjacent to her, regarding her quietly. With his arms folded, he sat back and crossed his legs. The picture of contemplation.

"What?" Her eyes narrowed with irritation.

"I'm just thinking I have a lot to do tonight, and I hadn't stopped to consider ravaging you. I'm not sure I have time, sweet. Then again, it is what sea captains do after they've pillaged. Do I have that correct?" He regarded her without menace.

She rolled her eyes, turning away. With her arms crossed, she closed herself off to any more of his ridiculous discussion.

Sitting forward, he breathed in deeply, placing his clasped hands atop the table. "We're both tired, Nicolette. I suggest you eat something—you look a little green—and then get some rest. Unfortunately, I have a lot to do yet."

She refused to look his way.

He stood, pushing his chair away from the table with the backs of his legs. "Is there anything else I can get you? Besides a jolly boat?"

She sent him a look. "No." The answer was short and crisp.

He nodded, then strode to the bed where he opened a drawer and withdrew a navy-blue wool coat. Like the one that Robert wore. "There are more blankets in the left drawer." He pointed to another drawer under the bed and made to leave, then stopped. "I don't know if Captain Donovan told you, but I've sent word to your uncle, and as we speak an investigation has begun to find your kidnapper."

She eyed him. "Oh? Did they catch the next boat? Because my captor is standing right here. You could have saved them the trouble by leaving me home." She tamped down the disturbing fact that someone else had, indeed, tried to kidnap her before the duke entered the picture. That wasn't the point.

He scratched his cheek, then plunged his arms into his coat

sleeves. To his credit, he looked tired and weary, and she knew she was being contrary.

She turned away again because the impulse to apologize was too great. Heavy steps sounded and then the sound of the door opening and closing. Again the lock jingled with a key.

Alone again. In all probability she would remain alone for the rest of the night. If they'd left without a full crew, all hands would be on deck, in which case no one would rest tonight.

The grumbling in her stomach demanded attention. To stay hungry was spiteful, and though she had been sniping since she arrived in this room, it wasn't like her to do so.

She swiped at her nose, then grabbed a piece of toast and picked up the teapot. She expected to see tea, but to her delight what came from the porcelain pot was thick and dark and smelled like chocolate. The bittersweet goodness spilled into a dainty cup. It looked freshly milled and tasted like heaven.

Dratted man, he'd brought the perfect drink. The one luxury she'd grown accustomed to and would be hard-pressed to give up.

CHAPTER 8

In the morning, Grant found some solace in the weather. Clear skies meant that at least above deck there were no storms. Grant couldn't fathom the storm brewing belowdecks. But for now there was nothing equal to standing at the helm and letting the fresh salted air flush his lungs. After the excitement of last night and the drawn-out conversation with Captain Donovan concerning what to do with their captive, Grant relished a moment alone.

In the city, amusements abounded, business knocked at his door daily, calling cards came in droves during the season, and his grandmother visited her opinion on him weekly. But this... this was something else. It was heaven. And despite—or because of—the impulse to protect this one small woman, Grant felt freer than he had in a decade. He didn't attribute that directly to her, but because of her he was sailing out in the middle of the ocean with no particular destination.

"Commodore," Captain Donovan said, scaling the steps to the bridge.

"Captain Donovan, how's our prisoner?" Grant's question got a smile from Robert. "Is she awake?"

Robert shook his head. "Not last I saw. I thought it best to leave her sleeping. I did leave her a bite of breakfast."

"I'm just happy she slept," Grant said and handed the helm back to Mr. O'Newel. "As I said last night, I think it best if you speak with her."

"She thinks I betrayed her." Leaving the bridge with one destination in mind, they crossed the quarterdeck. "It hurts like hell, I'm not embarrassed to say, sir."

Grant cast a cursory glance while keeping stride. "You're like family. I wouldn't expect her to feel any different. I can handle her anger, but she needs this information from someone she trusts."

"And I wouldn't have it any other way," Robert grunted. "I knew the day would come. My hope was that it wouldna come like this."

Robert and he rounded one corner of the quarterdeck. They spoke freely, Robert took a step ahead, and Grant stopped short when he caught a glimpse of the hellion standing on deck, still garbed in the maddening ball gown, hands planted on her delightful hips, the very vision of an angry goddess. The wind whipped her unbound hair like twisting taffy.

He watched as blue shimmering silk shaped itself around her limbs, lapping at her ankles, exposing a hint of silk stockings, and setting his blood on fire, which with some exasperation made him wonder what her silky legs would feel like wrapped around him. And because of that, dammit, he couldn't chase the word *silk* from his depraved mind. He pinched the bridge of his nose, praying that her rigid governess had packed something more appropriate.

"I'll bring her along and we'll meet you in my quarters," he said to Robert, sending him ahead.

"How could you?" She was already snapping by the time

he reached her. A storm brewed in her eyes, but he attributed most of her bluster to last night.

He stood before her, collecting his patience and reminding himself that she likely felt out of control, dismayed, afraid, and least of all but most potently, melancholy with nostalgia.

"You look lovely, Miss Bradenton. I wouldn't have guessed that a woman would fare so well at sea. But here you are."

She blinked hard and shook off the compliment. "I know whose cabin I slept in last night." Clearly she felt his action reprehensible. In the light of day, he could understand how the decision to whisk her away in the dead of night might seem like overreacting.

She swiped at the torrent of hair whipping at her face, then snatched a strand from her mouth and shoved it behind her ear, where it refused to stay. Watching her do it stole every suitable response from him.

These were not good thoughts to have this morning. The day was too serious and the information forthcoming quite heavy.

"May I suggest taking your voice down a tone? I know the wind is up and you feel the need to shout at me, but if you continue, these men will not only know where you slept last night, but they won't wait to find out where I took leave, and they'll make up their own minds."

That suggestion gained the action he needed. Nicolette squared her shoulders and smoothed the ridges from her forehead with considerable formality, placing a serene, boring look of nonchalance on her blushing face.

"Where did Robert go?" she asked, her tone now considerably calmer.

"He's waiting for you in my cabin. If you'd allow it, I would be honored to escort you." He purposed to keep his features relaxed, certain that her compliance was not guaranteed.

When she wavered, he added, "I'd come to believe my charm irresistible. I think you called it legendary."

"Oooph," she growled and snatched his arm. "I did no such thing. You're a scoundrel."

"So I've been told." Sparring with her warmed his blood and almost made him look forward to the day, except he knew better.

Grant tried to help her maneuver the steep laddered stairway that led belowdecks. Even though he knew she'd grown up here, it still surprised him to see her scale the steps without taking his proffered hand. With her one hand gripping the ladder rail and the other holding her skirts, she managed it quite well on her own.

They found Robert waiting in Grant's cabin, a look of grave concern dulling his eyes, a frown peeking through his beard.

Done with games, she strode to the same chair she'd sat in the night before. Even in that decadent dress she wore, when she wrapped her tangled hair around the front of one shoulder, Grant could see the girl she must have been here.

"Robert, you look so solemn. What can be worse than yesterday?" she asked.

Robert eyed him, and Grant took a seat across the room, allowing at least the pretense of space and privacy.

"Nicole, darlin'," Robert began. "You're no longer a child, love. As I said last night, it's time for ye to know some things." He took a deep breath.

Grant could only imagine the heart-pounding anxiety he must feel.

Nicolette said nothing, but her lungs stuttered with each breath.

"I want to help ye understand why His Grace brought ye here." Robert bobbed his head toward the far corner where Grant sat at an intricately carved mahogany writing desk.

Nicolette turned, her gaze darting over him until their eyes met.

Grant's lip twitched with sympathy, and he softened his gaze. "Nicolette, how much do you know about your father's death?"

Anger fell away as she spoke. "I know he was killed in a robbery on the waterfront. Why do you ask about my father?" She leveraged a hand on the back of her chair as she twisted to see Grant.

He sighed with a heavy heart while Robert cupped his forehead in his hand. Grant helped start the difficult conversation. "You deserve to know the truth, Nicolette. You're a bright woman and should have been told much earlier in my opinion."

That comment seemed to mollify her. She turned back to Robert, who scooted around the table and took her hand.

"Darlin', your father was not killed in a robbery. He was murdered."

"I know that. What else if not murdered?"

Robert braced himself with a steady breath. "He was *murdered*. Killed, but not for money. Those that did it took nothin' but his life."

"Why? And why has no one ever told me this?" Her posture did not change, and Grant wondered if she'd heard what Robert said or if the shocking truth kept her from accepting it.

The mind was a powerful instrument with enough will to protect a person, holding them up for years with lies.

"Because we thought it safer this way. Yer uncle agreed with me." Robert bent close and placed her cupped hand to his lips and closed his eyes. "John Bradenton was killed for his name. Your grandparents were killed for their name."

"And what... Are you going to try to convince me that my

mother was killed for her name too?" She snatched her hand away. Shock widened her eyes.

Grant was almost relieved at her show of emotion.

"No." Robert shook his head and straightened in his chair. "Illness took your beautiful mum. There is a legend of wealth. Treasure as large as a king's ransom that once belonged to yer great-grandparents. No one has ever seen it, or proven it, and most don't believe it. But there are those that figure if yer father's family are all eliminated, then this untold treasure will belong to them. If'n they could find it."

"Where is it supposed to be?"

"I don't know. It is but a legend. But the death of your family... that part is true. It's so true that your father changed his name when he met Elisabeth, your mum. His real name is isn't John Bradenton."

Grant could see that she was more confused than ever, so he stood and gingerly stepped behind her chair, ready to support her any way he could. He nodded at Robert to continue.

"His name was Bradley John Eton. He took pieces of the name and turned them around to start over. All the Etons are gone. All of them but you. Your father has gone by John Bradenton for so long that no one remains to remember the name Eton except me and your uncle... and now His Grace." He bobbed his head toward Grant. "That's what's kept ye safe all this time."

She glanced up at Grant, and he nodded.

"John wanted it this way. He wanted to protect his family. Thieves were lookin' for an Eton, so he changed that. But now someone has figured it out. We'd hoped that takin' yer uncle's name woulda' been enough to throw any fool still lookin'. Turns out we were wrong.."

"Now I understand why Uncle James insisted I take Thomas as my name." Her shoulders gave way a little.

"Yes. They love ye like a daughter."

She nodded, sniffling back tears.

"Nicolette," Grant said, coming around to kneel by her chair, "we need to know if the attempted kidnapping had something to do with your name. If that's so, then all of this is my fault because I called you Bradenton."

She turned her gaze away from them both for a moment.

"Robert, you said Papa was killed when his identity was discovered, but my father lived in Creekshire for most of my life. Everyone would know him there. Even if his name had been changed from Eton, why did it take so long to find him?"

"I understand why you'd ask that, but those that killed yer father's family did so in Scotland, where he's from. He changed his name before moving to Creekshire, so he had a clean slate. Only the townsfolk knew the Bradentons, and when Mr. Craddock moved his shipping business outta London, John thought the name would be further lost, which meant safety fer you. If Craddock hadna allowed yer father to bring ye here, he'd have quit the line and given up his ship." Robert paused to wipe a tear from her cheek. "The connection to ye took them longer to make. And now that they have made it, we believe yer in danger. That's why His Grace brought ye here."

Her throat bobbed and she wet her lips. "Will you answer me the truth?"

"Of course, love."

"Is Uncle James my family? Is he mama's true cousin?"

"Yes. They're yer real family."

"Are they in danger?" she asked in a quivering whisper.

Grant answered her. "We don't think so. It's the Eton family that has drawn the attention. Whatever nonsense surrounds this mystery belongs to your father's side of the family. And we need to find the ones responsible."

"Before they find me." She shivered, and Grant ran his

hand up and down her forearm. Surprisingly, she didn't shake him off or turn the typical caustic glare of distrust on him.

Robert asked, "Would ye like me to stay with ye for a while?"

"No, Robert, I'm sure you have things to do."

Grant nodded him on, and Robert stood.

"Nicolette..." With a gentle finger, Grant turned her face toward him. "I want you to know that before we left port, a message arrived."

Her eyes, doleful and wet with tears, watched him, hopeful.

"I sent a note to your family before we left, informing them where we'd make a brief stop during the night, and your uncle sent a reply."

She nodded and a tear escaped.

"He thinks it best that we stay away for several weeks."

Her head lolled forward, and her hands rested in her lap. "I understand. Would you mind?" She dismissed him with pained politeness.

His throat felt like a jagged rock was lodged in it. He swallowed down the sharp spasm of guilt. This was his fault. He took full responsibility. His lips parted to say something, and then he stopped. Against all propriety, he took one hand from her lap and squeezed softly. "I'll be available if you need me."

She nodded. Her silence was as gut-wrenching as if she'd railed and blamed him for everything.

CHAPTER 9

Grant left Nicolette to her privacy. She needed time, and he needed to nail down some ground rules. Captain Donovan was to escort her to lunch, where she could spend time with the officers. He still wasn't comfortable with her sharing time with the underseamen, although it was very possible that she knew most of them, or perhaps all of them.

Having a woman on board made him nervous, forget the reasons why. Things like men ogling her in that blue gown, men watching her hair come undone in the wind, men posting themselves on deck to catch a glimpse of her ankles. All things he'd done or thought about doing. Hell, he was a good man. He was only worried for her. He'd have done the same for anyone.

Not likely. But it was a good lie. Any other woman and he'd have intervened on the abduction and then left her family to care for her protection. Guilt had caused him to act further. Which, of course, was another good lie.

There was something about her. Something beyond his initial curiosity over a few faded, scrawled words on a jewelry

IT WAS ONLY A KISS

box. Words that might bring danger. For that reason, and because she already blamed him for stealing her home from under her, he would, for now, keep knowledge of the box to himself.

He strolled the deck, watched the crew tend to their individual duties, and looked for unfamiliar faces. According to Captain Donovan they had sailed with a skeleton crew of forty men, which meant that he was needed to fill in some gaps. On most ships, the captain's—or commodore's—prerogative did not involve the everyday running of the ship. Not that Grant minded; he rather enjoyed it. But if he were to continue enjoying it, he needed a change of clothes. And to change his clothes, he needed access to his cabin.

While Nicolette lunched in the officers' galley, Grant slipped into his quarters. Lemon mingled with lavender greeted him at the door. The scent of her was everywhere. The made-up bed caused him to wonder whether she'd slept in it or *on* it. And with a vision of her disheveled hair lying across his pillow, he tore out of his clothes and wrestled into buckskin breeches, boots, and a fresh lawn shirt. He adjusted his breeches and fought his body's irresponsible reaction, as if his brain were not connected to the parts of him that were currently demanding attention. He swore under his breath, swiping up his discarded clothing and laying it over a chair to dry.

With The *New Horizon* requiring a minimum of forty men, Robert admitted to filling in five positions in a hurry before they sailed, which meant not all the men were vetted. With that worry, Grant strolled the decks, concentrating on the fo'c'sle, the upper deck where the crew lived.

He wondered how Nicolette fared at lunch but avoided seeking out Captain Donovan for answers, and he avoided her at all costs. The rest of the day he busied himself. There were always supplies to check, schedules to approve, not to mention scouting for men he didn't know.

Just before dusk, he found himself on the quarterdeck under the eaves of the bridge. Leaning against the rail on his forearms, he turned a shilling finger over thumb while watching the current break from the hull. Wind like chilled fingers tousled his hair, and the sound of whale song in the distance brought comfort. For a year, the sea had been the only mistress he required.

Head over tail, he flipped the coin in his hand, wondering again if bringing Nicolette aboard had been the right choice. He'd been drawn to her since that first glimpse of her at the theater, seated demurely on the steps of a deserted stairwell. Beautiful women were readily available, but she was more than that. His feelings went beyond attraction. Her perseverance to survive in a world she'd not been raised in and the way she'd kept that indomitable, undisciplined spirit in balance was a thing to be admired.

This time he flipped the coin into the wind and watched it spin and tumble, the setting sun catching each side with a wink, until it disappeared into the surf. His churning thoughts of Nicolette, however, were more difficult than a flip of a coin.

Friends or lovers.

Gnawing desire plagued him. He could blame it on sentiment; after all, the woman needed safeguarding. But his craving to taste her lips had pursued him even before he'd known she was in danger or needed protecting.

Now he felt as if he were the one who needed protecting.

Blazes! It was this boat. The vastness of the sea and the endless sky always took his mind from home and made him believe there was more to life than what his grandmother insisted upon. Was he missing something? His father had found happiness. Not the kind that made his grandmother happy, but even in the face of such dire will, his father had defied her and made his own choices. Grant had always admired him for that.

The coach ride with Nicolette had dredged up old feelings.

She was like no other woman he'd ever known—sharp tongued, unhindered by propriety's concept of wit and charm. Grant couldn't know how long the investigation would take, but he did know that to survive this trip with sanity intact he would have to do everything in his power to avoid the vixen who had robbed him of his practicality.

He looked over the rail and wondered on which side the coin landed. It was best he didn't know, because the woman was untouchable for a dozen reasons.

Faint footsteps sounded behind him. Instinctively he knew it was her. He turned, his back to the sea, an elbow resting on the rail behind him.

Guileless blue eyes drenched in innocence met his. Cynicism clouded his vision, but somehow her presence cleared it.

She nervously wrung her hands. "I would ask one thing of you, Your Grace."

"Anything," Grant replied sincerely, trying to gauge her reaction to the brutal news Robert had delivered that morning.

"I should wish to be moved to more appropriate quarters. It is entirely unseemly for me to stay in the commodore's cabin."

Grant had grown accustomed to the scheming manipulations of the fairer sex, expecting a combination of hysterics, tears, and the inevitable swooning, but never courage, nor honesty for that matter. The latter two he had come to know in this one petite woman, and he was confused by his own response. She struck a chord he was not yet comfortable with and a feeling he could not name.

His reaction was to smile at the innocent request and nod. "Of course. Robert will sacrifice his quarters." She looked to protest, so Grant added, "Captain Donovan and I have already discussed it, and the arrangements have been made. We aren't sailing with a full crew; moving around a few officers won't be difficult."

Grant worried for her. Grief needed time, and he was painfully aware that hers for her father had been reborn.

"Nicolette, you may have whatever you need, but I would ask one thing of you in return."

"Anything." She mirrored his response. Her entire countenance changed. She stood before him, hands now clasped, wearing a lovely peach-colored walking dress, her hair, loosely pinned back, whipping wildly behind her.

She took his breath away.

"You mustn't continue to foist *Your Grace* upon me."

When she rolled her eyes, he had to bite back a fresh chuckle.

"I'm quite serious." He tried for stern, even dipped his head down and glared from under his furrowed brow.

"Oh heavens," she said, exasperated. "As you wish, pirate captain."

His head tilted at her charmingly unaffected defiance.

She relented. "Havenly." That she said with a straight face, prim and yet graceless.

"Close enough." If she wouldn't use his name, then Havenly would do. That is what his *friends* called him.

"I didn't thank you. I do apologize for that." The easy gleam was gone from her eyes.

He crossed his arms, genuinely uncomfortable with her gratitude. "For what? I've done nothing but cause grief."

"You aren't to blame." She squared her shoulders and lifted her chin, a confident air of instruction about her.

He suddenly became interested in the cut of his fingernails, checking the cuticles. "It was my blunder. My selfishness caused this." He peered up. "I shouldn't have called you Bradenton. It was wrong of me, and I don't deserve your gratitude."

"You have it nonetheless," she protested gently. "I am grateful. You quite probably saved my life."

He stretched his fingers, searching for a comfortable position to place his arms, his hands, his heart. This young woman made him nervous as a pup. Blood pulsed through his veins, keeping tempo with the headache that had tested him all day.

Nicolette reached out, gripping both his hands in hers. The feathery touch of her fingers doubled his heart rate. "You are not to blame. Do we understand each other?"

Seeking to knock his breathing into something more civil, he pressed his own point. "Not quite."

She sighed with a little laugh, jerking his hands as if she held reins. "Havenly. There, I said it. Now… do we understand each other?"

He placed her hands together and gave them a little rub. Her fingers were cold. "For now. But only because you're a clever girl who's difficult to argue with." He could feel his cheeks stretch, his eyes squint, into the kind of smile that one could not practice. Genuine. She did that to him.

She wet her lips against the wind, dragging her teeth over the full, fleshy bottom part. He couldn't tear his eyes away while his mind screamed for a taste.

Not appropriate. Not even close.

The thin wisp of muslin covering her arms fluttered with the wind, and he was suddenly aware of how cold her hands were. He shrugged out of his seaman's peacoat and flipped the thick woolen jacket around her shoulders. It hung heavily, and she looked down in disbelief.

"This isn't necessary. I'm headed back to… to Robert's cabin, I guess. I'm sure your need is greater."

"Keep it on." He grabbed the front lapel and overlapped it, tugging the double-breasted jacket closed, then pressed a gold button through a buttonhole. "Besides, your teeth are chattering, and I don't think you'd care to know what the physician does with broken teeth." He teased her into a smile.

She hugged the coat tight, the sleeves hanging beyond her fingertips. "Is there really a physician on board?"

"Yes, me." He looked purposely affronted.

"You're not a physician. What would you do with broken teeth?"

"I make necklaces. I've collected several," he said earnestly.

"Necklaces or teeth?" She chuckled up at him.

"Whichever will give you nightmares and cause you to keep the coat on."

"You don't scare me." Her laughter was like a familiar melody. "It's but a short distance to my cabin. I'll be fine."

"And you'll be warm." He wouldn't take it back.

"And you'll be cold." She tried to reason with him.

"Rakes are cold-blooded. I think you told me that."

She gasped, a chaste feminine sound, one that quickened his blood. "I never said anything of the sort, Your Grace."

He pinched her chin and bent over enough to make their eyes level. "If I hear you title me to death again on this voyage, I will kiss you into silence." He let go of her chin with a little tug, smiled wickedly, and cupped her cheek. "Your choice."

"You're a scoundrel. Shall I call you pirate captain, sir?" Pleasure was bright in her eyes, and her pupils dilated with the exchange.

"Only when I wear my eye patch. Otherwise, it's Grant." Never had bantering made him feel anxious.

"I cannot. It's too intimate."

He quirked a brow and conjured up his best roguish grin. "Under the circumstances, I'd say the consequence of applying my title will cost a greater intimacy. Choose wisely for my sake."

She rolled her eyes and gave a slanted smile. "We'll see... Havenly."

She turned to leave.

"Nicolette," he called, and she glanced at him over her now

overly padded shoulder. "I know this isn't easy. I am sorry, truly."

There was no condemnation in her gentle gaze. Her mouth turned up at the corners. "You say that too often, you know?"

He was dumbfounded, silenced by a slip of a girl. She gave him another smile and then left him to his foolhardy thoughts.

CHAPTER 10

Nicolette was thankful for the warmth of the navy wool as she made her way to the duke's quarters. She opened the door and found the room devoid of her things. The next logical place to look was Robert's cabin. En route, she passed the door that led to the captain's sitting room and another room that stored maps. These rooms had once been used for high-level meetings, and she wondered if they still were. She passed another companionway that led to the stern deck, making the helm accessible from the senior officers' quarters, mainly the commodore, captain, and chief mate. During her time on the *New Horizon*, only the captain and chief mate stayed in this part of the ship. The third room had belonged to her. Now she assumed this section held three officers since Havenly had taken a permanent room, the one her father had occupied. When she came to what had once been Robert's room as chief mate, she stopped and knocked.

No answer.

She tried the door. It swung open, revealing another room she remembered well. This room still belonged to Robert. It was nearly the size of the commodore's quarters, with heavy furniture, a nice bureau, a large bed, and a small stove for warmth. The drapes were pulled back from the windows, the room illuminated from outside by a stern lantern. It was enough light to locate an oil lamp and to recognize her valise near the foot of the bed. To her surprise, the table was set with several covered dishes.

With ease she lifted the half-empty valise to the bed. In Miss Blanchfield's haste, she had not packed nearly enough, and if the formidable woman were privy to the conditions under which they sailed, she'd be a flustered mess. Nicolette had broken so many rules she'd lost count.

Grant. How on earth would she manage to call him by name? She'd used his name in the coach, yes, but at the time her reason was muddied by fear and survival.

The man had apologized to her. This strong duke of a man, beyond reproach and beyond blame for anything as far as the ton was concerned, had deigned to apologize to *her*. His kind could get away with murder, literally. They fought duels at dawn, legal or no, and took part in all manner of debauchery —or so Frances had said—and few could touch them. Certainly not lowly maidens like her. And he stood right there at the taffrail and apologized for using her real name. The piercing intensity of his gaze made her stomach restless.

Her body shook, but not from cold.

She smothered herself in the warm wool lapel of his peacoat and inhaled again. Ah, there it was—bay rum, sandalwood, and the duke.

The lapel fell away and she shrugged one arm out, then the other, catching the collar as it slid from her shoulder. She hugged it to her chest, then hung it on a peg. Tomorrow she'd return it.

She found that she liked his company.

Perhaps she'd find more reasons to run into him.

Perhaps that was reckless thinking.

Perhaps she should just go to bed and stop the rattling between her ears.

More than just Aunt Lydia had called him a rake. The other girls had also, and Miss Blanchfield, and Arlienne, and... everyone.

Except she didn't see it.

He had treated her with the utmost kindness, with the manners of a gentleman, with the concern of a friend. But friends did not make her heart pound. They did not conjure thoughts so inappropriate that her face burned with a blush.

When he smiled and that delightful dimple showed, it reminded her of their first meeting at the theater. Behind the great curtain, when he stood behind her close enough that she could feel his chin on her head. And when she looked up at him, what, if not passion, would cause his eyes to smolder? And when he walked her to the door after dining with her family, what, if not passion, would cause him to look disappointed at calling her friend? According to him, he didn't keep women friends, and yet he'd called her friend. Then yesterday when they danced, he'd asked her to choose—friends or lovers. She'd had to count through the steps, concentrating to keep from falling.

Who was she kidding? She'd already fallen. Why else would she trust a rakehell with her well-being?

Her stomach protested like an echo in an empty cavern. She was ravenous.

Cheese and bread and a variety of thinly sliced meats along with a kettle of tea had been left on the table. A basin with a pitcher of clean water stood in the corner of the room. Everything she needed was here.

Coming into two nights aboard ship, she knew not where they headed. But tonight at least she had more answers, even if the questions were increasing.

NICOLETTE SLEPT BETTER the second night, waking early with the sun. Her wardrobe suited a walk through the park more so than a walk on deck, but she had little choice. It was the peach dress or the formal blue. When she had lived here, dressing in work breeches and a lawn shirt was the norm. For a moment she considered rustling through Robert's things, then discarded the idea. If Miss Blanchfield were to hear of such scandal, she'd have Nicolette back in training. Lesson one, lady's fashion.

No, thank you.

She ran a hand over the duke's navy wool coat, then set it aside. Today she'd return it. Her hands trembled, her nerves on edge with anticipation, making it difficult to dress. Thankfully, Miss Blanchfield had packed stays with front ties, because shaking fingers made the act of tying the stays awkward enough without having to reach behind and pull the laces without seeing. When she had donned the peach dress, she left the cabin, coat in hand.

On deck, one could not escape the wind, but today it was calmer and the tie that held her hair in place stayed put.

Where would the commodore be midmorning? Yesterday he'd been at the helm, but not today.

She walked the quarterdeck and finally gave in to asking a crewman.

"Strollin' the fo'c'sle, miss. At least 'e was when I last seen 'im."

"Do you have time to send for him?"

"O' course." The young man tipped his cap and rushed off, then turned back, skidding along a plank or two in haste. "Where should I tell 'im ye'll be, miss?"

"Here."

She waited in the same spot she'd left Havenly last night.

Clutching the coat in both hands, she laid it over the rail and let it cushion her body. At her height, the rail was chest high, making it easy to rest her chin atop her hands. The position served twofold—she could take in the smell of salt water and catch the heady scent of bay rum. Best of both worlds.

"Good morning." A deep voice came from behind.

Her eyes went wide, and she felt a warm flush of embarrassment battle the crisp breeze and win.

"This is my favorite time of day," Havenly said when she turned to acknowledge him.

Before a word could form, she shoved the coat into his broad chest, forcing him to catch it, and then rushed a reply. "Thank you." She wrung her hands, resisting the urge to pat her hair in place. "It was more than kind."

"You're welcome to borrow it for the remainder. I know it's too big, but it will guard you better than the cloak you brought."

If he only knew that his presence alone warmed her.

"You forget I lived here once. I'm not unaccustomed to a little wind and chill, Your... Havenly," she said, correcting herself. She breathed in the salty mist and turned toward the sea, gripping the side rail and pressing her body against the hard polished wood. With the cushion from the coat gone, she could feel the cool rail through her dress. The wind and mist kissed her cheeks, her eyelids, her lips, and she smiled against it.

Haphazardly he tossed the coat over the rail. Holding it down with his elbows, he leaned over the side, his hands hooked together, profile strong, face relaxed against the breeze, dark hair tousled with the wind. He seemed to enjoy this and looked as if he'd been born here.

She absently rubbed her arms and forced her gaze elsewhere, then placed her hands flat against the rail and leaned in, not over.

For two days someone had left food in her room. This morning when she woke, there was a tray of toast and another pot of chocolate.

"Who's been bringing my meals?"

He leaned a forearm next to her and watched her profile. "Captain Donovan."

She glanced sideways at him and pulled back a loose piece of hair that was whipping like a ribbon near her eyes. "Really? How kind. I'll have to thank him and let him know he needn't continue. I'm sure he has more important tasks at hand."

"One of those tasks is looking after you." He touched a finger to her arm, and it tingled as if he'd touched her skin. The thin fabric of her walking dress was no match.

"It isn't necessary, truly. I know my way around."

He gave her a pointed look, a measure of concern sketched in his brow. "Nicolette, do you *know* every crew member on board?"

"I'm sure I don't. But I know many of them. Why?"

"Because although it is safer here than in the city, there is still a modicum of danger to consider."

"What could possibly happen out here? There is nowhere for me to be taken, and I know enough of the men to enlist the aid of at least a dozen at a moment's notice." She managed to keep condescension from her tone, although it did rile her a little.

He quirked a brow and looked purposely overboard.

"Thrown overboard?"

"What better way? It's easy, fast, clean, and silent."

She comported her features and said as if he were a simpleton, "I can swim, and I assure you it would not be silent."

"Gagged and tied, I fail to see how you would fare well unless you are a magician. Besides, you have sailed long enough to know the ocean has been a coffin for many who've underestimated it."

"I'll grant you that." She relented for the sake of peace.

"And speaking of *grant*."

She opened her mouth to protest. She knew what he meant.

"Let's practice a little, shall we?" His smile drew her into a web of unsuitable dialogue. "I'll ask: How do you fare today, Nicolette? And you'll reply…" His hand made a rolling motion between them.

"I'll reply… I'm well?" When he stayed silent and continued to regard her, unblinking, she asked, "What if I'm not well?"

He simply stared at her.

She glanced skyward and sighed. "What if I'm not well… Grant?" Oh Lord, she said it.

Striking white teeth shone, and the smile he gave her produced the devastatingly handsome dimple. "Was that so difficult?"

"Yes, as a matter of fact, it was. Let's start with once a day, shall we? That is my suggestion." She batted her eyes for distraction, then looked back to the sea.

"Do you count that as one? Because I sense that it was unduly forced, but it should come about naturally. Don't you think?" It was clear he would not let this go. "Nicolette?"

She turned toward him, resting the opposite elbow on the rail. They were mirrored in stance, although her posture was a little awkward considering her height and the height of the rail. She shook her head, chuckling at the look of pure innocent delight—wickedly innocent delight—on his face.

"What did you do all day on a ship this size when you were a girl?"

"Are you engaging me in conversation just so I might have to say your name, or are you actually interested?"

"I'm afraid there is nothing innocent left to me. I boldly wish to hear my name on your lips." That silly grin challenged her again. "And, I might add, I am genuinely interested, if that helps my case in the least."

"Sometimes I fished," she said, daring him. "Do you believe me?"

"I have no reason to think otherwise. Did you bait your own hook? Clean your own fish?"

She tugged her mouth to the side. "You don't believe me."

He laughed, a gasping sound of disbelief. "Why wouldn't I? Clearly I am not privy to the odd behaviors of women."

"Clearly." She giggled. And then she slanted him a look. "And I cooked."

"That I do *not* believe. Women are terrible cooks."

"How would you know? Do your women friends cook for you?" she said good-naturedly.

"I'm still waiting for you to say my name."

"And I have all day to do it."

He held her gaze, pausing until the atmosphere turned. "Your eyes take on the color of the sea when you're near it. Did you know that?"

She shook her head, speechless. Men didn't talk with her the way he did. Jesting and teasing one moment and lighting her insides on fire the next.

"You aren't like other women, Nicolette. You aren't afraid to let your hair go free, to blow your nose…"

She pressed her lips into a straight, irreverent smile for that comment.

"You are unconventional." His brows were drawn together as he studied her.

"And was that a compliment, Your Grace?" She used his title on purpose, like a warning.

He palmed her chin, lifting gently until their eyes met. "Please say my name. I need to hear it."

She swallowed hard, willing her mouth to form the words, while her body warmed under his amber-flecked gaze.

He crooked a smile while watching her lips, then chucked her under the chin and broke the spell. "Yes, that was a compliment."

She chewed at her bottom lip. If she had said his name, would he have kissed her? Did she want him to kiss her?

Yes. She did. And it scared her.

"No need to thank me." When she continued to stare at him, confused, he added, "You're brave and rare and spirited, no doubt the very things Miss Blanchfield instructs against. And that, my kitten, is far more attractive than the usual accoutrement."

Thinking of Miss Blanchfield and trying to bring order to her addled senses, she replied woodenly, "Thank you. I guess."

He straightened, then knocked his knuckles on the rail, relinquishing the conversation. "I think Captain Donovan's expecting us for lunch."

"I should like to clean up first. I'll meet you there," she said, then scurried away.

She needed distance to rein in her rioting pulse. A quick detour to her cabin to freshen up was the perfect excuse to cool her cheeks and to cool the desire he fired with just one lazy smile.

CHAPTER 11

If asked, Grant would be hard-pressed to explain what this woman did to his good sense. He couldn't remember a time when he'd been asked to expound upon a compliment. Every time he went near her, his tongue became tied, his mind fled, and his insides all conspired by altering course. Avoiding her was the simplest solution. But although he tried—and he did try—he couldn't seem to shake the urge to see her. He found himself wandering near the galley, searching the quarterdeck, and nervously eyeing the companionway that led to her cabin.

She captivated him.

Just standing next to her aroused him.

Something had to change. From adolescence until now, he'd grown accustomed to the strategies of opportunistic females, but never had he come across pure, unadulterated innocence. She couldn't possibly know what she did to him.

He didn't just need her to say his name. He needed to kiss her, taste her, and God have mercy, he wanted her. This, in combination with his protective feelings for her, amounted to utter confusion, which until now had been a foreign feeling. She was like the perfect storm.

Eventually he settled on waiting in the galley for Captain Donovan and Nicolette to show for lunch. He propped his booted foot on a low bench and contemplated the unconvincing stories given him by two of the five crewmen taken on minutes before they'd launched. They might have been in the right place at the right time, but the convenience seemed suspicious. He couldn't reconcile their credentials because he had yet to find a man who knew them. Something wasn't right. Still, he didn't wish to alarm Nicolette with empty suspicions. Instead, he'd keep a close watch on the men in question and ask Captain Donovan to do the same.

When Donovan and Nicolette arrived, they exchanged the usual pleasantries with him and settled in for lunch.

During the meal, Grant listened to Robert and Nicolette chat comfortably. He had to admit a modicum of envy over the ease they had with each other. Like old friends, or family. It dawned on him that for two days she'd been without the usual female amusements, and he realized, with this female, he could not imagine what those amusements might be.

When they had finished lunch, Captain Donovan stood to leave. He rested his hands on Nicolette's shoulders and kissed her atop her head, then whispered in a tone of feigned warning, "Do yerself a favor, lass, and try not to make trouble." He winked at Grant. "Don't let her sway ye into lettin' her climb the shrouds to the top or the forepeak."

Grant watched with a mixture of disbelief and horror as Robert left. The top and forepeak were not for the faint at heart. A man could be entangled in the shrouds, and for the love of God, the forepeak was not much more than a standing mount around the main mast.

When he turned his gaze back to Nicolette, she was smiling like the Cheshire cat.

"Don't even think it."

She looked pleased with herself and laughed when he lifted a brow and squinted like a pirate. "Am I now to be terrified by rakish pirates? If so, you don't know me very well."

That reminded him why he'd sought her out in the first place. Her statement was correct. He knew her, but not well. And what he did know, he liked too much. However, his original goal involved finding out the origin of the jewelry box. In order to question her, he'd be forced to tell her that he now owned it. He couldn't think of a worse idea, but neither could he think of another that would suffice.

Later.

He'd tell her later.

"You'd do well to be a little terrified, because if I find you climbing the shrouds, I will beat you, as is the right of every good pirate captain." The words were jest, but he pierced her with an unwavering look, a warning against trying him.

She irreverently rolled her eyes, something he'd become accustomed to.

"I will not climb the shrouds or any rigging. Besides, I did that only once, and I assure you, Papa was none too pleased with me."

"Yes, but did he beat you?"

"No." She laughed. "But he forbade me to do it again and threatened to leave me at home. He looked as serious as you do now, so I complied."

"Glory be, there is hope." He exaggerated a sigh. "In all seriousness, is there something I can help you with to fill your time? Do you read?" He stopped short and held up a hand, closing his eyes against the sure-to-come reprimand. "I did not ask if you *can* read but if you'd care to read."

She nodded whimsically, as if she waited for him to insert his other foot into his mouth.

He pushed his plate away and cleared his throat. "I have a

small library you're welcome to. If you care to sew, I can rummage up thread and needle, although I'm not sure what you'd care to do with it."

He looked at her askance. She was still smiling impishly.

She shook her head. "I do not trifle with thread and needle. Miss Blanchfield insists I try, but I am a dismal failure at it."

"Noted. Do not allow Miss Bradenton near the sails."

"There is great truth in that, sir. I hate sewing."

"Then all punishment from here on will involve darning socks."

"I'll take the pirate beating if you don't mind?"

"Why should I mind? I am a pirate, after all." He gave the matter some thought. "Besides fishing, how did you spend your time as a girl?"

She opened her mouth to speak, then bit her lip and broke eye contact. "I worked on my studies, and I had chores. I scrubbed the rail during calm seas. And—"

"Out of the question."

She shot him a determined look. "What harm could come from doing a few chores? Am I a prisoner then?"

"Of course not, but I'll not have you patronizing the crew, and I'd prefer you had no contact with them at all."

"You're being silly."

"Am I? Do I sound silly?" Unblinking, he leaned toward her an inch.

"Yes."

"No." His word was final, but her raised brow told him he'd just thrown down the gauntlet.

She huffed a rather loud, unladylike sigh. "Then what do you suggest... *Grant?*" Her eyes flashed when she said his name.

"I'll take the name any way I can, Miss Bradenton. Even with disrespect."

She crossed her arms. "I'll read, Your Grace, because I like to read, not because you allow it. And I'll mop a deck if I see fit."

He consciously held off grinding his teeth. "Anything else?"

She searched his eyes, unwavering. "And as I said before, I like to cook."

He blinked twice. "I thought you were jesting." She surprised him at every turn.

"You believe I did deck chores, but you question whether I cooked?"

"Kitten, I think you'd dare anything, but I've never met a proper lady who cooked."

"I'm not a proper lady." That was not a self-deprecating statement she made; it was matter-of-fact.

"Point taken." He closed the space between them, bracing his forearm on the table, and held her gaze. "Reading and cooking if Mr. MacTavish, the cook, doesn't mind."

"Agreed."

CHAPTER 12

Nicolette spent hours in the kitchen every day and, when the pirate captain wasn't present, she availed herself of his library. But she failed to keep boredom at bay. With the added restrictions he'd placed, she no longer felt nostalgically cocooned. She felt confined. Surviving an endless trip to nowhere required a variety of activities and a change of scenery. If Havenly hadn't demanded her complete obedience concerning deck chores, she'd have never considered testing him. But she was just bored enough to let the challenge inspire the kind of adventure that only he could spark.

However, she was not foolish enough to call it to his attention. When she was a young girl, she'd worn men's clothes—breeches, shirts, boots—and assisted with easy chores. Polishing the rail had never taxed her. She considered climbing to the forepeak, but only for a moment. Even she recognized the folly of scrabbling up the shrouds, but the command to refrain from all chores struck a defiant chord.

Tamping down her absurd memories of donning trousers and boots, she delved into something even more irrational, something dangerous, something that changed everything.

She sought out Havenly.

Havenly. Grant. The duke. But mostly the pirate captain. At least that's what he looked like when she passed under the bridge, slanting furtive glances toward him while he stood at the helm. His dark hair whipped in the wind. His full white shirtsleeves billowed like sails while the open shirt ties flew about like snapping adders. But not his breeches. They were plastered to his lean, muscular thighs and disappeared into polished, knee-high black boots.

Holy Moses, he was beautiful. Not just handsome, but beautiful. Here, nature attended him like a doting valet. Where most men would have fallen like a reed, Havenly stood like a proud oak. More than anything, he looked happy.

Too soon she reached the opposite side of the quarterdeck, ran a hand over the smooth polished rail, and made a reckless decision. She headed back to her cabin.

A giddy feeling bloomed inside her while she rifled through Captain Donovan's trunks, looking for a pair of breeches small enough to cinch around her waist. Never would they fit, but a long cord of rope or a leather thong should suffice to hold them up. Havenly might have forbidden her to do deck chores, but he was busy driving the beast, and she was too busy thinking about it.

She needed this.

The knee breeches she settled on were almost long enough to reach her ankles, and her stockings covered the rest. Thankfully, Miss Blanchfield, in her mindless packing, had included a pair of lace-up boots. They were too nice for work but a better choice than the short-heeled blue silk shoes she'd been wearing on arrival.

With an oversized peasant's shirt tucked and cinched around her waist and her hair wound and tucked under a cap, she snuck toward the fo'c'sle, which the trunk of the foremast partially obstructed. Between sails, rigging, masts, and water barrels, her folly should go unnoticed so long as Havenly stayed busy at the helm.

Avoiding getting down on hands and knees and using a stone to scrub, she used a long-handled mop. For the most part, her contribution was more like a sweeping of the decks. By the time she finished a ten-by-ten patch of deck, however, she was more than exhausted. Her memories were apparently clouded by a girl's dreams. Her muscles screamed for rest.

For the next few days, Havenly focused on his work and she focused on hers, and somehow they managed to avoid one another.

Her innocent indifference to the rules was for the greater good.

That is what she told herself.

That is what she believed.

After three days of surreptitiously working on deck, she chose a day of rest. She happily donned the peach walking dress and opened the curtains of her stateroom. Close to the window, an overstuffed armchair beckoned her, and she sat, book in hand, her legs curled under her. She tucked her stockinged feet under the hem of her dress and supported the book of short stories against the armrest. The book wasn't terribly interesting, but it was distracting.

Robert brought lunch for her on the days she didn't show in the kitchens, so when the door creaked, she took little notice.

"Where the devil have you been?" That all-too-familiar voice echoed off the windows. There in the open door stood Havenly, exasperated, hands on his hips and looking every bit the pirate she'd called him.

"I've been right here. What do you need?" She did her best to sound as innocent as she hoped she appeared.

"I need to know where you are all the time. That's what I need. Or do you care so little for your own safety?" With one look, he pinned her to the chair.

"I am safe. Certainly there are crewmen aplenty to report on my whereabouts. Why not try asking them next time?" She was not a child. She failed to see the gravity of the situation. Somewhere, buried in her mind, she feared he might be privy to her secret activities.

"I've asked everyone! And every time I get an answer, it's another goose chase. Why do you think that is, Nicolette?"

"I'm sure I don't know. Most days I'm here or in the galley. Did you bother questioning Cook?"

A nerve twitched in his cheek. Either that or he was working the muscle. Neither one boded well. It appeared he was beyond angry. Or perhaps he was just angry with the men who sent him on empty errands. She felt guilty for that. Putting them in the way of his wrath was not what she intended. Staying out of it was her goal now.

"I can see you're upset. I shall endeavor to make myself more available if that's what you wish. I only thought to stay out of your way. I know you're busy." She hoped to placate him with that innocent bit of tripe.

He dropped one hand from his hip, and with the other he rubbed the angry lines of his forehead with his thumb. "I'm not upset; I'm worried. And"—he swallowed—"I hoped you might care to have dinner with me. I realize I've been remiss in my duties."

"You have no duty to me." She closed her book and put it aside. "I had planned to serve dinner for the officers tonight. I know most of them, and Robert thought it a nice gesture."

"Then I'd be delighted to dine with the officers this evening." He bowed his head toward her as if he'd just removed an invisible hat.

On the ship, meals were a simple affair. No courses, just the essentials—meat, vegetables, and sometimes port. But Nicolette surprised them with a special treat of caramelized apples and clotted cream.

When she left the room to retrieve coffee, Grant excused himself. He met her at the door leading to the galley, took the steaming pot from her hands, and set it on the side table.

"It's time the men finish."

"Yes, of course." She smiled wanly.

The officers stood and mumbled their thanks, each one with a dip of his head, and Grant gently took her elbow and escorted her from the officers' dining room.

When they'd cleared the doorway and had taken several strides toward the companionway, she wiped her hands on the makeshift apron, pulling it free of her waist.

"Do me a kindness and stop wearing that ball gown." The last part came out a trifle more exasperated than he'd meant, but she didn't seem to take offense; in fact, she was smiling ear to ear. She walked ahead of him and ascended the steps to the open deck.

When he emerged from the companionway, she was paces ahead, her hands braced behind her, the apron still clutched between them, her hips gently swaying.

She stopped at the rail and waited for him to catch up.

"You, sir, could use a day with my governess. Manners are her specialty. And I assure you that this gown is in the height of fashion."

"Therein lies my problem. I have no sense of fashion, Miss Bradenton."

"Of course you do not. Because if you did, good sir, you would know that debutantes are not encouraged to wear a ball gown more than twice. This one has exceeded the limit," she said regally. "How is it that you, having grown up among the entitled, are not aware of this rule? Your tutelage must have come from the school for libertines."

He was completely amused now. "Why is that, madam?"

"Because libertines are more interested in ridding women of their clothes than dressing them."

"Nicolette, sometimes you speak before you think." Her summation was partially accurate, but it was not at all the right thing to say to him at this moment.

"That may be true. To be honest, I rather like it here, where the rules don't reach quite so far, and I can say whatever I wish. Don't you ever feel that way?"

"All the time."

The seas were calm, the breeze an afterthought. And the moon, full and bright, lit up the deck. Their conversation was lively and witty and genuine, as always. Nicolette was nothing like the women who usually attracted him. They strove to look alike, dress alike, act alike, and somehow hope to stand out. But they paled like common wrens compared to Nicolette. She was unaffected by the strict standards set by the ton. Her identity could not be governed by a society that held itself to the highest moral standard—one that looked the other way whenever it suited those in charge. Nicolette had kept to the rules while in their presence, but they could not drown out the individual she was born to be.

The moment to safely confess that he possessed her jewelry box had passed. She would deem it an omission of truth, and he would well deserve her wrath. He should have told her days ago, perhaps weeks ago, but every time he planned to sit down with her privately, he was thwarted either by circumstance or his growing attraction for her.

"If you could say anything without repercussion, what would it be?" It was the right question.

He casually watched the moonlight dance on the waves and leaned his arm against the rail. Between his curiosity over the jewelry box and his wish to kiss her in the moonlight, he could think of little else.

"I confess my thoughts are too wicked and scandalous to mention."

"Must you always tease?"

He chuckled. "Nicolette, I am not teasing."

Her mouth parted in silent shock, mesmerizing him.

"Not to worry, kitten. I've no intention of acting on those thoughts unless you'd like to forgive me those repercussions as well."

She slanted him a grin. "I think we should change the subject. Something safer, perhaps."

"More's the pity."

"Does it offend you that I call Captain Donovan Robert?" She discouraged eye contact by throwing her concentration into folding her apron.

He straightened. "No. I'm concerned for your safety. Using his name in the company of the crew undermines his authority over them. A captain without respect or authority has a difficult time keeping peace." With a finger, he gently lifted her chin. "Why did you think I was offended?"

She pulled away, hugging the apron against her chest. Whatever she was thinking seemed to trouble her or embarrass her.

She focused on the swell of the ocean. "I thought you might feel slighted because I give Robert what I will not give to you."

"Aha! You admit to withholding."

"I beg your pardon?" She snapped a look at him.

"You refuse my respectful title. You withhold my name for spite."

"I do not." She hid a smile behind her denial.

"You do. And do you know what that does to me?"

Her brow knit.

He leaned in. "It makes me want it more."

Biting her lip, she held his gaze.

"You want to say it," he whispered.

She shook her head.

"I'll bid you good night if you do. Otherwise, I'm liable to forget the repercussions of my wicked, scandalous thoughts." He shrugged one shoulder and backed away just far enough as not to intimidate.

"Grant." The word came out rushed, forced, and accompanied by a sweet blush.

He took her hand and kissed the tips of her fingers. "Goodnight, Miss Bradenton."

"Goodnight." Her voice was a feather, and as he watched her silently walk away, he couldn't help but think that she was disappointed that he hadn't grabbed her in his arms and kissed her.

He'd come close. Too close.

He adjusted his breeches and cursed under his breath.

CHAPTER 13

Nicolette dressed for a day of chores in the impromptu work uniform she'd constructed from Captain Donovan's clothing. She whistled and smiled a secret smile, remembering the way Havenly had leaned in and suggested he had scandalous, wicked thoughts about her. She walked with a greater confidence in her newfound ability to set this one man off-balance. Considering the many times he'd been the cause of her teetering world, all things were equal.

The risk of exposure still existed, and caution could not be abandoned. Most of the time Havenly worked on the bridge until midday. So far, his schedule had not disrupted her routine, and the crew she worked alongside were all men she'd known as a girl. This felt like home.

She leaned against her broom, gripping the handle next to her cheek while she listened to Mr. Portman retell how he'd lost two days' wages at brag.

"Nicole, you need to play old Drew—he'd never have a chance." Mr. Portman laughed, using her all-too-familiar childhood nickname.

"I'm sure I wouldn't remember how." Her cheeks were

tight with smiling just being in the company of old friends. A good many of them were no more than ten years her senior, and some even younger.

Mr. Portman cleared his throat as if he'd swallowed a fly. "I think I ought to be about my work, miss."

"Oh yes. Don't let me keep you. I think I should be done for the day." Nicolette waved her friend on.

The small crowd departed. Actually, they all but scurried away. She gauged the sun. Almost noon. If her timing was right, she had a good half hour to change. She loosened her grip on the wooden broom handle, careful not to catch a splinter. It was an unusually warm day, and she looked forward to getting into her dress.

The deck creaked. The rigging overhead moaned. The shout of orders sent a warm feeling of nostalgia through her. A ship could be a loud place, especially when it was set to a good sail. Today it was fairly quiet. They scarcely coasted. After all, their destination was time, not port.

A cough sounded behind her and she turned.

And then froze.

With a hip against a rain barrel and arms crossed over his intimidatingly wide chest, the duke's eyes shifted to the forgotten broom in her hand. His mouth stretched into a hard, straight line, he crooked a finger at her.

She winced. No wonder everyone had scampered. He must have been standing there for several minutes. A hot flame of embarrassment—or fear—seared her cheeks.

"Me?" She pointed a finger to her chest as if there were any confusion.

He nodded without preamble.

She felt her lips twitch into a haphazard, shaky smile, and her words caught in her throat. She cleared it. "I can explain—"

"I doubt it," he interrupted. "Would this be the reason I

had a difficult time finding you the past several days? Do you listen at all, Nicolette? Do you have any sense?" The words came out rushed, thrown together end to end like one long sentence.

Implying that she had no sense stoked her ire, restoring a measure of false confidence. "I will not stand here and listen to you tell me I have no sense. Who do you think you are?"

She made a move to put away the broom, but Havenly took three giant steps and snatched it before she could put enough distance between them. She fanned her fingers, checking her palms for splinters, then nervously brushed her now-sweaty hands on her work trousers.

He seized one of her hands, checked the palm, and dropped it without ceremony. "They look fine to me." His voice snapped as sharply as his flashing eyes.

She sneered, wiping her palm again while anxiety pounded in her chest so intensely she could feel the pulse throbbing in her neck.

"What did I tell you about returning to chores?"

She shrugged. With her eyes wide, her voice evaporated under his continued glower.

"And let's not speak of the breeches. Because my ire is formidable, and my anger is only loosely contained at present!"

"You're shouting."

"Am I? You're lucky I'm not the beating kind." Scratching the side of his neck, he sighed almost as loud as he'd yelled. It was a gruff, irritated sound like an animal.

She opened her mouth to retort, but he interrupted again.

"What the devil do you think you're doing?"

One brow rose and she reared back. "Are you that blind?"

"Oh, for the love of God, Nicolette, do you seriously think you can outwit me on this one?"

She blinked and bobbled her head. "It's worth a try. It's better than listening to you rail at me."

"Your wisdom is lacking in this, I assure you. Did you not wonder what kind of impression you were leaving? Or the kind of trouble it might cause?" He blew out a harsh breath. He calmed, but only a little.

"I've caused no trouble." Courting defiance, she braced her hands on her hips and stood her ground.

"No? Your limbs are covered in men's breeches—that alone is obscene." He wagged a finger to quiet her. "It is, and you know it. I don't know what your father was about, allowing you the freedom to parade around like this. You're not a girl anymore. And these are men. Grown men."

"These men are my friends."

"Oh? And when's the last time you had contact with your *friends*?"

She rolled her eyes and let her mind drift, hoping he would spend his energy soon.

"You're acting like a child. You need to go change your clothes and start acting like a woman."

That insult seared her cheek like a slap. "Is that what you'd like, *Grant*? For me to act like a woman?" She smirked. "The blue ball gown or the peach walking dress? Which is your favorite?"

"Nicolette, sweet," he said far too calmly to be true. "You are trying my patience."

"I didn't know you had any."

The muscle in his cheek popped when his jaw worked back and forth, teeth clenched. She could see he was working hard not to yell, but she couldn't seem to help herself from causing him a little discomfort. After all, he was doing his best to embarrass her.

She let her pride go out of her shoulders and looked away. "I was only doing chores. Not even a modicum of what I used to do." She glanced at him. "I was bored," she said by way of explanation.

"So you thought it best to entertain the crew?" he asked on a quieter note.

"I was not entertaining anyone."

"Have you bothered to catch a look at yourself in a mirror? That costume you wear is far more seducing than the blue ball gown, I assure you."

Her mouth dropped open.

"You don't believe me?" He took a long stride, reached forward, and barely pulled the tie holding the neck of the peasant shirt together. It fell from one shoulder.

She looked down at the shirt and pulled it back up. "I don't wear it undone."

"You don't need to. It has a gap in it big enough to fit your head through even when it is fastened." Tugging the ties at her throat, he looped them, pulled them together, and tossed at her the remaining length.

"Sketch a bow, my dear, and I'll show you how entertaining you are."

She looked at the shirt again. Pulled it out from the neck and clearly saw what he meant. A quick glance down the front of the neck hole told her that bending over would show off more than the daring blue gown had ever hoped. No question of her gender.

His damnable brow was cocked when she looked back up at him, and his mouth was pulled into a smirk. "I can see that you now understand."

"You have made your point. I'll change."

"And you won't be wearing that again."

"Yes, as you've commanded. I will change. You needn't belabor." She clutched the throat of the shirt, embarrassed and now exasperated.

"Nicolette, do you know why the curtsy was invented?" He didn't wait for an answer. "So that kings with their smarmy, cunning ways might look down the dresses of all their women subjects."

"You're making that up."

"It doesn't matter whether it's made up, it's true. And every time you curtsy or lean over a bit, any number of men standing close enough to see are filling their minds with portraits of you without clothes on." He let that sink in for a moment.

She gasped. "Maybe the ill-mannered barbarians of the ton, but not the men on this ship."

"Every man on this ship would look, Nicolette. You knew them as a girl. You are no longer a girl."

Her heart pounded like a wild thing. She felt caught in a snare. There was no good argument for it.

A finger gently lifted her chin. "That's what men do."

"It's barbaric and rude." She knocked his hand away.

His chest rumbled at her action. "It's instinctual and guarantees the continuance of the human race."

"I'm sure Captain Donovan would do no such thing."

"I'll give you that. But only because you're like a daughter to the man. Why do you think I grabbed you from serving dinner the other night?"

She felt defeated. The settling sounds of the ship, the calm lapping of the water against the hull now trapped her and reminded her that she had nowhere to go. That getting away from this man would be near impossible.

"Why don't they teach young women about this when they're schooled in etiquette?" She was angry that Miss Blanchfield had not warned her.

"This should be your second season, Nicolette. Most women have figured it out for themselves by now and are purposely using their newfound knowledge to snare, catch, and otherwise cajole their victims into marriage."

She scoffed at that. "Well then, I guess it has some merit."

And then she added on another note, "Do you mean to suggest that I am an imbecile because I didn't know this?"

"Of course not. Your problem is that you were not raised among women who use their charms like an art. You are far too trusting—that's not a flaw, love. It's just dangerous." His voice was a bit softer.

"Why have I not seen it then? I've been to enough balls, routs, parties, teas, and I have not once, apart from you of course, been treated with anything but good manners," she said a bit too triumphantly.

"I realize that my morals are suspect, but have you seen *me* do it?"

There was too much confidence in his voice, and something told her that she would not care for his next words. "No. I haven't."

"Well, my dear, I can promise you that I have. Men tend to master the act of looking without looking about the same time as women discover what men want to look at."

There was an argument to be made for ignorance. It definitely sounded blissful. "You have made your point too well. Is it at all possible that you could be any more vulgar, sir?"

Grant smiled and contemplated. "Yes—I do believe I can. I generally reserve vulgar words like *the devil be damned* and *holy hell* for the men's clubs and refrain from using them in front of ladies. I believe that qualifies as indecently more vulgar."

"Well then, you have broken your own rule." She had him on this one.

He grinned unrepentantly. "Darling, you are wearing a pair of breeches. I don't think the rule applies in this case."

She began to laugh. "You, sir, are absurd."

"There are more if you're interested."

She choked on a giggle. "No!"

"Go change. And spend the rest of the day reading or cooking or darning a sock. But do not let me catch you doing this again. Or wearing a pair of trousers." His tone brooked no argument.

She rolled her eyes closed and sighed. "Yes, Pirate Captain Havenly."

He chuckled. "I love it when you do that."

Now she was confused. "Do what?"

"Roll your eyes at me. It's highly disrespectful. And all you."

"I'm happy to be of service." With the shirt pressed to her throat, she bowed.

"That was not a proper curtsy, my lady, and it doesn't count."

She gasped. "You're counting?"

"Only since I met you." He grinned roguishly. "I'll come take you for a walk when the sun sets. And do not be dressed in this costume."

She bit into a mischievous smile as he quirked a brow. Nicolette knew she'd pushed him this afternoon. Part of it had been exhilarating if she were honest, but she had little wish to try his patience again. However, leaving him with the impression that he'd won this round would not do either.

AFTER GRANT LEFT NICOLETTE, he gave orders to empty the quarterdeck of crewmen by sunset except for those officers changing shifts. He selfishly desired time alone with her where chaperones were not expected, needed, wanted, or available.

Something in him craved to walk in the quiet, to hear her laugh again, to feel unbound by a society she had not expected to emulate. He wanted and hoped, against his better judgment, for a witty repartee of disrespect because few dared challenge him so. Even his grandmother knew the limits. But not this girl. She'd dared to push him beyond measure, and in a short time he'd grown to appreciate that very thing about her.

Did he want more than that?

Probably, dammit, but he was a gentleman regardless of her defining him as a rake. Lord knows he'd done his share to deserve the title, but he'd never pushed beyond the boundaries of ruination.

Hell, it was just a walk.

Still too early to meet her, he washed up in his cabin and settled into a chair with a book on navigation, star charts, and constellations. In the North Atlantic, sailors navigated by the North Star, a star that had once guided three notably wise men. Tonight, if the skies remained clear, Ursa Minor would be in full view, and if he were a man of wisdom, he'd keep his focus on that brightest point instead of her ocean-blue eyes.

He flipped the book shut and haphazardly stacked it atop the others on the table. Books that normally interested him now held no allure, leaving him bored, frustrated, antsy.

Perhaps Nicolette had felt the same after spending a week at sea with little to do. He could hardly blame her for seeking other amusements. But mopping and sweeping decks? Good Lord, that hardly qualified as amusing.

He chuckled at the memory of her as she stood holding that broom and the moment she realized that he'd joined her audience. Whether she'd known it or not, she'd gathered quite an audience by the time he'd arrived. It seemed half the crew was not in their respective places. They'd gathered to watch the little hoyden sweep a deck. He couldn't really blame them for that either.

He rubbed his jaw as he watched his cursed foot bob up and down while propped on his opposite knee. These were nervous gestures for a young pup, not a man of his twenty-eight years. He consciously forced both feet to the floor as if they'd been nailed in place, then gripped the arms of the chair. He felt himself sawing his teeth back and forth.

Dammit, dammit, dammit!

He shoved out of the chair and threw on his peacoat, then spent an hour checking crew schedules, which could have been written in Latin for all he knew. When the sun finally kissed the horizon, he sought her out.

Right where he'd requested, surprisingly obedient, she strolled alongside the rail, concentrating as her fingers bounced along the wood like a tiny rabbit. Before she turned fully, he took in every inch of her from her lush dark blond hair to the bodice of that vexing blue dress.

Did she really need to wear that?

Her hair was drawn up in a loose twist, her forearms and hands sheathed in elbow-length silk gloves. She was a goddess. Stunning in her formal wear, she was still at home on a ship in the middle of nowhere, and she belonged. Truly belonged.

When he was close enough for his boots to sound, she glanced up.

"I see you've worn the dress again."

"You didn't precisely forbid it." She smiled while pulling a wayward strand of hair that had blown across her mouth. If the evening breeze kicked up, it wouldn't take long for the wind to pull the heavy mass from its pins. He said a small prayer to Poseidon.

"Where's your cloak?"

"I don't need one," she said with a confident smile before turning away.

The day had been warm, but the early evening brought a chill. He started to offer his coat, but she backed up a step and leaned her delightful derriere against the sideboard of the taffrail. One arm rested lengthwise on the top while her fingers hypnotically brushed back and forth against the polished wood. He had seen fit to have several lanterns lit, but for the most part he hoped to watch the sunset with her. Even now, directly behind her, the glowing pink of the setting sun and the shimmering blue of the ocean turned the sky violet.

"You have a mischievous glimmer about you," he said. "Or perhaps it's the coy smile and the way you watch me from under your lashes." That brought a blush. "Or maybe it's just the sunset."

She bit her lip. "Or maybe I have a secret."

"I'm good at keeping secrets." For God's sake, he had a secret of his own, one that could ruin their burgeoning friendship if he spoke of it now.

When she turned her face toward the last glow of the sun, he blamed the anxious flutter in his chest on her stretched and deliciously bared throat. In truth and more likely, his heart beat hard because he had too long delayed telling her why they'd met.

"You keep a secret, my lady? Will you tell me now, or must I guess?" He took her hand, intending to bow over it, but she snatched it back.

"I've broken a rule."

"Shocking." He gasped and held a hand to his chest. "You have my undivided attention."

"And will you have mercy upon me, pirate captain?"

"As much mercy as you've left me today, this I promise."

She hid a chuckle behind her hand. "Beat me, sir, and I shall call upon the gods to introduce you to the sea."

He appreciated the cut of her gown, the way it swayed in the changing breeze from aft to stern, the length plastered to the outside of her leg. The fabric, a smooth silk, appeared bumpy, not wrinkled as he would have expected. His brow furrowed. He glanced up and caught her laughing expression.

With a wink she lifted her skirt, then just as quickly she dropped it. Had he seen correctly? The shadow of dusk romantically surrounded them, but there was nothing romantic about the trousers he swore he glimpsed under her skirts.

"Miss Bradenton, where are your stockings?" He tried for gruff, a stern stance, and a serious cock of his head. She played with fire, which made his libido leap and his heart melt.

"I'm wearing them." Hanging on to her dress with one hand, she scrunched up the bottom of one trouser leg with the other, revealing a stocking underneath. Her sheepish smile radiated despite her attempt to hold on to the moment. "So you see, I am quite warm."

"How clever you are."

Brushing down her skirts, she added, "That's the last time you'll see me in trousers. I just couldn't resist, and the ball gown was the only dress I had that would hide them." She shrugged. "That's why I chose it."

"Is it? Are you certain you're not being contrary just to make sport of me?"

"No." She shook her head, and a fine line appeared across her brow. "I've no desire to anger you. I hope I haven't."

Did she really think he would be angry over a jest? After this afternoon, yes. Of course she would. "I think you're funny, and beautiful, and playfully wicked."

A smile teased her mouth, and she reached up to touch his right cheek. "Your cheek dimples when you smile so. Do you know that? Only one."

He took her hand and rubbed her gloved fingers, wishing she'd left the silk sheaths in her cabin. "So I've been told."

"But of course. Women fall at your feet like wilting lilies. I'm sure they've pointed out the oddity dozens of times."

He had yet to release her hand, and she did nothing to pull it away. Grant wrapped her arm around his, rubbing her fingers while they strolled the perimeter of the uppermost deck.

"Nicolette?" Face forward, they continued to walk slowly.

The sun was a tiny wink, the last sliver of flashing light before it disappeared as if the ocean swallowed it whole. "I owe you another apology."

She stopped, and he was forced to face her. She tilted her head back to look at him. "You apologize often. Why?"

Eyes like sapphires sparkled back at him, and he was lost just watching her speak. "I'm not accustomed to raising my voice to women. That alone deserves an apology. When I found my cabin this afternoon, I sat down and attempted to enjoy a book. Admittedly, it wasn't interesting, but at that moment I could understand why you were bored enough to try something so rash."

"It's not your fault that I'm exasperating." She grinned, tugging on the lapel of his coat. "This place brings out the worst in me, I suppose."

"I wouldn't say that."

"It certainly brings out the childish, disobedient part," she said impishly.

He chuckled, releasing her fingers from his lapel, but refused to let them go just yet. "That I would agree with. Still, you are a woman grown. You can make your own choices. And I'm not the best nursemaid."

She pulled her hands free long enough to smack her palms against his chest. "I don't need a nursemaid. But I do appreciate your looking after my welfare. I know you feel an obligation to my safekeeping. Besides, I'd not given much thought to how I looked dressed in men's clothing. You were right to bring it to my attention."

"Like a pirate. That's how you looked."

Her laughter was lost on the wind, but he was close enough to hear it like a siren's song.

Grant took back her fingers and brought them to his mouth. "Why do women where these infernal things?"

"Because they're fashionable and keep our hands clean.

Why do you find them annoying? I've never heard anyone complain so much about silly gloves."

"Are you game for an experiment?" He bent a challenging brow and held her hand to his heart until she answered.

"Ah, you prove once again that boys love their games."

He shook his head. "I'm not a little boy."

"All men are little boys, Your Grace." She slanted him a cheeky look. "Now, what's to be the experiment?"

"We shall seek to answer your question as to why I don't like gloves. May I?" He held her hand out between them and motioned to the gloves.

She nodded with a wary glance, then turned her gaze to his hands while he massaged her silk-covered fingers, making little waves on the shimmering fabric.

"Do you feel that?"

Confusion marred her forehead, her eyes absorbed by his actions. "I... I feel you rubbing my fingers." Her voice was scratchy and abnormally high. She cleared her throat, then swallowed. "It feels nice." She looked up at him again, her eyes registering the new sensation as she bit into a twitching half grin.

Grant gently let her hand down while lifting the other. When he began slowly, meticulously, slipping the other glove from her fingers one by one, her mouth fell open. She stole a look at what his hands were doing, and he could almost feel her reason slip away when he began to knead her now bared fingers. The gentle pressure of his skin against hers, his fingers spreading her palm open, tracing the fine lines, culminated in a fine blush that rose from the skin above her bodice into the thick, windblown wisps of her hair.

The tip of her tongue darted out to wet her lips, and her eyes returned to his, filled with wonder.

"And now? What do you feel, Nicolette?" He brought her

naked fingers to his lips and brushed a kiss to each fingertip. "Is it different?"

She nodded slowly, her eyes wide, the smile gone behind parted lips.

"How so?"

Her throat bobbed and her words caught between breaths. "Nice. Comforting."

"Is that all?" he asked in a low, throaty voice.

She shook her head and watched in fascination as he took one finger in his mouth and sucked gently.

Gooseflesh ran up her arm and she visibly shivered. Her eyes turned to liquid pools of desire, the pupils flared, and the little thrumming in her neck picked up pace.

He noticed all that and was shocked to find that his reaction was twice that hard. He placed the bared hand behind his neck and lowered his head. Before he came in contact with her lips, he asked, "Do you feel the difference, Nicolette?"

Her lips parted, but she only nodded, and he seized the opportunity to feel her mouth on his.

She gasped but didn't pull away, just tugged her other hand free and wrapped her fingers around the back of his neck. It was his turn for goose bumps. Her touch sent a wave of tiny tremors, starting with his neck and moving up into his scalp and ending with his hair.

The woman stimulated his hair, for heaven's sake.

Without stopping to think, Grant enveloped her, his arms about her waist, crushing her to him at the same time he took her bottom lip, nibbling lightly, teasing with his tongue. It wasn't his vast experience leading him now, it was her. The smell of citrus sunshine, the warmth of her hand, the way her breath mingled with his, and the sighs... Oh Lord, the sighs.

He'd been dreaming of this for days. When his tongue flicked her top lip, she opened on a sweet sigh and he plundered her mouth like the pirate she'd been calling him. Somewhere inside him, he knew this was not a good idea. But the side that lust controlled, the side of the brain that women laid to waste, that side he had no power over. Breasts pressed into his chest, soft and full, and if he continued much longer, he could no longer take responsibility for her safety. That not only proved that she wasn't safe with him, but he wasn't safe with her either.

This small woman, this inexperienced girl, met his passion with devouring hunger. When she touched her tongue to the corner of his mouth, a growl tore from his throat and he felt more than heard a gasping giggle come from her.

A giggle. A tiny sound slipping into his foggy brain, dousing the spell. His heart raced ahead of his breathing like he'd just finished a pugilist exercise.

Grant shook his head in disbelief and chortled through what felt like gasps of air. "Did you just laugh at me, sweet?"

Nicolette's hands slid down his shoulders, and she buried her grip in his collar, hiding her face. The scent of him was all around her, the thrill of his heartbeat next to her cheek. This was like nothing she'd ever felt and everything she wanted to feel again.

With hesitant shyness, she looked up at him from under her lashes, but the minute she saw the satisfied little crinkles at his smiling eyes, words froze in her mouth. Unfortunately, however, the giggle she'd let escape had no problem bubbling out of her. She buried her face again.

"I'm sorry. I can't help it." Nerves had always done this to her, sent her into a fit of giggles. Her belly tickled with it. Her face felt warm, and she had no idea how to extricate herself from the embarrassment.

His chest vibrated with a low rumble, and he wrapped his

arms around her shoulders. Never had she felt more protected than now.

"So, what did we learn?" she asked, muffled between his shirt collar, his coat lapel, and the scent of bay rum.

"To leave the gloves on," he said flatly, as if it were a given.

Nicolette laughed all the more for it and nodded.

Grant held her away and tipped her chin up. "All this jovial abandon—I don't think I've ever witnessed such a thing. Was it the kiss that amused or just me?" His smile engulfed her and made her forget where they were.

"Uh-huh." She nodded.

"Both? Me and the kiss?"

"Uh-huh." She nodded again. Her voice came out in little tittering missteps like the butterflies in her belly. "Was that the experiment?"

"Not exactly." He blew out a heavy sigh and rubbed both his eyes with the heels of his hands, successfully removing himself from her.

When he opened his eyes, he squinted down at her and held her captive with contemplative silence. What could she say? That her insides stirred to life every time he touched her? That her lips still tingled where he'd sucked and nibbled? That when he groaned into her mouth, it was as if a hundred dancing butterflies had been released?

Nerves. Fear. Inexperience. The perfect storm for her childhood malady: uncontrollable giggles.

Had she hurt his pride? He didn't look upset, at least not with her. Womanly instinct told her that he was working through his own fierce, passionate reaction.

"Nicolette," he finally said. With his hands warm on either side of her face, he held her gently. He rubbed the pad of his thumb along her lips and watched, absorbed with the action, then took her gloved hand and kissed the back. "Friends?" When he was done with that one, he picked up the ungloved hand and kissed her fingertips again. "Or lovers? It's still the same game."

She snatched her hands from his grasp. Shock took over any nervous hiccup she'd had. She couldn't decide whether she was angry with him for making a mockery of his little experiment or if he truly wished to teach her something.

"Is this all sport to you?" she asked, no more butterflies, no tinge of giggles. Her voice no longer sounded foreign to her ears. She was a trifle miffed.

"No." He bent his head back, closing his eyes against the stars. "Have dinner with me in my quarters."

"You're mad."

He looked back at her. "That's one explanation. But we both must eat and it's late. And I like your company. You can leave the gloves on." He dimpled a smile. "But God have mercy, please change that dress."

Nicolette walked away, her stomach in knots. She could feel his eyes on her until she left the deck.

What was she to make of him? One moment he was passionate and tender, and the next he was staring at her, appearing every bit as confused as she was now. And then as if that were not enough to send her into a mass of womanly insecurity, he changed course and steered toward teasing again.

"And now dinner?" Nicolette shook her head. What on earth does one discuss with a madman at dinner? One thing was sure, she had no intention of tempting his frustration any further by wearing the same dress. Or the gloves!

CHAPTER 14

Grant remained rooted to the deck, his pulse racing, his mind staggering to control the flood of emotion that had seized him with one kiss.

This woman was forbidden. He knew it. He'd vowed to stay away from her but found it nearly impossible. Every day for the past week, hour upon hour, he'd dreamed of kissing her, touching her, and now that he had, his desire was tenfold. His body couldn't take another hit.

He had no business having dinner with her tonight. He had no business kissing her. He had no business even thinking about what he wanted to do with her. Grant pinched the place between his eyes and argued with his conscience, his resolve weakened by the ghostly imprint of her scent. Forcing himself from his wicked thoughts, he went to fetch dinner.

And her.

Asking her to dine was the act of a madman. Although kissing her again tonight was off the table, Grant couldn't resist the conversation or her uninhibited laughter.

Nicolette was sweet and unknowing, stormy and misbehaved—a natural seductress, the best kind. Brazen and unrepentant. He was unable to find anything he didn't like about her. He wanted her and, cognizant of his need for her, knew if they didn't get off this boat soon, he was bound to behave against all polite decency and simply seduce her. It wasn't a far stretch. It was evident by her reaction that she wanted him almost as badly as he wanted her.

It galled him to think it, but without even being aware of her own power to entice, she had managed to breach his impenetrable self-restraint, lending to the irony that a notorious, practiced libertine was charged with protecting the virtue of a natural temptress.

He picked up their meal from the kitchen, whistling there and back to his cabin. He expected to find her obediently waiting, hopefully dressed in something else because that sinful blue ball gown was his undoing.

With both his hands full, he nudged the door open with his boot. Nicolette was nowhere in sight. He took the time to light a lantern and a solitary candle for the table. When she didn't show after ten intolerable minutes, he wondered if she'd expected him to fetch her in her quarters.

Of course she did. A schoolboy's blunder. He hurried past the map room, quickly finding the companionway that led to her room.

But she wasn't there.

Could it be she was avoiding him?

No. Something about this didn't feel right.

Grant returned to his cabin and retrieved his gun. He passed only three men, questioning each regarding Miss Bradenton's whereabouts. After the day's escapade of finding her doing deck chores, he was certain the crew would not lie for her now.

His gut clenched with dread, and he hoped his instincts

were wrong. He made his way to the opposite side of the quarterdeck, the empty side, the side where they'd shared an intimate walk and kiss. The deck, now wrapped in near darkness, illuminated only by the stars and a waning moon, was eerily overtaken by a fine rising mist of fog pouring in from the west. He heard her before he saw her. She seemed to be arguing with a man.

He approached with grave caution, curious as to their conversation. Both had yet to take notice of him. The night shadows were enough to keep him from their sight. He blocked out all sound but their voices. The crewman's tone was sharp. Nicolette's was barely audible, but she was shaking her head vigorously at the same time the man grabbed her upper arm, yanking her close.

The son of a bitch dared put a hand on her! That alone made Grant want him dead.

He leveled his pistol before he stepped from the shadows.

"Unhand the lady and step back." His voice was a low growl, strong enough to carry the distance without shouting. He didn't wish to alarm the man into a complete panic. He just wanted Nicolette out of reach long enough to beat him within an inch of his worthless life.

With an unexpected jerk, the man, whom Grant now recognized as one Mr. Tidwell, whipped Nicolette in front of him, pinning her against his barrel chest like a shield.

The fool didn't know he was as good as dead. It took less than a second for Grant to adjust his aim toward Tidwell's head. Nicolette's bound hair fell from its pins to hang over her face, blocking her eyes and making it almost impossible to read her expression. He didn't have time to wonder how afraid she must be; he kept his mind on the task of removing the bastard who held her. His chest constricted, seized with a painful panic despite his efforts. He had a straight shot at the man, close enough for accuracy. But there was no way of communicating with her to keep still.

"I wouldna do that, sir, or yer lovey's neck'll spill blood all over this 'ere deck."

Grant refused to get into a debate with the heinous man. Tidwell held a knife at her throat, close enough to her skin that even if Grant were successful in shooting him in the head, any jerk of the knife could cause a mortal wound. He couldn't risk that.

He cocked the gun, hoping the sound would send enough warning to cause the man to rethink his steps.

"Ye want her back, and I jist want what's comin' to me. I've worked for it. I deserve it," Tidwell spat out.

If Grant could just keep him talking... "What is it you want, Tidwell?"

"She knows what is and what ain't. She'll show me, and I'll be leavin'."

Grant could think of only one way he'd be getting off this ship.

Nicolette attempted to speak, the knife making it difficult. "I... don't..." It was impossible to hear the rest, her voice smothered against the pressure of the man's arm binding her chest and the threat of the blade at her throat.

It was a strangled sound, and it turned Grant's stomach. Calm was necessary for a steady shot. He inhaled deeply and exhaled slowly.

"You've made a mistake!" Grant yelled.

"No, Cap'n, you have! I know ew she is. Miss Bradenton is worth a fortune."

Her head inched back, her hair parting like a curtain, and now he saw her eyes. Yes, she was afraid, but there was something else there. Her mouth was set in a hard line with fierce determination.

It became clear that Nicolette was not getting out of this alive. If all the Bradentons—or Etons—had been killed, it stood that she would not receive any more mercy than they had. His eyes made a quick inspection of her. One hand gripped her skirt and the other gripped something else. In her hand, she held a long, hooked hairpin. His gaze shot up to hers and he caught a gleam in her eye. He recognized it. It was the look of a fighter just before they dealt the winning blow.

Grant took in everything about the scene: the knife, the arm belted around her, the sneering overconfident smile on her captor's face. If he shot the arm with the knife, she might have a better chance. Something lit in her eyes, and he could feel the tension spread from his chest to the tip of his trigger finger. And he knew she was about to move.

Swiftly, her hand in fluid motion, quick and sure, she jabbed the hairpin into Tidwell's knee. The surprise took the edge of the knife from her neck, and she fell forward.

Tidwell screamed and bent his arm back. Nicolette ran straight for Grant. And Grant leveled a shot where the shoulder met the collarbone, hoping to catch the man before he loosed the blade.

Nicolette stumbled once but never looked back. The knife dropped. Tidwell fell back with a thud onto the hard deck.

Still aiming his empty gun at the unmoving man, Grant caught Nicolette with his left arm. She buried her face in his shoulder, and only then did he let his pistol arm drop.

"Are you all right?" he said, low against her ear, all the while keeping an eye on the ghostly-pale man.

That's how Robert Donovan found him. Soothing Nicolette with one hand, he waved Robert over with the other. The shot had brought several of the officers.

Over Nicolette's head, Grant called to Robert, "Check him."

Everyone else stayed behind them.

Robert knelt by Tidwell and shook his head at Grant.

Good. He was dead. That would save Grant from having to beat him to death before he threw him overboard. He couldn't get answers from a dead man, but Tidwell had a friend who was liable to know something. There was time for that after he got Nicolette to safety.

He motioned to Robert, holding up five fingers, and mouthed, *Five minutes.* He meant to see Nicolette back to his cabin, lock her in, and seek out the other man.

When he led her through the door of his stateroom, she didn't protest. Her steps were slow and uneven, as if her legs were too weak to lift her feet as she shuffled a clumsy gait along the floorboards. Grant noticed the numb look in her eyes as he sat her at the table, steadying her like a rag doll.

As shock set in, her arms quaked. Grant grabbed the folded quilt atop the bed, then wrapped it around her shoulders and rubbed the sides of her arms briskly through the soft calico squares. He gently checked her for signs of bruises and pain. He swore under his breath when he saw a red welt on her neck, a hint of blood beading along the thin line.

In three long strides, he hurried to the washbasin and retrieved a cloth, which he wrung out with cool water. When he knelt next to her, Nicolette's eyes shifted to his face and his throat convulsed. The wound had already begun to swell, red and hot, and he grimaced with each dab. It had to sting, but like a stone, she didn't move a muscle except for her eyelids, which blinked trancelike while she watched him tend her injuries.

"It doesn't hurt." Her voice came out in a raspy whisper.

"That's the shock, love. It protects against trauma... at first." He sighed heavily and melted under her trusting gaze.

She reached out, placed a gloved hand against his jaw, and produced a wobbly smile. "I'm all right, Grant."

He closed his eyes against the relief, swallowing the sick

feeling burning a hole in his stomach. He'd promised to protect her, and here she was wounded, worried for him.

"Do you think you can answer a question? Or is it too much?" he asked gently. A warm glow of lamplight reflected in her eyes.

The quicker they found the other man, the better.

With a deep breath she nodded, sending a relief of color back into her chalk-like cheeks.

"Was anyone else there? Did you see another man?" Holding her hand, he felt an impulsive squeeze at the question.

She swallowed audibly and nodded.

"How many?"

She held up one finger.

"Do you know where he went?"

She nodded again, and her eyes welled with tears. A heart-wrenching drop fell onto his hand as he rubbed his thumb over her fingers.

"Where is he now, love?"

"I killed him," she whispered on a sob, her chin trembling with the effort. Her voice quavered. "He's dead."

She'd killed him? With practiced purpose, Grant squelched his shock at such news. His hold on her remained confidently strong without betraying a twitch of alarm.

"Can you tell me how?"

Nicolette drew a deep breath. "He fell overboard into the water, where the railing lies low." As if saying it soothed the burden, she continued, more determined now. "There were two of them, one behind me and one in front."

"And then what happened?"

The words came out rough, staggered between short breaths. "They both had the same look, disgusting and ogling, and then the one in front ran toward me, and I panicked and did the only thing I could think of." As she held his gaze, her eyes grew round with her confession. "I slid off my shoe and threw it at him. The heel hit him in the head and he lost his balance. He stumbled backward and fell over the rail." She licked her dry lips. "I killed him. I killed a man." Tears slid along her jawline, dripping from the tip of her chin.

"Nicolette, you did not kill him. You threw a shoe at him." The vision of it almost made him smile, but the seriousness was thick and heavy in the room. She meant it. And the guilt of it was in her weeping eyes.

"Well, because of my shoe he is now in a watery grave. Not even a waiting boat could have saved him. The sound of his body hitting the water is something I will never forget. No thrashing, no sound, no yelping for help. Nothing. He must have hit his head on..." she sniffled, choking on a sob.

The tail of his shirt was as good as any hanky. He pulled it from his waistband and wiped her eyes and nose, which actually pried a giggle from her. The sound of congested tears and mucus mingled with a chuckle was the best thing he'd heard since sitting her down.

"A man's blood is on my hands." She sobered.

"No, it's on your shoe."

"Stop. You're making me laugh and it's not funny, Grant."

"No, it's not. But humor heals." He wiped at her nose again. "God was surely watching over you."

She nodded and put the back of her hand to her eye, swiping at the corners where tears welled.

"If you hadn't acted so quickly, it would have been you over that rail."

She shrugged. "Perhaps."

"You doubt me? Nicolette," he said, "those men would have taken whatever it was they were hoping to find and then killed you. It wouldn't be difficult to fake an accident. And I'm guessing they had a jolly boat in the water in case something went wrong. Captain Donovan is checking on that and the missing man. Or don't you trust what I say?"

"I trust everything you say," she said without pause, seeming to gain strength.

"Good. Will you be all right if I leave you for a few minutes?"

She shook her head, and once again panic seized her breathing into shallow pants.

"Love, I'm going to lock the door. No one else has a key. I need to find Captain Donovan and see if he's discovered anything." When she looked like protesting, he added, "He needs to know how you fare and that your wounds are not critical. Do you not think he deserves that?"

"Of course." She turned doleful eyes on him. "Can't I go with you?"

"I thought you trusted me."

"I do."

"Then stay here. Don't open that door for anyone. Odds are good those were the only two, but I'm not taking any chances." He held her chin. "Fifteen minutes at most. No more."

She nodded and started to say something, then stopped and nodded again.

"Lie down if you tire. You have a quilt, and there are plenty of blankets. You'll stay here tonight. There's dinner on the tray if you're hungry."

Grant stood and brushed a kiss on her forehead. "I won't allow anything to happen to you."

Locking her in wasn't easy for him. He worried about her emotional state and didn't wish to be the cause of any mounting fear, but he needed an audience with Donovan to discuss their next move.

He found him where he left him, cleaning up the boards and taking care of evidence. They both decided to create a story pitting the two men in a drunken brawl that had turned ugly. A fight ending with a random accident wasn't all that unheard of. And the fact that Grant had shot one of them made it appear as if the commodore of the fleet had protected the crew. Those crewmen who had witnessed the end of the spectacle were trusted officers and would keep quiet or lose their jobs.

"Donovan, I'm moving Nicolette to my cabin. I'm not debating it. I can't take a chance." His voice brooked no argument. He wasn't about to risk her life over rules and nonsense.

"You'll no' get a complaint from me. I'm just as worried fer her." The ready agreement shocked Grant, but it did come with a hard look and an unsaid warning to behave as a gentleman.

They both agreed leaving her alone during the day was out of the question. Grant trusted only himself, and maybe Robert Donovan.

Maybe.

By the time he headed for his cabin, he was mentally and physically exhausted. Internally he wrestled with the sleeping arrangements. With only one bed, he had failed to consider the implications of staying in the same room alone with her for another week.

A man of his word, he'd been gone for no more than fifteen minutes when he returned to unlock his cabin door. Light from the same lantern he'd lit when he first went to find her for dinner illuminated his now sleeping captive. She lay in his bed atop the covers, her ruby-red lips against her pale skin like Sleeping Beauty waiting for a prince to wake her. But he was no prince.

She lay there fully clothed, her head resting against her elbow, which she'd flung across his pillow. Her knees were pulled up to her chest.

With a weary smile, he noticed for the first time she wore

only one shoe. The other one had done an admiral job of saving her life.

With the barest touch, careful not to wake her, he slipped off her left shoe, then grabbed the quilt, covering her feet. He contemplated the formal white gloves. If he removed them, she might wake. But leaving them on didn't seem right either. Comfort had him pulling them off slowly, edging each finger free from its casing and discarding the gloves on the bureau. He tugged the quilt up to her shoulders now and tucked in her bare arms.

A cursory glance around the stateroom turned up no real solution for a place for him to sleep. The bed had plenty of room even with his occupant, but there was no way to move her without waking her and no way to climb around her either. Not to mention the fact that sleeping next to her would cause him a great deal of discomfort.

The chairs at the table didn't look promising, but there were few other choices left him. With slow deliberation, he scooched them together, making as little sound as possible. With his back anchored and his neck cramped against the chair and table, he propped his feet on the other chair and tried against all odds to sleep.

The soft, even sound of Nicolette's breathing soothed him. How she'd stood up against the murderous kidnappers was the bravest thing he'd ever seen. Most women—hell, most men—would have frozen. But she had bravely, without blinking, looked Grant in the eye and stabbed the thief in the knee. A four-inch hairpin and a shoe had served her as well as any single-bullet gun. He was proud of her.

He shifted his shoulders, fought the chairs for a comfortable position, and drifted in and out of sleep. Before the sun had a chance to rise, he gave up trying. Fighting back a growl at the sharp pain between his shoulder blades, he stretched his tweaked neck, took a deep breath, and rose.

Nicolette slept on. He watched her for a long minute, his reasoning punctuated by feelings he could not explain. He wasn't quite ready for all the answers, satisfied this early in the morn to leave more than a few questions behind. He grabbed his navy wool coat, hung a spare key on the peg by the door, and then left, locking the door behind him with a click.

CHAPTER 15

*N*icolette woke in Havenly's bed, momentarily confused. She pulled off the blankets that covered her, took in the wrinkled midnight-blue gown she still wore from last night, and let the memories come. Long ago she'd learned that forcing down bad feelings didn't keep them at bay. It only prolonged their power.

The sobering light of day brought a deluge of chilling memories including one body smacking into the dark water and another thudding to the deck.

It was surreal.

And so was this odd sense of security.

Certainly being aboard the *New Horizon* brought feelings of security, the familial comfort of nostalgic memories, but this was more than that.

From that first dance when Grant held her, to sleeping in his cabin now, she felt safe, protected. Of course, the way he'd kissed her last night brought a measure of unease. After all, the man had called it an experiment. His touch even through her gloves had made her heart race. But when he took them off—Lord help her—the action turned her mind into a disoriented frenzy. Whether she could trust him she never questioned, although perhaps she should. All she was willing to consider today was that she was out of harm's way.

She swung her legs over the side of the bed, which sat high over drawers built into the bottom. Her feet dangled above the floor. Next to the table were two padded leather chairs haphazardly pushed together and a burgundy wool blanket laid over the back of one of them. It was obvious that he'd spent the night there. She had a difficult time imagining his long legs and body stretched between the chairs. No doubt the position kept him from sleep.

The subtle scent of his cologne was evident on the blanket he used, and she could smell the comforting, spicy scent of sandalwood on his bedding too. His presence was in every corner of the stateroom.

She folded the quilt with neat corners and righted the upholstered chairs, angling them in front of the small pipe stove across the room, then pushed the ladder-backed wooden chairs around the table. As an afterthought, she checked the door to see if, in fact, he'd locked it.

He had.

It would have been just as easy to lock her in Robert's old room, but fear would have discovered her there more so than here. Grant must have known that. Or he wanted her close. That thought sent a shiver of unexpected pleasure through her.

She then examined the ingeniously erected bath chamber that took up one corner of the cabin. The washbasin was a gift for sure, but what she really needed was a bath. The mere thought of that greasy character holding her up against his barrel chest and the smell of ale on his breath made her skin crawl. Such vivid memories required a good dousing in hot, soapy water. For a moment she considered pouring the water from the basin pitcher into the tub, but it wouldn't have amounted to even an inch, and what she needed was full submersion.

As if her thoughts were magic, she heard the turn of a key and the latch give on the stateroom door. She recognized Havenly's clipped stride as he entered the outer room.

"Nicolette?" he called.

She stole a peek through the shutters of the enclosed room that housed the tub. "I'm in here, Your Grace." In a partial state of undress, she hurriedly pulled the arm of her dress up over her bared shoulder.

He stopped where he was, keeping to the greater cabin, but tilted his head slightly to see her through the open shutter. "I've brought hot water if you're interested."

She sighed with relief. "You read my mind." She fixed her dress in place, then stepped from the little room. The minute she did, Havenly sprang into commanding action, his countenance steely and determined as if he were instructing the day's watch. He graciously stood in front of her, blocking the crew's view while he motioned for them to bring in several buckets of water. She could smell the steam-permeated wood of the buckets. With his arms crossed, perhaps to expand his back as wide as possible to hide her from seeking eyes, he rushed the shipmates in and out with the flip of one hand. No one paid her any heed.

"I can't thank you enough," she said when the men left.

"You're very welcome." His tone was soft as he kept his back to her. "Take your time. I'll fetch you later for luncheon."

She held to the same spot until the door closed again. While waiting for the water to cool, she opened the heavy wool curtains covering a wide expanse of windows that made up part of the bulkhead. The view was perfect. Sunbeams bounced from the water and lit up the stateroom. She spied her gloves lying on the bureau and realized that Havenly must have taken them off last night and covered her with the blanket.

She'd called him a pirate. But he was truly a gentleman. Her inner voice reminded her how decent and trustworthy and kind he had been. He had not undressed her last night but made her comfortable by removing her gloves and remaining shoe.

With a few acrobatic twists, she managed to unfasten her dress. She laid the blue silk on the bed. The hem had a small rent where it met the seam, which she supposed could be fixed, but the beautiful, detailed silver braid was torn, the sparkling threads shredded. But it mattered not; the memories alone would keep her from wearing it again.

Watching the door as if it might fly open at any moment, she dashed to the tub, dropped her chemise at her feet, and stepped into the steaming water. The heat soothed her cramped muscles. The sandalwood-scented soap rid her of an invisible layer of disgust. Water was a luxury on a ship, she knew that, and to think Havenly would sacrifice not just one, but three buckets was beyond generous.

When she finished, she dried her aching body. Two finger-sized bruises just above her elbow felt tender to the touch. She slipped her chemise over her head, adjusted the neckties, and then realized she had nothing else to wear. At first she considered Havenly's bureau—not a good idea after yesterday—then settled on a russet silk banyan that hung on a peg beside the basin. It smelled of bay rum and the same sandalwood used in the soap.

It smelled like him.

As promised, he returned later, but not before solving her clothing difficulty. As the key rattled in the door, her heart sprinted in her chest and she rushed to the shuttered room, hiding behind the closed slats. There was nothing for it—her dress lay on the bed and she was stuck in the bath enclosure, wearing a man's robe.

"Nicolette?" Havenly's voice hesitated, a tinge of anxiety blended with forced calm.

"I'm in here."

"Oh."

It was the first time she'd heard him sound uncomfortably awkward.

"It's... I'm..."

"I'll come back." His speech was hurried and apologetic.

"No, I'm finished with my bath. I need my valise. I've nothing to wear," she called out on tiptoe, as if that would help her voice carry.

"Oh." With an upward note, the comment was not so awkward but playfully ambitious.

"I feel you are on the verge of roguish jest. If you'd like, I could have chosen something of yours," she called out with just the right amount of cheek. "But I recall quite a scolding for my... hmm... unique efforts to fit in."

"You're killing me."

She giggled outright, opened the door a crack, and stuck out her arm, which was encased in his robe.

"Ah, so you are not in your prime?"

"Aren't I?" She wore her chemise under the banyan, and the robe covered her from shoulder to calf. With a deep breath, she stepped out from behind the door into the greater cabin.

His gaze began at the tips of her bared toes, skating upward to her hands where she gripped the silk neckline closed, then faltered on her mouth. When he finally reached her eyes, she challenged him with a bent brow.

He tsked, shaking his head. "Will you ever learn, Miss Thomas?"

Her shoulders lifted with a dramatic breath. "Apparently not."

"I'll bring your things." He looked toward the bed where her gown lay. "No more formalwear." He turned to leave, then called over his shoulder like the pirate captain he was. "Don't move."

"You're wicked."

Within minutes he returned with her bag and this time left her quietly alone.

From the traveling bag she removed the high-waisted peach walking dress. In Miss Blanchfield's haste, she'd unequally thrown in three pairs of shoes. Silk peach to match the dress, low-heeled boots, and oddly a pair of turquoise slippers trimmed in delicate lace, which made Nicolette chuckle. Poor Miss Blanchfield.

Her only real choice were the boots. Apart from yesterday, she'd been wearing them since the second day aboard ship. Thankfully, her underthings were easily tied in the front, but it took some doing to get the buttons on the dress exactly right. Before she'd donned the dress, she'd looped as many buttons as possible up the back and then shimmied into the bodice and skirt, careful not to rend the seams. The fabric-covered buttons at the top were the most difficult. With an exaggerated stretch, she reached behind her neck and barely managed to fasten them. She was quite out of breath when Havenly returned.

He brought with him a plate of cheese and apples and watched her with some suspension while he set them on the table.

"Do you need help?" The question was a serious one and not made with innuendo, something she'd become accustomed to with him.

With a self-conscious tug, she pulled at the skirt of the dress, which was bunched too high for all her buttoning efforts.

"No. I can manage."

"Are you hungry?" He pulled a chair out for her.

"Not very." She sat, but the sight of food curdled her stomach.

"You need to eat. At least try." His voice soothed and coaxed as he took the opposite chair.

A piece of cheese and a slice of apple went down like swallowing a rock.

"How do you feel today?"

"Better." She tried another bite. "The bath helped. Thank you for that."

"You were very brave." Fresh from the outdoors, his sun-kissed skin gave him a vibrant look.

"I don't feel brave."

"You were in harm's way, and you didn't freeze. Most men would, but you chose action."

"I chose the first thing that came into my head, like a shoe." She gave a half-hearted smile.

"And a hairpin. That was genius, by the way. And dangerous."

She swallowed hard, scooting back in her seat.

"If you'll allow, I'd like to check the wound."

She nodded silently, all sound stuck in her throat.

He knelt on the floor in front of her with all the calm and sensitivity he'd shown last night.

"It's fine. I hardly feel it."

But he didn't listen, just prompted her to remove her hands from covering her neck. Shyly hesitant, she obliged. Bending her neck to the side, she pulled her long hair over the opposite shoulder and let him take a lingering look. She could feel his eyes on her, and she fought her breathing to keep the hitch in her pulse from showing. He smelled of shaving soap. His hair, so close to her nostrils, smelled of the fresh sea.

"This needs salve. It's welting, but I don't think it'll scar." He disappeared into the little connecting room and came out with a strip of gauze and something in a little tin.

Nicolette didn't bother protesting. He was determined to

see her treated as if the wound were mortal. Then again, it could have just as easily been so.

Each time he dabbed the salve to the wound, he grimaced.

This strong, confident, intimidating man *grimaced*. Her heart melted, but when those amber eyes smiled up at her, crinkling laugh lines and all, it set her blood on fire. The cabin suddenly felt too warm.

"Better?"

She parted her lips, meaning to say something, but her gaze fell to his mouth and her words wouldn't budge. She simply nodded. From under her lashes, she watched him stand.

Too nervous to address anything else, she hooked the conversation around something less stimulating. "The quilt," she blurted.

His brows popped up over wide-open amber eyes.

Nicolette rose from the table and snatched up the quilt, then practically shoved it at him. "It's beautiful." Falling over her words, she added, "I didn't know men quilted, Your Grace."

A chortled cough came from his throat. "I imagine that some might, but I don't. Are you asking if I made this?"

"Not exactly. I've no doubt you did not." She took great pains to run her hand over the quilted top without touching him since he still held it in his hands. "So who did make it?"

"First, I prefer Grant, which I know you can say. And second, my great-aunt Enid made it."

Nicolette hid her surprise. She would have never guessed it was made by a proper lady of the ton.

"She must love you dearly to have put so much care into the stitches. Why do you keep something so precious here?"

"Because I like to be here, and this reminds me of things I like." He searched her eyes, and she did her level best to tamp down the heat rising in her cheeks.

When she swallowed, the gauze stretched at her throat. She pulled her hand from the quilt. "Thank you for its use."

He laid it at the foot of the bed. "At your service."

Nicolette cleared the nervous lump in her throat. "I think we need to discuss last night." She had his full attention. "You cannot sleep in two chairs again."

"I agree, as does my neck."

"It was a…" Her whole body shuddered. "…frightening experience, and it makes perfect sense that you should have kept me here, but—"

"Nicolette, you're not leaving. I'm not letting you out of my sight. Either you are safely here where the door can be locked, or you're on deck with me or Captain Donovan." A pointed look willed her to understand.

In truth she was almost relieved. She did feel safe here. The thought of returning to her room sent a foreboding shiver through her. But he was here. And everyone would know.

Except everyone probably already knew.

Her brain just made a mud pie of the whole dilemma.

"You cannot possibly mean… We cannot… I mean, last night was acceptable under the circumstances, but today," she finished, flushed and fragmented.

"It's a large bed. You take a side. I'll take the other. I'll even let you pick." His good nature disarmed her.

"But what happens if everyone finds out? I know people on this boat." That was her last ditch at propriety. After this, she would accept safety without the guilt of not at least putting up a modicum of resistance.

He rubbed a knuckle across his forehead and closed one eye as if his next words would unsteady him. "I cannot go without sleep, Nicolette. As for the men, there is plenty of gossip to choose from if anyone wished to do so. But I honestly doubt any of these men would deliberately cause you grief of any kind."

He let her come to grips with that. She nodded once. Any more would look as if she were thrilled, and if she were being truthful, she'd have to admit that a small part of her *was* thrilled. A very small part. A part that one would hardly notice. She sighed.

"Now that's settled, would you care for a turn on deck?"

If he could act normal, then so could she.

For the rest of the day, she wore a strip of gauze like a fine choker at her throat, a little unflattering, and then too, it was conspicuous, but no one asked. Grant had assured her that only a few were privy to the entirety of the event.

They stopped outside the companionway that led back to his cabin, and Nicolette turned toward the carved rail, placed her hands against the polished wood, and leaned in. With her face tilted toward the last vestige of midday sunshine, she closed her eyes and inhaled.

"A storm is brewing. Can you smell it?" She breathed in again, a mixture of salt and sea and the mist from a coming storm.

He leaned an elbow on the rail and watched her. "Are you afraid of storms?" Concern etched his voice, that same uncertainty she'd heard in his tone last night.

"Perhaps the bad ones, yes, but mostly I love them. Or I *loved* them." She gave him a half-hearted smile, then looked away. "Fearlessness is a youthful emotion. Growing up is a trifle more difficult than even I expected."

Beside her, she heard him take a staggering breath as if to speak, then he sighed heavily, leaning both his elbows against the rail. He gathered his hands and rested his chin atop them.

"Children don't expect to be separated from their parents. Even in aristocratic households where governesses rule, there's always the hope of them in the next room." He gave an ironic grunt. "Or in my case, the next county."

"People always remind me how blessed I was to have my

father until I was sixteen." Tears gathered at the corners of her eyes. She welcomed the incoming wind, like cold fingers entwined in her hair, grazing her scalp. "I was not blessed. Losing someone is not a blessing, and for that statement to be true, then someone must be lost. I miss him every day."

Too late she felt selfish, as if she'd dismissed his loss. She placed a hand on his upper arm. With his chin still resting on his fists, he bent a look at where she touched him, then slowly brought his gaze to hers.

"Of course, you know better than most. I didn't mean to deny you your feelings."

"And how did you do that?"

"Because I'm blathering over losing my papa when you lost both your parents at such a young age."

"You lost both your parents as well. Do you think it more difficult because I was younger?"

"I don't know. Was it?"

"Feelings of loss cannot be compared. To do so negates another's feelings, and all feelings are valid."

"You're very wise."

"I would accept smart. Wisdom, however, is another matter entirely." He tapped her nose, an uncomfortable gesture for a subject as heavy as the brewing storm.

"Did you know that Papa's original plan was for me to leave before my thirteenth birthday?"

He shook his head, his stance returned to leaning on one elbow. He clasped his hands at his waist, his posture that of a relaxed gentleman.

A very handsome relaxed gentleman.

"Robert told me a few days ago during one of our walks. Papa assumed if I left when still a young girl, no one would recognize me when I matured into a young woman. The crew comes and goes, and he trusted few."

"So what happened? What changed his mind?"

She wet her lips. "I imagine I did. He didn't wish to leave me any more than I wished to leave him, so he began hiring officers he trusted, and vetted the crew, taking on those who would stay for a long period. That meant we ran with fewer crewmen than most. Somewhere around seventy-five, I believe." She paused. "And he must have been correct about the crew because after Papa changed out the early team and let some of the men go, we found that a number of personal items went missing."

"Personal items?" He straightened, his brow creased.

"Small things."

"Like?"

"Nothing that mattered. Insignificant things that belonged to an officer or mate."

"And your father never pursued the men who stole them?"

"He could never be sure exactly who they were, and the lost items were replaceable. Things like combs. Silly things really. Except perhaps Mr. Knoll's watch chain left to him by his father." She shrugged. "Mr. Knoll was none too happy, but he said that people and memories do not lie in things but in the heart, like a treasure."

"I take it that you lost nothing then?"

She swallowed hard and looked away, avoiding his penetrating gaze. He knew too much of her. She'd revealed a part of her soul that had been long buried. The day her jewelry box went missing, she'd been devastated. Not wishing to worry her papa, she'd never told anyone. If Mr. Knoll's statement was correct, her memories could not be taken or stolen. Even the finest of things were not the same as having memories of the people who gave them, or wore them, or what have you. Besides, the necklace was the real treasure. She'd unwisely allowed that one trinket to become the memory of her father. Like an idol of her heart. She'd never give it up. Losing it would be like losing him all over again.

CHAPTER 16

If Grant were not so concerned for Nicolette's safety, he might have questioned his waning sanity that had allowed her twenty-four-hour access to his quarters. Hell, to his bed, the very place his mind and libido kept placing her. A mental picture of her lying there, wearing the be-damned blue ball gown, had kept him from finishing more than one task today. If he could, he'd burn it and the blasted gloves too.

Would good judgment not have left her locked in Robert's cabin instead? No matter, it was too late to wonder since Robert had taken back his room last night. The two had agreed that someone should be there in case they'd missed a third would-be kidnapper, or murderer, as it were.

Grant trusted no one, which was another good reason to keep Nicolette close.

A solitary drop of water hit the tip of his nose. He swiped it and looked skyward. The threatening storm had arrived. Coming in from the west, a gust of swirling wind picked up small scraps of paper, scattering them about the deck. He'd been watching the barometric pressure fall in small increments over the course of the day. The storm was no surprise. The force of it was yet to be seen, although he didn't expect anything dangerous or unforgiving. More importantly, any storm gave him an excuse to stay topside until it passed. With any luck, Nicolette would be fast asleep well before he turned in.

He retrieved his longcoat from the map room and pulled up the collar to protect his ears from a squall of wind seconds before a dark cloud released its burden like a primed pump. The ship was like a floating rain barrel. All hands were called, and the sheets were eased to bleed the wind.

Grant stayed near the helm for several hours, monitoring the storm and the waves. He was correct about its force. Drenching rain fell, but he'd seen far worse, none of which compared to the storm of anxiety in his gut. Somewhere around three in the morning, the winds calmed enough for him to return to his quarters. He had every hope she'd be asleep. His own exhaustion was curtailed by stress, which resulted in a wakefulness bent to the will of his body and not his mind.

With reserved patience, he quietly unlocked the door to his cabin, focusing on every creak of the hinges. He didn't appreciate how soaked he was until he stepped full into the room. Every layer of clothing from his coat to the insides of his boots was damp and cold. Short of shaking out the navy wool longcoat, he draped it over a chair, then without a glance toward the bed, proceeded to the privacy room.

Inside, he grabbed a linen towel and dried the excess water from his dripping hair before washing his hands and face. When he removed his sodden shirt, gooseflesh prickled across his chest. He wiped down his torso, then flipped the towel around his neck and opened the shuttered door, purposing to light the small pipe stove. Between decks one could find stoves for drying, but only the captain and first officer were allowed a small stove for their cabin. Some ships allowed none at all, but for Nicolette's sake he was happy for the small luxury aboard the *New Horizon*.

Resting on his haunches, he opened the door of the black iron stove, then chanced a glance over his shoulder at the bed.

He froze, quite literally. Nicolette braced her hands against the pillow and sat up halfway. By the light of one lantern, the streak of blond in her dark caramel tresses shimmered.

She blinked back sleep, squinting one eye at him. "What are you doing?" She sat up fully, pulling her unbound hair over one shoulder. The quilt covering her fell from her shoulders.

The little minx was wearing his silk banyan.

"Havenly, you're drenched."

Her gaze moved over him, and he realized too late just how undressed he was. Like an idiot, he looked down at his body. In his crouched position, he pivoted on his feet and rested a bent knee on the floor, gripping the towel like a horseshoe around his neck and pulling on it for balance. Surely, growing up on a ship she'd observed bare-chested men before. Why then did he feel so conspicuous? And guilty? And caught as if he'd entered the wrong room?

He pointed to the stove. "You let the coals go out," he said, glad for something else to focus on instead of wondering what she was wearing or not wearing under his robe. Which, much to his chagrin, caused him to feel even more naked and bare to the world. Not a comfortable feeling at all.

"I allowed the coals to cool because there was a storm and I didn't wish to set the cabin on fire."

No, he thought. The storm was all inside. Inside him, inside the cabin where fire sparked every time she made a move. "Noise and bluster. A gentle storm by sailing standards. When you were a girl, did you put out the stove every time the boat rocked?"

"Is that your idea of amusing?"

His gaze snapped to her. He knit his brow, confused. "Not

at all. I was simply curious if you were afraid of the storm. Some people are, you know."

She gave a half smile, and her eyes widened with mischief. "Are you?"

Hell yes was the only response in his head. His mouth went dry, and he turned to stuff kindling into the belly of the stove, wondering if he should apologize for his ill wit or his state of undress. His immoral crimes were mounting. Perhaps he should have stayed topside.

He twisted a piece of paper and then remembered the lantern was across the room. Cursing under his breath, he shoved the paper in with the kindling and grabbed the tinderbox. With any luck, it would spark on the first strike. Lucky that. He blew the tapered paper into a flame.

"You really loved living here, didn't you?" he asked between billowing breaths to fire the embers.

"I did." She cleared her throat. "However, I will admit—only to you, I might add—that a momentary wave of sickness gave me pause."

"I consider your trust in me a privilege, my lady." He kept his tone light while he watched the little fire.

"I trust you with my life," she replied with a shy, serious edge.

He half turned, resting an elbow on his knee, his hand still holding the flint that hung casually from his wrist. She had scooted to the edge of the bed, her bared feet a foot from the floor. She briefly met his gaze, then lowered her lashes. Her hands clutched the edge of the bedclothes, her arms straight as rods giving the appearance of a frozen shrug.

Fifteen seconds of uncomfortable silence ensued.

With her bottom lip between her teeth, she openly examined him. "You should get out of those wet clothes." Her arms relaxed. Her shoulders fell into place. "If you'll hand them to me, I can hang them by the fire."

He raised his brow. "Now?" He didn't dare stand with his sodden breeches plastered to his thighs leaving little to the imagination regarding the status of his libido. Good God, bare chested was one thing. Buck-naked was another.

Still on his haunches and feeling more cramped by the second, he turned his back. "I hope you are not suggesting I give up my clothes when you are wearing my robe."

She gasped, and he spied her over his shoulder. She scurried back until she sat directly in the middle of the bed as if it were an island and she the only tree. Truth was, she looked like a goddess, her hair nearly covering one eye, her legs tucked under her, hidden by a fan of silk from the burgundy-embossed banyan.

"I do not suggest you disrobe right here, good sir."

He'd come to recognize the *good sir* as an indicator of nerves.

She shooed him with a wave of her hand toward the privacy room.

He chuckled, a trifle relieved because her embarrassment made a good cover for him to turn away as he rose. With great care, he angled himself back to the little room. He shut the door and shouted, "I'll toss out my clothes if you'll pass me my robe."

He was quite satisfied when he heard the balls of her bare feet thump to the floor just before scampering in the direction of his bureau. First one drawer and then another scraped and buckled while he imagined her lovely face in a frenzy as she searched through his clothes.

With his hands braced on the basin table, he stared into the mirror and once more questioned his sanity. Knuckles tapped lightly on the door in a hectic staccato, and before he could open it, a shirt popped through a crack no bigger than two inches. It hung like a magician's hanky from her fingertips.

"And the robe?"

At that, she dropped the shirt and pulled the door shut with a smart jerk.

"Trous—?"

Again the door opened, and a pair of tan breeches appeared.

"—ers," he finished, nabbing them before they hit the floor.

He felt compelled to thank her and at the same time impishly ask for the robe again.

He settled on gratitude.

The sway of the ship slowed with the storm. The blustering rain clouds had provided the perfect excuse for staying away. But his hope that she'd be asleep upon his return had been dashed to hell. But who could sleep through a storm besides weathered seamen?

He chuckled to himself. She could. So why was she awake? Fear? Maybe. Or did she want him as much as he wanted her? He splashed his face in a failed attempt to tamp down his desire. The ice-cold water would have served him better had he poured it down his breeches.

He'd never had an innocent woman in his bed. An unexpected one, on occasion, but never an innocent one. And somehow he wasn't sure how to act or what to say. If he hadn't kissed her yesterday, perhaps he wouldn't be contemplating it now.

Wishful thinking.

He couldn't hole up in the bathing room with nowhere to sit but the hinged seat where the chamber pot was stored. He buttoned his breeches and felt like a bride on her wedding night.

When he exited the room, he first checked the fire and then turned to find her lying in bed, covered to her neck, pressed as close to the wall as possible.

The last time he'd gone to bed fully clothed, he'd been soused. A sobering thought.

He pulled back the blankets, careful to leave her mummified in the quilt his aunt had made. She avoided looking at him. Just as well because *he* was probably blushing.

Between the stove, his clothing, multiple blankets, and her, he was hot as hades.

He lay back against the pillow, his eyes trained on the beamed ceiling, his hands folded against his middle in a deathlike repose. "Are you cold?"

"No," she squeaked almost before he finished the question.

"Are you uncomfortable?"

She turned her head to the side and addressed him. "Well, I am in bed with a man." Her face showed no emotion, but her tone was sardonic.

She rarely checked her words, and he loved that about her.

Clearing his throat, he turned on his side, propping himself on the pillow with one arm, his head resting in his hand. "Yes, but are you uncomfortable? What I mean to say is, it's rather warm in here with the fire."

"Then douse it."

Easier said than done. "You didn't let me finish. Between the fire, the bed clothes, *my* clothes, and if you'll excuse me for saying, a beautiful woman in my bed, I'm roasting like a chicken."

Her mouth clamped shut and her eyes nearly teared. Her heretofore beautifully smooth skin, innocently softened features, and blossoming cheeks were all cinched, pulled together, fighting against... something... which turned out to be a loud guffaw. Laughter fairly burst from her. She sucked in a breath, then filled the rafters with laughter. With her head thrown back, pressed into the pillow, she brought her knees up, creating a tent of the covers. The next he knew, she kicked off the quilt.

"A chicken!" Unquenchable giggles bubbled out of her.

Grant watched in silence. Her laughter was, yes, contagious, but in his state, he was rather dumbfounded by it.

She turned toward him, mirroring his position, leaning on her elbow. The vee of the robe fell open, revealing a chemise underneath. Her hair cascaded to one side, covering the hand that propped up her head. With a deep breath she cleared her throat, dislodging the mirthful uproar. "It is warm. I concur. Shall we put out the fire?"

Too late. The fire inside him was already lit. However, the fire in the grate was easily remedied. He rolled out of bed and smothered the little fire with sand. When he turned back, she was in the middle of the bed on her knees, the quilt in her hands.

"Here, I don't believe I need this."

"You could always give up the robe." He took the blanket and tossed it on a chair.

"I doubt Miss Blanchfield would approve." She scooted back to her self-designated side.

"All the better."

"You're wicked."

"I've heard."

"But you're right. It's too warm." She grinned. "Did I tell you what Miss Blanchfield packed for me?"

"I think I'd remember if you had."

"One dress, three pairs of shoes, two chemises, and four sets of stockings. No night rail or robe."

"If you were proficient with a needle and thread, perhaps you could make something useful with the extra stockings."

"Pity that. But you can now understand why I wore the blue gown and the trousers."

"No." He shook his head and closed his eyes against the image. "I cannot. But I will keep my eyes closed if you'd like to rid yourself of the robe. It's not as if you're completely indecent."

He heard movement and fabric and imagined she'd flopped back under the covers. He opened his eyes as fine silk flew at his face. It passed over his eyes, slick and smooth like ribbon, and when it passed his nose, he inhaled. Before he recovered, she pulled the sheet and remaining blanket over her. The robe went the way of the quilt.

"You are a brave girl."

"Unwisely so, I'm afraid."

He raised a brow. "I thought you trusted me."

"Does a hare trust a fox?"

"Only if the fox prefers quail."

"Do you love birds, Your Grace? You reference them so often."

He moved close to her, directly at her side, and peered down into a face of pure mischief. "No, sweet. I prefer kittens."

She gave two prolonged blinks, her only input, passing the turn to him without a sound.

This young woman *was* a kitten full of mischief with large innocent eyes, cutting her teeth on bantering. But she didn't belong to him.

He took the silent opportunity to memorize her dark brown lashes, her winged brows of deep caramel, and her lips... Dammit, her lips he'd already memorized, emblazoned on his daft brain until they burned out all manner of reason. The scent of her was everywhere, a combination of sandalwood and sweet angel. It was a heady mixture that incapacitated common sense. Body heat could not be underestimated while they shared a bed. Hell, while they shared a ship for that matter.

Should he leave?

She reached up and touched the dimple in his cheek. "Right there. Even better when you smile."

He looped a finger around an errant strand of her hair, then tucked it behind her ear, surreptitiously checking the wound on her neck. It looked to be healing, the welt smaller than yesterday.

He heaved a sigh and made a move to return to his side of the bed, but she stopped him by plucking the loose tie at his throat. She tugged his shirt open at the neck.

"Your skin is so brown below your collar. Why is that?"

He tried not to think much of her actions since she'd watched him stoke the fire while shirtless. "I spent the past several years on this ship, learning the trade business from the merchant's perspective. I'd invested money in it, but I'd never been a physical part of it. There's nothing but men here." He glanced away. "Generally speaking, that is. It's not unusual, on occasion, to take up a chore without a shirt."

She ran a finger along his shoulder, causing a shiver that started at his neck and ran down his torso. The sheet covering her inched down with her every move. She didn't seem to notice or care.

Like the rogue he was, he dared a peek. Her neck curved into a glimpse of shoulder leading to a smooth, creamy collarbone that partially disappeared behind the thin veil of her chemise. His breath caught.

His hand hovered over the edge of the sheet where he battled with the idea of covering her again or just staring. Covering was the smarter choice, because before him were tantalizing breasts covered in a thin, filmy gauze of underclothes. When she took a breath, her chest pressed against the fabric, revealing two tempting, sweet buds.

This was madness. This hadn't been what he had in mind. At the base of his actions did lay good intentions. Too late, he realized the chairs might have been a better choice for sleep after all.

He looked up to find her staring at him. A gaze of blue

followed his hairline to the cut of his jaw and came to rest on his mouth. His pulse throbbed, and he couldn't think of anything past kissing her. He was transfixed. Possibly out of his mind. It was his last thought before he lowered his head and brushed a kiss over her lips.

He pulled away, heart pounding so loud in his ears it shut out the creaking of the ship. It was a dangerous sound. Blood pooled in places that threatened to tip the scales.

The little minx looked at his mouth, then touched her finger to his bottom lip. "It feels good."

God help him.

His mind grappled for the last vestige of sanity and lost. Leaning in, he took her mouth, completely sealing off any good sense that might have survived thus far.

Her lips met his tentatively, but when he nipped her bottom lip, she groaned and kissed him back with a fervor that rivaled his. One touch of his tongue laid waste to the rest of his begrudging guilt. The palms of her hands came to rest on his shoulders, and somewhere in the fuzzy parts of his conscience, he half expected her to push him away. What he didn't expect was for her to brush the opening of his linen shirt down past his shoulders. Her hands like feathers, not quite hanging on, all but floated over his skin, which did more damage to his control than if she had pulled him down against her. He whipped the sheets back and snuck a hand halfway round her waist, pressing her close.

The tip of his tongue teased her upper lip and her mouth opened. He was lost in a game he couldn't quit, a game he couldn't win.

Driven by uncontrolled desire, his hand slid up her side and over one barely covered breast. The nipple hardened under his palm. Nicolette kissed him back, grasping in the infinite somewhere for more.

Her chemise was tied up the front with three tiny blush-pink bows. He rubbed the satin ribbon between his fingers.

Dragging his mouth along her neck, he found her ear and whispered, "I hope you don't care for this shift, because if these bows are knotted, I'm going to bite them off."

A tiny giggle began and then quickly turned into a sigh of ecstasy when he sucked at the spot below her ear, massaging her neck with his tongue. She would not burst into a rail of laughter this time. His pride couldn't take it. Perhaps he had something to prove to himself as well as to her.

Two bows released, one more to go, Grant lifted his head and looked down at her. Glorious honey waves of hair across his pillow, swollen lips still wet from his kisses, eyes half-lidded with passion.

And breasts. Perfect, voluptuously blessed, and not just beautiful—they were lovely, something to be worshipped, slowly, deliciously.

He ran a finger in a straight line from the hollow of her neck through the little furrow between her collarbones with deliberate care, caressing the soft swell of one breast. A light brush and Nicolette's eyes closed and her neck lay bare.

He plucked the swollen bud and listened to her breath quicken when he gently rubbed it between his fingers. "Would you care to try another experiment, love?"

"God no."

He began to pull her underclothes back. And Nicolette almost panicked. "Please, no more experiments. The conclusions are"—she gasped at the feel of cool air—"final." A satisfied sigh came out when he held the bared breast in his hand, kneading and rubbing his thumb over the stimulated peak.

"I have one more test."

Her head shook, but Grant just gave a short husky chuckle and lowered his head, replacing his finger with his tongue.

He tasted.

She gasped.

He sucked the point of pleasure into his mouth.

She moaned.

He raised his head to bathe the other one with kisses.

Her hands grasped his hair and pressed him back down as she panted, "I like this experiment."

Grant obliged. First one perfect peak and then the other. Trailing kisses up her chest and back to her ear, rubbing his chest against her swollen breasts, and reveling in moan after pleasurable moan.

Taking one hand, he pressed her palm to his mouth and kissed it. He shattered his last reserve when he gazed into her glistening eyes. "Touch me, Nicolette. I need it."

She tugged at the tail of his shirt. He pulled it over his head and discarded it.

With her hands on either side of his face, she brought his mouth down to her parted lips. She devoured his mouth, pressing her body into his. Her hands held on to his arms, kneading over his biceps until they reached his shoulders, and then torturously, fingers splayed, she stroked a path down his chest, sending ripples of pleasure along his skin and blood pumping to all the pertinent places. She wrapped her arms around him, pulling him down until he half lay on her.

Running on pure instinct and no wisdom, Grant scooped a leg over his thigh, massaging her hip and using every inch of willpower he had not to trace his fingers to the core of her. He imagined her warm and wet. A hard grip on her hip, he pressed her so close that there could be no mistake that he needed her. Her sexy moan echoed in his mouth, and his heartbeat thundered in his ears.

The need for release was almost painful. But even more painful was the realization that he could not allow this heat between them to come to its natural finish. He had to stop. She could not possibly understand what she did to him.

One more minute, his body begged. He ravaged her mouth, nuzzled her neck, let her breasts fill his hands. And when his breath was beyond a frenzy and the power to stop had passed, he reached inside himself somewhere deep to the point of painful submission and pleaded with the gentleman he'd been raised to be. Never had he taken an innocent. Never had he taken a woman who didn't know what she was doing or asking when she kissed him back like this.

With great reluctance he pulled his mouth from hers, his breath stuttering. "Nicolette, this experiment cannot be finalized, love. Not by me."

He was mesmerized by the bite of her lip and glazed passion in her eyes—inebriation had nothing on this heated intoxication.

She ventured without shame, "You cannot convince me that this was an experiment, Grant." She said his name with purpose.

A roguish grin rewarded her honesty. His voice was thick and husky. "If it was, I'm sure we proved the hypothesis." Reluctantly he let her hip go and proceeded to tie up the loose ribbon of her shift. He placed a light kiss on each peak before tying the last bow.

Reality began its sobering return, but instead of being affronted, Nicolette's actions surprised him.

"What comes next, my lord?" she asked without so much as a blush.

A raw, quiet chuckle rumbled deep in his chest, and he was engrossed in her unwavering stare. "Usually I have the answer to that. This time"—he shook his head, confused—"I'm not sure."

A brow whisked into a lovely crescent, and a simple seductive smile played at her rosy lips. "I'm going to sleep now, Your Grace. You may sit there and stare at me. Or find your own pleasure."

He coughed and laughed. "Nicolette... Sometimes, love, I don't think you have any idea the things you say."

She shrugged and rolled over. "Probably not," she said in a full yawn. "Right now I'm just happy that it bothers you to wonder."

"You're a vixen." He kissed the back of her shoulder and rolled out of bed. He couldn't sleep until she did.

He'd probably not find sleep again.

With that in mind, he donned his shirt and coat and took his disturbing thoughts above deck. Alone, he leaned over the rail and watched the water lap the side, the spray and mist from the passing storm still damp in the air. He contemplated the coin he'd tossed in the water that first week and was fairly certain on which side it had landed. Tonight's thoroughly perplexing event could not happen again. He'd yet to tell Nicolette, but they were on their way home. It would take almost another week to get there. Three weeks away was just short enough for a believable reprieve from the season and long enough for her uncle to secure the Thomases' home.

All he had to do was keep his damn hands off her for five days.

Five more days.

How hard could that be?

CHAPTER 17

A bright light bursting through the seam in the curtains brought Nicolette fully awake. She stretched like a cat, doubtful it was still morning since she fell asleep just before sunrise, but it did feel that way.

She'd lost her bearings somewhere between kisses and sleep.

She whisked back the coverlet with an anxious energy. Trepidation was in each left step and a wanton eagerness in each right, which meant that every other step tipped her mental balance from adolescent crush to brazen lust. Memories of Grant's mouth on her skin, his nose nudging a nipple, his hands kneading her hip, felt deliciously naughty.

Was this feeling wrong? Was it normal? She could ask no one these questions, not even Frances. In the city, gossip was like candy and the ton like little children. A sale on sugar would make the sweetshop a crush. And what could be more tantalizing than gossip surrounding a young, eligible, newly ennobled duke?

No, these were questions and feelings she must bury.

For the next two days Captain Donovan and the duke rescued her from boredom with strolls above deck. Only Robert took meals with her, and she no longer had the distraction of cooking to fill time. She paced the cabin and tried reading from the duke's small library, but as she'd found before, most of the books were about navigation or deciphering weather patterns.

The seemingly endless silence had her humming, even talking to herself. At night she fell asleep before Havenly returned. Twice she woke to his even breathing and found his arm wrapped securely around her with her back nestled up against him. She felt safer than she'd ever felt in her life. But still he did not speak of that night, nor did he attempt its repeat.

Her body ached with wanting him. Her stomach fluttered with little butterflies at his presence.

Perhaps somewhere within her was a seductress, or perhaps she was just foolish enough to believe he'd enjoyed that night as well as she. Conversations with him had turned benign and trivial. Several times a day she questioned her sanity, wondering if she'd imagined that evening, but one glance in the mirror was proof enough. On her neck, below her ear, a scarlet bruise gave testimony as loudly as if she'd shouted it from the fo'c'sle. He had wanted her.

But what did she know of men? He was a practiced libertine if one believed gossip. And she was just confused enough *to* believe it.

She was careful to hide the love mark behind the gauze strip. Neither Havenly nor Robert had yet to see it. With luck, Robert would remain ignorant of the whole telling ordeal, because if he knew of that night or had any suspicion at all, then Uncle James and Aunt Lydia would likely find out.

The physical evidence of their evening was fading, but not fast enough.

Once again, she donned the peach muslin dress with the pretty sheer sleeves and puffed shoulders, now deflated as if the wind had been knocked out of them. She pulled without much luck at the wrinkled fabric that hung high on the waist with a single matching ribbon tied just under her breasts. Lord, she needed an iron. She brushed at the permanent folds and crinkles, swatting at the fabric with mild frustration. To top off the fashionable look, she could not forget the clean white gauze bandage at her throat. She gave up on taming her hair into a perfectly acceptable coil and instead chose to accept it in all its glorious freedom.

A rap sounded on the door, and she hurriedly tugged at her stockings, then struck a prim pose. It was like a game. Who had come to call? Robert or Havenly? One brought peace, calm, and a smile. The other brought the anxiety of unsaid words.

When she heard nothing else, she yelled, "Come in!"

The door eased open, and Havenly stuck his head inside. "I wasn't sure if you were up. I didn't see you with Captain Donovan this morning."

"Sleeping has become something of a habit."

"I think that is the definition of boredom." He opened the door wide, held out his arm, and said, "Come, let's see if we can alleviate some of that."

Her heart was already in her throat before she placed her hand on his sleeve. She no longer wore the gloves. They were a nuisance and dirty besides.

They strolled the quarterdeck from starboard to port, crewman and officers alike giving them a wide berth.

"Miss Bradenton, if I might be so bold, you are smartly dressed today." His voice was a little overeager to be believed.

She gave him a dubious slant of her mouth. "The weather has not been kind to you. I believe your charm has rusted, Your Grace."

"I understand that you are especially talented at scraping

the chains." He put a finger to his chin. Without missing a beat, he turned about, having reached the opposite rail, leaned his hip against it, and rested his elbow on his arm. He looked like a man in deep thought. "In fact, I believe you begged me to allow you the work."

"Very rusty indeed." She tsked, shaking her head.

He took a deep breath, clasping his hands behind his back. The sheer depth of his gaze almost buckled her knees. They'd hardly spoken in days. She couldn't guess at his thoughts.

"You are precious, sweet," he shocked her by saying.

"Only so much as my family should think of me. You may not think it. And that is not a proper compliment, I'm afraid." She tried for coy but couldn't tell if she'd achieved it.

"Ah, yes, you prefer kitten."

"Stop." She laughed.

"And I prefer Grant," he said with finality.

"If you will refrain from calling me kitten, I shall consider it."

He gave one of his most disarming half grins.

"What are you thinking?" she asked when he paused for more than ten seconds. He was a puzzle. Avoiding those perceptive amber eyes, she stepped toward the rail and looked over the edge. She enjoyed the feel of cool polished wood under her palms and the taste of sea salt on her tongue. There was a place inside her that wished they could stay right there, locked away from the world, from rules she'd had nothing to do with making.

"I'm not sure I can keep that promise… kitten."

She bit into her bottom lip and let a small chuckle escape. "You have no shame."

"None." He reached out a finger and traced a line on her neck, hooking his finger into the gauze bandage. "Actually, I am concerned with this." He gave a little tug but didn't remove the gauze. His tone was serious, perhaps even dire.

She turned her head, gazing up at him. Worry lined his forehead, and his mouth was hard. She put a hand to her throat.

"Is it bothering you?"

She shook her head. "No."

"You worry me. May I?" He fingered the strip of gauze that hung from the makeshift bow.

She paused, her words stuck between truth and truth. The question was which truth to tell, the one involving the all-but-healed knife wound or the not-quite-faded love bite. Ultimately it didn't matter because Havenly would find both. But his finding out was not her true worry. It was her dear friend Robert, the man who'd been like a father to her.

She smoothed the strip of cloth away from his reach. "I'm telling you it's fine," she said more sternly.

"Now I must insist. It should be healed at this point. If you're hiding an infection, it could cost your life. I've seen men fall for less."

She considered him, his tone, the worry in his eyes. "You may be disappointed by what you find."

His features hardened. "Now." The tenor of his deep, rich voice matched the command.

She dropped her hand. "As you wish, Master Pirate King." She could not pry the idea from his head, so she surrendered her neck.

He ignored the jibe, pinning her with a gaze, then gently tugged at the loose-knotted bow and carefully pulled the gauze away from her skin.

"It's almost healed," he said with some confusion and more relief. And then his entire face went lax. Putting a hand to her jaw, he leaned, tilting her head at the same time and exposing the other side of her neck.

From the corner of her eye, she observed the moment of

comprehension. A roguish grin of manly triumph stretched across his face, dimpling his cheek.

She pulled away with a sigh, rolling her eyes, pausing in that position for a sparse moment before her head lolled back and she stared at the sky. She absently watched a white cloud inch by. "The mark you left is far more condemning, do you not agree?" she asked without looking at him.

"I imagine that depends on whether a magistrate finds the knife wound or an uncle discovers the mark."

"Or a captain," she said with dismay as she watched Robert coming toward them with a determined stride.

Havenly handed her the gauze, and she made quick work fashioning a bow about her neck, then clasped her hands primly at her waist.

"Nicolette, darlin'. Ye removed the bandage. How's it fare?"

She snapped a look at Havenly, who cleared his throat and stepped back. Denying Robert a peek would only increase his concern, so she gripped the bandage and yanked the bow free, whipping it quickly from her neck. With strategic precision, she leaned the wounded side of her neck squarely toward Robert, hiding the other with an exaggerated tilt of her head.

"Lookie there, it's all but mended," he said, wearing a smile.

"Yes. As I've tried to convince our commodore, I am perfectly fine."

Robert rubbed a thumb on her cheek, a warm, fatherly expression crinkling his eyes. Her response was so automatic that she failed to hold her angle. Instead, she fully faced him, expecting a hug.

Robert's face fell, his smiling blue eyes going wide with angry surprise, his mouth pulled into a grim line. With his hands gripping her upper arms, he twisted her to the side.

"What in God's navy is this?"

"It's nothing," she said too quickly, slapping a hand over the mark and shooting Havenly a pleading look.

"Nothin'! This ain't nothin'." He turned the storm on Havenly.

"Robert," she pleaded while tugging unsuccessfully at his coat sleeve.

"My quarrel is not with you, Nicolette. It's with *him*." A weatherworn, callused finger poked Havenly in the chest.

"I do not answer to you, Mr. Donovan." Ducal authority was stamped on Havenly's unsmiling face. His voice, a thick jarring baritone, vibrated through her, so unlike the smooth, heart-fluttering richness that left her knees weak. The power behind his firm stance, the tense, strained lines of his face, even the way his hands absently rolled into fists, was warning enough.

Nicolette backed up a foot.

"Today I'm afraid ye do… sir." Robert all but spat out the *sir*, leaning in, bringing his face dangerously within the duke's reach.

Anger hissed through Robert's teeth. Before Nicolette could guess what he'd do, Robert pulled back his arm and cracked a fist into the duke's jaw.

She'd been so focused on watching Havenly for any violent move that she'd missed the signs in Robert. She'd never witnessed him act with righteous anger.

"Stop!" Nicolette tried to grab hold of Robert.

He jerked his arm from her grasp. Havenly kept an icy stare on him while he cocked his head and spit a mouth full of blood over the rail.

"Ye filthy libertine. I should never have trusted ye. Ye couldna keep yer hands off her, could ye! You've a depraved soul, *Mr. Sutherland*."

Havenly's lip twitched into a sneering curl and his eyes pierced Robert.

She took a position between the men, throwing Robert a pleading look. She knew what it meant to refuse to honor a title. Robert might very well lose his position. Add a heavy right cuff to that, and she wouldn't blame Havenly for sacking him.

Guilt sucked the energy from her, and she all but stumbled as Havenly pulled her arm, dragging her out of the way.

"It's not what you're thinking, Robert," she begged.

And before she could finish, Robert turned his garish temper on her. "And what am I thinkin', Nicole!"

"That I've done something untoward, but you're wrong."

"No! I think *he* did something untoward."

"For the love of all things good, Grant, say something." She used his name, attempting to inject some reason into the failing situation.

Havenly's eyes blazed a trail of pure authority from Robert's boots to the top of his head. "Captain Donovan, what I do and do not do on this ship is none of your damn business. And if you'd care to challenge me again, I have no issue with naming another captain," he said with quiet menace.

"Be my guest." Robert pointed to Nicolette. "Yer uncle will no' look too kindly on that, miss." He stormed off before she could form an answer.

Havenly let out a heavy sigh and ground his teeth until the muscle in his jaw danced.

Thinking only of Robert, she said, "You wouldn't take his job from him, would you?"

His nostrils flared with every heaving breath while he stared, unblinking, in the direction Robert had taken.

"This isn't his fault. If you want to be angry, be angry with me."

Havenly looked down at her as if he'd forgotten she was there. His features softened only slightly.

"Angry with you?" he asked incredulous. "Nicolette, none of this was your fault."

"Just promise me you won't be angry with him and take his job."

He closed his eyes and sighed, then reached out and cupped her cheek. "I wouldn't do that."

"To which do you speak? You'd not be angry? Or you'd not take his job?"

"Neither. You believe me a monster?"

"No. But the man hit you."

He crooked a slightly swollen lip. "Nicolette, I cannot in good conscience sack a man for defending your honor, now can I? I'd have thought him a coward had he not plowed a fist into my jaw. But I couldn't let that happen without some kind of retaliation else these men would not see fit to respect me. Or Robert for that matter."

She swallowed the rock in her throat that threatened to undam a gush of tears. "It's just that he's like a father to me, and I don't have my father anymore."

"You don't think I know that, love?" He reached out and pulled her hair slowly through his fingers, letting it fall over the front of her left shoulder. "Will you be all right? If Robert convinces your uncle, what then?"

"I'll be fine. You needn't worry. I don't think he'll say anything to Uncle James. I'll speak with him. He's always been soft where I'm concerned."

"Now why doesn't that surprise me?" He smiled genuinely, a hint of concern still in his eyes.

She didn't know whether he worried for her reputation or his own. After all, Uncle James and the duke were business partners. She couldn't allow her uncle's investments to suffer a scandal. Especially if the scandal were a lie.

Nothing had happened. Not really. A few kisses. A decadent caress or two.

Waiting for Robert's temper to cool used up the better part of the day, and then pleading her case with him burned through another two hours. In the end there was no way to discern whether he believed her. All that mattered was that he not discuss it with Uncle James.

CHAPTER 18

Still awake when Havenly returned to the cabin, Nicolette stood with her nose pressed against the mullioned window, her arms hugging her middle.

"I brought dinner. Cook said you didn't eat."

She half turned and watched as he placed a single covered dish on the table.

"Thank you. I wasn't hungry." She let out a deep sigh, returning to the view. The moon had passed early, leaving behind a dark sea that swallowed the sky, making a mirror for the stars. Topsy-turvy, one could hardly tell which was up or down.

She heard Havenly brush his hands together and peeked over her shoulder.

"You're early tonight. I'm usually asleep by the time you turn in. Is it Robert?"

"No." He shook his head, then looked away.

Her pulse quickened. He seemed to avoid eye contact.

Something was wrong.

"We're on our way home." With that announcement he turned his focus back to her. Their gazes locked.

She examined him for any sign of regret. She only saw worry. For her part, she could not bring herself to regret their time together, not yet, not while she was safely ensconced on a ship in the middle of the ocean, floating somewhere between right and wrong with no repercussions to make one choose. This situation was highly preferable to the stuffy ballrooms of London and the suffocating rules of the ton. On the water she could breathe. At home she would drown.

She turned back to the window. "I know."

"You know we're on our way home? How?" He walked up behind her.

She felt the familiar warmth of his hands on her upper arms and smelled the comforting scent of bay rum and sandalwood. It reminded her of the theater when she'd stood in front of him, peeking out into the gallery while his chin brushed the top of her hair. She preferred this view. She preferred the intimacy they now shared.

"I can tell by the stars. Two days ago the Great Bear's tail changed from starboard side to port." She tipped her head back and looked up at him.

"You're a smart girl." He kissed her forehead.

From her vantage he looked far too serious. "Is that why you've returned early tonight? To tell me we're going home?"

He gave her arms a little squeeze, then walked to the table where he uncovered the plate. He popped a slice of apple into his mouth before pulling out a chair and patting the back. "Come sit. We need to talk."

A dull churn of apprehension rose in her throat. He did have regrets. The way he looked away, the somber tone of his voice, made her steps heavy as if her soles were sinking in sludge.

She sat. He paced.

"Do you know how we met?"

"At the theater when you came upon me on the stairs."

"Partly, yes. That's the first time we spoke."

"That's the first time I ever saw you."

"The night of your aunt and uncle's dinner party, when you asked if I'd followed you to the stairwell, my answer was deceptive."

She turned in her seat and watched him fidget with the strip of gauze she'd left on the bureau. After this afternoon, there was little reason to wear it any longer.

"How so? You spoke about how you knew my uncle and Robert and then how Robert had mentioned me."

"My dealings with Lord Walborne had everything to do with you. It's true I need investors to expand, but you were the reason I purchased this particular fleet."

"Whatever for?" At any other time she might have considered that a flattering thought, but something in his demeanor told her that his observation of her had nothing to do with attraction. He'd acquired the *New Horizon* in a game of chance years before they met.

His grim mouth twitched. Clamping his teeth together, he tapped his chin with a knuckle while leaving her the perfect side view of his Adam's apple bobbing on a hard swallow. Whatever he had to say was not good news.

With her heart pounding in her ears, she asked if he wouldn't like to sit. He just shook his head, but he did stop pacing. With the table between them, he stood with his feet firmly planted on the floor and his arms crossed.

"The other day you mentioned that items went missing after your father changed the crew roster. Were any of those items yours?"

She stayed silent, her brow furrowing as she contemplated his meaning.

"Do you remember?"

She nodded and looked away.

"What are you missing Nicolette?"

Her lungs stuttered with panic. "Suppose you tell me what it is? You seem to be having a difficult time. Why should I make that easier?"

"You're right." He took a deep breath. "By happenstance, I came upon a pewter jewelry box."

"Shaped like a heart?" Her entire body went rigid.

He nodded. "I believe it once belonged to you."

Her gaze snapped to his. "Belonged? It is mine! How did you come by it? Did you take it like you took my home?"

"I didn't take your home."

"Yes, I know. You won it in a game of cards." Sarcasm was her defense against him.

"And I purchased the other two ships. Now we have that straight, I have some questions about the box."

She covered a gasp with her hand. "You... you *did* follow me to that stairwell. You charmed me with a tour of the stage so you might find answers about my property. How and when did you come by it?" She spoke, one sentence on top of the other.

"Quite honestly, I assure you. Like the ship, I won the pewter heart container in a card game. A different card game. A different person."

"You are worse than a rake. You're a thief and a reprobate! You speak of honesty after you duped me into following you backstage, knowing who I am, having followed me to the theater? How long were you spying on me? How far will you go? Is that what this is?" She flicked her hand to emphasize the cabin, the ship, the bed.

"Perhaps the title pirate captain better suits," he said mockingly and then sobered in an instant when she scowled at him. He cleared his throat. "My apologies."

"Thief!"

He raised an infuriating eyebrow. "I believe that is the

literal definition of pirate. A name you gave me, not one I've earned."

"You have no right to be incensed when you stole my property, a gift from my father, and I want it back."

"And I want some questions answered, like where it came from."

"Are you simpleminded? I just told you where it came from. My papa."

"Where did he get it?"

"I have no idea." It was the truth, but by the glare Havenly returned, he didn't believe her. And why should she care when he had little regard for her private things? And why did he assume he deserved answers? The little palm-sized jewelry box was a velvet bed for the crystal necklace her papa had given her.

"Why didn't you mention it when I asked if you'd lost anything after the crew changes?"

"I don't recall my business being your business."

He placed both hands flat against the table, leaning in so their eyes met. "If I had not made your business mine, you would not be alive."

"No. If you had not called me Miss Bradenton, I would not be here. Let's be clear."

As MUCH AS Grant wished to argue the finer points with her, he grimaced when she blamed him for her current plight. She was, of course, correct. It was his fault they were here. Even the argument they were having was his fault for not sharing his discovery with her sooner. He'd failed to make the situation easier by kissing her, touching her, wanting her. In fact, those last three sins had caused him to question his every move until he was no longer sure what he sought.

He blew out a heavy breath and stood. Her shoulders relaxed, and she leaned back in her seat. A small truce.

"Is it here?" she asked in a small voice, a far cry from a moment ago.

"No. It's at home. My home."

"Why do you find it so fascinating? It's nothing to you and everything to me."

"There's an inscription around the inside rim. The words are well-worn and somewhat illegible. Do you know what it once said or means?"

"The inside rim? I've only seen an inscription on the outside."

"Ah, yes. The outside has an intricate braid with letters laced in the weave."

"It's another language, I believe." She glanced at him, then closed her eyes as if she were trying to envision it.

"It's Gaelic."

Her eyes popped open. "That makes sense. The braid looks Irish." She bit her lip. "Or Scottish. Perhaps Robert can read it."

"No. I want you to keep this between us. Do you understand?"

"No." She fairly laughed, as if the suggestion were absurd.

"Nicolette, I think your father was killed for the jewelry box. Did it come with something in it?"

"Not that I'm aware." She looked away, a sure sign that she lied.

If she lied about the contents, she might lie about what she didn't know. There was no way to be sure.

"If you're suggesting that the box once contained a treasure big enough to tempt murderers and kidnappers, I'd say you're wrong. It's too small for anything of the like." She sat forward. "Where is there writing on the inside?"

"Just under the velvet lining. The lining looks newer than

IT WAS ONLY A KISS

the box itself. Someone must have put it there later, perhaps to hide or save the integrity of the writing. I think it's a clue to something bigger."

"Like what? Jewels?"

"Could be. If so, it's too dangerous to leave about."

She rubbed the place between her eyes.

"It's late. We can talk of this later."

She shook her head. "We'll settle it now. The box is mine. You'll return it to me, and that will be the end of it."

"The box is mine until I'm certain it doesn't pose a danger to you."

"You insult me, Your Grace, if you think I believe that you care for my person."

He swallowed, watching her for signs of womanly strategy. He found none. At this point she would refuse to believe anything he said, even truth. And the truth was he did care for her. Too much. It was time to put that aside. They would be home in a matter of days, and he wouldn't be seeing her again.

"Regardless what you think of me, Nicolette, I'm asking you to keep this between us for now."

"Your Grace, I shouldn't wish for anyone to know what is between us... ever. You may trust me on that account."

NICOLETTE STAYED out of Havenly's way for the remainder of the voyage. Robert took responsibility for her during the day. At night Havenly turned in after she slept and left before she woke. He could not be getting much sleep.

The morning of their final day, she woke to find Havenly still abed, lying next to her, his broad tanned back turned toward her. His breathing amplified the outline of his musculature. She'd lain next to him every night for a week, and this was the first real unhindered look she had of the man. How could she pass up the opportunity to touch him? Since his confession, they'd barely spoken.

She'd wasted an entire day, angry and resentful of his interference, but it didn't last. She missed strolling with him, talking to him, bantering, and to her dismay, kissing.

Tentatively, she reached for him. Starting with his shoulder, she ran a hand down his biceps, watching the muscle leap at her touch even in sleep.

In the morning chill, pressing her body up against his sounded like heaven, but she didn't dare. She did, however, press her forehead against his back. Sandalwood. Bay rum. Even the sweat of a fine day's work. She was going to miss the scent of him.

Before she could respond, a very awake Havenly plucked her hand from caressing him and wrapped her arm around his bared waist. Her heart gave a painful lurch. In all the nights he'd quietly lain next to her, she had never purposely touched him or held him. And now the heady warmth of him spread throughout her veins into every intimate recess of her body, creating a space in her heart that would soon be void.

When had he woken?

She swallowed a gasp of surprise, afraid of breaking contact. His warm body, his stomach, his back, were as rock hard as his arms. She risked rubbing her cheek against his shoulder blade. He said nothing, just brought her fingers to his mouth and kissed them, slow, lingering for a moment as if he didn't want to let go, then turned her hand over and kissed the center of her palm.

It didn't last.

Of course it didn't last. Why should she dream otherwise?

He rolled from the bed without a backward glance and walked to the bathing room. The sound of water splashing in the basin came from behind the shutters, but no words. When he emerged, he wore a determined grimness in the flat lines of

his forehead and the unreadable pull of his mouth. Outsi
door were buckets of wash water, and he filled the tub fo
himself, then left the room. Not a look or a glance her way.
even an utterance.

The sound of bellowing voices that hailed the rituals o
docking were all too familiar. If she closed her eyes, she could
almost hear Papa exchanging directions with Robert. The fact
that her father was not there, combined with Havenly's failure
to say goodbye, laid the first bricks against the nostalgic pain.

She wondered if she would ever adjust to sleeping alone
again. She wondered if they'd run into each other or if he'd
acknowledge her in public. And then she locked it away with
every other life-changing memory.

She missed him already.

Robert alone ferried her back to London in a rented coach,
much the same as when he carted her to her aunt and uncle's
at sixteen.

After an hour of stilted conversation, she gave up trying.

CHAPTER 19

"Glory be, child. I thought to never see you again," Miss Blanchfield said as she hurried into Nicolette's bedchamber. The woman was in a rare state of mismanagement and chaos, much the same as when Nicolette had left her three weeks ago.

Nicolette nearly burst into tears when she saw Aunt Lydia and then Claudia. Lavender curtains, a lavender brocade coverlet on the bed, and lavender water. Nothing had changed. It was all exactly as she remembered. When Miss Blanchfield was inclined to ask questions, Aunt Lydia silenced them. Nicolette had not been allowed in the study with the men who'd gathered to discuss her case and absence. She wondered if Robert would mention that she'd stayed with the duke. More importantly, she wondered if he would mention the fight with the duke or the mark left by said duke. For an hour she wondered whether Havenly would show up, until she heard his voice in the foyer and knew he'd arrived to join the other men.

She watched warily as Claudia and Aunt Lydia undressed her, swearing a sigh of relief that the mark Havenly had left was no longer visible. Even the welt from the blade had faded to almost nonexistent. No proof of those three weeks remained except the scarring ache buried in her heart. The bed looked lonely and large and empty, and she couldn't imagine lying there without him.

She lingered in a bath. For the first time in weeks, she felt completely clean from head to toe. She dressed in a fresh, clean, appropriately proper night rail and did not argue when they put her to bed in the early afternoon. They fussed over her as if she'd been ill.

Miss Blanchfield left soon after, and Claudia finished removing her laundry, which left Aunt Lydia sitting on the edge of her bed while Nicolette ate finger sandwiches.

"I imagine you're exhausted." Her aunt patted her knee.

"I am." At the mere suggestion, she yawned. "I'm sorry, Aunt. It feels good to be home." It wasn't an absolute lie—she was happy to be with her family, although waves of anxiety overwhelmed her.

"You don't look worse for wear. Uncle told us about the attack. Do you want to talk about it?"

"There's not much to say except it was frightening, of course. Robert and His Grace were vigilant in their care for me, and if I may say, Aunt Lydia, the rest of the time was like a holiday. The memories of Papa were everywhere, and when I thought I'd be too sad to revisit them, a warm feeling of love and contentment would overshadow it as if he were with me. In some ways it brought some closure."

Tears welled in her aunt's eyes. "That must have been terribly difficult."

She swallowed down a lump of buttered bread and cucumber while her eyes blurred. She sniffled. Her aunt handed her a handkerchief and pulled another from the side table drawer for herself.

"You can tell me anything, darling. Just remember that I'm here for you and that we love you dearly."

The statement gave her pause, and she wondered again what her aunt knew. It had to be guilt she felt, because nothing in her aunt's demeanor was suspect.

"Arlienne will visit tomorrow if you're up to it."

"I'd love that. And baby Andrew?"

"Of course."

GRANT ARRIVED an hour later than Robert, having first made a stop at Richfield's town house to exchange details. He was shown to Walborne's den, where the two men had been speaking, presumably about Nicolette's safety. Robert would surely keep their miscommunication quiet for the time—they had bigger things to discuss, like whether his team of private scouts or Lord Richfield had discovered any suspects.

"That's all the news I have," Grant informed Walborne and Robert. "My contacts found little to nothing. The hack worked several streets that evening and could not remember anything unusual about the passengers."

"I think we can agree that Nicolette is still at risk," Walborne insisted.

"Aye." Robert nodded. He sat in one of two high-backed leather chairs set at angles in front of Lord Walborne's desk. Grant settled into the second chair while Walborne took his place behind the desk.

They had agreed on three weeks away. It was long enough to make inquiries and short enough to make excuses for Nicolette's absence. As far as the ton knew, she'd taken ill and returned to the Thomases' country seat for a short respite. It wasn't unusual for women to fall ill every month for various delicate reasons. No one questioned the obvious cycle.

"If I could move her to my country home for the remainder of the season, I'd do that," Walborne added. "But it would cause too many questions, and truthfully, I don't wish her out of my sight."

"Havenly," Robert said, "yer sure ye can't remember anything about the man?"

Grant looked away. "Nothing important. He was average height, maybe five eight or five foot nine. And thin. Scrawny. The alley between the houses was dark as pitch. He appeared to be dressed adequately for a ball." He addressed Walborne. "You did check the guest list, yes?"

"First thing. No one suspicious. No one who left at that time either. He must have snuck in. It's not difficult to do. I crashed a few parties uninvited in my youth."

"Haven't we all," Grant mumbled.

Robert looked from one to the other. "I've never." When they turned in unison, Robert shrugged his shoulders, his bushy red eyebrows rising toward his hairline. There was a short pause of comedic silence.

"At any rate," Grant interjected, "although we have little news on the man's identity, what we don't know is almost as important as what we do know."

Walborne steepled his fingers, his attention fixed on Grant.

"After three weeks gathering information, if there had been more than one man, we'd have more clues. I think we can safely surmise we're dealing with a single force and not an organized operation. I suspect the two men on the ship had been scouting for a while, hired by the imbecile at the party. The man at the ball had to pass as gentry, or perhaps is, and I can't see him befriending two murderous clods other than to hire them to do his dirty work. The two don't mix. I imagine the blackguards would have been killed after they'd handed over their goods, the same way John Bradenton was killed."

"And where's the good news in that?" Robert asked.

"One man. One girl. If we continue to keep her within

reach, she should be safe. I can't imagine she's very often left on her own."

"Have ye forgotten the man tried to abduct her in the middle of a party?" Robert pinned Grant with an accusing stare. It was clear that Robert blamed Grant for more than the debacle at the Thomases' ball.

"I take full responsibility." He held Robert's gaze, then broke contact, allowing the man the win. Grant refused to feel guilt for kissing her, but the danger he'd put her in by using her name, that he'd always regret.

In the end the three men agreed to keep watch over her. Robert would, of course, return to the ship and keep his ear to the ground. Walborne would make sure she was properly escorted everywhere. He'd enlist his son-in-law if need be. And Grant agreed to watch from a distance, allowing a broader look at the overall company she kept.

Grant turned to Donovan. "Anything else you want to add, Captain Donovan?" There was no menace in the question. Grant almost wished for him to spill the secret. But Robert was too good a man to put her in that kind of jeopardy.

"Nothin'." He eyed Grant. "Except that our Nicole was very brave. I'd give her a few days, James. It wasn't an easy three weeks fer her."

Grant rubbed his jaw and gave an imperceptible nod to Robert.

The past three days *had* been hell. This morning, when he'd felt her silky fingers tracing his skin, her hands sliding down his arms, inflamed desire had surged through him. His heart had filled with panicked need. It had taken every ounce of his will to keep from turning in to her touch, especially when she rested her head against his back. He'd known he had to leave the cabin. Known that speaking to her would make it worse. So he chose silence and never looked back. It was a cowardly, selfish move on his part. He had little doubt that leaving her that way had caused her more pain and bewilderment than she deserved.

But his actions did not go unpunished. He had only to close his eyes to smell her, to feel her body next to his. She had woven her way under his skin, and there could be no easy way to extricate her from his memory.

"We'll keep vigilant," Walborne said, interrupting Grant's thoughts. He put out a hand. "Thank you, Your Grace."

"You have use of my men. Take advantage of it. And if you need me, I'll do what I can."

Grant left the Thomases' home.

He left Nicolette. He left the mystery.

But he couldn't leave the memory.

He had no right to these feelings, to feel as if she belonged to him. But he knew better. She'd never be his, not really. Sooner rather than later, her uncle would find her a suitable husband.

CHAPTER 20

For a week Nicolette resorted to pathetically tagging along with Arlienne and Richard like a third wheel, a wheelbarrow on a road with fine carriages. Richard danced with her at every affair to save her from a speculating audience who itched to hear about those unaccounted for three weeks. These refined beauties often dined on far less. Gerald Clifton, who was usually the instigator of gossip during the season, hadn't dared engage her in verbal battle after Havenly and the Earl of Richfield had "encouraged" him to cease his ramblings at the Thomases' ball.

But there were others brave enough to venture into the business of ruining reputations. People like Victoria Helmsley, Clifton's counterpart, and even a jealous old mistress to a certain handsome duke.

While she'd been away, one surprising, earth-shattering event had taken place. Frances, her dear friend, had become betrothed to a kind baron who was heir to a viscountcy. Banns had been read two weeks prior, and Nicolette had come home to Frances's bubbling wedding plans.

It was as if the world had spun out of control, and

although Nicolette wished her friend merry and was in fact happy for Frances, she preferred the unpredictability of the sea than to be anchored to this chaos. It only reminded her of the disturbing predictions the duke had made about her uncle finding her a suitor.

Against her cry for sanity, she agreed to attend the theater with Frances, a place too familiar, too full of distracting memories. Accompanied by Frances's mother, Lady Hebert, Nicolette sat quietly en route, listening while Frances talked them all into silence. Frances heedlessly gabbed about her dreamy and simply wonderful Daniel Rutledge, or more accurately, my lord Rutledge as Frances loved to say. Lady Hebert beamed a smile at Nicolette every few minutes in muted surrender to her daughter's enthusiasm.

When they arrived, Frances's mother left them to their own friends. They mingled and drank punch, then took their seats, much the same as she'd done that night when she'd met the Duke of Havenly.

After the frenzy of endless words, Frances finally took a breath when they were settled. "Are you happy for me, Nicolette, truly?"

Nicolette placed a gloved hand over Frances's. "I am more than happy for you. I am thrilled." She pulled her mouth into a joyful smile and took extra care, pouring every ounce of excitement she could muster into the statement while suffering her own feelings of trapped isolation. With so many changes, the butterflies in her stomach whisked a perfectly good dinner into nausea.

Avoiding any condemning details, Nicolette simply told Frances the story that Uncle James had decided on, that she had taken a rest in the country during those missing weeks. Nicolette allowed her friend to believe that she'd disappeared from the Thomases' ball because she'd been overwhelmed to the point of illness. It was all poppycock but easily believed in a world where women were expected to faint at the silliest things. The fact that Nicolette was new to this world made the ridiculous tale more believable.

Nicolette did her best to avoid stealing a glance in the direction of the Duke of Havenly's box. But it didn't matter because everywhere she looked, she saw him, or at least the memory of him, laughing with her, inviting her backstage and showing her the auditorium. She found herself drawn to the corner of the stage where he'd pulled aside the curtain.

She fought against a momentary pang of melancholy as intermission grew near, and she forced herself to hold on to a smile. Tonight she would stay by Frances's side and avoid the privacy of the stairwell. In her mind, he was there waiting for her with a dimpled smile and an outstretched hand.

When the curtain fell, Frances stood. "Are you up for refreshments? Mother has allowed me a glass of champagne."

"That sounds lovely."

When they cleared the aisle, Frances wrapped her fingers around Nicolette's hand and pulled her along through the crowd toward the anteroom. The later in the season, the more crushing the theater.

Per usual, Nicolette half-heartedly watched for Grant. So far, she had not run into him nor had she seen him at any affair. Whether lucky or not, she didn't know because her heart ached and lurched whenever a tall man with dark hair poked his head above the crowd. In her mind's eye she saw him everywhere.

Both ladies were decked out lavishly, Frances wearing a poppy satin and Nicolette a cream taffeta that fit her shape like a glove. Nicolette grabbed two glasses of champagne and handed one to Frances. With one hand tucked into the crook of her arm and the other hand holding champagne, Nicolette took a dainty sip and nonchalantly searched the anteroom.

A few sips of champagne later and Frances said, "Last time

we were here together, Pleasance and I searched this very room for suitors while you took intermission in the retiring room. Remember?"

Nicolette noted that Frances asked that as if they had matured in the past three weeks. Frances's engagement might qualify, but she was still the same Frances. As for Nicolette... Nicolette had grown up too much. She knew too much. She wanted too much. She missed *him* too much.

"You were always the wise one," Frances said, gazing randomly at passersby. "You didn't spend your time on such foolishness."

Nicolette did her level best to keep a pragmatic posture that reached the stoic smile plastered to her face. "We are all foolish, Frances. Each to his own fault."

She ignored Frances's confused look, then was startled when her friend leaned to the side, peering around her.

"Holy mother of Moses, the Duke of Havenly's here," Frances whispered, loud enough for Nicolette to hear.

Nicolette squeezed her eyes shut, deciding whether to flee or stay frozen to the spot and hope he didn't see her. Before Frances could take note, she pulled from within, calming her disheartened features. "How nice. Frances, let's go back."

Frances peeked a look at her and then back around. "He's with a striking blonde."

"Good. Are you ready?"

"Oh my, it's..." Frances stole another glance at Nicolette. "Do you want to know?"

"It has little relevance," she said evenly, hoping to hide the sudden rush of jealousy that threatened to spill out and reveal more than she was willing. Curiosity won an abbreviated peek. Dressed in black formal wear, the same as the night he'd taken her from her home, he stood with the same woman Nicolette had seen in his theater box over a month ago. Thanks to Arlienne, she knew who the woman was.

"Joanna Featherbe," Frances said unnecessarily.

She wondered if Frances knew more about the woman. When she'd asked Grant whether the woman was his mistress, he had denied it. Was it true? Had he lied?

"I've heard it rumored that Miss Featherbe is mistress material. Maybe even his. Who can tell?"

"Who indeed." Nicolette decided she didn't care. Not a bit. At least that's what her jealous heart screamed. But she couldn't prevent the somberness that crept into her voice. Miss Featherbe, no doubt, knew him better than Nicolette. If the woman was his mistress, then she knew how it felt to be wrapped in his arms, knew the flutter of butterflies in her belly from just touching his shoulders, knew he was scandalously tanned to his waist.

From her chest to her cheeks, the heat of frustration seeped from Nicolette's pores. If she didn't leave, fainting was next on her list of humiliations. Focused on the shortest distance to the doors, she rushed through the crowd and refused to steal another glance. The desire to get away was stronger than the fear of explaining herself.

In no way would she provide him with the illusion that she missed him. He'd obviously forgotten her. And why not? Miss Featherbe was no doubt more than available to accompany him on his midnight diversions.

CHAPTER 21

*G*rant had been home for two weeks, which meant he'd been absent from his weekly meeting with his grandmother for over a month.

"Havenly, I am delighted that you remember where I live," his grandmother said harshly. She sat, per usual, directly in the center of the settee. One could either sit next to her or across from her. Either way, her position dominated the room.

"Sarcasm this early in the morn, Grandmother?" From behind the sofa, Grant bent and kissed her cheek.

"I never let the sun rise without it, my boy. Now, sit." She patted the seat next to her and gave him no other choice.

"For heaven's sake, it's been a month since I've seen you. Where did you go?" Her eyes were astute, but he chose not to read too much into that.

"Business kept me," he said simply, leaning back, cornered by the arm of the sofa. He propped a knee negligently over the other.

"Gossip would say otherwise." The duchess was a sly old devil.

"Would it?"

"Yes. But gossip is nothing unusual when it pertains to you. One might think I'm used to it by now. And maybe I am."

"But?"

"But this time, my dear grandson, you may have ventured too far. Where exactly did you go for nearly a month?" Without a rising crescendo, her voice was still keenly authoritative.

"Oh, Grandmama." He tried for condescending. "Do you really wish to know *all* my exploits? I'd have thought you'd grown weary by now." One foot bobbed with ill-concealed nerves. It wasn't like him to let his grandmother rattle him, but he worried for Nicolette. If gossip were flying, it was bound to have something to do with her.

Seeing Miss Thomas last night at the theater had put him in a bad place. He was sure she'd seen him, but he had refused the acknowledgment. Staying away was easier. At least that's what he told himself. He did his best to avoid her at parties where she might attend, but he couldn't keep her from showing up in his dreams. Even Joanna noticed it. Miss Featherbe had asked him about Nicolette when it was clear he'd been drinking in every inch of Nicolette's cream gown.

Miss Featherbe had even offered to distract him from torturing himself with memories of Nicolette. Of course that was not an option. Joanna was the furthest thing from his mind. In no way had he escorted Miss Featherbe to the theater last night, although Nicolette probably assumed otherwise.

"Be smug, but it's obvious you're interested." The duchess gave a triumphant smile before wryly commenting, "I have it on good authority that you disappeared the same three weeks as a debutante by the name of Nicolette Thomas." She turned ever so slightly in her seat, looking at him askance, managing to hold her back like a rod of steel.

How did she do that?

Past experience dictated where this subject headed. Straight to the altar somehow. But Nicolette would not be his grandmother's choice. She had no title, no funds, nothing of consequence, and these were all prerequisites. So what was the wily fox getting at?

"I can see by your look that the gossip holds at least some truth."

"Lord Walborne is a business partner of mine, and Miss Thomas is his ward," he said dryly. Best to head her off at the pass before she ran away with the story.

"I really don't care who she is, Grant."

He arched a brow and regarded her.

"It matters little at this juncture except that I demand an explanation for your behavior, because if you took that girl away with you, there will be hell to pay. She may not be titled, but her family is not likely to take kindly to it."

"I'm sure it feels deliciously sweet thinking you have me over a barrel, Grandmother, but I assure you wherever Miss Thomas may or may not have been these past three weeks, her guardians were well aware. And if I were you, I'd quit listening to every yarn that Gerald Clifton weaves." There, that ought to put an end to it.

"I didn't hear it from Clifton."

"Then where?" He shot her look. Disbelief had him speaking too loud for someone who didn't care.

"I have my sources." She looked away, a stern, satisfied draw to her mouth.

His shoulders fell with a heavy sigh. "The old hens."

"They are better than the tabloids, I promise you that." She folded her arms under her ample bosom. "If you have behaved rakishly—"

"I have not," he interrupted with a cynical smile. "Why do you think the worst of me?"

"It is not me you need worry about. It is the ton."

He uncrossed his legs and sat forward, elbows to knees. "Why?"

"Why? Because they will not sit much longer, waiting for you to wed. I realize if it were your choice, you'd spite me forever, but the longer you stay single, the more elaborate this uncivilized polite society will become at weaving yarns. Mamas all over the city will begin gossip just to ensnare you. And at some point they will pick just the right person to use against you. Someone whose reputation you care about. Even if it's all lies." She watched him closely and let her statement sink in.

Irony would have the ton forgiving his peccadilloes because he was a man. But they'd fillet any woman over the tiniest infraction, even an imagined one.

His head fell forward. He rubbed his eyes with the heels of his hands, then rubbed the palms over his hair to the back of his pounding head. He clutched the ends of his hair in irritation before settling on rubbing the muscles of his neck. The gold that accented the starched white room begged for honesty.

"Then there is some truth," she said softly.

"What do you want from me?" His arms resting on his knees, he turned his head to look at her. "You say truth matters not, so I'll leave the city. I can take care of business from Havenly, and Miss Thomas can get on with her life. I won't bother you with the circumstances of my friendship with her; they are too complicated and frankly none of your concern."

"You ask what I want? I want you to choose a bride. That would put a stop to the gossip."

He knew exactly what she was saying. The duchess wanted him to marry one of the vapid females that she'd chosen. Title, money, old families with positions of consequence. Well, he would not allow that to happen. "Let it go," he finally said.

"I will not. I cannot. If you like this girl, then do what all men do in your position."

For that tactless suggestion, he turned a scathing eye on her.

"And how would you know what men do? This subject is offensive."

"To whom? You? Bother, Grant. I'm old, but I'm not an imbecile. You don't think I had offers in my youth? Your grandfather wasn't the only catch."

Now his curiosity was truly piqued. He straightened in his seat. "What are you saying? That Grandfather made such an overture toward you?"

"It's possible."

"And I see how well that turned out."

"Yes... Well, I get what I want. And I came from a good family."

"You mean a wealthy family."

"Call it whatever you'd like."

He stared at her for a long minute. Midafternoon sunshine burst through the window like a prism, the rays surrounding her head like a blinding halo, forcing him to look away.

"How long?" he asked in a curious tone.

Her head snapped toward him. "What do you mean, how long?"

"How many months before Father was born?" He grinned, challenging her for a change. He loved his grandmother and didn't wish her any real harm. Truly he meant it as a gibe, something to redirect the conversation like the sun had redirected his focus.

"There's no point in discussing this." The duchess heaved a breath. He could scarcely remember the last time he'd witnessed nervousness from her.

"I disagree." Grant sobered. "It is the point. You and I both know why I won't marry. Although now I might be inclined to call you a hypocrite."

"What do you know of it?" It was not so much a question as a sarcastic statement attributed generally to defensiveness or guilt. "I have always acted out of obligation to my family. It is for the best that I have done what needs be done."

"For whose best? For yours? For the family name? What good has come of it? I have an aunt I hardly know living in Italy—your estranged daughter, I might add—and a father who was perfectly happy with his choices but who could never quite make you happy. And what has that done for you, Grandmother? Has it made you happy; do you enjoy your grandchildren? I'm not the only one, you know. You not only denied yourself, you denied me." He let her absorb that last statement.

"Seven months," she said absently.

"What?"

The duchess turned to him and said again, unwavering, "Seven months. That's how long it was before your father was born."

Grant waved a hand as if it didn't matter and had nothing to do with the direction their discussion had taken. He was actually relieved to find his grandmother was human after all and must have loved his grandfather dearly to have thrown the rules of etiquette, and the church for that matter, to the wind.

"You're a man and so cannot possibly know the seriousness of the situation."

"I don't condemn you—it's none of my affair except to wonder why it made any difference to you that Father married outside your wishes after you were wreathed in your own scandal. You of all people should have understood."

"It is you who do not understand. It was a living hell, Grant. And I have done what I can to make amends for it by not allowing my children to put themselves in the way of cruel gossip. The ton can be most unmerciful. I fortunately had a husband who cared for me and who was of a great consequence to silence the lot of them."

"You had no right to choose for your family. You have no right to choose now," he said mildly without rancor. "No one of my choosing will make you happy, and no one of your choosing will make me happy. So why bother? I cannot see the good of bringing any more unhappiness into this family. I will not marry and watch you make one more person miserable with your unattainable expectations. If you need an heir, look to Grandfather's nephews."

"You are the Duke of Havenly. You must provide an heir, and you know it."

He, for one, had no feelings concerning marriage to waste his time on. He felt no obligation whatsoever to furnish the required heir. His father having died before he could be named the Duke of Havenly, Grant harbored no lingering attachment to the title and considered his distant cousin just as worthy as any to inherit.

By the time he left his grandmother's town house, he was in a foul temper. The gossip couldn't possibly be that bad. Could it?

Unsuccessful at arresting her newfound feelings of jealousy, Nicolette found herself in the unfamiliar and altogether awkward position of battling half a dozen emotions over the course of any given day. Anger replaced tranquility, humiliation took dignity's place, and jealousy ruled them all.

If things were not bad enough during the day, her nights were even worse. Sleep was slow in coming, and Nicolette often found herself lying awake, missing the man who'd stolen her good sense and wishing he were still lying next to her, keeping her safe and satisfying the hunger he'd created. The memory of his arms about her would not be fast forgotten. Aunt Lydia had warned her about rakes and their ability to seduce, making every woman they were with feel special. Nicolette realized belatedly that she'd been nothing more than sport for the duke, as evidenced by his failure to even say goodbye.

At the end of the week, Frances visited Nicolette. They converged in the cheery yellow salon.

"I'll have tea brought up." Nicolette did her level best to play hostess although she was engulfed in waves of depression.

"I'm not interested in tea. I'm interested in you." Frances opened the discussion without preamble, patting the sofa next to her.

Avoiding her gaze, Nicolette pressed herself into an overstuffed winged chair instead.

"Have you ever met Joanna Featherbe?"

Nicolette's brain fairly ceased all function. She cleared her throat. "No. But if what you said at the theater is true, then it is pure scandal to speak her name."

"Even here? I thought we were friends." Frances tilted her head, her brow etched with concern.

A fresh stain of pink warmed Nicolette's cheeks while worry kicked up a notch. "We are the dearest of friends."

"Then talk to me."

She sighed, grappling for emotional control. She searched for her next lie, but her pounding heart flooded her ears, drowning her best-laid plans. "I tell you the truth, Frances. I do not know the woman."

"You have to admit that your reaction to her name is suspect."

Nicolette determined to be brave and gazed up at her friend. "It's not *her* name that brings such a reaction."

Frances searched her eyes. "Then the rumors are true."

She took her now-sweating hands and gripped her skirts to dry them. "Mr. Clifton or Miss Helmsley?" she asked of the rumors. She could only guess at the content.

"Neither. It's coming from Miss Featherbe."

"That's nonsense." Nicolette swallowed, silently needling

out an explanation. Havenly must have told Miss Featherbe. Who else could have, or would have? And if that were true, then perhaps Frances was correct when she said the woman was his mistress. But the biggest question remained. Why did she care?

Nicolette could not deny the jealousy racing through her. The implications of the tales Miss Featherbe might tell were hardly a concern when her heart was breaking.

"It's only speculation," Frances was quick to tell her. "You know how these things are. Gossip this delicious is much too sweet to let temper." She was too good a friend to say anything else.

"How far do you think it reaches?" Nicolette asked.

"Everywhere?" Frances had the kindness to grimace and then quickly reassured her. "You know how the gentry can be. They gather pieces of truth and weave stories as thick as blankets to entertain themselves far into the winter."

"And what is it exactly that will keep them warm this winter?" Nicolette asked just in case she'd been mistaken.

"The rumors of you and a duke."

The air left the room. She closed her eyes briefly. "They're lies. No matter what she has said, it's all lies." She breathlessly stuttered through the words. It was not an explanation.

"The woman's a jealous snake."

Her eyes welled with tears. "She has no reason for jealousy." She swiped the corner of her eye. "What makes you think she's his mistress?"

"Are we speaking of the Duke of Havenly?"

"You know we are." Nicolette gave her a pleading look.

"Because I've heard that she was once his mistress."

"When?" Her curiosity won the battle over her reputation. She had to know.

"Years ago. It could be just the foolish whispers of young girls."

"What has the woman said?"

"Would it not be better to tell me where you were for those three weeks?"

"Ill. I was quite ill, becoming even more so with every passing day," she said, allowing frustration to drive her courage. If she was going to put a stop to Miss Featherbe, her tone would need to change.

"She points out that Havenly was away for the same three weeks, injecting enough venomous innuendo to breed rubbish."

What a ninny she'd been. "Frances, it is not entirely coincidence that we were away for the same period, but I promise you that whatever Joanna Featherbe is spewing is not true."

"Of course it isn't. May I tell you what I think?"

"By all means."

"When you weren't looking, I saw the Duke of Havenly admiring you."

The pain in Nicolette's chest grew tight until she thought she could bear no more. "I'm sure you were mistaken," she whispered.

"I believe she wishes to renew their acquaintance and is jealous of you because she saw what I saw."

"Why should she be jealous when he escorted her there?"

"Her?" Frances laughed. "He did not escort her there. He was there alone. I watched his box after intermission."

Nicolette's head snapped toward her.

"Nicolette, you needn't tell me anything at all. It is not my place to ask, and I'm sorry for that. But if you have feelings for the man, rest assured that he is not interested in Joanna Featherbe. But I do warn you, if she has her sights on him and she considers you in the way, she will not stop until she either wins him or destroys you."

"Or perhaps both."

LATER THAT EVENING, Nicolette lay in bed, conjuring up visions of Joanna and Grant. Was sleep to elude her until the end of this unbearable season? One thing was sure, if Frances wondered about those missing three weeks, then the people of the ton were sure to re-create them in their own light, and Nicolette was the one who would be burned. It might be the women who carried the torches, but men were the ones who lit them.

It was time to extinguish the flame.

CHAPTER 22

Grant was rarely bothered by the yapping of gossipmongers like Clifton and Miss Helmsley, but considering his grandmother's dire warnings, he kept a savvy ear to the ground for any whispered mention of his name or Nicolette's. He didn't hear much, however, not that he expected to. After all, rumor and gossip weren't subject to honest confrontation, often hidden from those who might be the most damaged by it. What fun is there in diluting entertainment with truth?

In the interim, hoping to eliminate the gnawing craving he had for Miss Thomas, he gave her a wide berth. He missed the scent of ocean in her hair, the defiance in her eyes that always left him grinning, and the way her body fit perfectly to his in sleep.

Between the memories of that damn honey hair, the way she looked garbed in that oversized peasant's shirt, and that saucy roll of her eyes, he couldn't sleep or eat. His mood grew surlier by the day. And Miss Featherbe's henpecking wasn't helping.

He continued to frequent parties to dissuade any more blathering talk.

At the Ashtons' lavish affair, Grant ignored the crowded ballroom aside from scanning the crowd for Richfield, and because he couldn't help himself, he furtively perused the crush for Nicolette. His surliness continued despite the gay atmosphere, or perhaps because of it. Couples dancing, people smiling, too much punch, not enough spirits. He hustled in the direction of the billiard room, a place where women were generally not allowed. There he found Richfield already involved in a game of billiards with Viscount Lawrence. It dawned on him that Lawrence was married to Lady Lawrence, who happened to be Nicolette's cousin, Lord help him.

With that knowledge he was bound to search for her all evening.

"Havenly," Richfield called. He stood next to a red baize billiard table with thick carved legs and polished mahogany feet in the shape of lion paws.

Grant asked a footman to bring brandy, although Irish whiskey would better suit his mood. He leaned against the opposite table to Richfield, amused by his choice of gaming partner. It took an excellent shot to beat Richfield, and Lawrence seemed to govern the table.

After Lawrence made the last point, Richfield officially introduced the viscount to Grant. The night of the Thomases' dinner party, Lawrence had been absent and Grant had only met his wife.

"A game perhaps, Your Grace?" Lawrence asked.

"If you managed to beat the earl, I doubt I'd fare better." He tried for nonchalant, but by the odd, brooding look on Lawrence's face, he'd failed.

"Are you certain? I'd be happy to pardon the first two shots."

Grant eyed him warily and tried to take no offense. He wasn't a poor player after all.

"I only suggest a small headway because I know you've had little time to practice of late."

Grant hid a flinch behind what he hoped was a formidable warning scowl.

Was the man daring to lead up to something by mentioning his absence? Did Lawrence have something against him? Grant had a hard time reasoning through a subject that left him disoriented where Nicolette was concerned, and if this horse's arse was in any way disparaging her name, he had no compunction about introducing him to a black eye or broken nose. Grant didn't stop to wonder over such violent thoughts about a man he didn't know.

These past weeks had turned his craving for Nicolette Thomas into something as insane as jealousy. For God's sake, he needed a woman. That was it.

That was all of it. It had to be.

Lawrence eyed him, opened his mouth to speak, and then shut it again.

"Something else you wished to say, Lawrence?" Grant's tone was a mix of irritation and boredom.

Richfield leaned in front of Grant and gave him a warning look, then grabbed a glass of brandy and handed it soundlessly to Lawrence.

Lawrence accepted it and cleared his throat. "No wife yet, Havenly?"

Grant's cheek tensed.

"Isn't it the way of things, to ruin one and court another?" Lawrence laughed.

But before he could say another word, Grant hauled the man up by his neatly wrapped collar, including a fistful of shirt, and without thinking—because he'd obviously lost his mind weeks ago—Grant pulled a right and flew with it, landing a fist on Lawrence's chin. Lawrence was not a scrawny man and did not go down easily. He hung on to his balance like a man accustomed to a brawl or two.

Richfield did his best to intervene by dissuading onlookers from giving the little tussle any serious note. He chortled and slapped Grant on the back as if it were a game. Then, with not so gentle prodding, he moved his shoulder aside and out of Viscount Lawrence's reach. But there was no need, Lawrence was grinning from ear to ear, swiping his hands down the front of his waistcoat where it had been sloshed by brandy.

It was then that Grant saw his own folly. He'd punched a man for innuendo. Lawrence had not mentioned any names. The man hadn't even clarified what, in fact, he was trying to say.

"Your Grace." Lawrence straightened. He worked his hand over his jaw, rocking it back and forth, but his eyes held no malice. In fact, he looked downright sheepish.

"Enlighten me on my crimes, Lawrence," Grant gritted through his teeth. He stretched his pained knuckles, then relaxed his hands at his side.

"Oh dear." Lawrence laughed. "You thought I was speaking of you. Isn't that rich? Me sporting fisticuffs with the likes of a duke who exercises in the ring? At least that's what I've heard. But you know how rumor is, Havenly. First you hear it from one corner, and then it spreads like the plague to another." Lawrence stretched out his hand to shake Grant's, but Grant was not quite ready for that.

"And?" Grant issued the question like a command.

"And I was speaking of my wife. When I met her, some old hen had spoken ill of Lady Lawrence and I was quite put out by it because her reputation was impeccable." Lawrence gasped dramatically. "Your Grace, you thought I referred to recent affairs?" He paused and understanding passed between them.

Grant watched while Lord Lawrence calmly but purposely smiled like a Cheshire cat, his demeanor a combination of humility and mischief.

Grant sighed, looking toward the open doors that led to the ballroom. "Nicolette," he said to no one.

"Yes. I'd forgotten that you know my wife's cousin." Lawrence's tone was suspiciously matter-of-fact.

Grant's head popped up, and he stared for a long minute at his sly opponent before swallowing his pride. "Is she here?"

"My wife?"

Grant's jaw clenched tight, and he drew in his chin and leveled Lawrence with enough contemptuous warning to cow a lesser man.

Lawrence managed to look quite satisfied with the animal reaction.

"Do you happen to be a bastard, Richard?" Grant used the man's name without permission.

"No, Your Grace."

"Then let me be the first to call you one. And the cuff? I spare you no apology."

"Understood, Your Grace."

"Grant." And then he popped Richard on the shoulder and left the room.

Whether Lawrence had done him a favor, Grant couldn't be sure, but one thing he did know—it was time to confront Miss Nicolette Thomas.

NICOLETTE REFUSED to allow Arlienne to bait her into answering questions regarding the elusive Duke of Havenly, not after she'd successfully tamped down every feeling she had for the man whether good or bad. She determined to remove him from her heart, doing her utmost to separate the veracity of her true feelings from the carefree facade she played for the masses. The heart-wrenching strategy was beginning to work. Rumor and gossip, if not eliminated, were at least diluted with dancing and smiles. In her book, that was progress.

Richard had disappeared some time ago into the billiard room, but Arlienne stood by her side, faithful and true, while she counted the minutes until they could respectably leave. The Ashton affair had turned into a circus, a crush of stampeding elephants. The entire room was crowded shoulder to shoulder, leaving little space to speak without shouting. She eyed the door to the terrace and imagined stealing away into the gardens and hiding behind a large potted hibiscus plant.

"My apologies, Lady Lawrence." The completely recognizable shout came just to the left of Nicolette's ear.

She shivered in a room that felt like the fires of hell. Her pulse tripped over itself, fluttering in her chest and bringing with it an all-too-familiar nausea. Dinner had yet to be served, thanks to small favors.

She refused to turn around, trying to ignore him.

"What do you apologize for, Your Grace?" Arlienne sounded pleasant, amiable. And to Nicolette's biased ears, like a conspirator. She wished that Arlienne would shoo him away.

"For your husband's appearance. I'm afraid we got a little carried away over a game."

With the barest movement, feigning complete indifference, Nicolette tilted her head, watching the benign interaction from the corner of her eye. All the while, her heart thudded like a thousand horses and drowned out the crowd, everyone but him. From her vantage, she could not gauge Arlienne's physical reaction, but she witnessed the duke take her cousin's hand and properly bow. Next the devil turned to her, startling her with a dimpled smile while placing her trembling hand on his arm. She'd not agreed to a dance but had little choice other than to follow him to the dance floor where a waltz had begun. Why always a waltz with this man?

Her quaking nerves took the scenic route through her body, eventually reaching her feet. She almost stumbled.

For three weeks the man hadn't bothered to look her way, and now he'd grabbed her and was dragging her to dance without bothering to ask?

"What do you think you're doing?" she demanded, forceful enough to be heard over the music.

"I think I'm dancing. I'm never quite sure what it is you do on the dance floor." He gazed down at her, his golden eyes playful.

Against her will, her heart leaped, and she missed a step.

"See what I mean?"

She could not believe his daring. He confused and angered her. His actions threatened to undo her measly attempt to recover from those three weeks alone with him. And now he was what? Trying to charm her, when she'd worked so hard to dissuade the gossips from inquiring about those missing weeks?

"No greeting? No curtsy? I can't say I recall even one. You must owe me at least five by now, wouldn't you say?"

"You'll have to treat it as a debt unpaid and charge it thus, Your Grace, or throw me in debtor's prison. No, wait. You have already done that, haven't you? I believe I paid the debt. I believe I'm still paying for it. And this little farce right here"—she looked at the space between them—"will cost me interest no doubt." She glared at him, leveling him with as much contempt as her heavy heart would allow. "You shouldn't be dancing with me. You've caused me nothing but trouble."

"I've caused *you* nothing but trouble? *I* have? You are like a song I cannot get out of my head."

"What a most unflattering description of how badly I annoy you. And please do not patronize me by trying to convince me that it was some kind of twisted compliment.

That usual bit of tripe won't work anymore." She was too angry to dance with him, could he not see that?

"Then tell me what will." His tone was as gentle and warm as his hand at her waist.

Her insides ached with memories of the way he'd held her in the middle of the night. "I get to choose? How very generous of you, Your Grace." She rolled her eyes in disgust, and the foolish man broke into a full grin. That ridiculous grin! If she could not stamp her foot in frustration, she'd strip him of that smile with a chilling glare. "It would work for me if you, hmmm, let's see… fell overboard when next you sail. Deep in the ocean, preferably where no shore is nearby, no lifeboat available, and no crew to notice."

"And will that come at the end of a shoe?"

He was trying to be charming, but at the mention of the shoe, Nicolette wanted to cry. Tears blurred her vision.

"Nicolette," he said gently. "You know that wasn't your fault."

She looked away, biting back tears.

"Nothing that happened was your fault."

She lifted her chin, trying for brave, trying to hate him as much as she thought she should. "Your Grace, you think you take responsibility for your misconduct, but you do not. And I am doing my best to not only take the blame for my part but to go on as well and forgive myself for being naive, because if I don't, I will live with the shame of it for the rest of my life." For the split second she glanced at him, she thought she saw pain register in his amber eyes. She wanted to say how sorry she was, that she wasn't ashamed, that she was simply confused as to why he had not contacted her, or said hello, or even looked her way until tonight. What happened tonight that changed that?

The muscle under her hands tensed, and he scanned the room. She felt conspicuous dancing with him, and uncomfortable, and crowded by his charm. And sad. Because in truth his arms felt safe, which added to the emptiness inside her. For weeks he'd left her alone. All alone.

He cut their dance short, leading her out onto the terrace that opened up into a beautiful rose garden, and at this point she was too pained to care who witnessed it. A path led from the steps of the large stone terrace, and Nicolette truly wished for an unaccompanied moonlit stroll through the fragrant gardens. Petals of vivid color sweetened the air. Yellow and red abounded, and in the distance a torchlight caught the blood red of roses. But all she could think of were the thorns.

"Life is unfair," she began when they stopped at the edge. She stared aimlessly over the landscape. "Men, who are so often the downfall of a woman's questionable virtue, are the ones left to whatever freedoms they so desire. While a woman, dangerous to no one, is leashed like a disobedient dog. It would seem the wild beasts roam freely, able to locate their poor unsuspecting prey, who have the unique misfortune of being tied up. It is far more convenient to be a man."

"If you think life is unfair, then change it. You're the bravest woman I've ever met. You don't think you're capable of changing things?"

"This is as far as I'm allowed to go. Right here, standing on the edge of a most beautiful rose garden. And I can't even walk out there." She pointed to the garden path. "I stand right here, keeping distance from scandal, distance from men, distance from women of questionable virtue, distance from gossip, unless of course it could be used as a stepping-stone. These are the rules." She looked at him. "I *can't* change things. I've been trying, and although I have never set foot into that rose garden, I have inadvertently fallen into all the things I've just mentioned. I've denied myself. And for what, Grant?"

She swallowed hard and then took a step down the stone stairs and walked out into the garden where she had been forbidden to go. It was not as glorious, nor as freeing, as she had once thought it would be, but she was damned if she was going to be a wallflower anymore and wait for the scent of roses to reach her.

She cared not whether he watched her go. She didn't care if he was afraid to join her or what he thought of her boldness. He could let her be, and she'd have wandered straight through until she was out of sight, invisible to the world, especially this one.

"Nicolette." He called after her in a strained whisper. Soon she heard his heavy footfalls behind her. "You're correct. Your description is painfully accurate."

When she picked up her pace, the clipped steps behind her grew wider, farther apart. She heard a sigh just over her shoulder.

"Follow me." He didn't look back to see if she complied. The man was too confident by half. It would seem he knew her too well, and perhaps she was shamefully glad for it.

Just like at the theater, she followed. Against her better judgment. She wasn't naive anymore, and she wasn't afraid of falling half in love either. She was simply curious what he wished to say.

He followed the winding path to the right and behind a lush bush bursting with buds, the promise of red roses to come. Taking her hand, he pulled her down beside him onto a stone bench. He grew pensive. Unusually quiet.

Nicolette began, "You know there is gossip, don't you?"

"I've heard a little." He wet his lips, then turned to look at her. "I shouldn't have come back. I should have left the city for the season; it would have squelched the gossip. But I didn't." His fingers flexed as if he wanted to touch her but dared not. "Nicolette, it pains me to hear you talk of shame when you have nothing to be ashamed of."

"This said by the libertine." Her words accused him. "Your

Grace, has nothing you've ever done shamed you? Or do you live this self-indulged, privileged life with your head in the sand, unaware of the wake you leave behind? I really want to know. I'm not even angry, I just don't understand." Anger waned in the face of exhaustion. She'd simply grown weary of the battle.

"You may not understand this or believe it, but I have rules I must live by too. I do have a moral compass. And I have lived by those rules as much as you have lived by yours." With elbows on his knees, he looked at the flagstone under his feet and heaved a sigh. "Until a month ago."

They both sat there, silent for a good sixty seconds. Nicolette turned over every muddled word spoken between them, looking for the truth and wondering what to do next. A month ago, she was sure he would have kissed her in this garden and then done something outrageous like smile wickedly and dare her to kiss him back.

What he did do stupefied her.

"Do you love me, Nicolette?"

She snapped her head to the side and looked at him with her brows drawn tightly together. She could not trust her ears. She met his searching gaze, pausing to remember what he'd said about love. "And what would you know of it, Your Grace?" she smirked, feeling a little braver. "You don't believe in it, so what could it possibly matter what I say?"

"Just answer the question," he all but commanded.

"No," she said, a hint of disdain separating them.

Grant pinched his brow together and closed his eyes. "No, you don't love me? Or no, you won't answer?"

Nicolette gave him a sideways smile; it lacked any luster and dripped with sarcasm. "You pick. I'm finished. I'm going back to my cousin and then going home. I'm going to fall into my bed, by myself, and relive the nightmare I've been having for the past three years, of people I've lost, of a home I thought

I'd never see again. And then I want you to leave me alone. Do not come and dance with me again. Do not take another glass of champagne from my hands. And do not, under any circumstance, rescue me again. I've had enough. I'd rather drown."

She stood, and he grabbed her hand like a manacle, but she jerked it away and rubbed her wrist.

He stayed seated, snaring her instead with a piercing gaze. "Be careful what you wish for."

She mocked him with an artificially sweet smile. "I know who I am, Grant... Your Grace." She dipped into a low, proper curtsy. "One curtsy will have to do. I hope you enjoyed the view. It shall be the last you see of it."

The action seemed to confuse him, but the words she spoke emboldened her.

Then she left him—the infamous Duke of Havenly— sitting there like a fool, wearing one of his signature grins.

CHAPTER 23

Nicolette stormed through the veranda doors, back into the heat of the ballroom, and straight for her cousin.

"I'm going home, Arlienne. You may follow or stay. I do not care which."

Arlienne exchanged a look with her husband, who motioned for her to leave. "I will make your excuses," Richard said. "For you both." He directed that toward Nicolette with a hint of regret.

After Arlienne joined her in the coach, Nicolette turned her attention out the window and hoped her astute cousin remained silent.

That hope died after they passed the second streetlamp.

"How were the gardens?"

The question did not bode well.

She snapped her head toward Arlienne and considered lying. But even in the dim light of the cabin, it was obvious from the commiserative gleam in her cousin's eyes that she understood more than Nicolette dared tell. Nicolette also knew that Arlienne would not let it rest until she knew everything.

Unladylike, she tossed her little reticule on the bench beside her in a huff, all pretense dissolved.

"It did not go well. I hate all men." Exasperation clipped each word.

"No truer words have been said by the best of us, and yet we marry and find room in our hearts to love."

Nicolette crossed her arms and tilted her head, glaring.

It didn't seem to affect her cousin. "Did the duke declare himself tonight?"

"Of course not! Why should he, Arlienne?" The force behind the words was too telling, even to Nicolette's ears.

Arlienne lifted a brow. "I don't know. Perhaps because he has feelings for you?"

"The feelings he has are of no consequence and wrought with a maze of pain and confusion. And I am the rat looking for the way out." Just angry enough to throw caution to the wind, Nicolette did something that would change everything. She unfolded her arms and gripped the bench on either side of her legs. Leaning forward, she asked, "Do you wish to know what happened those three weeks, Arlienne?"

Arlienne held her tongue and nodded.

Nicolette left nothing out. Not the sleeping arrangements on board the ship, not her foolish feelings for the Duke of Havenly, not even the kiss. She explained the nervous turmoil of returning home before the bruise on her neck had vanished, how Captain Donovan had known but had stayed silent for her sake. The entire time, she felt as though her neck and face were on fire.

Arlienne never gave a hint of disapproval. Just listened.

However, Nicolette would not discuss the conversation she'd had with the duke tonight. Anger and confusion kept her quiet on that subject.

"It would be best if I just forgot those three weeks, because remembering is keeping me from sleeping and eating and just about everything else." The confession sapped every ounce of energy from her.

"Men are idiots," Arlienne said simply.

Nicolette couldn't help but chuckle at that. "Absolutely. What does that make us then?"

"Momentarily insane." Arlienne's eyes flashed, and her words made them both laugh outright. The sound filled the cabin until Arlienne leaned forward and squeezed Nicolette's hand. It was a silent promise of understanding and trust. "Are you sure you do not love him?" Arlienne asked with gentle kindness.

"I can't. Loving the Duke of Havenly is like a nightmare." She looked at her hands folded in her lap. "It doesn't matter."

"And why not? What happened tonight?"

Nicolette held back a sob, letting out a shuddering sigh. She closed her eyes. "He asked if I loved him."

Arlienne gasped and changed seats, settling next to Nicolette. "Don't you see? The man loves you."

Nicolette chuckled pathetically. "No, Arlienne." She turned to look at her cousin. "The man does not believe in love. And besides, he asked if I loved him, as if I were a simpering miss without prospects. He did not, in any way, declare himself." She shook her head. "No. The question was meant to put me in my place, not to shake him from his. He simply feels guilty, the scoundrel."

AFTER A FITFUL SLEEP and a tasteless breakfast, Nicolette was sitting at her vanity and pinching her cheeks when Claudia found her.

"You've a package." Claudia placed a box, tied with a sapphire blue ribbon, on her bed.

"Is there a card?"

"Not that I can see. But the messenger who instructed that it be delivered into the hands of Miss Thomas was dressed in Havenly livery. I should assume it's from the duke. Miss Blanchfield gave her approval after she rattled it a bit."

Claudia's indifference calmed her some. That the delivery was of little concern to Miss Blanchfield calmed her even more.

"Thank you, Claudia."

Her perceptive maid left her alone, and Nicolette pulled the blue silk ribbon free of the rectangular box and lifted the lid. Inside were two more boxes decorated with shining blue silk like the bow. Atop them lay a card.

Dear Miss Thomas,

It was unfair of me to keep such memories from you. Inside, you'll find the heart-shaped jewelry box. Never forget that memories are the finest treasure of the heart. I believe your father would have been proud of the woman you've become.

In the second box is something I promised to show you. Caramels the color of your hair. Indulge me this one last contact if you will. It was never my intent to cause you distress of any kind. After this, I shall honor your wishes.

Your friend,
Grant

Two tears dropped, smudging the salutation.

"Scoundrel," she whispered. The inappropriate use of his name, the reference as a friend—if Miss Blanchfield had read that note, she'd have brought the box up herself along with a lengthy lecture.

Friends.

Or lovers.

She had her answer. Somehow the victory of last night did not sit well today.

The following four days, she was too busy to ponder the finality of that note or the gifts. Frances's wedding provided the perfect distraction, along with frequent visits from Arlienne's son, little Master Andrew.

Arlienne seemed preoccupied, but Nicolette credited that to mothering a toddling two-year-old. Aunt Lydia had taken up staring at her with a peculiar expression. She could not tell whether it was concern or curiosity. So when Uncle James announced that he and Aunt Lydia were to be away for several days, she didn't mind. It felt like a reprieve.

Arlienne stayed with her, along with her favorite nephew. And best of all, there was no more mention of the Duke of Havenly.

Two days after her aunt and uncle left, Nicolette woke to a half dozen trunks in the foyer. She clutched the banister and dared hope they were going to the Thomases' country home for the rest of the season.

"Arlienne, did you know about this?" she called as she descended the stairs from the gallery. It looked as if Arlienne was supervising the spectacle.

"I did," Arlienne said. "Excuse me, Mr. Graves."

Nicolette followed Arlienne to a waiting salon just off the main entryway. Tiny bright yellow painted canaries intermingled with pale yellow pinstripes papered the walls. What was notably a pretty room only reminded Nicolette of the pale prison she lived in. Faint to the discerning eye, but there nonetheless.

"You may wish to sit for this," Arlienne suggested.

Such words rarely spelled good news. Nicolette sat.

"What I have to say will either make your world or destroy it, Nicolette."

"Go on." Nicolette reserved an instinctual panic for the next sentence.

Arlienne wrung her hands, took two nervous steps, then pivoted. "It's Havenly House."

Nicolette's stomach dropped like a stone. "The duke's heritage estate? The home where he currently resides?"

Arlienne watched her closely. Nicolette squeezed her eyes shut and shook her head. She licked her lips and gathered her courage. After receiving the jewelry box, she'd thought her dealings with the duke were finished.

"Why?" Even as she asked the question, she knew. A little more than a week had passed since she'd confessed her sins to Arlienne. "Why would the Duke of Havenly invite us to his country estate? Why, Arlienne?" She panicked, taking gulps of air, a clip of accusation in her voice.

"He does not know. His grandmother, the duchess, invited us." Arlienne looked terrified.

"The duchess? Why would the duchess invite us?"

Arlienne wet her lips. "Because"—she swallowed—"because I wrote a letter." The words came out frantic and hurried.

Perhaps it was shock, but Nicolette did not rail or get angry. A single tear formed in the corner of her eye, and she felt dizzy and faint.

Through bleary eyes, she looked to Arlienne as the tear scorched down her cheek. She licked the salt of it from her lips. Through the haze, she saw Arlienne rush to her side and kneel beside the settee. She handed Nicolette a handkerchief.

"How could you, Arlienne? I trusted you like a sister. I spoke in confidence."

Arlienne nodded, silent tears gathering in her own eyes.

"What exactly did you write to the duchess?" Then she gasped. "Oh heavens! What did you tell Uncle James and Aunt Lydia?" Now she truly felt sick. She needed fresh air. Ironically, she was about to get her wish. Havenly was a ten-hour drive with posting stops, which to her embarrassed horror had already been prepared for their travel with fresh horses and instructions to deliver them posthaste.

It took only one wincing look from Arlienne to know how much she'd revealed.

"It is far too much to ask, but I do hope you'll find it in your heart to forgive me someday."

At the word *heart*, Nicolette remembered what Grant had written. *Memories are the finest treasure of the heart.* And the memories with Arlienne were that and more.

"Sooner than later would be nice," Arlienne suggested cautiously, biting her lip.

Nicolette was not proof against her cousin's tearful smile. She was brooding, and for what? She was in a fix of her own making. Gossip had begun. It couldn't get much worse. Perhaps they were going to Havenly to work out a strategy, because the ultimate option would not do. She would not be forced to consider the duke, and he certainly would not willingly submit.

Arlienne still sat at Nicolette's feet, gazing up at her. "Tell me what you're feeling?" she asked, resting her hand over Nicolette's.

"Everything. Mostly fear. But I want you to know that although I don't agree with what you've done, it was but a matter of time before Robert would have been forced to tell the truth. I imagine all hell broke loose?"

Arlienne nodded, then leveraged herself off the floor and sat beside Nicolette. "Mother cried, and Father bellowed that he would kill Havenly the minute he saw him."

"Oh dear. Are they all at Havenly now?"

"I believe so, but Father did calm down before he left. I think he'd even convinced himself that the duke would make a perfect match."

"He's wrong. But I wouldn't want to see His Grace get into a row with Uncle James. Besides"—she began to gasp with oncoming, nervous, laughter—"Robert already cuffed him while on the ship. You should have seen it. The duke was stunned. Robert smacked him right in the jaw."

Nicolette wiped tears of mirth from her eyes, the manifestation of laughter and fear bubbling over. She held on to Arlienne's hand and boldly looked her in the eye. "I'll work it out. Don't give up on me. I'm a survivor."

It would seem, as Nicolette pulled away from London, she was oft to find herself in a coach traveling to some frightening, unknown future. She had two opportunities for reprieve. One, to convince Aunt Lydia and Uncle James that this match would not do. The other was to convince the duke, which she was certain would take no convincing at all. In fact, she counted on his refusal. He did not want to marry her. He did not love her, and she was doing her best to fall out of love with him.

CHAPTER 24

The drive was breathtaking, Nicolette could not deny that. She'd toured the seas but not the countryside, apart from her aunt and uncle's home. Spring rains brought the hills and meadows to life with wildflowers and tall grasses. Occasionally they'd pass a large manor house. The posting sites, although not much to see, were welcoming, and as she'd been told, they were ready for them.

The drive was to be only ten hours. A long time in a coach but a short time to travel such a distance. The four grays that pulled the vehicle were steady, and the rented coach was well sprung.

Arlienne and Master Andrew rode with her, along with Claudia and Miss Blanchfield for the sake of travel time. Nicolette was still amazed how much luggage one could pack onto a rolling vehicle. It was not a cargo vessel by any stretch, but Arlienne had managed to pack four women into one coach, luggage and all. They traveled with outriders for safety, but the men stayed out of view, and Nicolette enjoyed at least the illusion of freedom.

Along the way to East Sussex, they passed several villages,

each with its own personality, but the last one they came upon before they turned off the main road had an incomparable charm.

Up over a rolling hill, she spied a little hamlet. At the end of the town, the road circled around a multitiered fountain set directly in front of a beautiful stone church with stained glass windows set in brick and mortar. The town church had to be at least a century old. The circle was crowded with shops of every kind—millinery, apothecary, bakeries and butchers, even a shop with sweet treats.

They passed an inn on their way through and a tavern as well. Too soon they were on the other side. Nicolette knew they must be getting close to their destination because the requisite ten hours had elapsed.

She grabbed the coach strap as they swayed to the left and turned right onto a private drive. They stopped at a large wrought iron gate, and the driver spoke to a man who opened the gate and let them pass. Against her will, she was enchanted by the dreamlike manicured lawns with shaped shrubbery and a driveway so clean of debris that she hardly heard the fine gravel under the coach wheels.

The ducal estate clearly boasted extensive lands, and the grounds were immaculately tended. It spoke of great wealth, and Nicolette could not imagine ever living in such a place. And then the house came into view—not just a manor house like her aunt and uncle's but a magnificent mansion boasting three stories and two large wings with massive stone steps leading up to the front door.

"Isn't it enchanting? What do you think, Nicolette?" Arlienne asked.

Nicolette swallowed, and the wonder from traveling through such a marvelous part of the country vanished. "I cannot go inside, Arlienne. I fear my legs will not allow it."

"Yes, you can, and you will, and everything will be lovely,

just as it should." Arlienne's words were not entirely empty, but they lacked conviction.

"Somewhere in that house is a man who is not going to be happy to see me."

"You don't know that."

Nicolette turned to Arlienne, ignoring the fact that speaking so freely in front of servants was not at all the thing. "I know it with all my heart."

She spared a glance at Miss Blanchfield, who looked elated. Elated! Her governess had never looked anything but stern. And Claudia, her cherished maid, remained silent.

Was he in there? Was he watching the coach pull up? Nicolette was more terrified by the *not* knowing than if the man had come straight out and greeted them himself.

FROM THE FIRST glimpse of the house, Nicolette had been in awe. The foyer alone was as large as a house, flanked by two wide, curving staircases and surrounded by a gallery that she furtively scanned for one sinfully dark-haired man with a dimpled smirk. But he wasn't there. And neither were her aunt and uncle.

She was shown to a room on the second floor, directly across from Arlienne's. The proximity to her cousin calmed her. Claudia did the rest. She helped her out of her traveling pelisse, her hat, her gloves, and then into a warm bath. After nearly eleven hours of travel, Nicolette was not expected to visit, meet, or otherwise occupy the same room with anyone else. Arlienne came to visit with her and informed her that Aunt Lydia and Uncle James would speak with her tomorrow after she'd been introduced to the Duchess of Havenly. Normally she would have been devastated to be kept from her aunt and uncle, but under the circumstances, she considered it a reprieve. Besides, she was exhausted.

MIDMORNING, Claudia roused her from the best sleep she'd had in weeks. How odd that after so many nights floundering, she would find sleep in the one place she'd least expect.

After the requisite toast and jam, Claudia chose for her a dress of periwinkle blue trimmed with gold thread, and delicate lace gloves. She felt like a dressed doll. Nothing about this was familiar or normal. Nicolette sat on the edge of the canopied bed, plucking nervously at the shimmering buttercup-yellow counterpane embroidered with tiny white flowers.

Claudia had pulled her hair into a loose twist that flowed over one shoulder and left tiny wisps to frame her face.

"Claudia, I look ghastly, do I not?" She pinched her cheeks and refused the handheld mirror.

"No, my lady, you look..." Claudia gave her another look-over.

"Terrified?" Nicolette laughed.

"Lovely and rested," Claudia finished. Her maid was a gentle, mothering figure, and Nicolette could not have survived these past three years without her.

"Did the dowager truly ask for me herself?"

Claudia nodded and brought matching satin shoes, slipping them onto Nicolette's feet and tying the ribbons. When Nicolette first came to be with the Thomases, she'd balked at having someone help her dress until she realized that between petticoats and stays, leaning down to fit one's shoes was quite a task.

At last she was led by a stately butler to meet with the duchess.

The salon where Her Grace, the Duchess of Havenly, was seated boasted two full sofas, five overstuffed chairs, a tea table next to every perch and a veritable garden of bouquets set in expensive vases. The room was done up in an understated color of pale blue, like a clear pond. It complemented the dove-gray dress the duchess wore, as if the room were decorated as an adornment for her. The back wall was an expanse of windows that overlooked a breathtaking courtyard, and at present Nicolette wished she were out there among the potted ivy and flowering hydrangea.

Instead, she was being greeted by the current Duchess of Havenly. A formidable woman indeed.

"Come in, child." Without the help of a cane or a servant, the duchess slowly stood.

Nicolette felt like she was wearing two anvils for shoes. She proceeded but couldn't help her gaze from traveling the length of the room and spying every corner for the duke.

"It's just us."

Nicolette knew the duchess meant to assure her, to make her feel more at ease, but it did little to stop the quaking fear in her belly.

When she was within a few feet, Nicolette performed a curtsy. "Your Grace."

"Nonsense, I'll not have that. Groveling is unnecessary." The duchess belied the commanding boom in her voice with a smile that appeared almost contrived except that her eyes had softened when Nicolette looked up. "Please sit with me a spell. I'd like to know you better, child." The duchess patted the cushion next to her.

Nicolette, with her heart in her throat and a great amount of uncertainty, lowered herself beside the older woman.

"May I call you Nicolette?"

"Yes, of course, Your Grace. I would be honored if you

would." She pulled from her store of lessons, breathing slowly to calm her voice while her nerves tripped and somersaulted against her insides.

The duchess leaned in, giving Nicolette's hand a little squeeze, then returned to a rigid, regal state as if she'd always been a duchess.

"Lady Enid Sutherland," the butler announced.

Nicolette's head popped up at the name. She stood and smoothed her gown, keeping her head bowed.

Lady Sutherland turned to the butler and pointed with her cane. "Shut the doors, Houldsworth." She then proceeded to the front of the settee where Nicolette stood gracefully still. She imagined the effect was more sterile and strained than demure and lovely.

Lady Sutherland put a hand to Nicolette's chin, gently lifting until their gazes met.

"There, that's better. She's beautiful, isn't she, Matilda?" Grant's great-aunt's voice was lilting, soft and full of hope, a stark contrast to the duchess's. She took a steadying grip on Nicolette's hand and then lowered herself onto the settee. Like the duchess, Lady Sutherland patted the seat cushion between herself and the duchess.

Nicolette dutifully sat between them.

"Grant is my great-nephew. I hope he has spoken well of me, if he's spoken of me at all." She beamed expectantly.

"His Grace"—Nicolette stumbled over the words—"has spoken very well of you, my lady." She turned to the duchess. "And you as well, of course. Of you both," she finished awkwardly, consciously keeping her hands from flailing like her tongue.

"Has he?" The duchess raised a familiar quizzical eyebrow, an affectation Nicolette had seen on her grandson a dozen times. "I would be surprised if that were true. He's a scoundrel." The duchess said that last part with equal parts conspiracy and mischief.

Nicolette's esteem of the duke's grandmother rose by degrees. "My thoughts exactly, Your Grace."

"I knew I'd like you," Lady Sutherland said beside her. "You speak your mind. Grant needs that. And if you're worried that any rumors of his rakish behavior are true, then know, my dear, that reformed rakes make wonderful husbands."

"Enid," the duchess scolded.

"Pish, Matilda, you know better than most." Lady Sutherland turned a sheepish grin on Nicolette.

Nicolette felt as if she were sitting in the middle of a chessboard. At any moment she expected one or both to shout checkmate.

With Lady Sutherland's statement, Nicolette was reminded of that first dance she and Grant had shared when she'd coyly asked if rakes could be ruined. The memory made her smile.

She promptly tamped it down. At present she needed her wits, which meant getting her memories of his rakish smile, rakish behavior, and rakish good looks under control.

"May I say that your grandson, and great-nephew," she said falteringly, "will not approve? He does not wish to marry me, and with all due respect, I do not wish to marry him. So you see, all this work you have done is for naught." She bounced between them. "He is not a man who can be forced, believe me. If you push, he will push back. And, if I might add, the last we spoke, I did tell him that he was not to call upon me, not for a dance, not for anything, not ever again."

The duchess chortled—her bosom shook with it, the lines at her eyes crinkled, but her posture remained unmoved. The woman was the epitome of the beau monde. "You are a prize, Nicolette. It's my guess that he never saw you coming."

"You are mistaken."

"No, child. I am not. I know him better than most. We are much alike." The duchess breathed deeply, as if the outcome had already been decided. "My dear girl, I don't know what happened on that ship, and I don't want to know. All I can say is that since his return, he's been quick-tempered, out of sorts, and far more passionate in his arguments with me than ever before. You, Nicolette, have done something no one else could do. You touched his heart. He had hidden it so well that I had given up that it should ever be found."

Nicolette sighed and allowed Lady Sutherland to hold her hand. "We are not at all suited. And he will never be happy, not with me, or with you for interfering."

"I have spent a lifetime trying to bend my family to my will, Nicolette. It has cost me a great deal. I have a daughter who is estranged, living in another country, and when Grant's father was a young man, he eloped with a woman who I did my best to make unhappy in this very house. Instead of blessing their union so they could marry here, I forced them to elope and caused the scandal I so wanted to avoid. The Sutherland men have all been rakes and have done whatever they pleased. But Grant won't marry because he's worried that I will make not only his life but the life of his bride miserable, as I managed to do his mother's. And now I have an opportunity to change things, to make it right."

"What I see is you hoping to make amends with the past by drawing absolution from the future," Nicolette said honestly.

"Spirit and honesty," Lady Sutherland replied. "She's perfect."

The duchess paused, tilting her head, scrutinizing Nicolette. She all but looked down her nose at her. The experience was daunting and somehow satisfying at the same time because she had the distinct feeling that this scrutiny, the sheer force behind the duchess's severe look of judgment of her, was something of a compliment that very few were gifted.

Since Nicolette could not convince the duke's stubborn grandmother and equally stubborn but kind great-aunt, she decided to let him do it. And then wondered if he hadn't already tried.

CHAPTER 25

Of course it had been a trick, but Grant had spent two days after his and Nicolette's last encounter so agitated that he jumped at the chance when his grandmother requested he return to Havenly for a week. He had not been notified of her travel, something she usually did so he wouldn't worry. Now he knew why.

The wily old woman was using his home against him. The countryside, the distance from London, were meant to keep him from escaping into another distraction. Little did his grandmother know that Nicolette had distracted him to the point of isolation. After the Ashton party, he'd not left his townhome until the request arrived for him to join the duchess at Havenly House. He'd sent the jewelry box to Nicolette, hoping to end his obsession with both her and the box. And it would have worked had his grandmother not imposed herself into his personal affairs.

Two days ago, he'd met with Lord Walborne. He'd had the distinct feeling the man wished him bodily harm. With great and delicate equanimity, he'd tried to help Walborne understand that there was no reason for the drastic measures his grandmother had suggested. Since then they'd come to an understanding of sorts, one Grant had not completely agreed with. Perhaps Nicolette would make them see reason where he had failed.

When she arrived yesterday, he was working in his study. Today he was hiding there. Because of his grandmother's interference, he expected to deal with Nicolette's wrath once again. Last time they'd danced, it was a decidedly stormy parting.

"I invited them."

Grant looked up from his desk. His grandmother moved with the stealth of an assassin. Her talents were wasted on tea parties, although she *was* doing a formidable job of destroying his life.

"Bravo, Grandmother." He stood against his stubborn will, then invited her to sit. Grant took a place by the sideboard and offered her tea. She shook her head, and he poured himself a coffee. "You invited them. You entertain them."

"I never thought I'd see the day when my grandson was frightened of a girl."

He slanted her a smirk. "Nice try. You lured a perfectly decent family here under false pretenses and the misguided notion that I give a care." In fact, he did give a care, but just now he needed the fight and a position of power. He returned to his seat behind his desk. It could be argued that he hid behind it.

She passed a shrewd look over him, one that bordered on triumph.

"Have you met her?"

"Yes. And might I add, Havenly, that I did not lure them here on false pretenses. You can blame yourself for that." His grandmother chortled, something he was unaccustomed to. It threw him a little. "Do you know what she said about you, Grant? Miss Thomas called you a scoundrel."

He knew she wasn't finished. "And?"

"And I invite you to do as you please. You always have. Let her return to the gossip, which I have on good authority is on the verge of becoming something truly ugly. She's a strong girl. She can ride it out to its natural end. Perhaps next year the ton will forget and she'll find a kind gentleman who won't exploit her momentary fall from grace. It will be painful. I can attest to that. But if she hides in the country, they will tear her apart. I guess it doesn't matter. She's lost so much family already, I don't think she'll miss not having one of her own."

Grant stared at her, biting back the fury that was probably visible in his throbbing jaw. He wasn't ready to ask the pertinent questions of himself, like if he was angry with himself or his grandmother. Because the woman was right. He was used to scandal. But Nicolette was not. She was not raised as he had been, to endure the politics of selfish people bent on having a season for the sake of entertainment alone. She was born of love. Just as she'd said he'd been.

The duchess was not quite done with him. "None of this was that sweet girl's doing. In fact, I'll admit she was distraught, so I suggested she tour the grounds to clear her head."

If his own self-loathing weren't enough, that did it. "Where is she?"

"I'm not certain. Houldsworth said she took off in the direction of the stables."

GRANT LEFT the back of the house in the direction of the stables. A groom pointed him toward the livestock where she'd apparently wandered next. *Wild-goose chase* sprang to mind when he found her near a pasture of sheep, standing just this side of the enclosure, with several hens clucking at her feet.

"Be careful where you step," he stated, causing her head to jolt up.

She immediately looked to her feet, then raised one toe and stepped to the side. The cackling hens rushed from under her feet but refused to leave their buffet of seeds and sprouts.

"The stable keep said the chickens roam free during the day. I suppose I've taken my cue from them." Her mouth turned up in a wan smile that didn't reach her eyes.

"I seem to have failed your last request, but I promise I won't ask you to dance." His jest was lost on her. She didn't look his way, just leaned her arms against the paddock, resting her chin on her fist. He cleared his throat, sidestepping a chicken on his way to join her. He leaned against the fence, his arms hanging over the top rail and his booted foot propped on the bottom slat.

Without looking his way, she said, "If I ask you something, will you answer truthfully?"

"I think I've always been honest with you."

She cocked her head and pierced him with a demanding look.

"Yes," he said. "If you'll answer a question for me." When she looked skeptical, he clarified. "I won't ask how you feel about me again, I promise. I learned my lesson."

She gave a quick nod, then turned her gaze back to the pasture.

Neither said anything for several seconds.

Grant broke the charged silence. "Do you want to start?"

She turned fully toward him, her arms folded tightly against her chest. "Did you send for me? Did you invite my family here?"

"No. I didn't."

She rubbed her neck, dipping her head, but not before he saw pain register in her eyes.

"I should have greeted you when you arrived."

"No, you shouldn't have. I was weary and went straight to bed. Ironically, the long trip did what counting sheep could not. I slept all night." With her arms on the top rail again, she laid her cheek on her fist and looked at him. "What is your question?"

"Did you tell your aunt and uncle about us?"

Both her eyebrows rose, and he had his answer. "Do I appear insane?" She lifted her head and smiled, actually smiled, genuinely. "Of course not. I was under the impression that the duchess approached my uncle and not the other way around."

He blinked, surprised at that news. "How did she know?"

"Rumor? A certain someone's mistress?"

"Whose?" he asked dumbly. "Mine?" He was incredulous.

"If the shoe fits. I have it on good account that Miss Featherbe has been spreading a few disparaging words."

He would have laughed heartily if he hadn't thought she'd clock him for it. "I'd prefer you not speak her name. It does you no credit."

"Why? Does it offend your sensibilities to hear what your paramour is saying?"

"No, it offends my sensibilities that you think I have one. And if others are calling her that, then it's improper—"

She interrupted his warning against gossip fodder with outright laughter. Ironic laughter with a hint of self-loathing. "You're serious? I shouldn't speak the name of your mistress because it might damage my impeccable reputation? That's rich, Your Grace."

"Is that what this is about?"

"I think it's funny is all. If she's your mistress, then say so."

"I believe I've answered that already."

She gave a little shrug. "Suit yourself."

"The truth? Is that what you really want?"

"It would help."

He was happy to allow her the upper hand, but if she continued on this topic, his patience would not last. "Miss

Featherbe and I were momentarily involved three years ago. Not three weeks ago. It isn't something I wish to discuss. In fact, I believe we had this same conversation on the way to the wharf."

She conceded, her body sagging on a sigh. "You're correct. It was bad form of me to ask then, as it is now. I'm just trying to make sense of my life. I can't figure out why I'm here."

"I believe my grandmother has plans for a big wedding."

She chuckled at that. "You know what, Grant?"

He smiled, and his pulse quickened at his name.

"Against my will, I like your grandmother, and I adore your great-aunt." A chicken pecked at her shoe. "And these chickens have won me over too." She gazed up at him. "So what do we do now? If my uncle is here to sign a betrothal contract, it can't happen. And the only hope I have is knowing you won't allow it."

"One has been drawn up but not signed. Not by either party." He reached out to take her hand, but she sidestepped him, turning on her heel. She walked ahead of him, along the fence with a handful of chickens in her wake chasing after the lace hem of her skirt. And like the chickens, he followed.

She called over her shoulder, "Did you know that every year, since my sixteenth birthday, I've been fitted for a complete brand-new wardrobe?"

"That's not unusual." He skipped around another hen.

She twirled about, her skirts catching at her ankles. "It is for me." With her hands clasped behind her, she pretended interest in the chickens while she talked. "Ball gowns, day dresses, shoes, hats, morning dresses, walking dresses, traveling costumes, gloves and stockings, and for the life of me I cannot fathom why, at least two riding habits as well." She looked to see if he was paying attention. "Two." She held up two fingers and raised an innocent brow. "I don't even sit a horse. Why do you think that is?"

"You've never been taught?" He grinned.

"No." She offered a half smile and the hint of mirth. "What I mean is, why would Aunt Lydia order riding habits for me when I do not ride? She insists my wardrobe be complete, but I say she has spent money needlessly."

"I doubt Lady Walborne sees it that way. Perhaps she's opposed to seeing you in men's trousers." He crossed one arm, resting his elbow on it like a pedestal, and rubbed his chin thoughtfully.

"She loathes them. At sixteen I arrived on her doorstep with a whole valise stuffed with them."

Grant failed to look shocked.

"She never made me feel odd. I came from a small town, where for ten lovely years I lived in a small house with a wonderful mother and a loving father. And it felt like home. And then when my mother died, I stayed with my father where he worked."

"On the *New Horizon*."

Nicolette nodded. "That felt like home too." She took a quick breath and looked away. "Then at sixteen, my father was suddenly taken from me, but he had lovingly arranged that I should live with these wonderful relatives I'd never met. Although Uncle James is my mother's cousin, they were more like brother and sister, raised in the same household. I had never met my aunt or uncle, and yet they loved me without reservation. And that felt like home too."

Grant watched her silently, listening closely, afraid he knew where this was headed.

"I pored over books on peerage and etiquette and the god-awful confusion over which fork to use and when." She glanced at him. "I wore the proper clothes and began to feel as if I belonged. My friends are from this world. My aunt and uncle are from this world. My cousin Arlienne is from this world."

"Nicolette." Grant tried to interject.

"Up until the time I left for those three weeks, I followed all the rules. I did everything I was supposed to do, and it has been for naught because I have ended up where I began. I'm of no consequence. A nobody. Gossip has soundly put me back where I belong."

"You're wrong."

"No, I'm not. I may not know where my home is anymore, but I do know where I don't belong. This is not my world, it's yours. It belongs to my friends, and my cousin, my relatives, but not me. I am as out of place as the riding habits in my wardrobe."

Grant realized his grandmother was right about one thing. Nicolette would not survive this. She was too transparent. Too kind, too honest, and had the good fortune to have been raised elsewhere.

Her eyes followed a butter-colored chicken with missing tail feathers. "She knows what I say is true."

Grant laughed at this. "The chicken?"

"Have you never heard of the pecking order?"

"Oh, for God's sake and mine, Nicolette—" With hands on his hips he looked up at the sky.

"Blaspheme all you care, but you cannot deny the comparison. That chicken has had her tail feathers plucked because she has assumed a position that does not belong to her. And"—Nicolette held up a hand to stop his next words—"she knows that if she continues to break that order, she may become wounded, even bleed, at which point the flies will come and... Well, the rest is too gruesome to speak of. Needless to say, she would not survive."

"Nicolette, you are not a chicken."

She whirled around, a look of disbelief on her lovely face. "Of course I am not a chicken." Then she shocked him by broaching the subject he'd originally come to discuss. "You do not wish to marry me. And I do not wish to marry you. If I had followed the rules, I would not be in this predicament."

"Nicolette, this *predicament* has naught to do with you. Not too long ago a brave, young, beautiful woman with hair the color of dark honey told me that I do not take responsibility for my conduct. She was absolutely right. And because of my usual selfishness, I hurt that woman. But I know you, Nicolette—you are not going to stand idly by and allow a throng of gossiping chickens to destroy you." He couldn't help smiling at the description.

Nicolette shut her eyes against him. "I cannot let you take all the blame." She then opened her eyes again, boldly, bravely holding his gaze. "I may not have recognized you when you approached me in the stairwell of the theater, but I knew exactly who you were when you kissed me on that ship. I know exactly who you are now too. There is some truth in every lie, and gossip does not always treat you kindly."

"You shouldn't believe everything you think you know." Grant found himself in the awkward position of defending his good name, and it galled him.

She smirked. "I know that you will not sign a betrothal contract because you do not believe in marriage."

He couldn't argue with that last part. "I have avoided marriage, that is true, but not because I don't believe in it." He held up a hand as she'd done to stop her next words. "My opposition was bringing a woman into my home that my grandmother would scorn." He shot her a telling look. "That is not a slight against you, sweet."

She rolled her eyes, crossing her arms, but stood firmly planted.

"She seems to like you very much."

"And you?"

"I like you too." He couldn't help the wide grin that broke across his face.

She shook her head. "I'm here, you're here, because of something that did *not* happen. Because I was so angry with you the last we spoke that I…" She growled, clenching her teeth and her fists. "That I told my cousin everything that *did* happen."

He scowled. "What the devil for?"

"Because I trusted her to keep it private, because in all honesty nothing happened. She's sorry now, I believe, and she did keep her promise not to tell my aunt and uncle, but what she did do was write to your grandmother. After that, I can only imagine the fiasco that ensued."

He scrubbed a hand down his face, then rubbed his chin and laughed.

"How can you laugh?"

Her hands were on her hips, and all he could think of was grabbing her around the waist and burying his face in her hair. "I've missed you, Nicolette."

"You're insane. It was only a kiss. Surely you've had more than your share."

He took several steps forward until he stood close enough to touch her. "None like this." Without touching her, he simply bent his head and brushed a kiss on her lips, then an inch from her mouth, he said, "After I sign the contract, which I will, it would not be unheard of for you to kiss me back."

She did not move. Did not back up an inch, and with her face turned up to his, she locked gazes with him. There was no retreat in this woman. She'd learned to stand her ground, balanced on a moving ship in a hurricane. Although he was convinced she created enough storms on her own, as she did now.

"You flatter yourself." Her pupils dilated, a hint of the storm ahead. "You're quite good at it when you have women practically pawing at your heels. Tell me, Grant, how many women have you held in the middle of the night? How many do you miss holding?"

He paused, drawn in by her challenge. How many did he miss indeed?

"Only one," he whispered.

She blinked and pulled back with an unsteady breath, but he wouldn't allow her to leave.

With one step forward, he grabbed her around the waist, bringing her up against his chest, her breasts softly pressing against his shirtfront. "I predict that before the day is out, you will kiss me back. What will your forfeit be?"

"I prefer not to play games with you because you cheat."

"Never have I cheated. Never once." He bent his head again, only intending another light brush of her lips, but when she sighed a little moan, he couldn't let her go. He caught her bottom lip between his teeth; he tasted every corner of her sweet mouth; he kissed her until they were both breathless. With his hands on her cheeks, he pressed his forehead to hers. "I missed you, Nicolette. I missed holding you at night." He kissed her nose.

"But nothing happened. Nothing to press a suit upon."

"No?"

She shook her head but stayed in his embrace, her arms wrapped around his middle. "It was only a kiss."

He watched several emotions play out across her face. She went from half-lidded passion to brow-knitted confusion to purse-lipped dissatisfaction. At the last, one of her hands fell to her side.

She looked away. "How did this happen?" Her voice had an edge. "Your grandmother, my aunt and uncle, my cousin, you've all had a hand in this manipulation. The part I understand the least is how you don't seem to mind when I know for a fact you don't love me. This thing we have going right now—the banter, the fun, the stolen kisses? They're very exciting,

Your Grace, but as soon as you claim what you want, you will grow weary. And you know where that will leave me?" She turned her gaze back to him. "Alone. And it will leave you to do as you please. To choose as you please. So if I seem a little unsettled about the whole affair—and I think I use the word correctly here—it's because I am a realist."

"And all this time I thought you were a dreamer." He wanted to be angry with her for that statement, but all he could see in her stormy eyes was heartbreak.

"Dreaming is what caused this mess," she shot back.

This mess was a direct result of the passion mark he'd left on her neck. It was visible and damning. But the mark she'd left on his heart was another matter. A private matter. And one he wasn't ready to address.

"You're good at this," she said weakly. "But you can't fool me. If you wish sanity for all your days, I suggest you put a stop to this madness. Or I shall."

CHAPTER 26

Nicolette returned to the house via the conservatory. Her heels echoed along the black-and-white tiled floor. Flat cushioned benches set between lemon trees invited a tête-à-tête. At another time she'd have enjoyed hiding from the world in such a place. Currently she was headed for the drawing room, where according to Grant, everyone was gathered. He'd kissed her hand and left her with the decision to join the signing or remain detached.

She chose to be there when her life was promised to a near stranger. After all, a few kisses did not a relationship make.

She composed herself outside the closed doors to the drawing room, then nodded for the footman to allow her entrance.

The room was full. These good people who would soon be family turned in her direction. Both the duchess and Lady Enid sat beside one another on the sofa while Arlienne was perched on the arm of the chair where her Aunt Lydia sat.

The decor was done in varying hues of cream and cocoa and accented with burgundy and gold throughout. The comfortable room with its iron-latticed windows was large enough to keep the deep colors from being oppressive and was made airy by several vases of fresh-cut flowers. It was quite a contrast to the room where she'd first met the duchess. This room looked as if the duke himself had decorated it. Perhaps that's why he was so interested in chocolate.

Uncle James stood next to an open mahogany secretary that overlooked the side yard. On the hinged table lay a rather thick stack of papers, no doubt the contract that would seal her fate. Funny how it did not require the signature of the female in question. In fact, if she refused to show for the wedding, a proxy could stand in her place since she was not of an age to know her mind.

Such rubbish.

"Nicolette, darling. Come sit." Aunt Lydia found her voice first. She absently patted the single seat of the chair she rose from.

"No, thank you, Aunt." Nicolette walked on wooden legs toward her aunt and kissed her cheek, then Arlienne's. Everyone looked as stiff as she felt. Stoic faces greeted her as if she might throw a tantrum or faint at any moment.

"Uncle James?" She swallowed hard and watched from the corner of her eye as Grant came toward her.

"Come sit," Grant said beside her, but her gaze never broke from her uncle's.

"Uncle James? Will you really sign my life away?" The question was rude and impertinent, everything she had been taught not to be.

His eyes softened apologetically. "It's in your best interest, Nicolette."

She shook her head. "If you'd only given me a chance to explain."

"His Grace explained."

"Then His Grace did a foul job of it, because there is no

reason for such a rash decision. No reason at all. Ask Captain Donovan. He was there the entire voyage."

"This isn't the place or the time," her uncle said.

"No, the place and time were taken from me, so here I am. Can we not discuss it now?"

"Child." The duchess's voice had the power to command a room at a whisper. "The contract is very agreeable."

"To whom?" She closed her eyes for patience. "With all due respect, Your Grace, you don't know me, and neither does he." She outrageously pointed to Grant, who looked as if he might say something until the duchess interrupted.

"Then tell me who you are." It was an ironic request from the current duchess to the soon-to-be Duchess of Havenly.

"I'm but the daughter of a merchant seaman. And my real family is not considered acceptable in your world."

"No, my dear, now you are telling me who I am, and it is but an assumption, perhaps a lie my grandson perpetuated." The duchess turned steely eyes on Grant, who was in the process of pouring a drink. He looked up too quickly, splashing brandy over the top of his hand. He flicked his fingers, grabbed a napkin to wipe his knuckles, and then with one smooth move bent over and mopped several drops from the toe of his boot.

Apparently he was as nervous as she. That alone eased her pulse and calmed the panic. Perhaps there was still hope that he'd not sign.

That hope died when he put down his drink and said, "The betrothal will be signed."

With hands on her hips, ignoring every other person in the room, she replied with hauteur, "I will not be defeated by pen and paper."

Grant strolled to the secretary, picked up a pen, then flipped to the last page of the contract and signed it. Uncle

James quickly added his signature before Nicolette could get so much as a gasp out.

"It is your fate you sealed, Your Grace. I warn you that I intend to make my own."

"Miss Thomas, I look forward to it," he said flippantly, arrogantly nonchalant.

She held his gaze, breathing deeply with her hands now digging into her waist. And Grant, he couldn't have looked more like a pirate if he'd been wearing an eye patch and had a parrot on his shoulder.

She heard someone clapping and turned to find Lady Sutherland, a smile beaming from her rosy cheeks, her cane resting against the settee.

And then she saw it. The Duchess of Havenly, always proper and austere, rolled her eyes at her sister-in-law.

Grant had told her on the ship that he loved it when she rolled her eyes. It was clear he thought more of his grandmother than he let on. It was also clear that she and the duchess had something of an attitude in common. Was that a good thing? Possibly, because the duchess seemed to be the only one who could rile the duke.

AFTER AN AWKWARD SILENCE, they filed from the room, each congratulating the bride and groom-to-be while wearing peculiar smiles that ranged from dismay on her Aunt Lydia to complete elation on Grant's great-aunt. It was a fiasco. A circus.

And then they were alone.

Grant stood in front of her, his hands rubbing her upper arms. "Would you like to read the contract?"

"If I did, could I alter it?"

"Everything is negotiable."

He put a finger to her lips when she took a breath to speak. "Everything but the marriage."

She rolled her eyes. "Never mind, Your Grace."

"Do you think we can dispense with the whole title thing now?" His voice had a smile in it. The deep, vibrating timbre rattled the bricks she was desperately laying against him.

Every time she built a wall, he destroyed it.

"You do realize this was necessary." He tilted his head to see her.

"It doesn't matter what I think anymore. Not that it ever did, of course." She shrugged his hands from her arms but didn't move away.

"Nicolette." He coaxed her to look at him. "Gossip is the favored pastime during the season. You and I are the current entertainment, and no matter what you have heard of me or think of me, I cannot allow my conduct to dishonor you. It's as simple as that."

Did he think to put her at ease with such foolishness? "Do you know how backward that sounds?"

"I can understand your misgivings, but a wedding will stifle the gossip and return everything to normal."

"For whom?" She huffed, throwing up her hands in surrender. "Then again, what do I know? Right? I cannot possibly know my own mind. Not a woman. And as for normal, God Almighty knows that I don't recall what that word means. The definition has become something other than textbook."

"Allow me the opportunity to help you adjust."

She looked at him askance.

"Or allow yourself the freedom to put aside everything that's happened before today and enjoy the respite from the city. Havenly sits on over one hundred thousand acres. One could get lost here. Not that I'm suggesting you run off, mind you." He dimpled a silly grin at her.

The betrothal was signed, as legally binding as if they'd

taken their vows. She hadn't willed it, but when he'd held her, kissed her, spoken her name with that silly grin, she couldn't stop hoping that perhaps it would not be a disaster.

She had fallen in love with him easily on the ship. She was not so naive to think that she could feel the same again. But she did miss him, she wanted him, and perhaps a small part of her still loved him. However, admitting such heresy to herself was different than telling him. In her life, she'd suffered too many heartbreaks. She would not willingly play a part in another.

"I shall waive my right to read the contract, but I will keep my right to annoy you with your title."

"I wouldn't expect anything less." He took her in his arms and held her for a few moments until her breathing slowed and her heart stopped abusing the inside of her ribs.

CHAPTER 27

Husband. The word was a thrill ride for nausea, like taking off in a hot-air balloon and wondering whether it would ever land. Nicolette imagined the scenery to be magnificent from such a height, but the possibility of failure wasn't worth the chance.

Taking her future *husband*'s advice, she exercised the part of her that could be coaxed to play in a storm, not that it took much to draw her into such a thing. Three feelings plagued her daily: Arousal. Confusion. And the most compelling, that sense of security he'd instilled in her from the first time they'd met. The rational side of her called it desire, a very persistent desire. The irrational side called it love. She found she had no fight left, no argument, and in truth she was almost glad.

For two days Grant doted on her. He took her to see his horses, which she refused to ride. He took her on an abbreviated tour of the property and described his other estates, including his grandmother's dower house left by his grandfather. Up until now, the dowager duchess had lived at Havenly with her sister-in-law. In the upcoming weeks, they would move into a manor house.

Nicolette had objected. She knew what it was to lose one's home. But the duchess insisted that newlyweds needed space for more than loud arguments. Great-aunt Enid had winked after that statement, and Nicolette had felt like she was standing in a hothouse.

She met several cottagers and was impressed at how well their homes were maintained, and she watched Grant with some pride while he spoke and listened attentively to their concerns and successes.

Nicolette gave in to his relaxed, elegant charm and allowed herself a few carefree days before returning to London. They were to be wed in two short weeks. One week spent at Havenly getting to know one another and one week in London to be seen in public without the presence of scandal. As for the banns, they'd been read with an understanding that a special license would be needed to forgo the third week.

While Arlienne and Master Andrew visited under the same roof, Nicolette seized the opportunity to spend time in the nursery with her nephew. She sat on the floor with the toddler, her skirts tucked around her legs. When his angelic blue eyes drooped, Nicolette scooped him up and rocked him where she sat.

Andrew smelled like a little boy, dirt and wooden toys and the sweet scent of sweat that curled the ends of his hair. She bent close and kissed his forehead, rocking all the while, allowing the tiniest thought of having her own family tickle her dreams.

She felt a light touch at her shoulder, then heard Grant softly whisper, "Shall we keep him?" There was a smile in his voice.

Nicolette shushed him over her shoulder; then her cheeks stretched into a full smile. "I don't think he's available."

"I guess we'll have to start from scratch then, won't we?"

The statement made her warm all over. Grant continued in a soft tone. "When you're done, I want to show you something."

"You'll have to help me up. He's too heavy." Nicolette half raised the toddler toward Grant as he stood, and Grant took Andrew carefully into his arms, a bemused expression on his face.

"What now?" he whispered.

She squelched a giggle, accepting a hand up while he capably held Andrew in the crook of one arm.

"You put him in his infant bed. Have you never held a babe before?"

He shook his head. "No." Grant laid him down gently and stepped aside while Nicolette tucked a blanket around him and smoothed his hair off his forehead.

She turned and whispered, "He's the closest thing I will ever have to a nephew."

After they left the room and shut the door behind them, Nicolette said in full voice, "I'm at your service. Where are we going today?" Seeing the baby had put her in a wonderful mood this morning. Even still, she could hardly believe they were to wed in less than a fortnight. If she dwelled on it long enough, it scared her to death. But not today. The duke appeared elated about something.

"It's a secret. Grab a cloak and I'll meet you downstairs."

There was a boyish mischief about him. He was definitely hiding something.

When she descended the stairs, wearing a wool cloak lined with cream satin that contrasted nicely with her rose day dress, Grant was waiting for her.

He held out a hand. "You stand out like a wildflower among roses."

Nicolette paused, perplexed by his strange observation.

"In a garden of roses, the rare jewel is the wildflower that blooms among them."

She covered her embarrassment and warm cheeks with a bonnet ironically ornamented with silk roses that matched her gown. "Thank you. I think."

"That was definitely one of my better compliments. I would have thought you were beginning to recognize my peculiar style of flattery." He smiled wide, showcasing the dimple that made him dangerously charming. He gallantly wrapped her arm around his and continued to beam at her while she tried to decipher his code for compliments.

His proximity did not bode well for her sanity, causing her to lose the ability to converse convivially.

They took a cozy curricle drawn by two beautiful bays and Grant at the ribbons. Since she and Grant were properly engaged, they were allowed to take an open curricle during the day without chaperone. Besides, much of the travel was over Havenly property, which in Nicolette's opinion was far more private than the ship, and since the damage had been done, as Miss Blanchfield dutifully pointed out, no one bothered to lecture them on comportment.

"You're full of surprises today."

He transferred the reins to one hand and with his free hand tugged on her satin bonnet ties, loosing the bow just before turning onto the road proper.

She gasped, her hands flying to the brim before a breeze sent it sailing. Hats were not high on her list of fashionable favorites, but the boyish grin on Grant's face made it worth wearing. She pursed her lips and shot him a scolding look while feverishly tying the ribbons again. Her stomach somersaulted, but secretly she liked this side of him.

He laughed. "Kitten, you're frightening when you're riled."

"That sounds like a challenge."

"Oh no. Not today. Today I want peace."

That alone was challenge enough for her. She smiled to herself.

The drive took them through the center of town where several villagers stopped to gawk. Grant dipped his head and smiled. She hid behind the brim of her bonnet.

"We cut twenty minutes off our trip going through town." He glanced at her. "Did you survive? You seem to be hiding."

"I'm not used to being conspicuous. They seem to love you."

"I suppose someone has to." He winked at her. "Honestly, I'm not here much and I think they're just surprised."

"You're good with people."

He lifted a brow, contemplating her as if he hadn't expected such praise.

"That's a compliment, Your Grace, just in case you were wondering."

He swallowed hard, turning his focus back to the road. "Thank you," he said uneasily.

If nothing else came of the day, she'd found out something new about this infamously confident duke. He was good at his business, he was successful in his life, he had friends, but it would appear that he had little experience with honest accolades. As a peer, he would be catered to in all things, which unfortunately included false praise.

Truth was important to her. For a man like Havenly, all truth must feel like a lie.

"Where are we going?"

He cleared his throat. "Astray." And just like that, his relaxed charm returned.

He was good at hiding his true self. She had a lifetime to find him.

The carriage lurched over a pothole. Without taking his eyes from the rough road, he reached over and held on to her arm, keeping her steady until they were well and good off the main thoroughfare. She watched him from the corner of her eye and was amazed at how at ease he seemed out here in the country, how disarmingly handsome and comfortable he was, riding contentedly through the countryside. He was a puzzle, to be sure. By the absurd grin on his noble face, it was apparent that he was incredibly pleased with himself over his little surprise.

The silence, however, did not detract from the view. It was superb. There were open meadows of green hawthorn spread throughout the sloping hills waiting for full spring. The beautiful meadows of wildflowers turned into groves of poplar trees and scattered oak.

The conveyance wound its way up a steep grade, and then she spied it—a wall of ruins surrounded by thickets of trees and veined with overgrown ivy.

"It's breathtaking."

They stopped when the road leveled out and Grant helped her down.

"There's a river in the valley," she said.

The moving water wound its way over the countryside as far as she could see in both directions.

Grant had left her to the view. "River Rother," he called from somewhere behind her.

She heard his crunching footsteps and turned to find him carrying a blanket and a basket.

"A picnic?"

"A picnic." He clarified before stomping through the brush, back to the waiting vehicle where he pulled another basket from a box adhered to the backside of the carriage like a small trunk.

She walked along the ruins. "What is this place?" She pulled off her gloves and flattened her palm over the cool jutting stones.

"Some say it's one of King Alfred the Great's fortresses. The burg would have been a defense against the Vikings who sailed up the river." When he reached her, he took the spare glove from her hand and then pulled off the other. These he stuffed in his pocket. "The river may have been wide enough at the time to accommodate a Viking longboat, but absolute proof is hard to come by."

He untied the ribbon of her bonnet, and before she could gasp, he pulled it from her head. "No gloves today, no hats, and if it pleases you, remove your shoes and stockings."

She peered around him, then caught his gaze.

"There's no one here. And don't bother with womanly theatrics, because it's no more scandalous than wearing men's trousers."

"Or following strangers at the theater?" Portraying a false innocence, she made her eyes shockingly round.

"If you'd like to faint now, I'll catch you."

"If I haven't fainted in the past week, I'm sure I don't know how." She smiled. "Besides, I hate hats, but the gloves I want back... later."

Grant looped the hat's ribbons around one finger, letting it dangle by his side.

"Shall we?" He offered her the opposite arm, but Nicolette, with a jaunty smile, took hold of his hand instead. She practically skipped beside him as they made their way toward the waiting picnic. Her fingers, cool from touching the ruins, sent a shiver of pleasure that started at his fingertips and ended everywhere else.

"If the Vikings made it this far, you may have Viking blood," she said eagerly, settling herself in the middle of a cotton blanket trimmed in embroidered roses.

"I doubt that is so." He joined her, then filled a small plate with cheese, cold meats, and grapes, which he served her. "But if it buys me favor in your eyes, then I should be glad to play the part. Which would you choose?"

Nicolette laughed. "The last time I was given a choice it made little difference."

"Remind me, what choice was that?" Unfortunately, he couldn't guess at her meaning. His male brain was still rattled from the feathery touch of her hands on his skin.

"Why do you make me speak of such mortifying things?" she asked shyly.

"I didn't know I was doing that. Perhaps you should review what you say before you say it. Although I rather like it better this way. Now, what choice did you make that made little difference?"

She took a deep breath, looked him boldly in the eye, and stated, "Friends or lovers."

He raised a brow and bit back a self-satisfied grin.

"No need to look so pleased with yourself. Your victorious grin is better suited for a Viking."

"Perhaps I feel like a Viking."

"Perhaps I prefer the pirate captain." She peeked from under her lashes and batted her eyes dramatically.

Grant burst out laughing. "I'll keep that in mind." He poured two glasses of wine.

"How on earth did you manage all this?"

"I have a wonderful staff that is rather well paid." He handed her the wine and decided she could spend the rest of the day calling him whatever name she pleased, even bastard, and it would not come close to overshadowing the way he felt when she voluntarily held his hand.

The picnic was the best idea he'd had all week. It gave them time to talk freely without censuring eyes, and even better than the weeks away on the *New Horizon*, they were completely alone.

The wine at lunch seemed to embolden her with unbridled playfulness. "I have a proposition for you." She giggled.

Grant was enjoying this side of her. In fact, he was beginning to suspect that she was not used to having more than a few sips of wine, or any spirits for that matter.

"In five minutes, I wager that I can catch a larger toad than you."

Grant slanted a look at her. "And why do I want to do this?"

"Because it's fun," she said as if the question was ridiculous. And then the real reason came. "And because I would love to see you play at teatime with me and little Andrew. That is the forfeit I call."

Her eyes shone with laughter and passion.

"You're foxed, my dear."

"No," she gasped. "I am not allowed more than one glass of champagne."

"You've had two glasses today."

"Yes, but this is wine. I do not have restrictions on wine, good sir."

Grant rolled to his feet, chuckling while he helped her stand. Her foothold was a tad unstable. He first satisfied himself that she could take a few steps before he let her go, then held up five fingers. "Five minutes. And you are not allowed anywhere near the steep grade. I'd prefer not to break my neck chasing you as you roll down the hill."

"That is satisfactory because the best toads will be up here." She said that with unwavering conviction.

"If I find the first toad, do I get to name a forfeit?" he called over his shoulder as they separated.

She yelled back without looking up, "Of course."

"Perfect. If I win, you will call me Grant for the next twenty-four hours."

She waved a hand behind her. "You're going to lose, so that is acceptable."

He had been just as content to watch her poke around under every rock, but now the stakes were raised and the game was on. He rolled up his sleeves and headed for the dank ruins.

He glanced up occasionally to see Nicolette bent at the waist, searching the ground. She wandered under a large oak, examining the roots where they bubbled up from the earth; then her head popped up and she shrieked.

"I found one!"

He straightened, brushing his hands together as she leaped over the clover and twigs to reach him.

"See?" She held out her hand, cupping the little green leaper.

"Keep looking, love. That one doesn't qualify."

She cocked her head and placed one hand on her hip, leaving the other an open platform for the little *toad*. It didn't last. She gasped as it jumped from her hand into the soft grass. Without a blink, she wiped her palms down her skirt.

"How can you say it doesn't count? Let me see your hands, sir."

Grant held them out, and she looked at the empty palms, then up at him with a raised brow.

"Nicolette, you did not catch a toad. You caught a frog."

She simply blinked at him, quirking her mouth sideways as if he were an imbecile.

He was not immune to her stance or the way she looked with her hair slightly undone and blowing in the breeze. "As you wish, I relent. It was a toad." And then he added insolently, "But it shall be noted in the records that you made me lie about it."

She rolled her eyes and sighed. Then went back to the blanket, bent down, and picked up her wine. Before she could take another sip, he came up behind her and grabbed the glass from her hand, setting it safely on the ground.

She turned on her heel. "You took champagne from me at our first dance. Why do you keep doing that?"

"I'm guessing you've never been drunk."

"And I, sir, am not now."

"I disagree." He silenced her by lightly pressing a finger to her lips when she looked to protest. "The mere fact you keep calling me *sir* is indication enough."

Just foxed enough, she kissed his finger as he moved it away, brazenly stared at him, and laughed.

"Nicolette." His voice was an unheeded warning.

She cleared her throat with a chuckle and stood before him with her hands tucked behind her. The picture of innocence she was not. There was a clear dare in her arched brow and blue eyes.

"What am I to do with you?" he asked, only half-serious. He certainly knew what he *wanted* to do with her.

She quirked her mouth. "You could kiss me."

Her matter-of-fact response threw him momentarily. He ran his hands down the outside of her arms until their fingers were linked, then bent his head and kissed the smile from her inviting lips. When he was about to pull away, she stood on her tiptoes, wrapped her arms around his neck, and kissed him back with an ardor that only comes from a lasting attraction. He had not expected that. If he had no scruples whatsoever—as his grandmother was wont to believe—he would have taken his future bride behind one of the ruins and made love to her right there.

Nicolette untwined her arms from around his neck and rested her palms against his chest. "How did you manage Miss Blanchfield this morning?" She changed the subject quite effectively.

"I told her we were going to church." Grant winked.

"I doubt she believed you. You don't look the type."

"Me? I attend more services than you might guess, my lady."

She bit away a smile between her teeth. "I have a confession to make."

"You know the difference between a toad and a frog and now declare me the winner?"

She watched her fingers play with a button on his waistcoat. "No. I wanted you to kiss me." She gazed up from under her lashes, beaming with mischief. Just foxed enough to tell the truth.

"Nicolette, you flirt dangerously."

"You see things as you wish, Your Grace."

"If only that were true." He had not stopped smiling since they left the house. He wrapped his hands around hers and kissed each palm. "I like it when you touch me."

"Why do you say these things to me?"

"I like to see you blush, sweet. And the flirting is rather nice too." He let her hands go and rubbed the pad of his thumb down her cheek.

"If merely touching you is a flirtation, which I should wonder at your definition, then what shall I do with my hands?"

He shook his head, his chest shaking with mirth. "Nicolette, you are making me insane."

She shrugged. "I told you I would drive you to bedlam. If I flirt with you, my lord, Your Grace, and Havenly, not to mention pirate captain, sir, it is only because you have eyes like the devil and you see fit to seduce every woman who has the audacity to stand in your royal presence." He might have taken that poorly except she ruined the whole effect by smiling cheekily.

"Miss Thomas, tomorrow I am going to remind you of this moment and verify who kissed whom."

"That will be perfectly fine. You are a rake. And I, being an appropriate debutante, would not know how to do such a thing." She was having difficulty suppressing the grin that played about her lovely mouth.

Later, Grant packed while she sat on a huge boulder overlooking the valley. He imagined, even in her slightly inebriated state, that she was thinking about how much her life had shockingly changed in the past month. He left her to her thoughts. He would remember this day the rest of his life. And if by some chance he found himself in the likely position of wanting to wring her neck, he would think back on today and remember how lovely, innocent, and genuine she was.

THE CARRIAGE RIDE home was not entirely silent. Before the wine wore off, Nicolette continued to speak enthusiastically and with little reservation, which suited Grant.

"Your Grace, sir, have you thought about our wedding day at all?"

"The day? No." A broad smile broke out across his face, and he clung to the reins, pushing aside all thoughts of a wedding *night*.

Nicolette missed his deliberate provocation. "Are ducal weddings always held in the city at Saint James?"

He eyed her. "If you could choose, where would it be?"

Peering at him sideways, she said, "Out on the ocean, where no one could follow." Whether deliberate or not, she'd left off the word *us*.

Grant knew she needed more time to accept the wedding. He also thought it an excellent idea. "What do you suppose the gossips would do with that?" He winked at her.

Shrugging, she said, "I really don't care anymore. They tend to say whatever they wish, truth or lie, it matters little as long as it entertains." Then she contagiously continued with the fantasy. "You could dress like a pirate."

He threw his head back, laughing. "Brilliant. If not a little odd, since I used to patrol the merchant pass, protecting against pirates during wartime."

"Truly?" She was amazed. "Is that when you learned how to sail?"

Grant nodded, keeping his eyes on the road. "And it's how I became interested in trade." He looked at her then and smiled. She seemed far too serious.

"That sounds frightening. You might have been killed."

"That is the general hazard. The Earl of Richfield and I served on the same ship. It's good to have someone watching your back. He saved me from a few bad moments, and I saved him from several," Grant said matter-of-factly. It was a decade ago when they were both just young enough to believe themselves invincible.

"Is that why you trust him so much?"

"I've known Mitchell my whole life. That's why I trust him so much." He glanced down at her, then back to the road. "I joined the Royal Navy because he did, and I promised his mother that he'd come home."

"And who promised that you'd come home?"

Grant shrugged with little concern. "No one, I guess."

Her eyes reflected the pain of that statement. "I'm glad you came home in one piece. Were you ever hurt?"

He sighed heavily and leaned into the horses. This was not a good subject. His wounds would have been fatal had Mitchell not been there to drag him to safety and then see him home. Ironically, they'd both gone to watch over Mitchell's brother Phillip, but the same battle that wounded Grant had taken Mitchell's brother.

He answered, removing the memory from his voice. "Once or twice." He reined in the horses, then reached over and caught Nicolette's hand. "Nothing more than a scratch or two. Now, can we talk of something else?"

Her grip on his hand, as if she were truly frightened for him, gave him pause. The tender gesture struck his heart. She smiled bravely up at him. "Well, if you came dressed as a pirate, I would bring an extra shoe to protect you."

There was a fierceness about her, a passionate goodness that often threw him off guard. He laughed at the reminder and appreciated her vulnerability to make light of a terrifying situation. Turning his attention back to the road, he put both hands to the ribbons again. He needed the extra grip for balance, something his life had been out of for a while. She captivated him. Every moment today had been full of laughter and fun and teasing banter. Not to mention a kiss he'd never forget because she'd initiated it, then admitted to wanting it. That had almost been his undoing.

"If I am dressed as a pirate, then what shall you wear? I really do think only one of us should be wearing trousers."

"I'll be a kitchen wench."

"Never. You'd be my captive." And then he thought of something better. "Or the cook. Yes, I think you should be the cook. You're rather good at it."

Her cheeks turned a rosy pink. "I think I'd like that." She turned her attention to the scenery, and they fell into thoughtful silence.

Grant pondered her questions and responses. This woman barely knew him, and yet she cared that he'd been injured. She cared that he'd come home. Truth was, he and Mitchell were both more than lucky to have returned at all. Of course, his grandmother had been happy when he returned for her own selfish reasons. She had been livid when he joined the war effort. Heirs were not to be risked on the battlefield, not even for a good cause. It was a duty for second sons. When he returned, his grandmother had chosen to punish him with silence.

It had taken place long ago, and yet this woman beside him responded with relief that he'd returned safely. Sincere, genuine, relief. He wasn't accustomed to being cared for with open honesty.

CHAPTER 28

Two days after the toad-finding contest, the household packed and returned to London to put the final plans in motion and ultimately attend the wedding. Nicolette felt as if she stood in the eye of a great hurricane. A frenzy of hands poked her with pins, measured yards of fabric against her body, and spun her about on a seamstress's platform like the rotors of a windmill.

She was happy to allow Aunt Lydia and Arlienne and even Miss Blanchfield carte blanche over fabrics, style, shoes, and invitations.

She would not voice her true wish to marry somewhere other than the city where her reputation had been damaged.

Soon the constant barrage of well-wishers, gifts, and flowers began arriving, all colliding with a stack of pamphlets being handed out by the best gossips in town with titillating information concerning a quick engagement between a duke and a most fortunate orphan.

Nicolette's nerves were raw and her emotions teetered somewhere on the brink of sanity—she felt her life had become quite insane some time ago—her soundness of mind being just out of reach.

Grant was no help on that accord. He showed up from time to time, reminding her as often as possible that they would be married soon and that the gossip seekers would then find their entertainment elsewhere.

He went out more nights than she, and jealousy surged through her to think he might be with the one woman who had the power to bring her down. Joanna Featherbe. It was no secret that he'd at one time been attracted to Miss Featherbe, and her fears, however unjustified, would not leave her alone.

As much as she tried, Nicolette could no longer deny her feelings. The jealousy, the bitterness, the pettiness, were all a result of this overwhelming desire to be loved by the man she'd fallen in love with. He had made no overtures to her, and because of that she refused to reveal her feelings. She had trusted him with too much already.

Grant escorted her to the theater, pairing up with Frances and her new husband, Lord Rutledge. They sat in Grant's private box. Eyes were trained on them, and she remembered how she'd secretly watched him from the gallery months before. She could only imagine what people were thinking, but according to Grant, whispers would die down or at least be ruled irrelevant in light of their engagement. Regardless of the pamphlets, being seen together eliminated the mean spirit from the billowing gossips and turned them into the couple to court.

Sitting with Frances did not cure her melancholy as she'd hoped. Seeing her friend beaming with happiness and the way her husband adored her with every touch, every look, every word, only reminded her that she'd been denied the only thing she ever wanted.

Grant tried, he truly did, but Nicolette's good nature was clouded with envy for her friend's relationship and jealousy of Joanna Featherbe, a woman she'd never met.

When the curtain fell for intermission, she stood and excused herself. In the country she could breathe, but here in London she felt squeezed and crowded. She understood the reasons for being here, but she couldn't shake the overwhelming urge to flee. She cut through the crowd, avoiding eye contact with everyone, and didn't stop until she'd left the building through the front doors. She doubted she'd find happiness in a marriage built on witty banter and tolerance for one another's company. Panic seized her chest; tears stung the backs of her eyes. She rounded a post and leaned against the opposite side.

She heard the quick clip of Grant's shoes before she saw him. He rushed around the pillar, concern etched in his brow. "What happened in there?"

"Nothing. I just needed air. The auditorium is stifling."

He leaned an arm against the pillar, creating a small bubble of privacy. "You scared the devil out of me." He couldn't yell or rail at her, not here. But she could hear it in his loud, hissing whisper so close to her ear that it made her shiver.

She leaned her head back against the hard stone and shut her eyes wondering if he was angry because she'd embarrassed him, or was it fear she heard?

Nicolette smelled a hint of cigar smoke in the distance. She heard the murmur of several stragglers who'd wandered outside for fresh air as she had done.

"Would you care to go back inside for refreshment?"

It was a simple question, a common question, and Nicolette understood Grant's attempt to make her feel comfortable. Anxiety knotted her stomach, and the suggestion of punch or wine made her throat convulse. She could not face the crowd again.

"No, thank you. But don't let me keep you."

Exasperation poured from him. "Nicolette, you cannot stay out here alone. I'm not leaving you if you wish to remain."

She gazed up at him. The moonlight turned his eyes a dark amber. She wanted him to kiss her, to tell her that he had fallen in love with her. That he adored her.

What a fantasy.

Instead, she allowed her frustration to overrule clarity.

"What I wish, I cannot have."

"You can have anything you want. You'll be a duchess, the envy of everyone. You'll live in a mansion large enough to lose yourself in if you care. You'll have the protection of title and name."

"I never wanted those things. I want someone who is obsessively in love with me. Are you? Can you say that?" She felt more reckless with each word.

He couldn't seem to answer. His silence said it all.

"Nicolette." His tone patronized.

"Don't say my name like that."

"Miss *Thomas*. I think what you're looking for doesn't exist. No one is that in love. I'm not even sure my parents were that in love."

Her frustration died away with that statement. "I feel sorry for you," she said. "I truly do. I know it exists because I've seen it. And if your parents ran off, as your grandmother claims, without permission or blessing, then they had that too. I don't know what you want, Grant. I've never quite understood that. You say I'm an enigma, but I am everything you see, and you are nothing I see. You're but a shell of the beau monde. You're exactly who they created you to be."

"I certainly hope that isn't true."

"I, as well, because whereas your life will change little, mine is a forever sentence. Men are free to do as they will. My only job will be to…" She couldn't finish. The picture conjured by the thought sent blood rushing to her cheeks.

He sighed and answered for her. "An heir. That's what you think your life will be about?" He glanced away, then looked back at her. "Nicolette, I have no intention of keeping you from the life you want."

"But you have already done so." She hated that her voice sounded pleading and weak.

"I can't help what's happened. I can't change it. I can guarantee that your uncle is looking out for your best interests because this love you seek is no longer possible."

"How so?"

"Because, kitten, your reputation would not survive long enough to find a proper gentleman." He cupped her cheek.

She shook her head, but she knew it was true. If she remained unwed, only the poorest of men seeking her dowry would pursue her hand. The men of the ton would treat her as fast; the vulturous women would treat her like carrion.

"I've tried to make this transition as easy as possible for you. I know I am not what you expected, and you are not what I expected."

Her gaze snapped back to his. After her outpouring, that was all he could come up with? Not even a hint of false adoration? She held her tongue, but she could feel her nostrils flare with each breath.

"Yours is not the only life that's taken a turn."

In truth, she'd been too self-absorbed to consider what he'd given up. All she knew was that she'd fallen in love with him all over again, deeper, more completely, and she was green with outraged envy and jealousy was the mortar. It was such an ugly thing. Her heart needed protecting, and fighting was the only way she knew to do that.

Grant closed his eyes for a moment and rubbed the bridge of his nose, breathing evenly, clearly trying for control. "Let me take you home," he said simply, quietly, without rancor.

Nicolette swallowed the painful lump in her throat, turning away so he wouldn't see how much she hurt. "What about the Rutledges? How will they get home?"

"I'll send a note to Lord Rutledge." He sighed. "Nicolette," he said more softly.

"I'm fine." She wiped a tear from her cheek with her gloved hand and stepped in front of him, letting him follow her, not caring whether anyone had witnessed their conversation or caught a glimpse of her tearstained cheeks.

She waited by the road for their coach, wishing for control, almost hoping that Grant would put her in the carriage and take a hack to wherever it was he went at night. She intended to go home and cry herself to sleep, feel sorry for herself, and then wake up tomorrow and begin to accept her life as it was, again. Her whole life had been a lesson in starting over.

Grant stood back and let the footman help her into the coach. The streets were not overly crowded tonight, but still the bustle of the season made its own heat.

"Are you sure you don't wish to grab another cab to take you wherever it is you go at night?" she said as he relayed a message to the footman concerning their friends, then followed after her into the conveyance.

"Nicolette, I go home at night."

She gave him a look that said she was not so naive as to believe him.

"A lot has been asked of you. I know this isn't your dream wedding, that I'm not the dreamy husband you'd prefer, but please do me one favor—do not believe everything you hear or think you see. Whatever lens with which you view the world right now would be anything but clear."

She knew there was much truth in his statement. It was gossip she believed. She had no real proof except what she perceived through her green-tinted spectacles. And right now those lenses were fogged and blurred by the tears that had started in the front of the theater, and she couldn't seem to stop them if she tried. Embarrassment flooded her with the onslaught, and she wished to be anywhere else.

Grant reached across the seats and firmly took her arm, pulling her over to sit with him. He wrapped his arms around her and held her, and Nicolette folded her arm into his body, wrapping the other around him, crying into his shirtfront. The last time she'd cried like this was when her father died.

She gripped him as if he were a lifeboat. When he handed her a handkerchief, she childishly flung it to the dirty floor and then felt his chest rumble. She warily looked up at him and saw him smiling. And then he crushed her defenses by doing something she never would have expected from this hard, powerful man. He kissed the tears on her cheeks. When she couldn't take anymore, she leaned up and softly kissed him on the mouth.

Like a feather, she lightly brushed his lips, and he responded by kissing her back, deeper, passionately giving her what she had wanted on the theater steps but minutes before. He chased the tears down her neck and gently sucked the soft skin, threatening to leave a mark that surely would last until their wedding day. Her hands were in his hair, and she felt him pull his gloves off. With one hand he supported her back, with the other he found the bottom of her skirts, then rubbed his bare palm up the inside of her thigh. His warm fingers caressed her skin while he plundered her mouth with kisses.

An aching need built inside her, reminding her of the things he'd made her feel on the ship, and she didn't want him to stop. Not this time. Opening her mouth against his, she gave back as much as he'd given, leaning in with her hips and coaxing him closer. She felt his hand move farther up her thigh, and when she didn't think he could touch her more intimately, he softly teased and caressed her most sensitive core. She heard herself moan against his mouth, and by some instinct she moved against his hand. When he slipped a finger inside her, the sound of carriage wheels, the clopping of horse hooves, and the jingle of tack all fell away along with the rest of the world.

The heat of his palm against her, the feel of his fingers inside her, were so delicious, so passionately wicked, that she could not decipher whether her racing pulse was the pleasure of his hands or the excitement of something forbidden. They weren't married. She wasn't even sure if married people did such things. Begetting heirs was one thing. This was something else. Something that had nothing to do with having children. It was devilishly erotic. When she didn't think she could feel any better, Grant shifted to rubbing the sweetest, most sensitive spot with his thumb while his fingers touched the depth of her soul. She writhed against him, her hips participating of their own accord, driven to the height of ecstasy without caution or shame. Desire shot through her veins and then straight to the place between her legs until she gasped in waves of pleasure. He held her still, tightly clasped to him until her heart slowed and the pulse between her legs stopped.

"God, Nicolette, I want you. Every sound you make, every breath, every little movement. You are in my blood, sweet," he whispered, a raspy sound against her ear.

She was surprised to hear his breathing as labored as hers. Did he feel the same pleasure? Grant buried his face in the curve of her neck and smoothed her skirts back into place.

It gave her time to catch her breath. She felt more relaxed than she had in a fortnight. She blindly reached up and stroked his cheek while hiding her face against his chest.

"Marriage may have some merit after all," she murmured against his shirtfront.

"Thank God." He let out a deep breath, and she felt him lay his head back against the seat.

CHAPTER 29

Somehow Nicolette survived the week leading up to her wedding. She survived the gawking gazes from across park meadows. She survived halted whispers during harmless outings. And she managed to gather her fear into a fake sense of security all because she wanted what Grant had said in the cab to be true. She wanted to ignore what she thought she knew, what she thought she saw, and believe in something that could not be true.

And when things could not get any more confusing, Claudia woke her the day before the wedding far too early for comfort. She handed her a piece of toast while hurrying her through her morning ministrations. Nicolette stood by and allowed her maid to dress her like a doll.

"A traveling costume, Claudia? Is this necessary? I thought I'd spend my last day around a pot of chocolate and a tower of scones."

"Not today, my lady. Today we travel." Claudia took a crusted corner of unfinished toast from her hands and hurried her onto the vanity chair. She brushed out her hair, then pinned a rather large hat to her head, one that she'd remove the minute they stepped up into the cab.

"And where did you say we are going?"

"It's a surprise." Claudia did not waste any energy on explanations; she simply used all of it to hurry Nicolette from the room.

What kind of trip does a bride make the day before her wedding?

Two coaches waited outside the parlor window, one full of trunks and boxes and one saved for occupants. The one with trunks pulled away with a heavy sway while the other waited with the steps let down.

"Where are we going?" she asked as Arlienne entered the room fully dressed for travel.

"Here are your gloves—it's time to leave," was Arlienne's response.

Nicolette pulled on the blue kid gloves dyed to match her ensemble and followed her cousin from the room. She turned to examine the cheery yellow room, the one with canaries and yellow striped wallpaper. She'd once considered this room like a cage. Now she only saw the beauty of the people whom she'd entertained. Arlienne had first asked her about Havenly in this room. She'd had tea with Frances, sitting on the yellow silk sofa with pillows that matched the wallpaper. She'd played with Master Andrew on the thick Aubusson rug that almost covered the entire floor.

She inhaled, allowing the crisp, clean scent of polish to paint a vivid memory of every good thing that had happened here. Before leaving the room, she breezed by the settee, picked up a striped pillow, and turned it on its side so that the stripes opposed the room's balance. Sometimes imperfection is the cornerstone of good memories, and she wanted to remember this place.

She met Arlienne and Aunt Lydia at the front door.

"Aunt Lydia, am I to be moved into the duke's apartments the day before the wedding?"

"No, darling," her aunt said while she tied Nicolette's hat ribbon under her chin. "The duke has prepared a surprise."

"Will I like it?" Anticipation turned over in her belly, and her nerves were alive with pleasure.

"I believe so." Aunt Lydia winked at Arlienne.

Just outside London, Nicolette realized they were headed in the direction of Havenly. East Sussex was too far for a day trip, and she was left to wonder how on earth she'd be married at Saint James tomorrow morning. Certainly the wedding had not been called off. To her surprise, just the thought of a postponement made her throat painfully tight.

She'd grown to anticipate the wedding because somewhere inside, at a time she could not name, she'd started wanting this.

When the glorious three-story estate came into view, the question of where they'd marry was put to rest. The grounds were decked in splendor with immaculately tended flowerbeds. New shrubs in large pots tied with white ribbon lined the drive. A canopy of vines had been placed for the guests to walk under on the way to the front door. The scent of roses filled the great entry hall, greeting Nicolette even before she stepped onto the marble floor.

A cascade of servants helped with the unloading, and an upstanding woman with jangling keys showed her to the master suites. Why she hadn't expected this, she couldn't say, except she'd never dreamed of such luxury, and now this was home.

Her rooms, decorated in muted colors of pale pink and cream, were not quite her taste but she could not dispute the beauty of them either. Claudia soon found her way to the grand room, and the two of them unpacked Nicolette's whole life.

When she came upon the little heart-shaped pewter box, she excused Claudia. Everywhere she had gone in life, the necklace in the box followed her. Since the age of five, she'd cherished the gift from her papa. Now it was the only tangible evidence of his love for her. Of his existence. She sat on the edge of the bed, lifted the lid, and pulled out the crystal necklace. Immediately the cuts in the glass caught a beam of sunlight and a spray of tiny spots in rainbow hues fanned across the walls, the ceiling, the floor. She tilted it back and forth. When she was young, it all seemed like magic. Now she understood the science, the way the cuts in the glass bent the light just so, how it created a colorful mosaic of fine polka dots. She understood too that it was the memory of her papa that made it priceless. Miss Blanchfield had forbidden her from wearing it, but she'd never need worry on that account. Her father had said it was like a magic bean and that she should leave it in its box where the giants could not find it.

Although she no longer believed in giants, she left the necklace hidden. It was her little secret treasure of memories. And thanks to Grant, she now had the box in her possession again. She hid it back in the top bureau drawer and chided herself on not thanking him for its return. She'd been unforgivably churlish these past weeks. She rarely stopped to think that this was not what he had expected either, that he had every right to be angry, and yet he'd held her while she cried and kissed the tears on her cheeks.

Somehow she'd make it up to him. But first she'd have to survive the festivities.

She didn't see Grant until the next morning. He'd slept in another part of the house, leaving her to wonder where the connecting door in her room led and what his rooms looked like. Would he come to her room, or would she go to his? Life was simpler on the ship where there had been only one room and one bed to occupy.

Claudia and Aunt Lydia were up early, and by nine o'clock Nicolette's room felt like a ship ready to sail. Servants like stevedores filed in and out of her rooms with arms full of wedding paraphernalia. And just when she'd thought everything was finished, a seamstress showed up to sew fresh lilac around the hem of her gown.

"It's a madhouse out there." Arlienne buzzed with pure joy as she waltzed into the room. "Richard said everything's in order, the men are prepared, and the servants are running."

Every room at Havenly would be filled by evening's end, along with the inn in the village. The gala would continue for three days, replete with activities from hunting to whist and croquet. At least one hundred of the ton's most elite and those closest to the families had been invited to the festivities along with the villagers.

Claudia made beautiful work of Nicolette's hair, piling it loosely atop her head in graceful waves and curling tendrils. There were no fancy adornments, just a simple veil attached to a ring of wildflowers including sprigs of lilac to match her hem.

The dress, a remarkable understatement, lacked the heavy lace and ruffles that, in general, brides managed to only get lost in. Nearly white satin made up the bulk, covered with a sheer, shimmering overlay of lavender. It was unpretentious in its simplicity and beautiful for all that. It hailed a low, decadent neckline, high waist, and flowing detachable train to make mingling and dancing easier, which delighted Nicolette. No tripping over gowns, no stepping on toes. Well, perhaps a few toes. She smiled at her reflection and allowed a moment of pure pleasure. Then she stepped off the pedestal in her room and gave over to the butterflies flapping madly in her stomach.

"Oh, Nicolette, you're beautiful," Arlienne said.

A knock sounded and every head in the room turned in unison. Aunt Lydia opened the door and returned with several black boxes too small to be anything but jewelry.

"I believe these are for you," her aunt said. "We'll leave you to the note and meet you downstairs." Her aunt gave her a kiss on the cheek.

"Arlienne, will you stay?" Nicolette asked. If it was indeed jewelry, she'd need help with it, and besides, she'd been hoping for a moment alone with her cousin.

Nicolette broke the wax seal on the note and read.

"Well, is it from the duke?" Arlienne asked impatiently.

Nicolette shook her head. Holding the note, she dropped her hand to her side. "It's from the duchess. She said these belonged to his mother and that she wished for me to have them." Nicolette's hands shook as she put aside the note and picked up one of the boxes. In one velvet-lined box was a brilliantly understated single-drop diamond necklace and in the smallest box, a pair of diamond drop earrings that matched. But the third box was the most curious of them all. Inside was a note addressed to Grant's mother.

Nicolette sat at her vanity.

> *My love,*
>
> *Although we make haste, I purchased these in the village where we changed horses. I wish it could be more, but you outshone every precious jewel. You granted me your love, and I would grant you your every wish from this day forward. If we must wake the vicar, it will be but a fond memory to share with our children.*

IT WAS ONLY A KISS

I would give up a dukedom to love you. You are my heart.
My soul. My strength to face another day.

Yours always,
David Arthur Sutherland

With tears threatening, Nicolette handed the fragile note to Arlienne to read.

"Holy Moses," Arlienne breathed.

"Arlienne, they named him Grant because of this note. *You granted me your love*, he says to her. Havenly told me that his parents loved each other. This is proof." She pointed to the note now in Arlienne's hands.

"It's very sweet."

"It's an apology from the duchess. I wonder if Havenly knows."

"You must stop calling her the duchess because, my dear, in a short hour you will be the Duchess of Havenly. Do you understand?"

"Arlienne, this is proof of what I told him."

"And you can tell me all about it later. If you have not forgotten, it's your wedding day."

She took the note from Arlienne then packed it neatly back in the box. She allowed her cousin to help her into the jewelry while her insides turned with anticipation. Grant's parents had loved each other. That gave her hope. And even more so that his grandmother had made sure she knew.

She grabbed her train and followed Arlienne to the side entrance under the portico where coaches were loaded and unloaded. Beside a navy-blue lacquered coach, the ducal seal stamped on the side, stood her betrothed.

Aunt Lydia met her as soon as she cleared the back of her dress from the open doorway. She hugged her, then kissed her cheek.

"His Grace has been wonderful. The surprise was all his idea. Enjoy, my love," her aunt whispered in her ear, then stood back. Arlienne hugged her next.

Uncle James waited halfway between her and the coach with a proud fatherly smile. Her uncle bowed over her hand as if she'd already become the duchess, then kissed her cheek. "It will all work out; you'll see."

"Thank you, Uncle. I'm sure it will."

Her legs felt weak; her heart felt like a racing horse. Grant bowed over her hand. He helped her into the coach, and for a moment she wondered if bad luck was due since she'd seen him before the vows.

Her soon-to-be husband sat directly across from her, far too handsome for comfort, wearing a contagious grin.

He cleared his throat as if he were as nervous as she. "You're absolutely gorgeous, love."

She shyly looked up from watching the bouquet she held in her hands. "As are you, Your Grace."

The horses shook their tack, eager to move. Oddly, one whinnied as if announcing the private spectacle.

"They're outspoken," she said as the wheels underneath them gave a little kick forward. They were headed somewhere, and by the look of it, they were completely alone on the journey.

"Since I lost the toad-finding contest and there's no time for a rematch, I wonder if you'd perhaps take pity on me and use my name today?" He smiled while he asked, but his voice had an underlying pleading tone.

"A wedding present perhaps? If it pleases you… Grant." How could she deny such a small pleasure on her wedding day?

"It pleases me more than you know." He examined her with a certain amount of adoration, not the kind that speaks love but the kind that sparks a fire. "Are you curious where we're headed?"

"If you must know, I'm dying to find out. I can't imagine why you'd risk such bad luck, seeing the bride before the nuptials." She'd never been one for superstition, but today of all days, she might have been tempted to practice some just in case. "Are we doomed, Your... Grant. Have patience with me. I am trying."

"You've been a lesson in patience since I met you." He said it with a smile, but the statement rang true. "And I believe we would be doomed if I'd begun this day any other way. It is something of a tradition in my family. One I find selfishly pleasing, in fact."

She looked at him, eyes narrowed.

"You want a clue?"

"No. That would spoil the fun." She bit her lip and placed the bouquet next to her before folding her arms while scrutinizing the man, who gave nothing away. He scratched his bottom lip, and suddenly she didn't care anymore where they were headed. Her thoughts were on a kiss. Then it dawned on her. She pointed at him. "You're eloping with me, aren't you?"

He gazed at her thoughtfully, tilting his head. "If I say yes, would that please you?"

Overwhelmed with feelings she could not control, Nicolette turned her focus to the scenery out the window, swallowed back tears, and nodded. "It's the ruins." She looked back. "Isn't it?"

She didn't need an answer; it was in his eyes. His entire countenance softened, and for a moment she made believe that he adored her, loved her, and they were a happy couple. That day of the picnic had been special. And now this special place would mean even more.

Forty-five minutes later, they were driving up the hillside, gently curving back and forth until they reached the top. To

Nicolette's delight, Frances and her husband, Lord Rutledge, were waiting for them as witnesses. Robert Donovan stood as clergy between Frances and her husband. A ship's captain was allowed to perform marriages aboard a vessel, but not on land. However, she could think of no one better to marry them.

Grant took her trembling hand and led her to stand before Robert. She hugged Frances and tried not to cry. "Thank you for being here." Nicolette then turned back to her soon-to-be husband and watched as he took both her hands in his. The breeze picked up the veil and tugged gently on her skirt, and in the distance she could see the place where she'd scooped up the little toad—or frog as it were. She saw the winding river that, a thousand years before, brought Viking longboats through the valley. The atmosphere relaxed her. She felt as if her papa were watching proudly.

She felt at home.

Captain Donovan smiled warmly. The words, the questions, he spoke were serious, and when he prompted Nicolette with *do you take this man*, she dutifully said, "I do." But when it came time for Grant to repeat the vows, she wanted to flee.

"Do you promise to love her, to cherish her?" Captain Donovan spoke the rest, but it was the word *love* that stopped her mind from moving.

"I do." Grant sounded sure, confident, honest.

She knew he lied—he cared for her, yes, but love was still foreign. Nevertheless, his thoughtfulness in bringing her here was love enough for her today.

The best part of the ceremony came when Nicolette promised to obey. Grant stopped the vows and surprised her by asking for an amendment. He handed Robert a piece of paper. First Robert eyed it, then the duke. He put on his most serious captain's expression, his bushy brows pulled together in the middle, making one fuzzy caterpillar-like eyebrow. "Do you promise to think twice before wearing another pair of trousers and to trust your husband in all matters concerning fashion?" Robert held her gaze without flinching.

Speaking was impaired by the bubbling laughter she couldn't squelch. "I..." She giggled, one hand pressed to her stomach. "I will try." And then, because a legal marriage required an agreement, she relented. "I do." She rolled her eyes skyward, smiling cheekily at God.

Before she knew it, the simple ceremony was over. Without regard to the company, Grant pulled her to him and kissed her beyond all decency until Robert cleared his throat and she heard the three attendees move away. The noise of jostling coach reins and the teeth-jarring sound of horses' bits jangled.

Robert yelled from the distance, "We'll see you at the estate."

Nicolette broke free, patted Grant's cheek, and waved at the entourage.

"Thank you so much," she said when they were alone in the meadow. "It was perfect. Did you really do this because it's tradition?"

He shook his head and brushed back a lock of her hair freed by the breeze. "No, I did this for you." Then he pointed to the simple wildflowers she carried and the ones adorning her head like a halo. "And these?"

She smiled shyly and shrugged. "I chose them for you."

He tipped her chin up and kissed her softly. "Thank you, love. A wildflower among colorless roses. Stunning."

After they were seated in the coach, Nicolette wasn't sure what to do. She smoothed her dress, trying to ignore the beautiful man seated opposite her. Whether they were truly married she wasn't sure, not until they came to the village and Grant stopped the coach at the little church.

There they had a very fast, legal ceremony with a vicar, and Nicolette was thrilled to see her Aunt Lydia and Uncle James, along with Arlienne and Richard, present. To her surprise, the vows were exactly the same, including the amendment. This time she only stopped long enough to glare at Grant. Somehow he managed not to break form, appearing the adoring husband throughout.

Breathless, Nicolette took her seat once more in the coach, wondering a little if her new husband had anything else up his sleeve.

The moment he climbed in, Nicolette was entranced by his smile.

"One more stop, love."

"No. You cannot mean it." She laughed, fanning her cheeks with her hands.

He nodded with a shameless grin. He let out a deep sigh when he sat, then took the hat from his head and laid it on the velvet seat cushions. "Just home."

"You wretch," she said with a side-glance. She loved this teasing side of him, the man who surprised her, the adoring man who didn't seem to mind her company.

He leaned his head back against the seats, a self-satisfied smirk on his face. "Did you know that our elopement makes three? I think we can consider that a tradition maker."

"Your parents eloped and we eloped." With a finger to her lip, she considered who else might have done the same.

His eyes shifted to hers and his brows lifted. "Guess."

"Hm." Then her mouth dropped open.

"Yes." He chortled.

"Your grandmother? But she's the one you said was adamant that you marry within your rank."

"Ah yes, my dear. But then she insisted I marry you. She is not as conventional as it would seem."

"Apparently not. Grant?" she said shyly. "Your grandmother sent me a gift this morning."

The sudden crease of his brow told her that he knew nothing of it.

"The earrings and necklace. Do you recognize them?"

He leaned forward and fingered the diamond drop at her throat. "I can't say I do." He sat back. "I should have sent you something."

"No, this was more than perfect. It came in three boxes, one for the necklace, one for the earrings, and one for a very special note." She watched him. Surely his grandmother would have shown him that.

"From her?"

Nicolette shook her head. "It was on old parchment paper. A note to your mother from your father on the day they eloped."

He swallowed and turned his focus out the window.

"You needn't say anything. I should have told you later when I could show it to you."

He turned to her, reaching across the seats again. He took greater care this time in fondling the little diamond drop.

"They're here with us, Grant. Your mother and father and my papa, they're all here. Will we be a happy couple for them?"

He looked up from under his lashes. "No, we'll be happy for us."

She took advantage of their proximity. Placing her hands on either side of his cheeks, she rubbed his mouth with her thumb, then leaned forward. She kissed his forehead.

He chuckled, removing her gloved hands and kissing each one, then leaned back against the seat. "I think you missed."

"I never miss."

"I look forward to you proving that later."

She felt warm all over, her cheeks burning. "What will the guests think when they realize the wedding took place elsewhere?"

He nonchalantly cast a glance out the window. "I wouldn't worry about the guests. They didn't come to see a ceremony or even to celebrate our marriage. They came for a party and days of revelry and minor misconduct." He grinned. "They will not be disappointed in that. An announcement will be made before we arrive that we are well and good and married. That should satisfy even the old biddies."

CHAPTER 30

When Nicolette entered the Havenly mansion, it had a decidedly different feel. This was her home now.

Frances and Arlienne converged at the side entrance so they might rush her to her room and help her prepare for the wedded couple's announcement. First Frances, with care, dislodged the veil from the wreath of wildflowers, then helped Arlienne unhook the train from her gown and replaced it with a wide floral-embossed ribbon that circled her waist and tied in the back with a generous bow. She barely had time to preen or replace a few errant tendrils of her hair.

Frances kissed her cheek. "You are like no bride I've ever seen. The dress will have the crush downstairs chattering for weeks. I predict the weddings next year will be mimicking a certain confidently understated duchess." She said that last part with a nasal tone and her chin held high.

They giggled and Arlienne, like a mother hen, shushed them and hurried them toward the entrance to the ballroom. With nerves strung tight as a violin bow, she met her husband at the top of the stairs that led into the great room. Frances gave her a little squeeze just before Grant took her hand. He raised it to his lips, kissed the back, lifted those fiery amber eyes to her, and smiled like a newly married man.

She took a deep breath. Her first tour of the ballroom had been almost two weeks ago. Then it echoed with the softest sound. Today the room swallowed the moving conversations, the tinkling of glasses, the whoosh of taffeta. The sounds did not echo off the white walls but were thrown about like the wind on the sea. She caught the hint of a word here and there, but for the most part it was like the cacophony of an orchestra tuning up, each instrument blaring a discordant note. And then Houldsworth announced them, and the entire symphony of voices went still.

"Are you ready for this, Duchess?" Grant asked.

Her brain was frozen until he said *duchess*. "What have we done, Grant?" She looked up at him. He didn't falter, nor did he look disconcerted in any way at her question.

"I like my gift." He bent to whisper in her ear.

"I'm terrified," she replied without hesitation.

"I know. It's like a dance. Let me take the lead." He covered her hand on his arm with a reassuring squeeze.

This man beside her who'd been all but forced to marry her held a smile as if this had always been his plan. As if he adored her. He'd prepared in secret the most glorious morning so she might be happy. Was he proud to introduce her now? She hoped so.

They descended the stairs slowly, she imagined in part to keep her from tripping and falling on her face, but it was also apparent that he wished for everyone to have their fill.

The ballroom floor had been polished to a shine. The beautiful inlaid wood in varying shades of blue and ivory made up a striking braided pattern that encircled the entire floor. There were doors that opened from the east and south sides, lined with windows that showed off the magnificent gardens beyond with a titillating view of a hedge maze. The requisite billiards and gaming rooms were off to the right, and behind the staircase were the tables of lavish food and flowing drink, taking up the large dining area. All these plans had been made without her lifting a finger. She spied her aunt and uncle in the crowd but refrained from waving.

To Nicolette's surprise, a cleric waited to bless them as they reached the bottom step. They bowed their heads, received a prayer, then Grant pulled out a tiny box from his pocket. He opened it toward her, and she beheld an exquisite ring with an oval amethyst surrounded by a dozen sparkling diamonds.

Her eyes misted. Without thinking about where they were or who was watching, she reached up on tiptoe and kissed her husband modestly on the mouth. "Thank you." She wasn't sure what was expected next. Would he put it on her finger or was she to take it from the box?

"Do you like it?" he said for her ears only.

"No, I love it!"

Grant turned to the crowd and shouted, "She loves it!"

The room erupted with cheers. He put up a hand to quiet the crowd and did one more outrageous thing that made Nicolette blush and laugh at the same time. He handed the box and ring to the cleric.

When he turned back to her, he proceeded to undo the buttons of her gloves, then carefully tugged one finger at a time until both gloves were removed. Next a waiter brought a large silver canister. Grant dropped both gloves inside the bucket, took a lit candle, and then set the gloves ablaze. As soon as a flame licked the edges and everyone could see spiraling smoke, the servant capped the canister, putting out the fire, then bowed and took the ashes away.

Grant cheered to the entire room. "To the official burning of the gloves! May my wife, Her Grace, Nicolette Marie Havenly, never touch me again with the damnable, pain-in-the-arse gloves that she insists on wearing to every event I have ever escorted her to." He looked at her wolfishly and wickedly kissed the palm of each hand.

Only a duke would dare curse in front of a sea of guests at his wedding breakfast.

With the ceremony complete, she was now pledged to the enigmatic man who held her trembling hand. They started the dancing. Before Grant released her to mingle, he said firmly, "One glass of champagne, do you understand? One."

She threw him a jaunty smile as she sauntered away. "Then I'll stick to wine."

Formal introductions continued all evening. Lines formed wherever the couple landed. And on more than one occasion they were separated to play host and hostess. Nicolette knew very few people, but most of them treated her with the grace and honor and respect due her new title. Frances then came and curtsied in front of her, causing both girls to giggle themselves into a fit, at which point they excused themselves from the room for a breath of fresh air.

"Nicole, you are ravishing. I mean it. And the way the duke looks at you... Well, it's simply adorable." Frances was beaming. "I'm so glad you were the one who met him that night at the theater and not the rest of us. We would have made cakes of ourselves and embarrassed our mothers no doubt."

Nicolette smiled, drying the tears caused by the kind of irreverent laughter she and Frances were famous for. "I am happy about that too, God help us all. Well, mostly God help Grant." And the giggles started all over again.

She didn't notice how long Grant had been standing there, but when he spoke it was with grave concern.

"Nicolette? What is it?"

The man must think her in tears. Frances was good enough to stifle a giggle behind her hand and left the two of them alone. Nicolette cleared the laughter from her throat and straightened to her regal height, all five feet, four inches of her.

"I'm sorry." She tried her best to look contrite, but it wasn't working.

"I'm not sure what I married." He grinned, shaking his head in mock disbelief.

"I warned you about bedlam. I told Frances that I was glad I married you, but then I ruined it all by saying, 'God help us all.'" She bit back a smile. Her throat quivered with mirth.

Grant checked over her head, then spoke with all earnestness. "How many glasses of wine have you had?"

She reared back with feigned innocence. "Why none, Your Grace. And no champagne either. I am simply drunk on laughter."

Gerald Clifton and his entourage of bores, including one Miss Victoria Helmsley who had spent more than her due weaving a basket of lies during the past several weeks, approached them for the requisite bow, curtsy, and mannerly adulation.

Nicolette could not clear her head of the words *toady* and *harpy*.

Wishing only to move on and forget the pain these people had caused, Nicolette requested a dance from her husband. It was the first time in her life that she had ever asked a man to dance. It seemed appropriate. And Grant seemed more than pleased to oblige.

It was nearly two in the morning when they took up their last dance. The party would continue until dawn, but the bride and groom would retire, leaving the guests permission to do as they pleased.

"You are smiling at me like a pirate. What will our friends and family think?" she asked.

"Our friends will snicker, and your family is liable to cuff me in the eye… again," he answered cheerfully.

"You'd drag me away from my own wedding celebration?"

"Aye. I'll carry the lassie oop the stairs if'n I moost, sweet." He cocked a brow and winked a piratical eye. The accent and winking made her legs feel limp and wobbly.

"I shouldn't like to disappoint the pirate captain."

He smiled warmly. "You could not if you tried."

He picked her up slightly as they whirled around. "If you step on my foot one more time, I'm going to be limping to bed and people will wonder if I have gout."

"That kind of flattery will take you about as far as the first step." She bobbed her head toward the staircase.

"Perfect. I can manage from there." He twirled her off the floor, linked her arm with his, and escorted her toward the stairs.

When they had taken the first step, he stopped and turned to her. "Shall I carry you the rest of the way, or do you think you can manage it?"

"Have you not caused enough scandal, Your Grace?"

"Not nearly. You do remember the way I carried you onto the ship?" The mischievous gleam in his eye told her that he had no compunction about repeating the same act.

"I'd prefer to walk if it's all the same."

He bowed and wrapped her arm around his. They took each step regally and then, against all propriety, when they reached the top step he turned and swung her up into his arms. The room was alight with boisterous laughter. She could do naught but tuck her head, hiding her fiery cheek on his shoulder.

"You wicked man," she whispered.

"Champagne, Duchess?" he asked without a hint of remorse.

She nodded into his shoulder. He then, to Nicolette's great mortification, turned once again toward the crowd and shouted, "The bride is demanding champagne!"

Between the loud guffaws and the cheers, Nicolette heard a few encouraging phrases from the male population, making her glad to hide behind the duke's wide shoulders.

They reached the master suites, and Grant grabbed her close and whispered in her ear, sending a chill down her spine and causing gooseflesh to appear on her bare neck and naked arms. "You take one minute more than an hour, and I will come find you."

"How provoking. And if I bar my door?" She leaned against the door to her suite.

Grant pounded a fist on the closed door. "Then the Viking shall come to break it down."

She tilted her head and bent a brow. "I believe you would."

"Darling, it isn't always necessary to play nice." With his hand on the doorknob, he leaned in for a kiss.

She heard the door click, the hinges move, and she almost fell into the room. He caught her arm and chuckled. "One hour."

CLAUDIA HELPED Nicolette bathe and dress. With only an hour, Nicolette had little time for nerves. She enjoyed kissing, enjoyed his touch, and was shamelessly hoping Grant would do more of what he'd done in their coach two days ago, but beyond that, she had no idea what to expect.

Claudia lifted a gown of gossamer silk over her head. The fine blush-colored fabric hung from her shoulders by thin lace straps tied in a bow. Its beauty lay in the long, simple design and delicately embroidered cream flowers. With her every move, the soft silk tickled and caressed her skin.

"Your Grace." Claudia interrupted her thoughts.

"Please, Claudia, do not call me that. My name is what I

need to hear." She turned to the maid who had served her kindly and well these past three years.

Claudia smiled. "Nicolette, my lady, you are a dream. I hope the duke appreciates you."

Nicolette's smile wobbled, a knock sounded on the connecting door, and she froze. Of course it was Grant. Who else would it be? Her heart beat a thundering pace.

"Claudia, thank you. I'll be fine." With forged confidence, she steadied her voice, excusing her maid for the evening.

Nicolette watched her hand as if it belonged to someone else. Her fingers gripped the roped brass handle of the connecting door, then turned it to the right. She pushed the door open.

Grant stood tall and handsome, wrapped only in a robe.

His bare neck reminded her of the nights they'd already shared.

"I had hoped to break down the door." He flashed her his best Viking imitation.

"That won't be necessary. I'm fully willing to make good on my wedding gift." Nicolette lifted a corner of her mouth and did her best to look alluring and flirtatious, hoping to keep him off-balance if only for a while. Guessing by the shocked look on his face when she passed him en route to his suite, it worked.

Grant stood dumbfounded. "Nicolette?" He spoke in soft tones. "If your gift is to torture me, you have my undivided attention."

She called over her shoulder, "And to what do you refer?"

The master's rooms were done in dark tones of green and gold, the walls opulently paneled in rich mahogany.

She turned slowly, standing by his large, masculine bed. "My gifted obligation was to call you Grant." Saying his name was her first command of the evening since she knew he liked it and she didn't always oblige.

He shut the door, gave a throaty laugh, and conceded, "I'm

not sure if you've figured out your currency or if you're innocently playing me."

"Well, my lord, that sounds like your dilemma, not mine." She was, however, not entirely sure just whose problem it was. And at the same time, it really didn't matter because the passion in his eyes was greater than any she'd seen yet.

Only two candles burned in the large master bedroom, one on the mantel of the fireplace where a warm cozy fire was lit—adding to the romantic illumination of the bedroom—and one by the bed.

She had little time to think after that observation because Grant made quick work of the space between them. She backed up along the side of the four-poster bed, one hand on the coverlet for balance, her eyes never leaving his. And he stalked her with a decided gleam. She halted her retreat. Grant stood close enough to her that she felt his body heat as he devoured her with his eyes. At the same time, she was distracted by the rippling pulse in his corded neck.

He took her hand, bringing it to his lips. His countenance changed and his eyes were lit with confusion and awe. "God, Nicolette, do you know how beautiful you are?"

She shook her head, and for a moment she felt what it must be like to love and be loved. It was her wedding night, and she would dare to dream it. She would dare to dream it all.

"I don't deserve you." He rubbed her cold hands while her insides quaked.

She let that sink in and then replied with a courage she did not own. "I must agree with you."

He looked at the floor, a wide smile spread across his cheeks. "You make me laugh. You never cease to say something I don't expect. I like that about you."

"And I like this." She pointed to his dimple.

He held her hand to his cheek.

GRANT JOLTED AS SOON as her bare fingers touched his skin. The innocent gesture sent pangs of desire straight to his loins. He cupped her hand against his cheek and took a deep breath, then kissed her palm. Before she could do or say another thing, he swept her up in his arms and laid her in the middle of the bed, leaning over her with a knowing smile.

She gave a surprised hoot at the sudden movement but settled under his gaze while holding eye contact. With a finger she touched his lips.

"You scare me a little, Grant Havenly, but I do like your kisses."

He took her hand and held it against his heart. "I don't want to scare you."

"I know." She pulled in a cleansing breath. "I have a confession."

Her voice was dire enough to cause his brow to crease with worry.

She blinked twice. "I have no living idea what I'm doing." Then she giggled. "I hope you do."

He laughed outright. "God, I hope so too." He rolled onto his back, then changed position, propping himself on one elbow so he could gaze down at her. She rested against a pillow, honey-blond hair fanned out like a burst of sunshine. Not for a second did he believe she had abandoned all maidenly shyness with that comment. He leaned back, reached behind him, and grabbed the opened bottle of champagne from the bedside table. He poured two glasses.

When he turned to set the bottle back, Nicolette sat up on her knees and plucked a glass from his hand, almost knocking the other from his grip.

"We should toast," she said. "To wedding gifts?"

"Yours to me is torture. Consider me a most agreeable

husband," he said lightly, but the sudden finality of what they'd done filled the room. Married. He was married.

While he sat there like a dolt, she threw herself into the moment, clinking her glass with his, wearing a broad infectious smile.

She tilted the glass and promptly swallowed half the contents. "I do like champagne."

"By all means, love. That is your one glass." He was quite serious. He had not planned this marriage, but he had damn well planned on this night.

"Grant," she warned through a grin, "if you even dream of taking another glass from my hand, you may consider yourself exiled from this room." She downed the rest.

"Might I remind you whose bed you occupy?"

She rolled her eyes, the first signs of an inebriated smile played about her mouth. When he took the empty glass from her hand, she lifted a challenging brow.

Instead of refilling it, he happily handed her his glass.

She took a petite sip before handing it back, then trailed a finger down his arm until she reached the end of his sleeve where his hand rested on the bed. With a caressing touch, she traced each finger, intently watching as if she memorized each knuckle before sliding her hand over the top of his. She looked at him through her lashes, her smile gone, a smoldering passion behind her half-lidded gaze. She wanted him.

He wanted her.

Grant put down the glass, pushed himself up into a sitting position, and with both hands on her cheeks, he took her mouth in a searing kiss. His intoxicating wife grasped the lapel of his robe, no doubt for balance since Grant felt a little off-kilter himself.

He moaned against her lips, then grazed her jaw with kisses, tasting the curve until he reached her ear and sucked the soft lobe. He explored more thoroughly that part of her neck that had resulted in his downfall on the ship. The place where this night had been put into motion. He'd lain awake many nights dreaming of her, in his bed, beneath him, soft, willing, and his. Not until this moment had he believed they would finish what they'd started. Now the entire royal guard could not pull her from his arms.

The wickedly sheer gown she wore outlined her body, the peaks and valleys, the delectable indentation in the soft swell of her stomach, the shadow of womanly curls between her thighs. The gossamer silk was nothing compared to her skin. He traced the vee of her neckline until his finger disappeared between the heat of her breasts. He trailed a finger to the erect peak, teasing and taunting. She was his. Finally his. Every moan, every movement, every sexy curve.

She gasped and pulled him in closer for a maddening kiss that challenged the promise he'd made to himself to go slow, to not frighten her or hurt her. But at the moment her hands were in his hair, combing over his scalp, then gripping a handful of strands in her fists.

God have mercy, she was a passionate woman. His need to possess her was so great it went far beyond a husband's right by law—he only wished to honor her.

Before his animal instincts had the expensive silk that worshipped her body torn to rags, he pulled back and inhaled deeply.

"Do we stay kneeling?"

He almost choked. So caught up was he that he failed to notice their position. Both of them kneeling on the bed, face-to-face, a nose length apart. He laid his forehead against hers and settled his pulse before answering, barely managing to shake his head and chuckle. "No, my sweet."

In his mind he tortured himself with her question. Another time, he thought, and he'd kneel before her and show her the more erotic pleasures. Tonight, surprisingly, she was showing him how erotically pleasurable innocence could be. This was an experience foreign to him. She was a true gift and much more than he deserved or expected.

His mind tortured him for answers to the feelings that warred in him, and then he gave up and did what his heart desired most. He made love to her.

With a hand at her shoulder, he pulled on the lace bow, then leaned back and steadied her. She didn't look away as he let go the other bow on the opposite shoulder. He saw her swallow, heard her intake of breath when the delicate sheer fabric cascaded into a pool around her knees.

He traced the same path between her breasts and watched her eyes close, felt her surrender like it was his own. When his hand claimed her, he felt the tender nipple under his palm rise, harden, and he needed to untangle himself from his clothes. With one hand behind her neck, he pulled her in for a devouring kiss and shrugged one arm out of his robe, then repeated the action on the other.

He held her face and kissed her, her jaw, her neck, and this time he let himself taste the sweet hollow between her shoulder and collarbone. Cupping both breasts in his hands, he stroked her nipples, hard and soft at the same time. He bent his head and caressed her with his tongue, nudged her breast with his nose, and brushed his eyelashes against one swollen tip.

Nicolette's hands squeezed his shoulders until he felt the prick of her fingernails. It was a pleasurable assault. Supporting her back with one hand, he kissed her, pressing her onto the pillows. Once again, her hair splayed out like sweet strands of caramel. He untangled the last of her gown from her bare legs and flung it from the bed so he could see every delicious inch of her.

Her eyes remained shut. He couldn't fault her for that. But she breathed heavy with passion, the rise and fall of her breasts hypnotizing him.

The effect aroused him and left him staring, studying her as if he'd never seen a woman before. Then his fogged brain registered where he was. He saw her brows pulled together with confusion.

"What is it?" Her voice came out in a sweet whisper, a mixture of frustration and concern.

"You're just"—he almost couldn't speak—"you're the most exquisite creature I've ever seen. And I can't believe you're here."

A smile curved up her lips, and she stretched a hand toward him. Unfortunately, her eyes followed the reach, and she glanced at the standing evidence of his arousal. One eyebrow cocked, her gaze traveled the length of him, past his abdomen, his chest, and lingered on his neck. Without the sound of the crackling fire, his heartbeat would have echoed throughout the room.

She took his hand and pulled him down. "Kiss me, Grant. Before I'm afraid."

"Oh, sweet. Please don't be afraid of me. I couldn't stand it."

"Then kiss me," she said against his lips.

He did as she asked. This time when he trailed kisses down her neck, she was writhing beneath his hands while his fingers rolled each nipple, pulling gently until his trailing kisses reached her breast and he replaced his hands with his tongue. First swirling around the hard tip, then sucking gently, tugging with his teeth until she moaned with pleasure.

He massaged her hips.

For the second time that night, she grabbed his hand, but this time she pulled it down between her legs and shamelessly pressed his finger into her wet desire, showing him exactly what she wanted. He stroked the most sensitive part, sliding his finger over the swollen bud and then inside her.

"Please." Her husky voice was his undoing.

Her boldness shattered his control.

Grant could not believe what she'd done. Not shy, not afraid, just needing him as badly as he needed her. He obliged her happily, kissing her mouth and laughing when she moaned, disappointed as he took his hand away. And then he replaced it with his body. He eased inside her, slowly at first, hoping to make this as painless as possible. But his brave Nicolette pulled him deeper, tearing a primitive groan from him. It was pure torture. The kind she'd promised. Nature took hold of her, and she wrapped a leg around his waist, pulling him in. There was longing in her smoky blue eyes, and he drank her in with a lingering gaze.

She nodded up at him and he took her mouth in a fierce kiss, pressing his hips closer to hers, inching deeper. She answered by meeting his thrusts until he felt the barrier. His heart beat painfully for her. But Nicolette's beautiful face was tense with ecstasy. Her eyes squeezed shut; her nails clawed at his arms.

"You're mine, Nicolette." He said the words against her ear and quickly thrust past her maidenhood. He felt her chest heave with a shallow whimper. Her arms tensed. Her thighs tightened around him. And then she breathed. Looked bleary-eyed at him and wordlessly brought his mouth down on hers.

It was Nicolette who first moved beneath him, starting a craving he no longer wished to stop. She enraptured him with her passion. Every sound she made brought him closer.

He pressed her knees back, exposing the most sensitive part of her into contact with each thrust until he heard a moan. He chased the sound with each movement, listening to her, allowing her to lead him with a comfortable rhythm. He couldn't know if her whimpers were ecstasy or discomfort until he felt her pulse with pleasure around him. When her breathing settled a little, he picked up his own frenzied rhythm, welcoming the last pangs of her pleasure as he climaxed.

Her body went limp and soft beneath him. Arms and legs fell away, and he wondered for an irrational moment if she'd fallen asleep. Holding himself above her on his forearms, he looked at her resting. Soon he saw her cheek move and stretch into a wide grin. She gave him a sideways glance, and he raised both eyebrows.

"That was even better than the carriage ride." She stretched like a cat.

"I made some minor adjustments." He pulled away, blowing out the candle by the bed, then flipped back the covers and retrieved a clean towel from the bathing room. He dipped it in the fresh basin water, wrung it out, and brought it back to the bed. After handing it to her, he turned his back, assuming she'd wish some privacy even though they'd just completed a most intimate act.

"Minor adjustments?" she repeated, sounding a little preoccupied. "You're wicked, Havenly," she chided, then nudged him.

"Love, I think I'm nothing compared to you." He took the towel and tossed it through the open door to the bathing room, then slipped between the sheets next to his wife.

It was true. He was nothing compared to her.

As many times as his jaded path had brought him to ecstasy, never had he felt like this. Making love to her was intoxicating, refreshing, innocent and complete.

Sated, he held her close, her head nuzzled up against the side of his chest like she was meant to be there.

Stroking her love-tousled hair, he listened while her breath evened out in sleep, and he allowed himself to drift into a satiated fog.

"Grant, are you asleep?" The question came out in a loud whisper that sounded more like a clap of thunder in the dead of night.

"No." He sighed. His body convulsed with silent mirth.

"Do you think people know what we did?"

"Nicolette." He cracked a smile. "Go to sleep." The fact that she could change from pensive and serious to this delightful, animated state was beyond his comprehension. And he loved every minute of it.

"I can't sleep."

He rose on an elbow and looked at her in the dim light of the fire. "And why can't you sleep?"

"It's rather embarrassing, don't you think?"

He laughed and fell back onto the pillows. "Are you embarrassed?"

"I think I should be, but I feel too good to be embarrassed. Do you think that's normal?"

"I don't think there is anything normal about you, thank God in heaven."

CHAPTER 31

*G*rant arranged to breakfast with Nicolette in their room. Though it was his bedchamber they slept in, he considered it theirs. In fact, he'd planned to refurbish her rooms and hoped by the time it was completed she might choose to stay in his bed every night.

He left her to her morning ministrations and went in search of coffee. The sun-filled morning room reserved for family smelled of freshly ground coffee beans and boasted one other occupant, his grandmother. Ignoring the sideboard of eggs, ham, and breakfast tarts, he headed for the silver coffeepot.

"No satisfied smile this morning?" The dowager's eyes raked him severely.

"Of course, Grandmother." He smiled, refusing to fall for their normal grumpy repartee.

She eyed him suspiciously like she had something on her mind.

"Nephew, you're awake," Enid said as she breezed into the cheery room.

"Do me a kindness, ladies, and keep my wife company this morning while I join our guests for a morning ride?"

"I imagine Nicolette is not feeling up to it," Aunt Enid stated. "I remember my wedding night. I do hope you were gentle, nephew." She sat opposite the dowager at a quaint round breakfast table.

Grant nearly scalded his throat, stepping back just in time to miss spilling coffee down his white lawn shirt. He swiped a hand down his chest, reassuring himself that he'd managed to sidestep the hot black brew, but the conversation was another matter.

"Enid!" His grandmother tried a reprimand but ruined it by turning a devilish smile on Grant.

"My wife is well. I have not beaten her, I assure you. I only ask because Nicolette does not sit a horse. She had little time during her childhood to learn the sport, and I feel at least one of us should be present this morning." He topped off his cup. "She's also not used to playing hostess. If you'd lend your support, I'd be in your debt."

The dowager slid a gaze—minus a monocle—over his entire person. "I'd say you already are, dear boy."

"You win, Grandmother." He kissed her temple.

"We both do."

Nicolette and the Dowager Duchess of Havenly sat quietly in front of a bay window overlooking the back lawns, a checkered board placed between them. The dowager set the round tokens in their appropriate boxes, intent on placing them directly in the center of each square.

"Thank you for the company. His Grace insisted I stay behind this morning." Nicolette concentrated on her burgundy-dyed tokens, feeling somewhat guilty.

"Grant is a good man." The dowager slid a black piece diagonally to the right.

Nicolette could not be sure whether the dowager meant to compliment her grandson or if she questioned Nicolette's feelings about marrying him. After all, Nicolette did agree that he was a scoundrel that first day she came to Havenly.

"I've never doubted that he's a good man." Nicolette put her hands in her lap and paused the game until the dowager looked up from the table. "Do you think my hand could be truly forced into a marriage if I didn't think the man good or kind?" Her purpose was to reassure, but she feared the question came out a bit brash.

"Nicolette, I used to think Grant had met his match in me, but I was wrong. The universe goaded me along with a false sense of superiority where he is concerned until you were grown and ready to challenge his sanity."

Nicolette knit her brow but couldn't help the sheepish, satisfied smile that snuck up her cheeks. "His sanity?"

"Oh yes." The dowager's eyes gleamed with pride, something that Nicolette assumed never happened, at least not often. "He will never be sane with you by his side. But for all that, he'll never be bored or unhappy or disillusioned or interested in another woman." She raised her brows, picked up a black game piece, then jumped it across the board, snagging two of Nicolette's red disks.

Nicolette watched her in awe, not for her game play but for her wisdom. "Are we playing draughts or chess, Your Grace?"

"You may call it whatever you wish, my dear. You are a duchess. Although I suspect you have a natural fortitude that doesn't require the title." The dowager's eyes softened.

"Thank you," she said sincerely. "As I suspect you do, madam."

"Never doubt it," the dowager said with mock severity.

THREE HOURS LATER, Grant entered from the back of the house, dusty from the morning ride, a little hungry and curious where his wife had gone. She didn't appear among the whist players, nor had he seen her on the grounds playing croquet. But he did see his grandmother and his aunt Enid sitting quietly over tea in one of several open salons. Careful to stop and greet his guests, he slowly made his way from threshold to settee where he hoped to glean something about Nicolette's morning adventures.

He reached his grandmother and bent over her chair to kiss her cheek.

"Your wife is a gem," she said as he straightened.

He greeted his aunt in the same way.

The rooms open for games were each provided with finger foods for those not interested in luncheon or those who'd missed it completely.

"I imagine I played her into boredom, but we had a lovely visit this morning."

He motioned for a servant to fill a plate from the side table. "Would you happen to know where my wife is?"

"She spent several hours with the guests, then went off to find her friends," his grandmother offered.

Enid added, "I saw her climbing the stairs not long ago. Perhaps she's resting before dinner."

"You're probably right." He turned to leave, then changed his mind, addressing his grandmother and aunt once again. "How would you say she's doing? Does she seem to be enjoying herself?"

"I suggest you ask her. The woman knows her own mind." His grandmother dismissed him with a hand, then winked.

He followed Enid's advice, taking the stairs to the west wing where the family apartments were. After discarding his jacket on the lounge in his dressing room, he rolled up his sleeves and washed his face.

When he emerged from his dressing room, he eyed the adjoining door to the mistress's suite, debating whether to knock or walk in. If she was napping, which would not be surprising, a knock would disturb her. If he barged in and she was indecent...

Done. With an anxious grin, he decided on surprise. He'd yet to meet a married man who failed to learn things the hard way. There was nothing wrong with trial and error, he told himself.

He did, however, compromise on a short knock while opening the door.

"Grant!" Nicolette yelped, jumping back a pace from the bureau she was rifling through as if he'd caught her in the act of misbehaving. She wore only her thin chemise and stays.

A warmth of embarrassment was his reward for such folly. He wished for pockets to jam his hands into, but his riding breeches had none.

"Forgive me for startling you." He was truly contrite.

"It's your house. Do you need something?" she asked while scouting the room wildly until her focus landed upon a robe haphazardly draped across the bed.

Although he was rather pleasantly arrested at seeing her half-dressed, he lost his smile over her comment about *his* house. He wrinkled his brow, snatching up the robe. He walked the short distance, holding the fine silk at arm's length, then turned his head away when he reached her, taking note when she slipped her arms into the sleeves. He let the fabric settle over her shoulders and took a seat a safe distance away on her bed, sinking into the thick rose-colored counterpane.

Scanning the room, he couldn't imagine the decor being to her liking, and her comment about this being his house upset him. What their individual roles would be after the marriage had not been discussed. The past several weeks had been a whirlwind of planning and, with the exception of that first week at Havenly when the betrothal had been signed, they'd spent little time alone.

"I brought food if you're hungry."

"I had a bite earlier, thank you." She shut the top bureau drawer, tied the sash at her waist, then turned to address him, leaning back against the maple dresser. She licked her lips and examined a porcelain atomizer shaped like a rosebud resting on the bureau. "I played draughts with your grandmother today. I like her."

"She adores you."

He saw a wisp of a smile on her lips before she turned back to the dresser. "She told me that I challenged your sanity." A long, tapered finger dusted the edge of the pristine maple.

"She's perceptive but not always right."

"I imagine we all fall somewhere on that spectrum." Her shoulders rose on a deep breath. "I don't wish to make you insane." She bit into a smile.

"Don't you?" He padded up behind her, placed his hands on her shoulders, and kissed her neck. She tilted her head to give him better access. "I'm in your debt, kitten," he whispered against her shoulder.

In his position, he could see her fumbling with the heart-shaped jewelry box. He'd never asked about it again and he wouldn't now either, not while she was in such a good mood.

She crossed her left arm over her chest, blindly reaching for his hand resting on her opposite shoulder. Her fingers closed around his, and she used the grip to twirl around until they faced each other. With her other hand, she traced her fingers down the length of his arm until both their hands were linked.

Pressed close, holding hands, with her face turned up to his, he lightly kissed her nose.

"The Earl of Richfield didn't come—why not?"

He kissed the side of her mouth. "Because our wedding was planned quickly, and he had business to attend. Rest assured he's loyal to a fault. I think you'll like him."

"We'll see. If he's anything like you"—she gripped his shirt and playfully yanked—"I'm bound to find fault." She stretched on tiptoe while pulling him down for a proper kiss.

As soon as he leaned in for a deeper connection, she let her hands fall away and ducked her head, a giggle on her lips. She twisted around until her back was to him.

His arms felt empty when she pulled free. This yearning inside him to be in constant contact with her was foreign. That this small woman could make him feel so deeply was humbling.

She focused her attention back to the drawer, then pulled out the jewelry box. "I never thanked you for this."

"It was wrong of me to keep it, but I'd been searching for the rightful owner so long that I fancied it mine."

"Do you really think it holds the secret to treasure?" She held it between them, a finger caressing the molded braid that wrapped around the edge.

"Doubtful, but someone believes it does or you'd never have been in any danger. Perhaps it has a curse. It certainly did something to me. For all my curiosity, I was shackled with a bride."

She punched him lightly in the gut for his answer, her blue eyes shining with mirth. "This pewter heart started it all. If you weren't planning to return it, then why did you bother finding me and then following me to the theater where, I might add, you mentioned nothing about it?"

He had to mentally shake his head for such a blunder because his entire purpose for following her was to glean information about the inscription engraved in the metal. "I had hoped to covertly gather evidence. Instead, I found a woman who intrigued me more than the mystery."

"I intrigued you?" she asked, pulling in her chin with a satisfied smile.

"Very much." He traced the curve of her jaw. "Too much. A first-year debutante following a known scoundrel into the unguarded chambers of the actors' realm? Who wouldn't be intrigued?"

She blinked slowly. "I wouldn't have followed just anyone, you know."

"Oh? Shocking." He grinned unrepentantly. "What made you follow me? You compared me to an alligator."

"I believe it was a crocodile," she said, correcting him. "Besides, I found you equally intriguing. What kind of mysterious, self-important man seduces an unsuspecting girl to follow him into an actor's parlor unless he has something nefarious planned?"

"Self-important? Seducing? I'll accept mysterious, my lady, but I did not seduce you."

"But you wanted to." She held his gaze without wavering.

He blinked and shook his head with mock severity. "I am shocked at your innuendo."

She chuckled. "After the trouser fiasco, I didn't imagine shocking you was still possible."

"Oh yes. Very much so."

Her cheeks pinkened, and she shyly refocused her attention on the jewelry box. "Until this was stolen—not suggesting that you stole it," she clarified, "I kept a necklace that my father gave me as a girl hidden away in this little heart. Papa told me that I was his heart and that it was only right that I should have it and the necklace."

He stepped back, his brow knitted with a certain amount of curiosity now hindered by a growing alarm. What else had she not told him? Perhaps the engraving wasn't the only clue to this mystery. He waited for her to speak. The last thing he wanted was to lead her in the wrong direction and create danger where none existed.

"Thankfully, I was wearing the necklace at the time it went missing."

"So it was empty?" he said more to himself than to her. He stepped away, rubbing his jaw. With his back to her he asked, "Where is the necklace now?"

"Back where it belongs. In here."

He turned half around to see her open the box and pull out a thin gold chain.

"It may be a rather ugly, worthless crystal, but it's priceless to me." She wore a nostalgic smile. Part grief. Part joy. "Miss Blanchfield forbade me to wear it. Of course I would not, but there is a measure of fun in taunting her."

What connection could there be, if any, to the necklace?

"Would you like to see my favorite part of the crystal?"

He nodded, forcing a smile, one he hoped didn't look as if he were covering up a newfound alarm. He followed her to the window where she practically stuck her arm outside, dangling the necklace from her hand. It took everything not to jump forward and snatch it up before she accidentally dropped it into the bramble bushes two stories below.

With fists at his sides, the muscles in his face contorted each time she twisted the chain, rotating the gem.

"There isn't enough sun left. Here." She walked to a lamp and turned up the flame.

"Nicolette, you're going to start a fire."

"Wait." She held up a hand before he could turn down the lamp. "See?" she asked, rocking the gem under the light.

On the walls and part of the ceiling, the necklace bent the light like a prism into a hundred scattered, sparkling dots.

"It's by no means a beautiful piece, but you can see how a little girl might like it." Lost in the memories, her gaze darted over the ceiling. "It's like a kaleidoscope."

"Who else knows about this necklace?" he asked cautiously.

Without looking at him, she answered, "Just my family and Claudia and Miss Blanchfield."

"Robert?"

She stopped and frowned at him. "Yes. Why?"

"May I see it?" He held out his hand.

By the chain she dangled the gem over his palm, settling the weight of it in the middle and letting the chain fall like a coil, still warm from her touch.

Testing the weight of it, he examined the fine edges that made it sparkle. Whoever cut the piece had no training in the art because it was quite ugly.

"Who told you the stone was crystal?"

"My father. Why do you ask?"

"Because"—he turned to look at her—"it's not a crystal; it's a diamond."

She laughed and gave him a wry look. "It's no such thing. You tease because I'm acting childish over a silly bauble."

"I say that because it's true. I've purchased enough fine gems to know."

She looked down at her hand, and for the first time he noticed she wore the ring he'd given her. Confusion knit her brow as if she tried to compare the two gems.

"Bring me a book."

Nicolette did as he requested and then he turned the stone over and placed it on an opened page. "If this were simple glass, you'd be able to read through it. If it's a diamond the refracted light won't allow you to see the letters clearly."

She bent her head and looked to see if what he said was true. "I can't read a word." She breathed in awe. "It must be worth a fortune considering its size. Papa couldn't have known, else why would he trust it to a child? If he'd sold it, perhaps he'd still be here," she finished on a sad note.

Grant had his own suspicions. "May I keep this for you? I'll put it in a safe place."

"You're not telling me everything. I can see the worry in your eyes."

He flashed the diamond in the lamplight again and had Nicolette look at the ceiling. "Do you recognize anything peculiar about the pattern?"

She studied it, her brows drawn in thought.

"Think, love. You've seen this before."

"When I was younger, I fancied the sparkling dots as stars because they looked like constellations."

"You fancied that because you were a very bright girl. You know the heavens, Nicolette. This diamond was cut to resemble the night sky for some reason."

"A map?"

"That would be my guess." Grant looked at her, thoughtful now. "I think your father was killed for this diamond. I think the attempt on your life was because of it."

"How can that be? My attackers never asked me anything about a diamond. It seems rather odd they would go to the trouble of killing me without even inquiring over the reasons for it."

"Robert said the Etons—or Bradentons—were eliminated over a legend, a possible treasure that rightfully belonged to the family. If no family existed to claim it, then whoever found the hoard would be free to take it, no questions asked. That one diamond alone might possibly drive someone to kill a single person but not wipe out an entire family. I don't think your assailants knew about this pendant. But your father did, and he obviously didn't think it worth his family's lives to reveal the secret. Moreover, I think the necklace works with the jewelry box. If I'm not mistaken, the half-rubbed-off letters are Gaelic. Irish or Scottish, I can't tell."

"Robert's Scottish. Do you think he could decipher them?"

Grant ground his teeth. Without proof, he didn't wish to disparage Captain Donovan's name, but he certainly wasn't letting the man anywhere close to Nicolette again either. He had to have known the two pieces went together. The question was if he'd ever translated the words himself. For now Grant felt Nicolette was relatively safe because Robert Donovan had returned to the *New Horizon*. Until he could get the words transcribed, he meant to keep all the pieces locked away together. And his wife safely locked away with him. Being newly married certainly had its advantages.

In the parlor connected to his suite, he moved a bookcase that hid a safe where he locked the necklace and jewelry box inside.

From behind him, Nicolette watched his every move.

"Do me a favor." He turned and placed a finger against her lips to hinder her from interrupting. "Please," he amended. "Do not, under any circumstance, tell anyone about the diamond." She nodded her head mutely, but he continued, remembering her disregard for the rules on the ship. "Not Robert, not your aunt and uncle, not your cousin or your friend, and especially not that governess and maid of yours."

She lifted a dubious brow, taking his finger from her mouth, which only made him want to kiss her.

"I understand."

"Do you? The last time I gave you instruction, I recall your absolute disobedience."

"That was before our vows, good sir. Now I have pledged my obedience." Then she impertinently added, "However, I do recall it only included some kind of disagreement on the subject of trousers and may not apply here."

"Nicolette, I'm serious. If this information falls into the wrong hands, it could mean your life."

"I understand." She looked pointedly at him. "I truly do. I quite like my throat just as it is," she said with great sincerity.

"Good. So do I." To prove it, he bent close and placed a light kiss behind her ear, resulting in a satisfying shiver of gooseflesh on the back of her neck. There was time for this mystery later. He ran a finger down her slim throat and leaned in for a kiss, only to be rebuffed.

Nicolette backed up an inch, swatted his hand, and then laughed when he scowled. "I came up here to rest before dinner, but it's too late for that now. We have guests, husband. It's time to dress."

He playfully grabbed the sash at her waist and pulled the bow free.

She clutched the edges of the robe and layered them with her crossed arms. "I did not say *undress*, wicked man."

He chuckled. "Disobedient little wench."

"Pirate," she countered.

Dinner that night was a painfully long experience. It tried every ounce of his husbandly patience. After dinner, when Nicolette joined in another round of draughts with his grandmother, he whispered in her ear, "I had your maid draw you a bath." To his grandmother he said, "If you'll excuse the duchess, she has other duties."

Nicolette's skin turned a bright pink while his grandmother rested a hand over Nicolette's. "He's not nearly as adept at this game as he thinks. Make sure he knows that." Refusing help, the dowager levered herself into a standing position, then straightened to her full aristocratic height, which was daunting even at five feet two inches. "Good luck, dear boy. And you're welcome."

Nicolette watched the dowager leave, a faint, enigmatic smile on her face.

CHAPTER 32

When Nicolette reached her rooms, Claudia had prepared a nice warm bath with lavender-scented water. The decadence of having a room for just bathing was something Nicolette had never dreamed of. However old the duke's estate, it had been updated frequently to keep up with current trends including the newest breakthrough of indoor plumbing. Pipes had been set in the wall for pumping cold water. The servants would still need to bring hot water from the kitchens, but just having a supply of fresh water to the room was a luxury. Likewise, there was a pipe for draining the tub. The floor was a mosaic of white and pink tiles shaped like roses, and the walls were papered in pastel pink and gold.

"Claudia, you're a gem," Nicolette said as her maid helped her undress. She sank down into the water, the heat rising off the top like a cup of hot tea. She leaned her head back against the high end of the lion-clawed tub and closed her eyes.

"Let me find you a clean robe. I'll return shortly to help with your hair," Claudia said, backing out of the room while picking up a handful of stockings and underthings.

When Claudia shut the door, Nicolette let out a soothing sigh, losing herself in the scent of lavender and letting her arms float atop the water. The gentle movement of lapping water reminded her of the nights she'd shared with Grant on the ship. The thought caused her flesh to prickle even under the hot water. As she relaxed, the day fell away until she heard the click of the door.

"You may leave the robe at the door, Claudia. I think I'll just soak for a while."

The sound of boot heels on the tiles brought her up short, hands flying to her breasts and water sloshing over the edge of the tub. Soap stung her eyes, and without her hands to wipe them, she squinted.

"Oh dear Lord, Grant! This is indecent. You shouldn't be here. What if Claudia walks in and sees you?" She sank lower in the warm water, careful to cross her legs just so in order to hide herself. The water was milky from soap, but she had little doubt of its translucency from a standing vantage point.

"Darling, if this is what it takes to hear you say my name, I'll be doing a lot more of it." He pulled up a short stool, the one her maid used to help with her hair. He managed to look comfortable in his shirtsleeves, his elbows resting on his knees —which sat unusually high because of his size in comparison to the small stool—and his arms loosely crossed while his hands hung casually between his legs. He also managed to look like a man who intended to stay for a while. His dark hair was slightly damp, and she imagined he'd just come from his own bath.

He smiled while he scanned the water. "I don't give a radish what your maid thinks."

She scrunched a brow. "Did you just say, 'I don't give a radish'?"

"I didn't think you'd care for what I had in mind. Would you like me to repeat it?"

"No! And if you want to speak to me, hand me a robe and leave the room," she said, then in afterthought added, "Please."

His gaze circled the room. When he glanced back at her, the grin on his face was anything but charming. It was full of mischief. "No robe, darling."

"You are wicked, and not at all a gentleman." She did her best to not look flustered because the more nervous she became, the larger his smile.

"If I were *not* a gentleman, I would suggest that you find a robe for yourself right now while I wait and watch. In fact, I'm just enough gentleman to only *hope* that you will do that while I am less inclined to assist. Unless, of course, that's a game you'd like to play?"

Nicolette just rolled her eyes, which only caused her to squint again as an errant drop of water fell into her open eye. "If you'd like to help, you may call Claudia and not return."

"I relieved your maid of her duties. But if you'd like help with your hair, I'd be more than happy to oblige."

Covering her breasts with one arm, she wiped her eyes with her now-freed hand.

With his knuckle, he rubbed the part of her shoulder that surfaced like an island, and she was surprised at how one tiny touch could arouse her.

"I'm willing to sacrifice my evening to help." He added just enough innocence to almost sound convincing.

Her body tensed and she shrugged her shoulder, hindering his touch while her pulse sounded in her ears. She swallowed hard. Without looking at him, she asked, "What would you know of washing a woman's hair?"

The question hung like fog between them, a silent pleading for reassurance. The answer was more important to her than she wished to admit. Was there not something of him that belonged only to her? Would there ever be?

"Ask me, Nicolette." A serious tone broke the playful spirit.

She looked at him askance. "Why? So you can lie?" The surly question was uncalled for.

"I don't believe I've ever lied to you." His eyes were soft, forgiving almost, as if he understood. "Ask. I won't answer until you do."

Did she want to know? What would it gain her at this point? She calculated her next move and decided to try something different. "Why did you marry me, Grant? You didn't have to. A duke can do as he pleases, especially if the person he ruins is a nobody like me."

"You'll never be a nobody." He caressed her cheek. "And I don't believe I've ever ruined anyone."

She thought about that for a moment. If what he said was true, then he'd never lain with a virgin. True, he'd probably been with more women than she'd like to know about, but he'd never been with anyone like her.

"Thank you for using my name, by the way," he said sincerely.

"Of course, Your Grace." She couldn't help the taunt. It wasn't in her to pass up the opportunity to tease him.

He playfully tugged her hair. "You know you can ask me anything. Always. If you need to talk about my past, then we'll talk. Even if it makes me uncomfortable."

Truly she didn't want to. She'd rather put it all behind them. In fact, his past was just that—*his* past.

She shifted in the tub. When she looked at him, he wasn't staring into the water for a glimpse of her, he was gazing expectantly into her eyes, somehow understanding that the vulnerability she felt was more than the condition of her contorted nakedness, but rather the hideously distorted wound of jealousy.

"I have never washed another woman's hair. I have never even seen it done. Never, in fact, have I had the pleasure to witness a woman bathing. That is the answer to the question you would not ask."

He had avoided answering the question of why he'd married her, but she was just as happy to hear that he'd never sat at the edge of a bath next to another woman. In that she would always be the first.

"Thank you," she whispered, swallowing the catch in her throat. This perceptive husband of hers was more than she could have hoped for in a marriage not of her choosing. Whether she would choose it now was something she wasn't ready to contemplate.

"My pleasure." He leaned in and kissed her temple. "Now, the real reason I'm here."

"Do you mean you're not here just to vex me?" Now that she felt better, a little banter was in order.

"Perhaps a little," he said, a dimple of a smile on his very kissable mouth. "Actually, I wished to discuss something with you."

When he offered no other clue, she became concerned. "What is it?"

"Nothing as dire as your look, sweet, but I do want you out of this bath in fifteen minutes." He rose from his perch. "In my room. Fifteen minutes," he repeated, flashing her first ten, then five fingers.

With her hair already floating like ribbons on the water and no other way around washing it, she shooed him with a little splash. "It will take me at least that much. Now get out, you heartless man." She leaned her hands against the tub, using the sides for a shield.

He laughed on his way out the door, only to return a minute later with a fresh robe that he hung on a peg just inside the doorway. He poked his head inside, a silly half grin on his face. "You said your last curtsy to me would be my final view. I just want to thank you for the reprieve."

"Beast!" She threw a soaked sponge at the hastily closed door. When he disappeared, she giggled until her head was submerged and her laughter turned to bubbles.

When she finished, she tiptoed through a puddle of water with a towel wrapped around her head. She slipped into the robe hanging on the peg, then opened the door to find her wicked husband standing by her bedpost.

"What now?" She pulled the towel from her head, and her heavy hair in loose tangles fell over her eyes.

"I thought you might require an escort in case you lost your way."

Through the wet strands she could see his gaze drinking in every inch of her.

"You're devouring me with your eyes." She combed her fingers through her hair, twisting it into one big spiral curl.

"It's currently all I have time for."

At the bewitching gleam in his eye, her heartbeat took off like a lathered Thoroughbred. She clutched the lapel of her dressing gown, managing a well-composed voice despite her befuddled senses. "Fifteen minutes is hardly enough time to bathe and dry my hair."

"There's a fire in my room. You can dry your hair while we talk."

"May I dress first?"

He strolled to her vanity where he picked up a pair of slippers lying next to the seat. "These will do."

Marching toward him, she threw up one brow and grabbed her slippers from his outstretched hands, then preceded him through the connecting door that joined their suites.

True to his word, a fire burned hot in the grate. She stood by it and began to separate her heavy hair with her fingers, wondering at his unusual behavior.

There were two chairs and a round tea table close enough

to be warmed by the blaze. He led her to the chair closest to the fire, then raised a silent brow for her to sit.

"Does that take long?" he asked of her hair.

Subconsciously she twisted it around her hand and brought it over one shoulder. Drops of water from the ends left wet spots on her robe. "Twenty minutes or so by the fire." She regarded him warily. "You are awfully curious this evening."

"Am I?" He picked up a polished wooden box from his dresser and brought it to the table.

Too big for jewelry, too small for an elephant. What on earth was he up to?

He finally sat in the chair opposite her, leaned back, and relaxed his elbows on the thick upholstered arms. "We need to discuss the sleeping arrangements."

She paused her grooming efforts. "Oh? If you're suffering fatigue—and I can understand at your age how that might be an issue—I have no qualms about sleeping in another part of the house if it pleases you." She sat up primly, making her eyes as widely innocent as possible without breaking into laughter.

"Your generosity is overwhelming, Duchess. And your concern for my age is more than I could ask. Surely you understand such delicate matters, what with being a year late for your own debut, and all because of your inability to dance."

She gasped. "You go too far." Then she ruined it all with pent-up laughter.

He winked. "Well done. However, I'm serious about the sleeping arrangements."

She blinked twice with confusion.

He ran a hand over the mysterious box on the table. "I was thinking about what you said—that this is my house. And I remembered the way you described your home on the *New Horizon* and then with the Walbornes. And I must admit I'm a bit jealous."

She was taken aback by his confession.

"I want you to feel at home here, and I can't help but wonder if your room isn't fitting of your personality. You are a wildflower among roses, yes, but that room does little more than swallow you up."

"It verily screams every time I enter. Your room, however—the rich green, the heavy wood, the gold accents—is perfect."

"Exactly." He sounded almost relieved. "I thought it only fair that you should have a say in your room's design."

Her heart sank, but only a little. Secretly she'd hoped he would ask her to stay with him. Since their time on the *New Horizon*, she'd felt alone in her bed. Did the upper echelon ever share a bedchamber aside from the obvious reasons?

"I took the liberty of enlisting some help to begin clearing furniture tomorrow. I realize our wedding week isn't over, but I don't think I can look at that room any longer." He paused to breathe. "If it's reasonable to you, I thought you could stay with me until it's completed."

She scratched her nose to hide her joyous smile. "That would be agreeable. I suspect it will take a long time."

"The longer, the better. Until then, or always if you prefer…" At that, he looked up at her hopefully, and her heart somersaulted. "I'd like you to think of this as your home and this room as ours."

She sniffled, fighting the well of tears gathering in her eyes.

He drew in a deep breath, clapping his hands together and rubbing them briskly as if they'd put the subject to bed, so to speak.

Her parents had shared one room. She knew the ton did not welcome the practice, but her husband was offering at least the appearance of what she most wanted. A love match.

She swiped at an errant tear that escaped while her thoughtful husband busied himself with the carved wooden box. From inside, he pulled out a pile of tokens. He placed them, perfectly stacked, on the table and then returned to the box and produced a deck of cards.

He glanced at her from under his brows while he fanned the cards out on the table and sifted them with his hands.

"If I were not so delicate a creature, I'd guess you're a betting man, and those, sir"—she pointed to the coin-shaped tokens—"are for betting with."

"Close. The tokens will represent the stakes."

"May I see one?"

He flipped a coin toward her, and she grappled to catch it. On one side was the ducal crest and on the other a monogrammed *H* stamped into the brass.

"You had gaming tokens made with your insignia? Brilliant." She wanted to clap her hands while her insides turned over with excitement. The tokens? The cards? They could mean only one thing.

"Would you care to share your gambling prowess?"

She sat forward in her seat, her hair all but forgotten, and nodded her head. She could feel her cheeks stretch with anticipation. She was almost afraid to speak for fear of revealing her confidence. She'd been taught to gamble on her father's ship—not a pastime he'd approved but one he'd purposely ignored for her sake. The games were harmless, but the strategy had stuck.

"Vingt-et-un, hazard, or brag? Brag has the best strategy." Oh, she hoped he'd say brag.

"Brag it is." He brought the cards together, tapping each side on the table until the edges met. "We'll use the tokens to wager, but the cost must be something else."

"The cost?"

"Yes. The coins are but a token of the real stakes."

"You suggest we bet with real money? Oh, this is rich." She started to get up. "I think I have a little pin money in my room."

He held up a hand to stop her. "We bet only what we have with us."

She looked down at her robe like a ninny, shoving her hands in the pockets despite knowing they were empty, then looked at him, confused.

"My pockets are also empty, kitten." His smile told a different tale.

"Finally the nefarious plan is revealed. I knew you weren't a gentleman." Her words were laced with teasing sarcasm, a reference to when first they'd met at the theater.

"The crocodile and the duck," he said, a wolf in sheep's clothing while he dealt four cards.

"I've only ever played three card."

"You must discard one—the chances for a better hand are greater, turning bluffing into an art form." He pulled a card from his hand and returned it to the bottom of the deck.

"I take it my ante has something to do with what I'm wearing?"

"Aren't you the perceptive one?"

"Grant Havenly, you lured me in here without allowing me to change." Her tone was accusatory, but she warmed to the challenge.

He answered with a smirk and a cocked brow.

"You do not play fair."

"I'm playing by the same rules, love. I've nothing else to offer."

"No? You're wearing shoes."

"You're wearing slippers." He bobbed his head toward her feet.

"Yes, and a robe." She paused until he peeked over the top of his cards, hiding the telltale signs of an overeager grin. "And *nothing* else. While you, sir, have stockings, trousers—"

"Breeches."

"Breeches, a shirt, and a hastily tied cravat."

He reached up with one hand and untied the already loosened knot, then tossed the silk scarf on the table. "Now we're even."

"Hardly so." She squinted her eyes and tucked her chin. "But I'll accept your challenge with poise and good humor."

"Yes, that's all fine and good, darling, but would you care to ante, or have I frightened my kitten away?"

"No." She laughed. "Are you trembling in your boots, good sir? If so, I can divest you of those first."

He laughed outright, a sound that rattled her momentarily. She was accomplished at cards. But better than her husband? That remained to be seen.

"You may, without cards, divest me of it all, my sweet. But I like the odds." He looked her over with barely concealed lust, and a part of her wanted to throw down her cards and skip the game.

She slid a two of diamonds in place next to its sister card, a two of clubs, and waited for the betting to commence. With only two players the round took less than a minute. If they continued in this way, she'd be naked in five short minutes. Her ego refused to take such a beating, but she did win the first hand. Pride filled her when he pulled off one boot and placed it beside his chair.

After she won another hand, leaving her husband's trembling feet without his boots, he removed himself for a drink. She watched as he poured one glass and then picked up the sherry for her.

"If I'm to play cards like a man, I want a man's drink."

He pointed a questioning look toward her with a dubious brow raised, and then he put the sherry down. To her surprise he brought two glasses, both filled with amber spirits.

"Irish whiskey, my dear. Compliments of Mr. Ethan Strong." Ethan, she'd learned, was a friend of Grant's who owned a club.

She lifted the glass to her nose. A sting tickled her nostrils.

Grant watched her from over the rim of his glass. "Don't feel the need to drink it," he said just before taking a nice swallow of his own.

Nicolette tilted her glass in a silent toast, then took a tiny sip. It burned her tongue, but by the time it hit her throat, the overwhelming, smoky bite had mellowed and slid down smoothly. She wasn't sure if she liked it, but she did like the wolfish gleam in his eye.

"Is there any possibility that you might find me a comb for my hair?"

The question was said with so much honey he squinted his eyes, clearly wary.

"If you can't find one, there's one in my bureau, or the bathing room, or maybe my wardrobe. Sorry, I'm not entirely sure where Claudia stores them." It was almost the truth. She kept one in her bedside table, but whether Claudia stored them in her dressing table or among her toiletries, she didn't precisely know. It didn't matter. She only required a moment of privacy. The goose chase would provide that.

He was gone for a full three minutes.

"I found a brush, will that do?" Grant returned, holding up an ivory-handled boar-bristled hairbrush.

"Perfect!"

He placed the brush next to the glass of whiskey and looked pleased when she took the glass for another sip instead of picking up the brush.

"I suggest we adopt an acceptable alternative to our current wager."

"Such as?" he asked, his curiosity piqued.

"I've never played with four cards, but I do believe betting on the extra card is good form. Then we play out the hand as usual and use the total pot for the paid win. In other words, the game will last longer."

"Which, I imagine, suits you?"

"I'm only trying to offer you greater opportunity to win with strategy, Your Grace," she said with sham innocence.

"Why do I get the feeling I've been played?" He anted, looked at his fourth card, then put it aside before discarding so they could add another bet to the pot.

"Are you afraid? If so, I can go easy."

"Please, don't put yourself out. I'm afraid it's my advantage since I care little whether I win or lose. The outcome will no doubt be the same."

"Bragging rights?" she asked without looking at him, laying facedown her fourth card and sliding out two tokens. She stole a glance at him. He was studying her, looking for any sign of change in her demeanor. She returned his stare, blinking accordingly and enjoying the ever-so-slight slant to his brows. The man was thoroughly confused.

He slid out three tokens. She added another. And so the game went. Divesting him of his stockings gave her a boost.

After an hour of play, it was obvious she knew a great deal more about the game than he'd expected. She had been successful, in fact, at bluffing two hands before Grant caught on to the subtle changes in her body language. She could see it in his eyes. Her tell, as it were, was too telling indeed. He had been divested of his boots, socks, and shirt while Nicolette had only lost her slippers and the sash.

The game was, however, ready to take a turn because not only had Grant been able to decipher her body language, but Nicolette was finding it difficult to play the game while he sat nonchalantly across from her at the small table, stripped to his waist. No matter how hard she tried, she could not keep her eyes from wandering down the length of his chest to where his torso disappeared into his breeches. He appeared completely relaxed, as if this were most proper. He sat, his legs crossed at the ankles, stretched to one side while he lounged back and contemplated his hand. If she failed this next bluff, she'd lose the robe.

"I see you." Grant called the bet before she had a chance to force his hand. The sly quirk of his mouth involved a fair gleam of mischief, and she knew she was had. He laid down a pair of tens.

"You know this is not fair. I was to bet again." She tried to stall.

"I see your bet, sweet." He repeated the call, patiently gloating.

"Grant?"

He simply smiled at the sound of his name.

"I have proven I am a better player, but it was unfair that you should have more to bargain with than I." There, that was perfectly reasonable and called for another hand in Nicolette's very biased opinion.

"You have plenty to bargain with, wife." He put a finger to the table. "Cards. Now."

"Then I choose to fold?"

He slowly shook his head.

She laid down her cards, not even a pair, just a high queen.

"I won't do it," she said stubbornly.

There was a playful challenge to his gaze.

"Besides, you are even now imagining it's gone, so what's the difference?"

Grant held out his hand, prompting her to pay up.

"One more hand?"

He shook his head. "Nicolette, you have won more hands than I already."

"And that is my point. You at least have kept something of yours, while I, even though you agree that I am the more accomplished player, have lost everything."

He simply stared at her, unrelenting.

Her mouth curved into a secretive smile. "Do not say I

didn't warn you." She took another fortifying drink of whiskey, having known it would come to this. She'd known it the minute she stepped into his room—their room.

As for Grant, he sat back, arms crossed, quite satisfied. He licked his lips while he watched her pull back the lapel from her choking grip. The silk slipped away from her shoulders, and she allowed it to fall over the back of the chair where she sat, all the while never letting her gaze move from his.

"For the love of God." He breathed in awe. It was clear as to what he'd expected. What she gave was something else entirely.

She was, in fact, wearing the sexiest piece of clothing she'd ever dared—if what he'd said on the ship were true. She pulled the tie on the billowy peasant shirt she'd stolen from his wardrobe, feeling it slide off one shoulder and baring her to his gaze from her neck to the top of one breast.

"Is that all you have to say?" she asked, a coy purr in her voice. It would seem she'd found herself somewhere between her vows and this moment.

"It's the best I can do." He couldn't stop looking at her.

It was the best compliment she could have hoped for. The tail of the shirt rested on her naked thighs, leaving her legs exposed all the way to her feet.

"You haven't won yet, my lord." She bit her lip.

"And you are a cheat, Duchess." He shifted uncomfortably in his chair.

"No. I have simply evened the odds with my own currency." She blinked and did her best not to hide herself but to show him how much she trusted him.

"Oh, they're not even, my sweet, not by a long shot. You were not wearing that when you came into this room, were you? When and where did you find that shirt?"

She shook her head shamelessly, brushing her still-damp hair over her shoulder, the wet strands sticking to the cotton muslin and making it transparent wherever it touched. "No lies tonight, Grant. I sent you for a comb, and then I found this in the first drawer I opened. Now, I realize that I vowed to consult you about trousers, which is why I'm not wearing any..."

Before she could say another word, he was on his feet, rushing to stand behind her. His warm hand caressed her shoulder, and he bent to bite her ear. "You are a minx."

"As I was saying before you rudely interrupted. I promised not to wear breeches, but I never made a promise regarding your shirts." She tilted her head back to look at Grant standing above her, behind the chair. But he was not looking at her face—his eyes were smoldering and fixed on the opening of the blouse. "I didn't think you'd mind."

Nicolette shifted her body, turning about until she was kneeling toward the back of the chair. She curled her fingers over the top of his breeches, tugging just enough to make him look at her. The skin against her knuckles was warm, and she could see the pulse in his neck increase.

"Truth, Grant." Tilting her chin up she asked, "What is it that you want?"

A myriad of emotions passed over his face, from pure lust to tenderness. He looked down at her hand clasping his trousers, his eyes full of fire, the evidence of his arousal apparent. He gazed into her eyes. His mouth opened as if he couldn't speak.

Then finally he took a shuddering breath. "Just you." His voice was full of longing, a raspy whisper against the crackle of the fire and the otherwise quiet of the room.

He coiled her damp hair around his fist, rubbing the strands between his fingers and palm. "What's your truth, Nicolette?"

She nervously rubbed her lips together, determined to tell him what she'd known for weeks. To give him the real answer to the question he'd asked her in the garden when her pride had swelled painfully. Now her heart ached for him to know.

"I love you, Grant."

His breathing increased, his pupils dilated, and in that moment it mattered not whether he returned the sentiment because she understood him better each day. Everything he did, he did for her. He overwhelmed her with his patience, his willingness to protect her reputation at all cost, to the end of himself, even so much as a wedding. And more than anything, she was overwhelmed by his tenderness, something others missed when they sought him out for his political position or his title.

He swiftly plucked her up into his arms and carried her to the bed where he carefully laid her down as if she were fragile, watching her as if she might disappear like an apparition.

Above her, she took his face in her hands, relishing the evening shadow of his beard. She coaxed him with a gentle pull, drawing him down for a kiss.

He nuzzled her neck, covering her shoulder in whisper-soft kisses. He lifted the makeshift gown slowly over her head, allowing the crisp, cool cotton to stroke her skin until the shirt was completely removed. With studied gentleness, he slid his strong hand down the side of her body, over the side of her breast, until it came to rest on her hip.

"God, Nicolette, you feel like heaven. I missed you after that last night on the ship. I couldn't say goodbye. It killed me to even think it."

Bay rum and sandalwood assailed her senses, combined with the fresh scent that was all him. She was drawn to it in a way she could not explain. It comforted and delighted her.

"Please love me, Grant," she pleaded in a whisper.

He answered with a drugging kiss full of a passion so much greater than lust.

He kissed her eyes closed, and then he touched her. He

verily worshipped her with his hands and mouth, and then, oh yes, his body.

She released her mind to the euphoria of being loved by him and found pleasure in the power of desire.

This was her husband, body and soul. And he wanted her. That much she knew.

And tonight?

Tonight he loved her.

CHAPTER 33

*G*rant woke smiling, a curiously foreign feeling to him until this week. He couldn't believe his luck in finding a woman who thrilled him, rivaled him with her bullheadedness, and promised a life without a dull moment to spare. He'd fought against the possibility of happiness for so long that he'd almost forgotten how it felt.

This morning it felt like satiated satisfaction, and the bringer of such happiness was pressed into his side with her arm draped over his middle. He could have stayed there all day and would have if it weren't for a hundred guests waiting for a last day of festivities.

After a short breakfast in their room, they saddled up for a tour of the east property, which was lined with weeping willows and a sprinkle of poplar. From there, they followed a wide creek to the three-acre lake that fed it. Early wildflowers spotted the open meadow. Spring at Havenly was a sight he often missed and one he was delighted to share with his new wife.

"You're doing well with Butterscotch." He nodded his

approval toward the winter-white mare Nicolette rode. "She's as docile as a lamb."

"She's actually very sweet, but I would have preferred to ride with you."

"We can make that happen another time, I promise." He clucked his tongue and gave a gentle tug of Brewster's reins, pulling him in close to Butterscotch. He leaned heavily to the side, grabbed a pommel of Nicolette's sidesaddle and planted a bobbing kiss to her cheek.

"Butterscotch for a white mare, and Brewster for a black Arabian? Who named these horses?"

He laughed. "Explanations can be conveyed in two words: Aunt Enid. She likes to name the animals." He winked.

With the lake now in view, he could see the guests already gathered on scattered blankets. Thankfully the week had spared them even a drop of rain, leaving the ground dry enough for an early luncheon. The servants were ready to bait fishing lines for the men and pass out nets to the women for catching butterflies. However, it was more than likely that the women would drink champagne while they oohed and aahed over a three-inch bluegill brought in by a proud fisherman. Flirting was generally the first thing on the menu at such affairs. Activities were but an excuse.

"Without shame, I admit that I don't want to share you today," Grant said over his shoulder just before they reached their final stop.

"You're a duke—are you not able to send them all away?" There was not a cinder of malice in her voice, only mischief. A servant came forward when she was within reach and took control of Butterscotch, leading her to a mounting block.

Grant dismounted and then proceeded to help Nicolette from her horse. He forewent the mounting block for her to step onto and swung her down by her waist, loath to let her go. He placed a kiss on her smiling mouth and basked in the desire that such a small gesture sparked in her ocean-blue eyes.

Without any shyness, she reached up and cupped his cheeks, and when he thought she'd kiss him back, she simply said, "I love you, Grant."

Those three amazing words had been on her lips all morning. The damned question she'd refused to answer when they argued at the Ashton ball was something that had haunted him. He wanted it so badly, so why couldn't he say it in return?

There was still a fear inside him that his grandmother would destroy his happiness as she'd done his mother's. It hardly made sense, but then childhood trauma was not something he could explain.

His grandmother loved him, that he knew. And she had fairly insisted that he marry Nicolette although he didn't quite know why. He'd lived his life trusting very few people, a natural cynic, refuting the existence of true love at every turn. Unsure if his heart would ever understand it, he still couldn't stop himself from wanting to hear the words. He had needed it weeks ago. He craved it now.

Nicolette greeted their guests with an ease he'd yet to see in her. Before today she hadn't seemed interested in visiting with them, but now she seemed relaxed and free, much like he remembered her while aboard the *New Horizon*. She'd found her home time and again. His heart ached for her to find home with him now, here at Havenly, in the city, in a coach, on a ship, everywhere. For the first time in a long while, he felt at home. And for the first time in his life, it had nothing to do with a structure. Not a ship. Not a house. Just her.

NICOLETTE WATCHED her husband mingle with old friends. She tried to imagine him as a little boy fishing this lake or sailing paper boats on the water. She wanted to see a happy little boy racing his first pony or battling Sherwood Forest in the copse of trees nearby. But all she could see was this man, formal and loyal, answering society's call to be the duke. Lord knows she wanted a daughter, but she secretly hoped their first child would be a son because she wanted Grant to see what his childhood as a little boy looked like, one where the parents were devoted. She wanted to raise children to search for happiness under every rock, whether toad or frog, to kiss a prince or princess because sometimes life is what you dream. She'd known many homes, but she was happily content to name this her last and most cherished, and it was not the place but the person. In her mind she saw Grant laughing on the steps of the theater, discussing the peacock plumage of a patroness of the arts, as it were, and his teasing smile every time he complained about her waltzing on his feet.

She didn't know when she'd come to love him—the time was of no consequence—she only knew that she did.

And he loved her. He had to, because although she had yet to hear him say it, she felt it, truly felt it. He'd made love to her last night with such tenderness, holding nothing back. He gave her everything, even time.

He was not like anyone she'd ever met. Unlike the beau monde who rarely shed their hauteur, Grant had spent time earning a living, increasing his estates instead of depleting his reserves. Change was inevitable, he'd told her. Those that understood the business of that change would survive, and those that did not stood a good chance of losing their fortunes. Entailed properties would remain, but whether they fell into disarray or flourished relied on the titled gentry who had the responsibility to care for them.

She was proud that her husband cared enough about his family's future to preserve it. And even more proud that he cared for the cottagers and those who worked his properties.

After midday, the guests began returning to the house, so when Nicolette witnessed a lone rider approaching at a fast pace, she knew it was more than a late arrival. As the rider closed the space, she recognized the Earl of Richfield, Grant's trusted friend.

Beside her on the blanket, he put down his glass of wine and rolled to his feet. "Excuse me, darling." His tone was light, but something about the way his eyes darkened disturbed her.

When Grant reached Richfield, the earl did not dismount, just bent low in the saddle and spoke with him. The conversation appeared serious. At one point Grant turned back to look at her, then called out for Mr. Jenkins, the underbutler overseeing the festivities.

Mr. Jenkins returned with a message, speaking to her as she saw Grant mount his horse and ride off with the earl. He relayed that *His Grace was needed for a minor matter and that she was to remain in the company of the guests until he returned.*

GRANT'S HEART hammered in the galloping rhythm of his horse's hoofbeats. Richfield's late arrival was not what concerned him, it was the message he'd delivered concerning Amelia Covington, an old friend and an unexpected guest. She'd come to stay at Havenly several days ago per Richfield's request. The plan was for her to hide away until Richfield returned to retrieve her. Grant would never ask why she needed shelter; he only knew that Mitchell needed the favor. Although the house was full of guests that might recognize a previous member of their society, Amelia had been given the nursery to stay in and access to the servants' stairs where she could come and go without notice from the guests. Sometimes hiding in plain sight was the safest option.

After all they'd been through, he would have given his life

for Mitchell. They were better than brothers—they were the truest of friends and always would be.

According to Richfield, Amelia had been accosted by an uninvited guest. The man had tried to threaten her into stealing something of great import from the Duchess of Havenly, Nicolette. The squirrely man hadn't had a complete description of the item he needed, but he had guessed it might be jewelry. Grant now understood what the killers were after. The star map. The oddly cut diamond that he'd locked in his safe.

Fortunately, because of Amelia's description, he also knew the identity of the man. Henry Milford, Emmett Craddock's nephew, as in the former owner of Craddock Shipping where Nicolette's father had been employed. It was Henry Milford who'd lost the *New Horizon* in a game of chance. And it was Henry Milford who all but lost the entire shipping company—which he'd inherited after the death of his uncle—before Grant purchased the other two ships in the small fleet.

Grant had always thought Craddock's heart attack came at a convenient time shortly after John Bradenton was killed. He'd suspected Henry, and possibly Craddock as well, knew about the history because the timing of their deaths was too coincidental. Robert had praised the former owner, Emmett Craddock, but had nothing good to say about the nephew.

After he questioned the servants and very nonchalantly sought answers from several guests, he and Mitchell determined that the man had left the property. Something had obviously put him off. For now Nicolette was safe, and Grant left it to Mitchell to protect Amelia.

He rode back to the lake for Nicolette but kept the full story, and his suspicions about Henry Milford, from her for now. He had no wish to worry her, but when she heard about Amelia Covington's scare, she insisted on seeing her.

IT WAS ONLY A KISS

After Grant sent Nicolette to look in on Amelia, he joined Mitchell for a drink in his library.

"I'll do whatever needs be done," Mitchell offered without question.

"I know. Mitch. Thanks." Grant drummed his fingers on the desk and sighed in thought. He'd already made up his mind. "I've told Nicolette only what she needs to know. If I'd said nothing at all, she would have needled me to death. Now she's free to comfort Amelia." Grant rubbed his forehead, guilt over the attack on Lady Amelia eating at him. "I'm sorry about her, Mitch. I hate that Milford threatened her, but at least we know who he is and that Lady Amelia is in no danger."

Mitchell stood from where he sat in front of Grant's desk and pensively walked to the window.

"I'd never ask about her, you know that, but this friendship works both ways." Grant said, hoping to cool some of Mitchell's fears.

"I don't know what to do with her," Mitchell admitted quietly, his focus elsewhere.

Grant knew his friend didn't need advice, just an ear, something he understood well. "Nicolette's gone to see her. Maybe she'll share with my wife what she won't share with you."

Mitchell nodded. "Perhaps."

"If nothing else, they can compare their secrets. Threaten to blackmail one another."

Mitchell turned to find Grant with a wide grin spread across his face. He chuckled lightly. "Maybe, my friend. Lord knows they're both a cauldron of scandalbroth. Clifton could sell two seasons worth of stories between the two of them."

Grant sobered. "I'm grateful she was here. If that lunatic had spoken to anyone else, we might've never known. Now we've got a good description."

"We shouldn't have any problem finding him." Mitchell walked to the sideboard and poured a drink. "I'm keeping Amelia with me tonight. Do you think we can keep that under wraps?"

"Without question. Although my wife may blister your ears for it, she'll understand."

"Amelia doesn't feel safe. I can't see that changing. I'll take her back tomorrow. And hey"—he shot him a stiff look, apologetic and regretful—"I didn't mean to miss it."

"You didn't miss anything. Just the best damn wedding of the year." Grant grinned. "How did the job…?" He didn't finish. He didn't need to. Grant worried for Mitchell's safety more than Mitchell did.

"It's done." Mitchell cleansed his lungs with a fresh breath, like the world had just changed. "And now I'm done with it. For good."

Grant was one of the few who knew the kind of work Mitchell had been involved in to keep the Crown safe, and sometimes even the world. The group he affiliated with acted far and wide, looking out for the interests of justice, although justice wasn't always clear. It was the unclear part that Grant knew his friend grieved.

"Grant!" An exasperated Nicolette announced herself with a flurry of rustling skirts, strolling into the library with the confidence of someone who truly lived there. Grant was happy for that. "We cannot leave that poor girl up there without food. The servants are suspended from the room, and she hasn't eaten since yesterday." She then turned her freezing blue gaze on Mitchell. "And you, sir, what have you to say?"

Grant shrugged his brows at Mitchell, and Mitchell comically returned it. "I'll… see to it, Your Grace."

"Yes, you will. But give her twenty minutes. I've had a bath sent up. And you, sir, are to keep your distance." She pointed, very unladylike but very Nicolette-like, at Richfield.

"Understood," Mitchell said helplessly. When she turned on her heel and left, Mitchell added, "Lord, you have your hands full, my friend."

"Don't I know it." Grant looked away, a possessive smile pulling at his mouth.

The two of them had enjoyed their bachelorhood—their freedom—together, and now they stood in Grant's library, worried sick over two women.

He put his drink down, absently rubbing his thumb up the side of the glass. "The wedding guests will be gone tomorrow. We'll move back to the town house in London and wait."

"You mean to draw him out?" It was a sound strategy. "When you find him, Grant, send word. Promise you won't do this alone. You know I'll be there."

CHAPTER 34

While Nicolette gladly said goodbye to her wedding-week festivities, she found little excitement in the family's return to the London season. With Parliament in session, she understood the necessity for Grant to be there and she wouldn't dream of leaving him on his own, but she did hope to spend most of her evenings alone with him. To her delight, they enjoyed a week of peace punctuated with invitations that Grant turned down in lieu of spending time with her. He seemed to take pleasure just being in the same room with her. So she sat in his study while he worked and read. She teased him into laughing when he looked far too serious, and she learned to seduce him with a smile.

He filled her days with his devoted company. When they retired for the evening, they did so together. There was nowhere she'd rather be than surrounded by his arms every night and tangled with his legs as she slept. It was the same safety she'd felt on the ship during the weeks they had sailed, and she relished in it now, knowing it was hers for a lifetime.

They had been in the city for five days when Nicolette remembered the absurd and indecent wager they'd made almost two months ago. The paying of the forfeit was due. This was one game she was happy to lose. If Uncle James had not seen fit to insist on preserving her reputation, she would not be now married to Grant. Although she'd married a man she loved, she conceded the forfeit on the grounds that she would not have chased a suit if not for the scandal. So in her mind, she'd married without choice, and for Grant, he'd married at least without the knowledge that he loved her. In fact, he'd still yet to say it. But he would. Soon. Or she would torture him with kisses until he relented.

While Grant busied himself with contracts and the purchase of three new ships, adopting plans to deal in cocoa as far as the Americas, she wrote out a note.

Grant,
No need to gloat, darling. I will be waiting at the wooden bench in the back garden where the pink royal azaleas grow. I'll bring the forfeit. You bring champagne. I respectfully acknowledge my loss. Although even as the choice to marry was taken from me, I shall never forget how you signed the contract without reading it and granted me what I had secretly longed for but was too proud to admit. I was not aware at the time that you would fall in love with me, but I know that now even if you do not.
I do love you, Grant. I have loved you since you stole that first glass of champagne from my hands. But darling, you never stole my heart… that I gave to you. And only you. Forever.
I will love you always,
Nicolette

She left instructions with the footman to deliver the note at noonday, at which time she'd be waiting in the garden with one gold sovereign.

Grant would spend the next two days rereading that note, suffering her disappearance. She was right, he did love her— he'd loved her since the day he'd first danced with her and she had asked if rakes could be ruined. He would have to answer *yes* to that question now, and he would do so gladly. He hadn't told her he loved her, not in words, and now he couldn't because he didn't know where the hell she was.

After receiving the note, he'd smiled to himself, remembering that special coach ride to the docks where she'd laid her dreams out, how she'd revealed her heart and insisted that he'd find love because he'd been born of it.

He'd followed her directions, grabbing a bottle of champagne, two glasses, and heading for the bench out back where the pink azaleas grew. He expected to see her there, sitting primly, perhaps wearing a pair of trousers just for good measure, because he couldn't imagine her losing anything gracefully.

She'd roll her eyes and laugh. And he'd serve her champagne, then take her to bed and devour her sweet mouth, pour wine on her soft belly, and drink in every inch of her. And then he'd tell her how he felt. He'd tell her what she already knew and deserved to hear.

But that was not to be, because when he arrived at the bench, there was no Nicolette. No note either, only one gold sovereign that had fallen between the slats of the bench, hidden behind the forward wooden peg. He found it after frantically realizing that she wasn't hiding or playing a game. He'd torn the bushes of flowers apart, looking for a clue, and then he found the pound sterling and knew she wasn't there. The town house yard was big enough to hide for a short time but too small to get lost in. She wouldn't have strayed outside the property, not after he'd begged her to stay within the garden walls. But someone had found her waiting in the garden. Someone who'd come for her at the wedding.

Henry Milford. The little twit was going to die when Grant found him.

She was brave and intelligent, and if there was a way to leave a clue, she'd have thought of it. The money was evidence she'd been abducted.

Grant called for Walborne and Captain Donovan. Forty-eight hours passed without a note or notice. Lord Walborne had come quickly at the summons, but Robert was not to be found. Robert had been the one to dissuade them over involving the authorities, telling him he thought they might be involved. The plan was perfect. If Grant had never enlisted the help of the Bow Street Runners, Robert would have ample time to get away with murder. Grant was also confident, maybe because the alternative was too painful to consider, that Nicolette was still alive because the diamond pendant remained in his possession. She was the only person besides himself who knew the secret of the necklace.

"How can you believe that Robert would have anything to do with this!" Walborne shouted, exasperated with Grant. The situation was taking a visible toll on both men.

While Grant paced the library, Walborne poured another drink.

"Because he's not here!" Grant barked, snatching up a fistful of note cards from his desk and flinging them into the air. "The man is hiding something; can you not see that?"

Lady Walborne entered the room at the sound of shouting and closed the study doors. Mitchell would have been here too except he was scouring the city for evidence. "I can hear you shouting in the hallway, James. And as for you, Your Grace, Mr. Donovan could not possibly have anything to do with this."

Grant was angry as hell, but he reined in his temper for the sake of Nicolette's aunt. When she was not angry, she was close to tears. He sighed heavily and sat down in the leather chair behind his desk. "And why is that, madam?" he asked as calmly as possible.

"Because Robert Donovan and John were as close as brothers," she said simply, as if that explained everything.

And perhaps it did. Grant could understand a friendship so deep that one would keep every secret, do everything in their power to help, even as far as giving up their life. Didn't he have that same kind of friendship with Mitchell? Still, he'd never known Nicolette's father, and he couldn't afford the luxury of trust.

"Excuse me, Lady Walborne, if I doubt your word, but where Nicolette's life is concerned, I will never lift my guard. His absence screams conspiracy."

Walborne put an arm about his wife. "Your caution is appreciated, Havenly, but what Lydia says is true. When John was a young man of seventeen, he'd foolishly gone in search of the treasure. The clues left by his parents had taken him to an island off Scotland where he'd been followed. The thieving murderers happened upon Robert in the village pub, asking him about a man who fit John's description, and Robert had sent them after him."

Grant was not amused, and he hissed through his teeth, "This is not helping."

"After several days of piqued curiosity, Robert went in search of all three of them. He'd been given a position on a merchant ship and was leaving within the week, but he couldn't put the foreboding feeling about the two strangers to rest. So he set out to find John, and when he did, his conscience stung with guilt. He took Nicolette's beaten father in and nursed him back to health. He also found the two men who'd thrashed him and... Well." Walborne took a deep breath and slid an apologetic look to his wife. "Robert killed them both. They weren't residents there, and Robert was leaving town, so their disappearance was never questioned. But there was the matter of John. Robert felt responsible for what had happened. He convinced his new employer to take John on as part of the crew, where he obviously thrived to the point of captaining the *New Horizon*."

"How much did Craddock know?" Grant was seeing the pieces fall into place. If Emmett Craddock had known even a small piece of this history, it was possible for his nephew Henry Milford to have come upon it somehow. And highly likely that Milford killed Craddock for it, as well as John.

"That I couldn't say. But Robert pledged to keep the secret. When John met Elisabeth, he changed his name on the off chance that someone might still find him. He loved her too much to risk her life, and then of course Nicolette's too. We'd already agreed to take in Nicolette before John's death. Fearing he'd been found out, we decided to give Nicolette the use of our name. It served two purposes, both of which we've told you. It gave her a fresh start and would hopefully throw John's murderer off the trail."

Grant covered his face with his hands in frustration, sucked in air between his fingers, and willed his pulse to steady. Robert Donovan would remain a suspect as long as he stayed away, but Grant now understood the bond.

He looked at the mess he'd made on the floor with papers scattered about his feet. Although the pieces of the story were coming together, it wasn't fast enough.

"I wish someone had thought to tell me sooner," he said, walking around his desk, randomly picking up items like a pencil, a few note cards, and a round pewter paperweight embossed with his ducal seal. He flipped the heavy paperweight a few inches in the air several times, thinking about the engraving on the jewelry box. "Does Robert know what the inscription on the jewelry box means?"

Walborne looked at him curiously while Lady Walborne's stunned expression snapped to her husband. She grabbed his hand, her movements stiff with tension. "What jewelry box?" Walborne asked.

"The one John Bradenton gave to Nicolette along with a necklace. Isn't that right, Lady Walborne?"

"Lydia?" Walborne's question was quiet, but his look of appeal to her was real. He hadn't known.

She shook her head, her eyes wide like a frightened doe. "I've seen the necklace many times, but never a jewelry box. I knew the pendant was special to her, but I had no idea why."

That sounded true enough. She'd obviously not known about the box. "You wouldn't have seen the box until recently because I've had it for the past three years. It was nothing more than a curiosity to me, and a needed distraction for a while."

He'd explain later how he'd won it, how it had led him to Craddock Shipping, how it had spurred him into approaching Milford about the shipping company. Grant knew Milford was broke. He'd overborrowed against the small fleet and was in danger of debtor's prison when Grant purchased it. To Grant's dismay, he realized he'd not only given up Nicolette's name at the ball where Henry overheard it, he might have inadvertently sent Milford in the Thomases' direction simply by purchasing the fleet and then bringing in Walborne to partner with him.

His chest squeezed with the part he'd played. The pain of it almost brought him to his knees. He'd never forgive himself if something happened to her. He'd never forgive himself for the events that led to this point.

A commotion sounded in the foyer, the faint bluster of a servant and the clipped beat of boot heels approaching.

"They're expecting me!" Richfield called to the butler before he burst through the door.

Grant sprang to his feet.

"Excuse me, Lady Walborne, would you rather I wait until you leave?"

Nicolette's aunt shook her head and grabbed her husband's hand as she sank down onto the dark burgundy-and-cream sofa. Richfield sent Walborne an apologetic look, then turned to Grant and tossed a handkerchief with the initials NMH—Nicolette Marie Havenly—embroidered on it. Grant recognized it as his wife's. His stomach lurched at the blood-red stain in the middle of the stark white muslin.

Grant turned it over in his hands, then looked at Richfield and nodded. Overwhelmed with nausea and panic, his life shifting in a storm of anguish, he confirmed, "It's blood."

"It may not be hers." Richfield offered hope.

"Houldsworth!" Grant didn't even bother ringing for the stately butler; he knew a shout would be just as effective, and right now he needed to release a measure of tension because when he found the bastard who'd hurt his wife, he was going to tear him to shreds.

The unflappable butler showed immediately and then went to have the horses brought round as Grant instructed.

Next, Grant turned to Richfield. "Where is my wife? Where did you find that? And don't tell me it's a dead end, by God!"

"I discovered it on the wharf in the hands of a drunk. He found it on the floor of a tavern and liked the way it smelled. My guess is she's there. I found Captain Donovan wandering outside the tavern. He'd apparently been seeking his own clues, so I left him to keep an eye out and came back for reinforcements."

"James," he called for Walborne, "see to the horses. I'll meet you in front in five minutes. There's something I need to get." He took the stairs by twos, running to his rooms where he grabbed a gun and the necklace that had created a lifetime of havoc. If Milford wanted the damned thing, he could have it. All Grant wanted was his wife. Safe. At home. To hell with family heirlooms and memories. People were far more important. Nicolette was everything to him.

Out front, he met up with Walborne and Mitchell and mounted his horse, and the three took off for the Wayside Tavern. It was in a seedy part of town, but then most of the taverns along the wharves were seedy and dangerous. He couldn't linger on that though—he had to believe she was all right.

They entered the tap house from the back, covertly watching for Robert. There were a dozen tables in the main room, filled with men drinking and gaming, waiting for new charges to sail. It smelled of cheap ale and rancid cigars.

They elbowed their way past two men who were arguing loudly while stepping over a third man passed out on the floor. Walborne asked the proprietor if he'd seen a man fitting Robert's description. The owner nodded and pointed to the staircase to his left.

"There's a pretty lassie up there too. If ya all be goin', I'll be wantin' some pay for the use of my rooms."

Grant threw some coins at the hideous man and stifled the urge to shove his fist down his throat. Walborne and Richfield followed Grant to the second floor. The vile tavern boasted only two rooms, and Grant checked the first room they came to, opening the door slowly and wincing at the creak of a rusted hinge.

The room was devoid of people.

He jerked his head toward the second door, gun in hand, and motioned for Mitchell to take sentry on the opposite side of the doorjamb where Walborne joined him.

The tavern inn boasted no outside balcony, no other entry

or exit to the upstairs. Barging in with guns blazing could mean a bloodbath if they weren't careful. He made eye contact with Mitchell. Not much more need be said.

"This could have been avoided, you greedy bitch, if you had just stayed put."

Nicolette sat on the dusty wood floor of a small inn, by the look of it. Or possibly a tavern, by the smell of it. The lunatic aiming a gun at her spat every time he said a word beginning with *P*. The worst part was that she recognized him as the man who'd tried to abduct her from her home.

The sharp, thin cut of his jaw seemed harder with two days growth of beard. He stood perhaps four inches taller than she, but the gun he held made him appear bigger than life, like a towering menace, and the white powder in his snuffbox seemed to make him more dangerously belligerent.

"Like all women, you let your extravagant lust for the finer things get in the way. None of you are capable of anything greater." Henry Milford spat on the floor at Nicolette's feet. The white powder he snorted shook the mumbling right out of him, making his speech sickeningly clear.

She turned her attention to Robert, who lay unconscious on the floor next to her. She held a rag to his bleeding head where Mr. Milford had hit him with the butt of his gun.

Unlike the other previous attempt, Nicolette had been taken quietly, rendered helpless by a dose of laudanum clamped over her mouth. She awoke in the dirty room two days ago, unhurt otherwise, but fearing the worst was yet to come.

Henry Milford stood in the sparsely furnished room, spurred by desperate greed, rambling on about an heirloom. The same greed that drove the men who'd attacked her on the ship. They had died for that heirloom, and now Milford was ready to kill for it. After the discovery she'd made with the help of Grant, she now knew they sought the necklace.

"If you might see reason, Mr. Milford, I can give you what you want." Then, more desperately, "I have what you seek. It is in my husband's safe." Nicolette cared not for the unproven stories of treasure. The necklace held only sentimental value for her. But her life and Robert's were worth more than memories, even good ones. While Mr. Milford railed on, she loosened the knot at Robert's wrists. She'd grown up around knots; there wasn't one she couldn't untie.

"Shut up and leave him alone! You're nothing but another man's hussy, Miss Bradenton, and it will be my pleasure to drive the filthy memory of your soon-to-be-dead husband from your mind." He grabbed her by the arm and hauled her off the floor. He had made sure that Robert's hands were bound; conversely, his low opinion of women caused him little fear, thinking them completely defenseless, and so Nicolette was left untied, at least during the day. As for the night, she'd been tied to a chair. Proof that the man was not a complete idiot.

"It will soon be over. Your foolish husband is bound to show, and if he doesn't, I'll write a ransom note... you for the treasure. Very simple. Then he'll be dead, and I'll be rich. Oh, and did I forget to mention that you'll be the resident whore on the next ship out of here? Men do get lonely at sea, but I guess you know that." Henry ran a finger down her neck and locked it in the fabric of her dress between her breasts.

Fed up with his nauseating blather, she refused to satisfy his ego with fear, because she knew something he did not—she was not a weak-kneed, frightened girl. She had never been that.

Leaving her unbound was his first mistake. Underestimating her husband was his second.

CHAPTER 35

The raised voices from behind the closed door came through with revolting clarity. Grant heard Milford in a rage, saying vile things. He heard Nicolette's pleading voice and swallowed down the lump of cold hatred he had for the man who'd dared lay a hand on his wife. He nodded at Mitchell, who lifted his booted foot and kicked in the door.

Grant rushed the maniac as he pivoted on his heel. The craven bastard grabbed Nicolette, swinging her about, pinned up against his foul body much the same as her attacker on the ship except for one thing. Instead of a knife to her throat, Milford held a gun to her temple.

Her eyes were wild with panic, but she looked in one piece. From the floor to his left, he heard a man groan and spared a glance to see Robert crumpled on the floor. He motioned for Walborne to check Robert while he and Mitchell held vigil with guns drawn.

"Touch him and I'll shoot her." Milford's voice grated, a clear warning that he had no intention of losing control.

"No one's going to do anything, Milford." Grant looked to Mitchell and Walborne, and the three dropped their aim.

"Flattered that you remember me," Milford said with an odd, appreciative gleam. His ego was his weakness. If he felt like he had the upper hand, they might have a chance.

Grant held eye contact with Milford, but he couldn't help stealing a cursory glance at Nicolette, deciphering her condition. Had she been physically assaulted? He'd already guessed the blood on the handkerchief was Robert's, but he couldn't stop worrying about her emotional and physical condition. Her throat bobbed with a hard swallow, her blue eyes bore into him a silent message, and he realized that her hair was unbound and remembered what she'd done to the man on the ship. For a heartbreaking moment, he was tempted to examine the hem of her gown for a peek at her shoes. Was she still wearing them? He couldn't tell. What he did notice was the gleaming hairpin in her clutch.

He shook his head as he looked back to Henry lest he think he and Nicolette were communicating. The last thing he wanted was for Nicolette to stab this man in the knee. Whereas the knife was more difficult to wield in pain, a gun would take little to jostle the trigger. The danger to her was greater than it had been before.

"Grant." The calm of her voice belied her quivering chin. "Mr. Milford has the impression—"

Henry gave a hard jerk, his arm cutting off her words.

Grant seethed. It took everything inside him to keep his feet planted and his hands from Milford's throat. "Mr. Milford, you're already dead. You must know that by now." Inside, he was pulverizing the man for daring to touch his wife.

"Unless one of you is willing to see this charming woman harmed," he ground out, inflecting just the right amount of sarcasm at the word *charming*, "I'll be walking out of here, but not until I have what I want."

"There's no treasure."

"So you say. I'm willing to take my chances." Despite his

arrogant words, Milford was faltering. His voice trembled. If not for his tights, his knees would be clacking.

Nicolette's eyes were wide, her mouth taut as she covertly bent a brow at him.

He gave her a ghost of a smile. The odds were not in Grant's favor because Milford still held her. Perhaps the necklace in his pocket would change that. The diamond alone would bring a nice price. He hoped it would be enough to appease the scoundrel, although Grant would never stop searching for him. He wouldn't be satisfied until Henry Milford swung for his crimes. Grant knew the odds were not in his favor. Milford still held Nicolette, but Grant held what the bastard valued most.

From his pocket he pulled the necklace responsible for so much heartache and dangled it from his outstretched hand. Bright dots created by the oddly faceted gemstone flashed back and forth on the walls and the ceiling while Henry's glazed eyes gleamed with anticipation, the telltale sign of an abuse of laudanum or something else. Even more dangerous than a greedy man was a greedy drugged man.

"This is what you want, Milford."

"How do I know for certain?"

"It's what you seek, Mr. Milford. My father gave it to me when I was a little girl. The cuts made in the stone create a star map." Nicolette's voice shook while her eyes plotted.

Grant held up his other hand, one holding the pendant, the other holding his gun. "We'll slide our guns across the floor. I'll give you the pendant, you give me my wife."

"Nice try. You slide your guns across the floor. Nicolette will retrieve the necklace while I hold a gun at her back. When I have the necklace and the lady, we'll be leaving. I'll release her somewhere along the docks when I'm satisfied that no one has followed." His ego, clearly revealed by the smugness in his voice, would be his undoing. "Take it or leave it, gentlemen. I'll make no other offer."

So sure of himself. And to Grant's alarm, so was his wife. She begged him with a dance of her eyebrows and a woman's commanding stare that he should allow her to secure her own position, but the risk was too great. For all of them.

"Nicolette," he said pointedly, "take the necklace and give it to him." He was confident that Milford would not be leaving the tavern with his wife. The man was simply outnumbered, and if that were not enough, then Mitchell's special skills of both finding people and making them disappear was a real option. Either way, he had no intention of letting Nicolette out of his sight.

Henry shoved her forward. Grant wanted to grab her and run, but now was not the time. He took her hand, the one that held the pin, and slid it from her fingers, then pressed the necklace into her palm.

She looked up at him, bewildered and not a little angry.

He rubbed her cheek and whispered, "Not today."

She sighed, visibly upset that he'd taken her only defense. He just couldn't take the chance, not with a gun pointed at her.

"That's enough," Henry snapped, irritable and patience starved.

When he waved the gun around, using it as an extension of his talking hands, Grant wished he still held his own gun. Henry's erratic behavior at the sight of the diamond left him open and vulnerable. Before he could work out a plan to grab him without getting shot, a pop of gunpowder shattered his focus.

From the floor where Robert lay, he saw the smoking barrel of a gun. Walborne had kicked his gun close enough to Robert to be reached. It had been his first impression that Captain Donovan was unconscious. Apparently he'd woken, and just in time.

Grant lunged for Nicolette as he saw Henry fall to the ground. A piercing wail of pain came from Milford, blood soaking his breeches while he clutched his upper thigh. If he managed to survive the wound until his trial, it didn't matter, because the man was bound to be charged with John Bradenton-Eton's murder and possibly Emmett Craddock's as well. His fate was inevitable. Punishment for murder meant the gallows.

Walborne helped Robert. Mitchell took care of Milford, and Grant whisked Nicolette away, her head covered by his coat. On his way past the barkeep, he tossed him some coins for the busted door and continued out the front, not stopping until he lifted Nicolette up onto his horse. He slid in behind her, propping her into his lap, instructing her to hang on.

When she wrapped her arms around his middle, laying her cheek against his chest, he could have wept. She was safely in his arms again. Never again would someone take her from him. They'd make the news public, even give up the clues and let treasure hunters have their day. He was done with all the nonsense. His own curiosity had almost been the death of her.

They came to a jarring halt outside his town house where Nicolette's Aunt Lydia stood at the door, dried tears on her cheeks, a hand at her throat as she watched Grant bring Nicolette into the house. He cradled her in his arms.

"I'm all right, Grant. You can put me down now," Nicolette insisted.

"Not before I see for myself that you sustained no injury." He set her on the sofa in the drawing room and gently lifted each arm, checking for bruises, and then her ribs and legs, much the same way he'd done the night of her attack on the *New Horizon*. Satisfied that she was indeed all right, Grant summoned Houldsworth and gave him instructions to bring the doctor.

"I will not let you call a doctor. Can you not see that I'm perfectly able?"

Grant knelt beside her, continuing his examination of her limbs. She placed a small hand over his, lacing their fingers to stop his ministrations. She cradled his hand against her soft cheek. Her hair was mussed from two days without a brush, and she still looked beautiful. Every inch of her.

"You're shaking." Nicolette kissed his knuckles.

Grant looked up into her eyes and swallowed hard. He had been running on a mixture of outrage and fear. His nerves had kept him awake for two days, not allowing him to accept anything but hope. He had come to realize how much he needed her. In all his life, he had been unwilling to meditate on his future, not wishing to bring into the picture a wife whom his family would ostracize or have children who would undoubtedly be sent away, raised by schoolmasters just as he'd been. To be humbled by this woman, to finally accept defeat where his heart was concerned, and then to come so damn close to losing her had taken a toll. After two days putting up a strong front, his resolve broke. She was alive and she was real, and Grant couldn't stop shaking. He'd done battle for his country, had taken down every adversary in his way whether enemy of land or business, and had done all of it with a steely determination. But now he was glad to surrender wholeheartedly.

He laid his head on Nicolette's lap, and instead of being appalled by his obvious show of what the ton would consider weakness, his beautiful wife leaned over and hugged his shoulders, covering him in a shower of caramel hair. She kissed the top of his head and then nipped the top of his left ear, whispering all the while how much she loved him. She spoke in a whisper with a soft catch in her voice. He looked up to see her eyes swimming with unhidden joy and longing.

"I knew you'd come for me, Grant. I never worried of

that." She leaned over, his face cradled in her hands, and kissed him with all the love she'd been born to share.

"You humble me, Nicolette."

"Love begets love, my lord."

"Then I shall look forward to completing the tradition."

Voices in the hallway interrupted his thoughts. He got on his feet and raised her hand to his lips. Nicolette's aunt and uncle and Captain Donovan, who had a red welt on his forehead from his injuries, filed through the open door to the drawing room.

Lady Walborne hurried to sit at Nicolette's side. She hugged her niece, sniffles punctuating the teeming commotion. At once James Walborne and Robert began talking, and Grant lifted a hand. His foggy head could not make out the overlapping conversation.

Robert bowed to James.

"Richfield hauled Milford away at gunpoint. I imagine we'll be hearing of the coming trial in the next several days." Walborne then nodded toward Nicolette, who was engulfed in her aunt's embrace. "How's Nicolette?" His worry was evident, and Grant felt for the man.

"She appears to have suffered only minor abrasions from the ties at her wrists. And the effect of laudanum doesn't look to be a problem, but I've called for the doctor just in case."

"Which I don't need," Nicolette chimed in.

All three men turned in unison toward the sofa.

James replied, "Do us all a favor and allow your husband, just this once, to take care of you." The sentiment was laced with just enough lighthearted teasing to keep Nicolette from responding, but she did give Grant a hard lift of her brow, then broke into a smile.

"I owe you an apology, Captain Donovan," Grant said with all humility. "When you didn't show after Nicolette disappeared, I assumed the worst."

"As ye should," Robert replied. "How could ye have known? I'd been tryin' to follow the man's trail since"—he checked that Nicolette couldn't hear—"since John's death. I've no doubt that Milford killed him."

"There's a trail as long as my arm from the death of Craddock, the inheritance of the shipping company, and his clandestine presence at our wedding. You did well, Robert. I'll forever be indebted."

"You jest take care of my wee moppet," Robert said of Nicolette. "An' we'll be best of kin."

Grant breathed with relief. "I can do that."

"She loves ye," Robert added.

Grant nodded, smiling with respect for the man who was like a father to Nicolette, which made him the closest thing to a father-in-law to Grant. He was happy to put all the animosity and distrust behind him.

"Her Grace, the Dowager Duchess of Havenly," Houldsworth announced just before Grant's grandmother showed up in the doorway.

The pale pallor of her skin worried Grant, and the way she leaned on a cane he'd yet to see her use before concerned him beyond measure.

"Your Grace," Nicolette said, coming to her feet. "Grant, hurry." She rushed to the dowager's side, Grant on the other, while they guided her to an overstuffed velvet chair that managed to swallow up a woman who, before this debacle, could not have been beaten into bowing.

Nicolette's concern grew. Her aunt and uncle along with Robert stood far enough away to give them ample room. They didn't greet her, for fear of causing her any more distress.

The dowager duchess squeezed Nicolette's hand with a

strength she'd have not guessed while tears not only welled up in her hazel eyes but fell in record number, slipping down her cheeks to make little gray spots on her lace-trimmed fichu. Nicolette knelt at her feet and kissed the dowager's shaking hands, then laid her cheek against them. Shuddering with tears, the older woman embraced Nicolette, resting her weary forehead against the top of Nicolette's head.

This woman, whom Nicolette had never seen cry, never seen out of control, openly sobbed.

"I thought you'd left me." The dowager's words wrenched her heart.

Nicolette swallowed a hard lump in her throat while she caressed the dowager's cold hands.

"I could not hold up against another loss. You are a gift, Nicolette. My granddaughter-in-law."

Nicolette chanced a troubled look at Grant, worried for her health. But Grant was caught in his own gut-wrenching cloud of discovery. His face brimmed with irrefutable truth at how his grandmother truly felt about his mother, and all the guilt she'd carried for so many years was in every tear.

"Not again," the dowager cried. "Not again." She lifted her hand toward Grant and gripped him like she'd never let go. Straightening in her seat, she accepted a handkerchief from her grandson, an unmistakable mist in his golden eyes.

The dowager sniffled, dabbed at her nose, then demanded as only she could, "Who is this man?" Her gaze fell upon Robert Donovan.

While she remained at the dowager's feet, Nicolette held out a hand toward Robert, who gathered by her side. The dowager placed a protective hand on Nicolette's shoulder. "Captain Donovan, this is my husband's grandmother—"

"I am *her* grandmother-in-law," the dowager said, her usual stern countenance returning with every word.

"The Dowager Duchess of Havenly, my grandmother-in-law," Nicolette finished, falling over her words, much the same way she stepped on waltzing toes. "Madam," she continued.

"Grandmama," the dowager sternly said.

Nicolette happily conceded. "Grandmama, this is Captain Robert Donovan, my…" She choked back a sob and continued with a catch in her voice. "…my surrogate father by lifetime friendship."

Robert bowed over the dowager's hand. "Yer Grace, it is my honor."

The dowager examined him with hawklike precision. "He is a Scot." The statement came out like an accusation, but no one in the room dared take it so. Nicolette had learned this was her newly appointed grandmama's way.

"Good God," the dowager continued, "how did you ever teach this girl to speak a speck of proper English with that accursed accent?"

Nicolette turned wide, pleading eyes on Robert, willing him to understand the dowager's remarks were not meant to offend.

"Aye, Yer Grace, we whipped 'er inta shape, we did." Robert put in an extra heavy burr and managed not to look like a pirate when he said it.

The dowager squinted her eyes. "Nonsense, this child could do no wrong, not in my eyes." She turned a genuine smile on Nicolette, then said with finality, "Welcome to the family, Captain Donovan."

Nicolette's heart melted at the dowager's acceptance of Robert into their private family. From here forward, every time the woman tried to be gruff, she'd remember the day tears poured from her eyes and she wept in Nicolette's hair. She was finally home. For good.

IT WAS ONLY A KISS

LATER THAT EVENING, after Nicolette had taken some much-needed time to soak away the memories of the past two days, she wandered out onto the back terrace, following the scent of roses into the small courtyard. It wasn't long before Grant joined her. She was instantly alert to his heavy footsteps and wasn't at all surprised when his arms snuck around her, pinning her back against his chest.

"I missed you," he whispered, nuzzling her neck.

"I've been away two hours." She smiled, purposely misunderstanding.

"You've been away two days." His tone was heartbreakingly serious. He turned her in his arms so he could see her face. The moonlight poured down on the courtyard, illuminating the gardens in the near distance where they should have met for the payment of the forfeit.

"I don't know what I'd do without you, Nicolette. When I couldn't find you, I knew real fear for the first time in my life. I wished so hard that no harm had come to you. And when that was not enough, I prayed. I prayed that God would help me find you. That He would protect you. My mind was tormented with horrible images of you lost somewhere, knowing that you needed me to find you, that you were counting on me. If I'd failed you, I couldn't have lived."

Nicolette reached up and smoothed a strand of wayward hair from his forehead. "As I said before, I wasn't afraid. I knew you'd come for me, Grant."

Grant held her for a long time in silence, the two of them finding comfort in the simple embrace. There was no one about, just them and the night sky. He held her cheek cradled against his chest and brushed his fingers through her hair. She felt and heard the steady rhythm of his heart. The sound reminded her of lying next to him after they'd made love.

With her face between his hands, he kissed her nose. "I want to discuss something with you."

"Oh? Are cards involved?" She flashed a coy smile.

He chuckled. "No, not this time. I propose that we make the clues to the treasure and the story public. It will do two things: stop the threat on your family and open the possibility up for treasure hunters. We'll offer a large reward to whoever finds it, even if there's nothing left of it. If it does exist, I have to believe that it's only monetary and not memorabilia, else your father's family would have kept it back. In fact, Robert suggested it's a diamond mine."

"That's brilliant! But how will we know if it's found? What if hunters steal it?"

"Does it matter? If it has the Eton name on it, there'll be little question, but if it doesn't, it will belong to anyone who finds it." He held her cheeks, rubbing them with his thumbs. "We don't need it, kitten. And I need you safe, always. I can't live this again."

She nodded, placing her hands over his. "My father died for that treasure."

"No, love. He died because of it. I don't think he ever meant for you to find it. He only wanted you safe."

She swallowed down tears. She knew he was right.

"Your uncle shared how Robert met your father in Scotland."

"Yes, Robert told me the story an hour ago. No wonder he and my father were so close. They remind me of you and the Earl of Richfield. He told me what the Gaelic words say: *The little bear and a new moon at the end of the journey*."

"What do you think it means?" he asked.

"Ursa Minor. It's somewhere in the Northern Hemisphere, under a new moon, whatever that means. The etchings under the velvet look like numbers as well as the letters *E* and *T*. Eton, I imagine."

Grant nodded. "And longitude and latitude."

She nodded, then stood on tiptoe, wrapping her arms tight

around his neck, bringing him down for a long, lingering kiss. No reservations, just a promise to love him for a lifetime.

It was quite some time before Grant relinquished her mouth. He ran his hands down her arms and linked his fingers with hers while she gazed up at the night sky and wondered at the constellations.

"When we were on the ship, you knew because of the stars where we were headed. So where are you now?" His voice soothed her while she breathed in the night air.

She gazed at his handsome, beloved face. "Right here with you."

"You can tell that by the stars?" He grinned at her.

"No." She smiled back. "I can tell by my heart."

He gathered her close once again. He raised her chin until their eyes met. "And where are you going, Nicolette?"

With all the love she had for him shining in her eyes, she answered genuinely, "With you, wherever you go." She hugged him tight around the middle, pressing her cheek against his heart, reveling in the feel of his arms about her again. This was where she had always felt safe; this was home.

"I love you, Nicolette," he breathed softly into her hair. "I've never said that to any woman before. But you're not just anyone. You're mine, for a lifetime, forever. And it's not enough."

"And my brilliant husband finally speaks truth." She tilted her head back until their eyes met. "I've known that for a long time, you know. That you love me."

He held her tight. "I've known it for a long time too. I'm sorry it took me so long to say it." He pulled back and looked down at her. "I found your forfeit."

Her eyes drifted to his mouth. "You know I lied about the payment? Neither money nor chores are the usual forfeit." She gazed up into his eyes. "Do you know what it is, Grant?"

He shook his head, a lustful smile on his face.

"It's a kiss. Generally a familial peck on the cheek."

He seemed as equally distracted by her mouth as she was by his. But just as his head descended toward her, she said, "However, you have apparently already collected the gold sovereign I dropped, so there is no need."

He deftly, without betraying a trace of movement, reached into one pocket and pulled out a gold coin, then tucked it into the tight-fitted bodice of her dress, sending a shameless shiver straight to her core. "I'd rather have the kiss."

THE END

MY DEAR FRIENDS

If you enjoyed sailing with Nicolette and Grant, please consider leaving a review on Amazon and Goodreads. It would mean the world to me.

Interested in the **Epilogue** from *It Was Only a Kiss*? Get the FREE download when you Sign-up for my newsletter.

Thank you for supporting Indie.
   Let's keep in touch,
   ~Shannon

ALSO BY SHANNON GILMORE

Ruined Rakes Series

It Was Only a Kiss

Every Time You're Near

A Lesson For All Time

My Everything

And more to come…

ACKNOWLEDGMENTS

Heartfelt appreciation for: Kathy and Meg, the brave guinea pigs who waded through that first draft without complaint. To: C. P. Rider, who inspires me to be better; Lisa Dworkin, my safe place to fall; Kate Pembrooke, for reading those first 50 pages which created an ongoing conversation that I'd like to never end; Justine Covington, for asking the right questions; Liana De La Rosa, losing a contest to you was perhaps one of the greatest opportunities of my life—without that, I might never have met you. My RWA sisterhood of Golden Heart Omegas, you guys rock! And the lovely Janna MacGregor for taking time out of your busy schedule to buy me a coffee. I love your shoes, lady!

For my editors. Without you there would be no book.

Anne Victory. You ironed out the wrinkles and made this baby shine. I'm so glad I found you.

Sue Brown-Moore. You, lady, are my word-wizard. You never cease to be a light of encouragement even when you're killing off some of my favorite characters. I love you my friend.

Special thanks to my kids for sacrificing much so that I could dream.

And to the real man with the single dimple and amber eyes…I love you so much Margie.

ABOUT THE AUTHOR

Shannon Gilmore writes historical romance. *Every Time You're Near*, of her debut series, **Ruined Rakes**, is a RWA Golden Heart® finalist. She resides in California with her husband and three rambunctious Ragdoll cats.

Made in the USA
Monee, IL
23 November 2021